Gemma Hill is the author of *The Twins' Twins*, her first well-received and well-read fictional novel. A storyteller, poet, and playwright, she has a way of crafting plots and creating characters that tempt the reader to stay up all night and read her novels. A retired lecturer in Communication, Social Science, and Health and Social Care, she loves nothing better than penning stories, long and short, that have a strong element of fiction based on her own life experiences and upbringing in Co Donegal as the fifth daughter of a small shopkeeper and café owner parents in a market town in Ireland.

To my late father, Tommy, who was born in the railway station house in Fermanagh when my grandfather, Tom, was a signalman there with the GNR in 1915.

Gemma Hill

ORPHANS AND STRANGERS

AUSTIN MACAULEY PUBLISHERS
LONDON * CAMBRIDGE * NEW YORK * SHARJAH

Copyright © Gemma Hill 2025

The right of Gemma Hill to be identified as author of this work has been asserted by the author in accordance with sections 77 and 78 of the Copyright, Designs and Patents Act 1988.

All rights reserved. No part of this publication may be reproduced, stored in a retrieval system, or transmitted in any form or by any means, electronic, mechanical, photocopying, recording, or otherwise, without the prior permission of the publishers.

Any person who commits any unauthorised act in relation to this publication may be liable to criminal prosecution and civil claims for damages.

This is a work of fiction. Names, characters, businesses, places, events, locales, and incidents are either the products of the author's imagination or used in a fictitious manner. Any resemblance to actual persons, living or dead, or actual events is purely coincidental.

A CIP catalogue record for this title is available from the British Library.

ISBN 9781035879786 (Paperback)
ISBN 9781035879793 (Hardback)
ISBN 9781035879809 (ePub e-book)

www.austinmacauley.com

First Published 2025
Austin Macauley Publishers Ltd®
1 Canada Square
Canary Wharf
London
E14 5AA

My thanks to Austin Macauley Publishers for supporting me in becoming a published author with my first novel, *The Twins' Twins* and for accepting my second novel *Orphans and Strangers*.

Chapter 1

William watched, dead-eyed, as the hilly ground held fast against the best efforts of the pallbearers to force the flimsy wooden box into the narrow slit in the ground.

He glowered at the sombre-faced undertaker. He'd delivered Margaret's coffin from Blesswell Hospital. "It's not to be opened. We don't want tuberculosis spreading in Fermanagh," he'd said, grim-faced.

William closed his eyes and held fast to the image of Margaret's face framed in a halo of hair the colour of ripened corn. It felt as if this was happening to somebody else. There was some mistake. The person in that box, they were preparing to pile filthy clay on, couldn't be his Margaret. His eyes fell on his daughter, Trisha. *It should be her I'm burying,* he thought savagely.

The rain running in rivulets down his collar did nothing to cool the burning rage that bubbled inside him. He wiped his wet face with the sleeve of his badly fitting grey demob suit the Red Cross issued him with when he was discovered as a prisoner of war in Poland in 1946. He could smell the strong odour of mothballs that permeated its every fibre. *It fits no better, twelve years on,* he thought, looking down at the rain dripped off the too-short trousers onto his farm work boots.

He started as a clump of thick mud and stones, loosened by the heaving of the pallbearers, fell with a clatter on the coffin wedged half down the grave.

An old woman, kneeling on the muddy ground, discreetly fingered her rosary. "At least she has the decency to pray," William said to no one in particular.

He straightened his long back. Looking out over the head of the assembled mourners, he focused on a group of people standing on the periphery of the graveyard. *Most of them wouldn't bid us the time of day in the street. Mother and that old poo-faced hypocrite of a clergyman saw to that,* he thought bitterly.

He stared at Reverend Snodgrass, standing under a black umbrella, droning on as the shivering altar boy stood beside him.

Eight-year-old Trisha shrank back from the look in her father's eyes.

"Stop moving about," her fourteen-year-old brother, George whispered. "Da's watching you. You know what happens when he gets angry."

Above her head, Trisha could hear grown-ups talking in low voices. Gusts of wind snatched away some of their whispering, but she heard them ask why her mammy wasn't being buried in the family plot where her grandad and granny Armstrong and wee Sarah were buried.

She wondered where heaven was, and if Sarah be there. She didn't remember when her big sister, Sarah, fell into the well. But she remembered Miss Lillian, the Sunday school teacher, had given her a new doll. Her eyes kept coming back to the dark gaping hole in the ground.

Looking at the men leaning on their shovels, she tightened her grip on her brother's hand. She wondered if her mammy could hear the plop of rain falling on the lid of the box that covered her face.

George looked down at her. "Don't cry," he warned, seeing her lower lip beginning to quiver.

"I'm afraid of the men with the shovels," she said too loudly.

Her father turned and glared at her. "Keep her quiet or I will," he growled at George.

Trying not to look at the shovels, Trisha watched the branches of the trees casting dark, swaying shadows on the puddles of water at her feet. Every time a gust of wind came, the shovels made a grinding, whining sound against the stony ground. The gravedigger nearest to her straightened up. Unable to hold back any longer, a scream erupted from Trisha throat.

"Oh mammy, mammy," she shrieked.

Reverend Snodgrass stopped praying and frowned over the top of his half-moon glasses. He glared at George as he thumbed through his prayer book. Where had he left off? "May she rest in peace," he said, giving the gravediggers a curt nod of his head.

There hasn't been much of a collection for this burial, he thought. *I would have expected the usual five shilling, but with the decline of the Armstrong farm, it's not enough to bring me out on a morning like this!*

He glanced surreptitiously around the windswept graveyard. The Hamiltons and Robbie Black, William's nearest neighbours, had come to offer their support.

He nodded at the postman's wife and a few other villagers. The Kieltys from the hotel were there too, but Annie Swanton, the postmistress, hadn't come.

"I suppose it's what one would expect under the circumstances—burying a papish in a Protestant graveyard," he murmured.

His eyes slid to William, standing forlorn and hapless at the graveside. He felt a twinge of guilt. His mind stole back to the promise he made to Sarah, William's mother, on her death bed. He had made an exception to that promise today when he'd let Margaret's corpse and William into the church.

"I'm depending on you, Geoffrey," she'd hissed, her words coming in gasps. "See that it's done."

"Rest now, Sarah. We can talk about it tomorrow," he'd said.

"No! We'll talk about it now. I can't go to my grave knowing that William and she would be welcome in my church."

"Think what you're asking me to do, Sarah! And as for the farm, William is still your son. He has a right to inherit the farm." Geoffrey had remonstrated with her.

Sarah lay quiet for a minute. Geoffrey thought she had fallen asleep.

"The day William puts a weddin' ring on her finger, be it in church or chapel, is the day he ceases to be my son."

He could hear her husband, Samuel, moving around outside in the yard. Did he know what Sarah was planning to do?

"What does Samuel have to say about it all?" he'd asked gripping his Bible.

Sarah's fingers had twitched on the bedsheet. "Samuel is a good husband and father, but he's not able for William. Aye, and even less able for his daughter, Lisa," she sighed. "Promise me, Geoffrey, that you'll see to it." She'd shifted in the bed and turned perceptive eyes on him. "Farm and all the land as far as Hamilton's was left to me. It's mine, not Samuel's. I'll see the renovation to the church—new electric light—done the way you want it," she vowed, gripping his hand tightly.

Geoffrey shook himself out of his melancholy and looked around for Lisa. *William will need his sister more than ever now,* he thought. She hadn't made it home from Scotland for her mother's or father's funerals. But she had always been close to William, and he was sure she'd be home for Margaret's funeral.

Yes, a bit of a rough diamond; her father's favourite, and unlike William, she had her heart set on working the farm, he mused. He furrowed his brow, wondering why Sarah hadn't left the farm to her daughter. *Maybe she would* have if Lisa hadn't run away and married the first man that asked her, after the American GI stole her bloom and left her with child, he sniffed.

The rumbling in his stomach reminded him that his cooked breakfast would be getting cold. *But I have one more job to do before I can enjoy it*, he thought guiltily, looking around for the couple he had seen near the grave.

"Poor Margaret didn't last long," he said in a suitably conciliatory tone as he shook hands with Fergal and Maureen, Margaret's parents.

"We weren't told she was sick," Fergal said.

"Your dear daughter is at peace now," Geoffrey said, a note of tetchiness creeping into his voice. *It's always the same,* he thought, *family members snub each other for years and then turn up expecting to be treated like the chief mourners.*

"Were you with Margaret at the end?" Maureen asked.

Geoffrey noted the incongruity of the woman's brogue amongst the chatter of northern voices around them. It irked him. "No, I wasn't," he said curtly.

"Did she receive the Last Rites of the Catholic Church?" Maureen asked, tears running unheeded down her cheeks.

"The hospital chaplain saw to all that," Geoffrey said, anxious to talk to them about William and the children and get home to his breakfast.

"William is not a well man," he said without preamble. "The war, you understand, had a devastating effect on his… mental capacities." Geoffrey let his words die away as he tasted the half-truth on his tongue. He shrugged. Nothing was to be gained from going on about their son-in-law's past behaviour. What he wanted to impress on them was that, with Margaret gone, their granddaughter might feel the full force of William's episodes of war weariness.

He cleared his throat. "With their mother gone, William will need support with the children. I was hoping his sister Lisa might have been here…"

He held up his hand as Fergal Furling opened his mouth to speak. "The farm is in a very rundown state. And then there is the fear, even with the new medicine, the children might contract consumption."

"Hold on, hold on a minute," Fergal Furling said, a shocked look on his face. "You're telling me Margaret had tuberculosis—TB!"

Geoffrey nodded realising this was going to be a more protracted conversation than he had anticipated. He held tightly to his patience. *What part of what I'm trying to tell them do they not understand?* he thought irritably. "There's been talk in the village…"

"Margaret had TB!" Fergal repeated, unable to take it in. Taking him by the elbow, Rev Snodgrass steered him away from the group of locals who were eavesdropping.

Fergal looked at him in utter bewilderment. It had been an unspeakable shock to receive word that Margaret had died. But to learn she had died from TB! "When did it star—how long…"

Geoffrey briefly recounted their granddaughter Sarah's untimely death from drowning. He paused when he heard Maureen's sharp intake of breath.

"Sarah drowned… in the well on the farm," she said in an incredulous voice.

"It was a terrible loss to William… and Margaret," Geoffrey added. He firmed his stance on the uneven ground against the rising wind as he avoided thinking about William's appalling behaviour the day his daughter drowned.

"Your daughter never really recovered from the loss," he said, moving his thoughts on swiftly. "She had a breakdown and was admitted to Blesswell Hospital." He fumbled with his vestments, trying to keep them from blowing in the wind. He sighed. "Sarah was the only child William took to when he returned from war. He was inconsolable when she drowned." Geffrey paused. "He simply never came to terms with her death. And then… Margaret contracted tuberculosis." He sighed again as he placed a steadying hand on Fergal, who was obviously shocked from what he was hearing. Feeling weak, Fergal leaned against the railings of an old grave.

"God almighty, if I had only known things were so bad. I didn't want her to marry William. But my god, I wouldn't have wished this on her or my grandchildren," he said. Fumbling his hankie out of his pockets, he swiped at his tears. "I thought she'd have full and plenty," he said helplessly.

Geoffrey cleared his throat and tapped his fingers on his prayer book. "Yes, well, mixed marriages bring their own problems. The Armstrongs became estranged from their son, as you did from your daughter," he said, a niggling sense of guilt worming his way around his gut. "Now, the present problem: the children. If you intend to help, this would be the time to do it."

I've done my duty, Geoffrey thought in the silence that followed. He cleared his throat. "I must have a word with Doctor Coles…"

Straightening his shoulders, Fergal stepped between the haphazardly laid-out graves in the direction of his son-in-law.

"We're staying at Kielty Hotel. Come and have a bite to eat with us, William?" he said. He had met William once before, at Margaret's nursing graduation at Queen's University Belfast. William had been non-communicative and withdrawn, but nothing like this dishevelled, angry man trying to brush him aside.

"Ah don't need your charity," William growled.

Mindful of Reverend Snodgrass's veiled warning, Fergal held fast to his mounting concern. "If you'll not come, let the children come."

"George is needed on the farm; he has no time for eatin' in hotels."

"What about her?" Fergal asked, nodding to where a girl stood, shivering.

William's face darkened. "Aye, her," he said spitting on the ground.

"Margaret is—was—our daughter, man!" Fergal said losing his patience. "And these are our grandchildren. With poor Margaret lying in her grave, all we want to do is help if we can."

William balled his fists. Fergal flinched, sure William was going to strike him.

"Oh, so she's your daughter now!" William spat. "And where were you the past fifteen years? Answer me that?" He turned blazing eyes on Maureen. "You sent her a wedding dress she had bought to marry another man," he said.

Margaret hadn't dressed in white for their wedding day, but as she'd got sicker, she had begged him to dress her in the wedding dress for her funeral.

A grim smile flittered across his face as he caught sight of the black-coated undertaker gabbing with Reverend Snodgrass. *No doubt he's telling him how I prised open the coffin; stripped the harsh calico shroud from my wife's body and dressed her in the white wedding dress,* he thought.

Maureen glanced at Fergal. She hadn't told him about posting the white frothy wedding dress Margaret had set her heart on.

Tentatively, she touched William's arm. "I'm sorry;" she said. "I just thought how beautiful my daughter would look in it on her wedding day."

William jerked away and faced Fergal. "Your daughter, is she? The day she turned her coat and married me, you turned your back on her," he bellowed into Fergal's face.

Fergal drew in his breath. It was true.

Standing in the barren graveyard with the icy rain beating down on his daughter's miserable grave, he remembered the day that changed their lives forever.

Margaret was home for a few days' holidays before she took her final nursing exams.

"Fergal, Margaret has something to tell you." Maureen had said.

"What's that?" he'd said, opening the evening paper.

"I've met somebody else, Daddy."

He'd turned to the sport pages and shook out the paper. "You're pulling my leg," he'd joked. "Tomas is the love of your life. Awk, it's just wedding nerves, love. Tomas is a grand lad. You'll want for nothing. Isn't that right, Mother?" he said, glancing at Maureen.

"Tomas knows about it," Margaret said. "I wrote and told—"

Fergal had sprung from his chair. "What are you saying? Tomas is away fight a war—could be killed by Hitler at any minute—and you broke off your engagement in a letter?" He'd slapped the Herald down on the floor.

Margaret's long, corn-coloured hair had bounced off her shoulders as she faced her father. "He's Protestant from Fermanagh," she shouted. "And I'm marrying him."

Fergal had listened to the clatter of her high heels as she raced up the stairs and the blare of the music as she turned up the volume.

He was jolted back to the graveyard by his wife asking William something.

"…We could take the girl until you get things sorted?" Maureen was saying.

William stared at Trisha. *What does it matter where she goes as long as I get rid of her,* he thought.

"We'll take good care of her."

She turned to the boy. Her heart twisted. *He's the image of his mother when she was young,* she thought, watching him push his dripping hair back from his forehead. She guessed when it was dry, it was the same soft corn colour as Margaret's had been. Maureen wondered if it was against the law to take your grandchildren across the border into Southern Ireland without their father's permission.

Fergal smiled at his granddaughter standing beside her brother. "What's your name?" he asked, bending down to her and holding out his hand.

"Her name's Trisha," her brother George said, trying to keep his guts from rumbling.

"That's a fine Irish name. It suits you," Fergal said, taking stock of the tall, stick-thin girl with the startling dark eyes and sloe-dark hair like her father's. She shrank back as he pushed a strand of wet hair from her forehead. Shocked at the look of naked fear in her eyes, Fergal let his hand drop.

A physical pain tore across his chest. *These are my daughter's children, and I am a stranger to them,* he thought. He sank down on a fallen headstone covered in lichen. "Come on, William. A bite to eat will warm us all up," he said wearily.

"No! That's that, an end to it," William growled.

"Let me take the girl," Maureen persisted. "I'll bring her back. I promise."

William's head jerked as Maureen's words resonated with him. "You'll bring her back?" he asked, his dark eyes boring into hers.

"I will, William. I promise," Maureen babbled, terrified he'd see the lie in her eye.

Gripping Trisha's shoulder, William dragged her away from her grandmother. He didn't want her back. *If Lisa doesn't take her, I'll find some other way of getting rid of her,* he thought, pushing her up the rutted graveyard path in front of him.

Chapter 2

Lisa shoved her daughter's hands away. "Stop pawing at me," she cried, tension making her voice sharp. Ten-year-old Isobel stalked away and threw herself down on the sofa bed beside her father.

Lisa eyes scanned William's postcard again. *As usual, he writes everything in a few short sentences and explains nothing,* she thought.

Dear Lisa,
Margaret is sick. Come and take Trisha to live with you.

William

Lisa thumped the postcard with its view of the Fermanagh Lakes down on the table. It had been a week since it had dropped through the letterbox. *William thinks all he has to do is dump his troubles on me and I'll solve them for him.*

You always have, a small inner voiced mocked.

"Well, not this time," Lisa muttered under her breath, searching for a cigarette.

"Who's the postcard from?" her husband, BJ, asked, flicking a quick glance from the racing form he was studying. Lisa glared at him. *I must have been insane to marry him,* she thought, looking at his unshaven face and mop of unruly greying hair. The people in the tenements called him Big Jim—BJ for short. Fifteen years of no money, no life; washing cooking, and cleaning for them all, including BJ's Granny Mac, Lisa fumed as she stuffed her brother's card back into her apron pocket and started to fold the basket of washing she had brought in from the line at the back of the tenements.

"Well, are ye goin' to tell me who's sendin' you postcards?"

"It's from William. Margaret's sick, and he wants me to come to Fermanagh and bring the youngest bairn to live with us."

Her husband looked at her as if she had taken leave of her senses. He leaned back and pulled the stub of a pencil from behind his right ear.

"She's aye sick. William should've married a farmer's daughter like your Ma wanted." BJ said, licking the end of the pencil. "You had to stick yer nose in. Margaret wasn't reared to live on a farm in the backside o' the lakes o' Fermanagh."

Lisa's conscience pricked her. "How was I supposed to know she'd get sick with her nerves? I never thought she'd marry him."

BJ retrieved his work boots from under the sofa bed, his gut tightening. He'd never dreamt a popular, good-looking lass like Lisa would marry him. The fear was always there that one day Lisa would go home to Ireland and not come back to him.

He squared his heavy-set shoulders. "You're no' goin' to Ireland. And she's no comin' here," he said, stuffing the racing form into his hip pocket. "William must think we're like him wi' a farm at our backs."

Lisa eyes glittered in fury. "If I want to go and see my brother, I will. You only married me, Jim Mac Knight. You don't own me. Its years since I was home."

Ten-year-old Isobel screwed up her face. "She's no' sleepin' wi' me. Bairns smell like piss…"

"Isobel," her mother warned. "What did I tell you about using street language in this house?"

"She can sleep beside Andrew," Isobel huffed. She let out a yelp as the end of the towel Lisa had been about to hang on the overhead pulley line whipped across her legs.

"I hate you, Ma," Isobel screeched.

BJ gave his daughter a perplexed look. *Tongue likes a razor, just like granny Mac who reared me,* he thought.

"She'll no be comin 'here," he soothed, stroking his daughter's red hair as her mother took a menacing step towards her.

"Let her be. You're aye at her," BJ said.

Fourteen-year-old Andrew, sensing another row was brewing about his mother's brother in Ireland, capped the glue he was using to assemble his model aeroplane. "A'll go down and show Gordon Gurley ma new Spitfire," he mumbled, edging towards the door that lead to the outside stairs.

Lisa felt her anger dissipate as she looked at her son. A sense of pride welled up in her. *He was the one thing that made life bearable in this place. He's growing into a fine, handsome young man like his father,* she thought. Hurriedly, she clamped down hard on her train of thoughts.

"Go on," she said, ruffling his hair.

"It's time that brither o' yours learned to take care o' his family. And no' always be runnin' to you," BJ snorted, pushing his arms into his working coat.

"Away you go," Lisa snapped.

Listening to the woman in the flat below screaming at the baby to shut its gob, Lisa pulled the curtain back from the window of the third-floor flat. If she focused on the gap between the tenements opposite, she stood could see the fields and hills in the distance that reminded her of home.

She turned and looked around the overcrowded flat she had come to share with BJ and his granny when they'd married in Gretna Green in 1942. It was supposed to be a stopgap until Granny Mac got her time out of the place. *Then we could get our own place,* she mused.

Granny Mac had died, but they were still here. BJ jokes he'll be carried from the flat feet first like his granny. *But not me,* Lisa thought. *Not me. One day I'll have a new house on the new developments springing up on the outskirts of Glasgow.*

"Any place as long as I don't hear the people next door arguing or making love," she sighed.

Putting the kettle on top of the grey Old World gas cooker, her hand went back to William's card in her pocket. *Poor Margaret,* she thought, *sick again. You gave up your family and your fiancé to marry William, and look what you got in return? My mother turned you and my brother into outcasts.*

Sipping her tea, Lisa let her thoughts drift back.

"Now that all the gossip about William marrying a Catholic has died down, wouldn't your mother like to see her grandson?" Margaret had said. "William is naming the baby, George, after the King."

Lisa sighed. Her mother had loved everything Royal.

"William is named his son, George, after the King," Lisa had told her mother.

A flicker of interest had washed across her mother's face. "Has he got William's way?" she'd asked.

Lisa knew what she meant. William rarely spoke to anybody except his mother or her. "No. He's a lovely smiley baby. He doesn't look a bit like

William. He has Margaret's fair hair and blue eyes." As soon as she'd said it, she knew she'd put her foot in it.

White-knuckled, her mother's hands gritted the bedclothes. "Aye, and the Church of Rome blood in him."

"Where's your Christian charity?" Lisa said exasperated. "William has joined up and is fighting a war. He could be killed. He'd want his son George to know his grandparents."

Sarah heaved up in the bed. "William betrayed his own kind. Tainted the good bloodline of his ancestors before him and fouled the blood of those that will come after him."

And I could have stopped him if I hadn't been so intent on getting back at you for putting him in front of me all the years we were growing up, Lisa had thought.

Guilt assailed her. She tried again. "Margaret wants to be part of William's Church and bring George up Protestant."

Her mother Sarah's rheumy eyes, glassy with pain, stared at her incredulously. "She's a papist and she wants to go to William's church?" she wheezed.

Lisa nodded. "And have George christened there."

A sob had squeezed from her mother's throat. "It must be true what the old folk said—Catholic girls cast some kind of a charm over Protestant boys…"

Lisa's heart ached. Her mother knew death was near, but she wouldn't forgive William for his 'betrayal,' Lisa thought, wiping a tear from her eye.

BJ's cheery whistle broke Lisa's reverie and galvanised her into action. She had been sitting there thinking of Margaret and home for hours!

She heard BJ call a greeting to their neighbour, Mary Potts. Without looking out, Lisa knew the old woman would be down on her hands and knees scrubbing her front doorstep, as she did every Friday.

"I thought getting married was my ticket to freedom," Lisa muttered. "Instead, it turned out to be a one-way trip to poverty," she thought, looking down at the potatoes swimming about in the cracked Belfast sink, waiting to be peeled for BJ's dinner.

"See the Telegram Boy on the street," BJ said as he came in.

"Yeah, and another family is moving out. Maybe I'll get moving soon as well," Lisa said.

BJ slapped her playfully on the behind with the paper. "We're fine here, lass." Lisa slapped a mug of tea down in front of him. If he dared to boast tonight that he'd be carried out of the tenements, feet first, she'd throw it around him.

Lisa's heart fluttered as the whistling Post Office boy pushed a telegram into her hand. Fingers trembling, she turned the buff-coloured envelope over and tore it open.

Come home straightaway William needs family, she read. It was signed by Dr Coles, her old family doctor.

A feeling of foreboding assailed her. *I should have gone home last week when I got William's card,* she thought, passing the telegram to BJ.

"Where're ye goin?" BJ asked as she pulled her red-gold hair into a ponytail and put on her coat.

"I'm going down to Madge Gurley to borrow the fare for the boat," she shouted, letting the door slam behind her.

"It's a cold night to be out," Madge Gurley said, ushering Lisa up to the glowing fire. Lisa looked at this old woman—a stranger, not a drop's blood to her—more of a mother to her than her own. The old feeling of antagonism rose like bile in her throat. She had always known her mother preferred William to her. She drew out the telegram and the postcard.

Madge's weathered face became perplexed as she read the words on the card. "It's a lot he's askin' o' you, hen. Raisin' your ain bairns is one thing, but…" She pursued her lips and let her words taper off.

A fit of red-hot anger blazed through Lisa.

"William thinks of nobody but himself. That's the way my mother reared him," she burst out. "When I was young, my job was to keep William safe from the school bullies. Even on her death bed Mother insisted I agree to always look after him." Lisa paused. "I need to go home, but I've no money for the boat."

Madge poked the fire into a blaze.

"Well, hen, a wee loan will no' be a bother, and warm winter outer garments if ye need them too," she offered, eyeing Lisa's thin coat.

"You're no' borrowin'!" BJ shouted. "Where will ye get the money to pay her back?"

Lisa stood with her back against the kitchen sink and looked up at BJ's broad frame. In the mood he was in, it wasn't the best time to tell him her news.

"I'm taking a part-time job as a cleaner at the Dispensary," she said, keeping her voice as steady as she could. BJ's face went brick red and then puce. He balled his fists.

Lisa stiffened. Some of the men in the Close beat on their wives, but not BJ. *I've pushed him too far this time,* she thought, feeling frightened. She straightened her spine.

"Money doesn't go as far today as it did in your Granny Mac's time," she smirked to hide her fear. "And Andrew has his mind set on joining the RAF Cadets. I'll need money for him."

BJ's mouth fell open. He opened and closed his fists in rage. "Andrew, Andrew, it's always about Andrew! Ah had a job at his age. Ah'll get him a start down the Cooperation. What about her?" he roared, stabbing his finger in the direction of Isobel.

Lisa glanced at her daughter. She knew only too well what it was like to compete for a mother's love. Her love had always been for Andrew. She'd never felt the same about Isobel.

"You're not bullying me out of this wee job this time, Jim McKnight. I'm taking it as soon as I come back from Fermanagh."

BJ look down into Lisa's blazing eyes. Her fiery Irish temper and her golden hair, which shone as bright as a flame when the sun caught it, were what had attracted him to her. He felt himself getting aroused. *She's still a good-looking woman despite having the bairns,* he thought. Standing toe-to-toe with her, he could feel the angry waves of heat radiating off her body.

Lisa gave him a satirical smile.

"Don't you even think about it, Jim Mac Knight. All you think about is getting me in bed and backing the horses."

BJ backed away. "You're no' goin' to Ireland, and William's bairn is no' comin' here. Do ye hear me? William was fit for Hitler. He's fit to look after his own bairns."

Lisa sat down at the table. She glanced surreptitiously at BJ. She had never seen him so enraged. Despite her best intention not to cry, tears fell down her cheeks. "BJ, I have to go. I promised my mother on her death bed I'd look after William. You read the telegram. He needs family," she sobbed.

Chapter 3

George stole a backward glance at the broad-shouldered man with the grey moustache and the woman with eyes like his mother's. They must be the people in the photo his mother kept hidden in a drawer. When his father was out, she'd take it out and rub her fingers over the faces in the picture.

His stomach rumbled. He thought about the warm soup and sandwiches he could be eating if his father had let him and Trisha go with their grandparents. He looked down at his little sister. Her oval face was pinched and tear-stained; her long dark hair hung in wet cats' tails; the ribbon he had tied it up with before the funeral was now a soggy band around her neck.

Glad to be away from the graveyard and the shivering weeds that smelled like rotten vegetables, Trisha held tightly to her brother's hand. "Will Mammy see our Sarah in Heaven?" she asked, her dark eyes trusting him to have the answer.

"I don't know… maybe," George said. He'd been taught his Bible, but he couldn't believe in a God that had let his beautiful mother die. He kicked at the loose gravel that lay along the side of the road. *Mammy's grave is ugly*, he thought, *not like the Armstrong family plot they'd buried Sarah in when she drowned.*

He visualised Sarah sitting on his Granda's knee like she used to, as he told her stories about when he'd married their Granny. Sarah was called after her. He could hear his sister's voice in his head, as he often did.

"When I grow up, I'll dance and dance," she'd say whirling around the kitchen and taking a bow front of an imaginary audience.

His father used to laugh out loud at Sarah as she swooned and dipped. He never beat Sarah or put her in the dark barn the way he did with Trisha.

In a way, I'm glad they didn't bury Mammy in the Armstrong plot, he thought. *Sarah's dead eyes might have stared up at him like they did the day I helped Dr Coles pull her from the well.*

"Mammy said Sarah was with the Angels," Trisha said.

Her father slowed his step and plucked a stick from the hedgerow that bordered the lane to the farm.

"No more, talking," George said. "Pick some flowers, and we'll put it on Mammy's grave tomorrow."

"Why is Mammy's box not in the big grave where Granada and Sarah sleep?"

"Shush," George said, jerking Trisha behind him as their father turned.

Con Callahan, the postman, drew his Post Office bike to a stop alongside them on the lane. "Margaret was a good woman, Sorry for your troubles," he said, extending his hand.

William ignored it.

Keeping in step with William, silent and brooding, Con thought back to when Margaret's letters with their Belfast postmark started to arrive for William in 1941.

"He's keepin' you busy," Samuel, William's old father, sighed as Con put yet another letter on the kitchen table.

"It's no bother," Con said.

"Did ye hear about William's courtship with this woman he met on the train?"

Con feigned surprise. He daren't tell Samuel that the rumours about his son hell-bent on marrying a Catholic were all anybody was talking about in the village.

"It can only lead to vexation," Samuel sighed running, a gnarled finger down the spine of the old Bible he had on his knee. "William's not one for the women. What woman, other than his mother, Sarah, would understand his ways," he'd sighed.

"William was never like other youngsters. I think that foul mustard gas from the war did something—interfered with nature. He was born when I got back from the war. Aye, the war to end all wars. Now Hitler's knocking on our door, wanting us to let our sons suffer the same terrible fate we suffered," Samuel sighed, casting a worried look at Con. "William has joined the Home Guard," he continued. "The next thing you know, he'll be joining up. He's not fit to marry or fight a war," he'd stated.

It got that I hated to see that Belfast postmark with its distinctive copperplate handwriting, Con thought.

He dragged his mind back to the present. "I hear Robbie Black is goin' to help you on the farm, William?"

William glowered at him. "Still deliverin' the post and carryin' the gossip, are ye?"

Con let the jibe pass. He knew what William was driving at.

He had walked in on a row between Samuel and his wife, Sarah, about William marrying. "You know William all his life, Con. Do you think he's the marrying kind?"

Con had balked at the straight question.

"He'd need to marry a special kind of woman," he'd hedged. The Postmistress Annie Swanton, and the gossips were puzzled why a nurse from the Royal Victoria Hospital, with a fiancé away at war, would be writing so many letters to the likes of William Armstrong.

He'd startled when William had stepped from the room off the kitchen. He'd fixed eyes of cold steel on him.

"Tell the Postmistress and anybody else you like, I'm taking instructions to become a papist, and I'm marrying Margaret in the Catholic Church if she'll have me," he bawled.

Con had edged towards the door. "Well, I'd best be off. Does Sarah need anything from the village? I'll likely be this way with another letter before long." As soon as the words left his mouth, he'd cursed himself for his stupidity.

"I'll get whatever needed. You have enough to be doing carryin' the post and the gossip," William had spat at him.

Walking behind Con and his father, George felt bone weary and bewildered. He stared at his father's stiff back. Con must be mistaken. His Da hated to be questioned, especially when someone else was there, but he couldn't let his Granda's cattle be looked after by Robbie Black.

"Da," he said tentatively, "Granada Samuel never wanted Robbie about the farm. Granada said Robbie Black was…" He backed up as his father stopped walking.

"Your Granda said a lot of things, George. He's dead; just like your mother. I'm in charge now," he said, beating the stick against his legs.

George gulped at the mention of his mother. "But Da, what will you do if you don't have the cattle to look about?" he persisted, his heart beating a wild drumbeat in his chest.

What will I do? William thought? *What I really want to do is crawl into the grave beside Margaret,* he thought despairingly. He turned unseeing eyes over the fields that linked his farm and the Hamilton farm where Robbie Black stayed. "Without your mother, it doesn't matter what I do," he moaned, turning into the farmyard. "Get in the house and get that sister of yours out of my sight," he ordered George.

"Nearly forgot," Con said, proffering a letter.

"Make Con a mug of tea," William said, in an abrupt change of mood at the sight of the letter.

"It OK. I'll be goin'. I have a parcel for Mrs Hamilton."

"It's no bother," George said. *Con knows everybody's business for miles around. He'd keep his father talking long enough for his anger to pass about Trisha crying out in the graveyard. Enough time for me to work out how to get us back to Kielty's Hotel and our grandparents,* he thought.

"The village and the train station are a lot is quieter without the Yanks," Con was saying as George handed him a mug of tea. He shot a glance in his father. Mention of the war sent him into a wild rage.

"There's nothing left to eat, Da," he said, interrupting Con. "I'll take Trisha and get us some things," he said.

Intent on reading the letter Con had brought him, William didn't answer him.

Con shifted his weight against the upturned water barrel and looked around the farmyard. An old cart, its shafts covered in weeds, stood rotting in a corner of the yard. The doors of the outhouses and milk dairy badly needed a coat of paint, he mused. Milk churns, their lidless mouths gaping, lay rusting. Con sighed. *It's a far cry from when the old folks were alive and Margaret was in good health,* he thought.

"Your barn door could do wi' a lick o' paint, William," he said.

"That's what comes of living a stone's throw from the Border and the wind that comes off them Donegal Hills," William grunted.

"Bad news?" Con said as William crushed the letter into a ball and flung it into a pile of rubbish under the kitchen window.

"It's from Lisa in Glasgow."

Con remembered Lisa. *A bit too free with her favours as far as the GIs were concerned,* he mused. But all he said was, "When's she coming? Will she stay long?" He turned to see William eyeballing George.

"Get your Granda's suitcase from the top of the wardrobe," he ordered.

Hope flared in George. He was going to let them go with their grandparents after all. His body sagged in relief. With his mother gone, he didn't think he could protect Trisha from his father's rages.

"Pack your farm boots. You're goin' with me to work in England. We're goin' on the night's boat."

George's face blanched. The steely glint in his father's eyes cautioned him not to question his decision. Con furrowed his eyebrows. *What was this? The day of the lad's mother's funeral wasn't over yet, and he wanted George to pack for the boat!* He cleared his throat. "Is it not a bit too soon, especially for the wee girl with her mother just buried, William?"

"She's stayin'."

Con felt his mouth fall into a gape. "Here, in the house—by herself?" He couldn't believe what he was hearing. "Why don't you wait till Lisa comes?"

William eyeballed him. "Lisa doesn't want her. Do you want her? Whoever wants can take her."

Sweet Mother of God, Con thought, rising in panic to his feet. *William has lost it this time.*

"William, she's not more than a babby; you can't leave her here by herself. There's a storm comin'," he spluttered, gesturing to the dark clouds gathering on the distant Donegal Mountains. "It'll be a rough crossin' tonight, William. Come home wi' me. The missus will make you all a bite o' dinner." Tentatively, he placed a hand on William's arm. "Wait till the mornin'. You'll be fresher then for the journey," he pleaded.

George's chest heaved "You can't, Da. You can't leave Trisha..."

William's face darkened.

"Get packed," William repeated "And get her into her mother's bed."

George looked pleadingly at Con. "Mrs Hamilton said nobody was to sleep in mammy's bed. She said the mattress and all the bedclothes in mammy's room were to be burned..." He backed away as his father moved towards him.

In a panic, Con grabbed his bike and started for the lane. *Mother of mercy, William would have to be stopped. The wife would know what to do.* Then, on second thought, he turned and headed for the shortcut that would bring him out near the Hamilton farm. He could phone Annie Swanton, the postmistress, from there. She'd get a message to Dr Coles. He'd *have to do what he should have done years ago,* Con thought grimly. *He'd have to have William committed to the mental hospital.*

"Don't cry. Auntie Lisa is coming for you. Scotland will be nice. I'll come to see you, and you can come and see me in England." George stopped speaking at the sound of his father's heavy step.

Coming into the room, William gave Trisha a rough shove, sending her sprawling on the floor. "Get to your mother's bed before I take my belt to you," he ordered.

"I'm ready, Da," George quaked, tying the laces of his old farm boots together and slinging them over his shoulder. Without a backward glance in Trisha's direction, his father pushed him out the door, slamming it behind him.

George stopped at the turn in the lane and looked back. Trisha's tear-stained face was pressed up against the bedroom window. A sense of blind rage engulfed George. *I'll make you pay, one day I'll make you pay,* he promised.

Chapter 4

William glanced in the direction of the graveyard and heaved the kitbag higher on his shoulder. Margaret was up there in a pauper's grave. His heart was as heavy as the quarry stones he knew he and George would have to break in England if they wanted to get work.

Wrenching open the door of the first carriage of the train, he sank into a seat.

He felt the train tremble in anticipation, like a thoroughbred waiting for the starter pistol. It took him a minute to realise George wasn't among the other passengers in the carriage. He lurched to his feet as door after carriage door slammed shut and pushed his way out into the narrow strip of corridor, his frame momentarily blocking the path of the ticket collector as he started his rounds.

George shrank back from the carriage door. His father had half walked, half ran the five miles from the farm to Ballet Railway Station. George had prayed he would meet someone on the road. He'd even wished he could meet nosy Kathy Swanton, who went to the same school as him.

He glimpsed his father's glowering face and his wild gesturing for him to get on the train. Once he was on, he wouldn't be able to tell anyone about his father leaving Trisha alone in the house.

The stationmaster blew lustily on his whistle. Pocket watch in his hand, he gestured at the train's guard, who put a whistle to his mouth and blew one long, continuous blast as the station porter hurried along the wheezing train, slamming doors.

George held his breath as the train started to move. He'd done it. He could go home and look after Trisha, as he'd been doing almost from the day she was born.

The piercing whistle shrilled loud in his ears. The porter was beside him now.

"What are ye doin' standing there with yer mouth hangin' open? Get on before she gathers speed," he barked.

With a one deft movement, he hustled George and his case in through the open carriage door and banged it shut.

George stood, stupefied, watching the station buildings slide past as if in slow motion.

It hurt William to look at George. His mop of strawberry-gold hair curled around his cheekbones, giving him an almost girlish look. His gaze travelled over George's long, slender hands—not the hands for a pick and shovel. Margaret had had big plans for her only son. She'd schooled him herself until he'd won a scholarship to the local prestigious grammar school. Pain stabbed at William's heart. If Margaret had lived, there was no way George would be on his way to work as a navvy.

He was jerked back to the present by a sharp dig in his ribs.

"Will you have a drink wi' us?" the man beside him offered, proffering a spittle-covered bottle.

"Never touch it," William replied curtly.

"Is that so," the man said, his eyes widening. "Hear that," he shouted to a group of men sitting opposite. "He never touches the stuff. Just like meself," he grinned, tightening his grip on the bottle. Letting out a roar of a laugh, he thumped William on the knee.

"Sheamie Foy's the name, Donegal born and bred," the man belched, sticking out a broad, browned hand.

William cringed. He could smell the sour stench of stale drink and cigarettes on the man's breath. "Alcohol's the devil's brew," he said brusquely.

"Foy, you playing cards or not?" A man asked, dealing out cards on top of a suitcase on the carriage floor.

"'Course I'm playin'," Sheamie shouted. Cursing loudly, he fell over the suitcase, scattering the cards among the legs, feet and cases on the floor. Immediately, a chorus of cursing and profanities broke out among the card players.

"We need to find someplace else to sit, Da," George said in a low voice as a heated argument broke out.

William felt his body burn with shame. *What madness possessed me to bring George into the company of drunks and gamblers?* he thought. He began to sweat. Margaret wasn't even cold in her grave, and he'd already broken his promise to her to keep her son safe and at his education. Agitated, he shook his head from side to side.

The rattle of the train on the track seemed to mock him. *"Soldier boy, back from war, crazy now, crazy now."* It was the rhyme the village kids chanted as they played their skipping games.

"I had to do my duty," William muttered.

"Your duty sent people to an early grave, especially your mate Spud Donnell," his inner voice sneered. William could feel the trembling coming, feel sweat pooling as it trickled down his neck.

He flung the carriage door open and stumbled out into the narrow walkway. Leaning against the emergency door, a thought came to him. It would be so easy to do, and he'd be with Margaret, he thought.

Wrenching sobs shook his body as he stared out at the darkening scenery as it flashing by.

"Da!" George's voice was like the crack of a bullet slicing through William's skull. Wiping the sweat off his face with the sleeve of his coat, he backed away from the emergency door and slumped among the rubbish littering the floor.

"Da, get up! People are trying to get past," George grated, attempting to pull his father's twitching legs out of the way.

"Here, young fella—A'll give ye a hand," Sheamie Foy said. Bending, he hauled William to his feet as if he were weightless. Dumping him in the far corner of the carriage, he tapped him with the toe of his boot.

"That's no answer to anything," he muttered.

"Is he your oul' man?" he belched, turning to a red-faced George.

George nodded.

Sheamie narrowed his eyes. "You goin' with him on the night's sailin to Heysham?"

"Da did his training for the army in England. He says he'll get work there."

Sheamie sucked air through his teeth and looked from the man to the lad. "Your Da knows somebody that givin' him a start?" From the look on the lad's face, he doubted it.

"He only decided after my mother's funeral. He took me and left my sister Trisha behind."

Sheamie's ears pricked at the undisguised venom in George's voice.

"You got family—friends you can stay wi' in England'?"

George shook his head. "Da's only got one sister, and she lives in Glasgow. I think my sister is going to live with her."

The rattle of the train on the track intensified as it gathered speed. The sounds and the overcrowded carriage took William back to the train journey he was taken on as a POW after his unit surrendered to the Germans. Piled like cattle into wagons, not knowing where they were going, they were sent on a long journey on the train.

Mixed-up images like film reeds flashed across his mind making his shudder—faceless bodies, limbless torsos, mud red with blood, and his mother's accusing eyes staring at him.

Margaret is a respectable moral woman, Mother, he muttered over and over again, the words beating like a drum inside his head.

"What's he raving about?" Sheamie asked, nudging George.

George looked at his father muttering incoherently. "He's talking about mammy. She was buried this morning."

"This mornin'!"

Sheamie Foy felt the cold finger of fear stroke his spine. *What the fuck is he doing going to England the day his old lady was buried?* he wondered.

"Your mammy—was she sick for long?" he asked.

"She hasn't been very well since Trisha was born."

Sheamie let out a long, slow breath. *Jasus, for a minute I thought the bastard had killed her,* he thought, glaring at William still muttering to himself.

"England is a big place. What part are you and your Da goin'?"

George was silent.

Sheamie wiped a large hand over his weather-worn features. "He doesn't know where he's going, does he?"

George's lip trembled. "I don't think he does," he mumbled, looking at is father still slumped where Sheamie had dumped him.

"Here, get the other side of him," Sheamie shouted to one of the card players as train slowed, approaching Belfast Harbour.

George followed as the navvies half-dragged, half-carried his father up the gangplank. Standing at the ship's rail, George looked down at the thrashing water as the ship's engines shuddered into life.

"If he tried to go overboard—this time I'm not stopping him," he muttered angrily.

Chapter 5

Fergal Furlong ignored the numbness that was creeping down his right arm. He waited by the grave until the other mourners left. Taking out his hankie, he wiped at his face. The salt of his tears tasted bitter. He stared in despair at the ravaged, rotting vegetation and the narrow, brown-topped slit that would be Margaret's home from now on.

It was on the junction of two paths and had been dug to accommodate the gradient of the ground, with one side higher than the other. He reached in his pocket for his hankie again.

The gravediggers sighed impatiently. Fergal realised they expected him to give them a tip for their work; he thrust two Irish five-pound punt notes at them.

"That funny money, no use up here," one of the gravediggers said inelegantly.

Rage burst from Fergal. "It's more than your worth. Did you see what happened when they tried to lower the coffin into the grave? It got stuck on one side," Fergal choked out to Maureen. Images of the cheap plywood box rose before him. It had reminded him of a flimsy wooden pencil case he'd once had. The lid had split at the first fall, leaving with a deep gash from its splinters. He thought about Margaret's face just below the lid.

A primal howl pushed its way up his throat.

Tears ran unchecked down Maureen's face. Before Margaret was born, there had been successive miscarriages and one stillbirth. But Margaret had pushed her way into the world six weeks early, and survived, determined to be born.

"A small wisp with a big personality, a shock of red-gold hair and a stubborn, determined streak that never left her," she murmured.

She had left Fergal's bed when he had rejected their daughter. For the past fifteen years, they had lived behind the façade of husband and wife. But behind closed doors, they were like two strangers sharing a house.

"She's at peace now. Nothing can hurt her anymore," she said in a low voice.

In the distance, she heard what sounded like a factory horn and a church bell chiming.

"They serve early lunches in that hotel we're staying in," she said.

The dining room hummed with the buzz of voices and the rattle of cutlery. *Life is going on as usual,* Fergal thought with a bitter heart. He looked across the table. His wife's face had a closed, shuttered look. He wanted to get down on his knees in front of all these strangers and beg her to forgive him. He had deprived her of their daughter's wedding, the birth of their grandchildren, and the pleasure of sharing their lives as a proud granny should have been able to do.

He thought about the two youngsters he watched being forced down the graveyard path; water squelching in their shoes and the clear look of fear in their eyes.

"Is that the man Rev Snodgrass called Doctor Coles?" Maureen asked, nodding in the direction of two men talking intently at a nearby table. Fergal glanced at a squat, balding man pushing back a strand of hair that insisted on falling over his forehead.

"He must be a widower," she commented.

Fergal looked back at the man.

"Why do you say that?"

"He looks a bit scruffy and threw together compared to the other man," his wife said, taking in the younger man's smart suit and matching shirt and tie.

A heavy silence fell between them.

"Can I get you something to drink while you're waiting for your meal?" a waiter asked.

"No." Fergal said, flexing his arm. Then, on impulse, he said, "Yes, yes, bring us two hot whiskies—plenty of sugar."

"You and Margaret were very alike in nature, you know—stubborn and proud, afraid to lose face, afraid to admit you were both wrong." Margaret murmured, cutting her roast beef into small pieces. It tasted like compressed sawdust in her mouth. She couldn't get it swallowed past the lump in her throat. "When George and wee Sarah were born," she went on, "she wanted to come home. She knew then she'd made a mistake." She thought back to Margaret's unhappy letters home.

She had urged her to get on the Belfast-to-Dublin train and bring herself and the two children home.

What have you to stay for, she'd written. *Your husband William is in some foreign land fighting a war. You don't know if he is alive or dead. You're living in an old railway station house, long abandoned. And your mother-in-law, Sarah, hasn't broken breathe to you since you married her son.*

She'd visualised meeting Margaret at Connolly Station and bringing her and the children home to Waterford. But her daughter had stayed just as she had stayed with her father.

"That's what woman do in this country," she muttered.

"She stayed in Fermanagh but you wrote and sent her stuff from the shop, didn't you?" Fergal said defensively.

"I did. I sent her clothes for the youngsters and things she couldn't get during the wartime," she retorted. "You pretended not to notice," she said bitterly. "Just as you pretended you didn't look at the baby photos or read the letters she sent."

A pain shot across Fergal's ribcage, and he winced. "All I could see was that Meggie betrayed me, turned her back on her own religion, and left her fiancé, Tomas, her childhood sweetheart, in the lurch. He had enough to face being labelled a deserter for leaving the Irish Army to join the Brits and fight Hitler without Margaret breaking off their wedding plans."

Maureen snorted.

"Tomas Maloney didn't do so badly. Yes, he and his family were treated like traitors because he joined the British Army and took the King's money, and he had to move up the north to get a job. But it wasn't long before he forgot about Margaret and married a Belfast girl," she snorted.

Fergal sighed. He had kept adding to the money he was saving for their daughter's wedding. He thought his prayers were answered when Margaret wrote to say she had leave coming up and would be home for the May Day Celebration. That had been in early April. She never came. He wondered if Maureen knew he had coaxed Tomas, on a short leave pass, to go up north and see Margaret. He had a faint hope if she saw her childhood sweetheart again, she wouldn't marry William. It hadn't worked. She'd married William in a hurried, clandestine service in a Protestant church outside of Belfast.

Maureen heart lifted a little. Fergal had called Margaret, "Meggie," the pet name he'd called her when she was a baby. Tentatively, reaching across the white tablecloth she clasped his clammy hand.

"It's too late to do anything for Meggie, but maybe we can help our grandchildren—and William…"

"Complements of Dr Coles," the waiter said, breaking their conversation and placing two more hot whiskies down beside them. He was about to turn away when he stopped.

"Sorry for your troubles," he said, his words coming out in a rush.

"Thank you," Maureen said. Somehow, the customary words of condolence comforted her, and the kind gesture of the doctor made her feel less of a stranger.

She put down her fork and knife and leaned closer to her husband.

"Maybe… maybe we could go to the police… or somebody. Explain what the clergyman said about people talking. Say we think they're in danger."

"Maybe we could just get the kids in the car and drive them across the Border," Fergal muttered.

Maureen bristled.

"You let your daughter down. You put religion and your bigotry about the North being still under Britain before her. Kidnapping her children is not the way to help them."

Chapter 6

Doctor John Coles finished the last dregs of his tea and debated whether Aengus might be right about contacting the authorities regarding the Armstrong children.

"William's mental state was manageable until after Trisha's birth and Margaret 'baby blues'," his father sighed.

His son, Aengus, bristled. "You saw him yourself. I thought he was going to thump his father-in-law. He hasn't been mentally well for a very long time. He should have been admitted for treatment years ago," he snapped.

His father sighed. War had been good and bad for William. His detached attitude had worked well for him in ambush situations. He had proved to be a good leader of men. On the other hand, continuous exposure to death and terror had exacerbated his own fragile mental balance, and he had not done well since coming home.

The locals had no stomach for war-traumatised veterans, and William had all the classic symptoms of "war weariness". He was hyper-vigilant to sounds and smells. A car backfiring sent him into a trembling fit. He suffered from flashbacks and vivid nightmares of what he'd seen and done.

"No moral fibre," the postmistress, Annie Swanton, called it.

"He looks like a man hanging on to a cliff by his fingernails, if you want my professional opinion," Aengus said. "His children would be off in the care."

Mutely, his father agreed. But a children's home wasn't the right answer either.

"I wonder if I could persuade William to have a civilised meeting with his in-laws," Dr Coles Sr said, looking across the hotel dining room at the Furlongs.

"Those children would be better in care," Aengus stated again, wiping his mouth and preparing to rise from the table.

"Why don't I have a word with the grandparents," John Coles said. "If they were willing to help, the children would be better off with them."

"You will wait until William harms that daughter of his. Why can't people around here do their civic duty and report these things?" he hissed.

"Country people don't like to wash their dirty linen in public. The Armstrong's least of all," his father said tersely.

"What about the drowning of the middle Armstrong child.? That was hushed up pretty fast."

John looked at his son. Sent away to boarding school at eight, after his mother died, Aengus seemed to have lost all his understanding of his hometown country's ways.

"That was just a simple farm accident. You'll attend plenty of those before you're much longer in practice. Go on. After this morning's, funeral patients will be lined up for the late surgery," his father sighed. "And when the busybodies start spreading their nonsense information about how you can catch tuberculosis, everybody and their mother will be convinced they, or somebody belonging to them, has it or is getting it."

He sat for a moment and watched his tall, well-groomed son walk out Kielty's door.

"Maybe I sent him away too young. Perhaps I should have let him go to the local town school for a while longer," he sighed.

He wondered if he would chance having a drink. Aengus didn't approve of drinking earlier than the customary pre-dinner drink.

His son's probing questions about wee Sarah Armstrong's drowning had struck a raw nerve with John. The image of her body, hair streaming out behind her as she lay on the rough ground clutching a rag doll, her brother George trying to breathe life into her dead body, haunted him daily.

He had been too far away to hear what was said between William and Margaret's father at the graveside this morning, but it was obvious it wasn't convivial. *William has a lot of his mother, Sarah, in him,* he thought. *Too much religious fervour...* "Folks round here have long memories," he muttered to himself.

Fergal rose and shook the doctor's hand. Dr Coles waved him back. "Don't get up, don't get up. I'll sit down for a minute if I may. I want to extend my condolences. Today must have been a very difficult day for you both," he said, noting the man's red-rimmed eyes and the dried tears where the woman's make-up had smudged.

"You're the doctor who wrote and told us about Margaret's funeral," Maureen said.

The doctor nodded. "I feel as if I know you already. Margaret talked about you and her childhood in Waterford," he said. "Are you feeling unwell?" he asked, registering the pallor of Fergal's skin under his shock of tight curly salt-and-pepper hair. He knew Margaret's father owned a drapery shop, but this man had the build and stature of a football player. *I suppose in his part of Ireland he was reared on Gaelic football and hurling,* he thought.

"Margaret was your patient?" Maureen said.

"Yes, I've been the Armstrong family doctor for longer than I care to disclose," John said, a hint of humour in his voice. "I'm retired now, but I still keep an eye on things. Aengus, my son, followed me into the business, and you know these young ones—full of textbook learning and new-fangled ideas."

"Yeah, nothing like life's experiences to teach you," Fergal said caustically.

"I wonder," John said, catching the waitress' eye, who was taking longer than necessary to clear their table, "if you have a little time to spare, could we have a talk? What about a strong cup of tea in the snug? We will have more privacy there."

The Furlongs looked at each other and nodded. *This might be the opportunity we need to see what could be done about the children.*

"Kathy, is the fire in the snug lit yet?"

"No, Dr Coles, but I'll put a match to it right away," fourteen-year-old Kathy Swanton said, blushing at being caught eavesdropping.

Giving the reluctant flames a blast with the fire bellows, the doctor smiled. "Kathy, the young waitress, is Mrs Swanton, the postmistresses' granddaughter, and what gossip her granny doesn't hear, Kathy hears it here," he smiled. "Speaking of grandchildren—was today the first time you met George and Trisha?" he asked, his face sobering.

Shamefaced, Fergal stared at the carpet. "Yes, doctor, I'm sorry to say it was."

"Margaret sent photos—when George and Sarah were babies," Maureen said. "But we never even knew Trisha had been born… or that Sarah had drowned." She paused. "Margaret wrote for the first five years she was married, and then she just stopped writing, and I never knew why," Maureen said, her hands shaking so badly the tea slopped into the saucer.

I can guess why, the doctor thought. *William came back from war and put a stop to it.*

As if he had read his mind, Fergal said, "I tried to talk to William this morning. I suppose it wasn't the best time to do it. It was just that we thought we might not get the chance again." He flexed his arm. "Revenant Snodgrass, the clergyman, seemed to think the children might be in danger from their father, especially the girl," he said bluntly.

"Have you ever met William before today?" John asked cautiously, trying to gauge how much they knew about their son-in-law.

"Margaret brought him to her nursing graduation, but he didn't really involve himself. He seemed distant," Maureen explained, turning to face John.

John was startled by the woman's resemblance to her daughter: the same clear blue eyes, the straight nose, and the soft textured skin. Margaret had looked like that before she started taking the tables… before he had started trying to help her get over her 'nerves'.

Margaret would never permit him to contact her parents. "No. I won't let my father see what way I'm living or how my marriage has turned out," she'd argue. He'd remonstrated with her, even offering to get Robbie Black, who was old Samuel's solicitor and whose firm had offices in Dublin, to give a lift home to Waterford. "It'll be a short break for you and the children," he had coaxed.

"No. I won't go cap in hand," Margaret retorted, her eyes dull and depressed. "My father would be ashamed of me and my children. He'll say I should have listened to him and married Tomas Maloney."

Now, he would have no need his late patient's permission. Her parents had seen and were about to hear firsthand the life she and her children had lived, and the seething, unreasonable hatred William had for his youngest daughter.

John drew in a deep breath. Aengus would have a spluttering fit if he ever knew what he was about to tell Margaret's parents. He'd consider it a breach of confidentiality, he thought. *I couldn't even begin to imagine what he would say if he knew even half of the things I've done for the Armstrong family over the years,* he mused. *He'd probably have me certified along with William,* he thought. *And maybe he would be right,* he thought wryly. He straightened his spine. Nonetheless, the grandparents needed to know what they would face if they took on William and their grandchildren.

Maureen studied the doctor's face. She could see a small vestige of brown in the doctor's hair. A pair of rimless glasses peeped out from his breast pocket, and the smell of tobacco clung to his clothes. She guessed he was a pipe smoker, and from the telltale sheen of pink on his cheeks, he liked his drink. She had the distinct impression that behind his warm and cordial greeting, there lurked an unease and nervousness.

The doctor cleared his throat. "As I say, I have been the Armstrong family doctor for many years. Bringing William into the world was one of my first duties as a newly qualified doctor." He gave a short laugh. "I don't know who was the more scared, his mother Sarah or me. Samuel and Sarah married late in life. They didn't expect to have children. William's birth was like the second coming of John the Baptist—a miracle in their old age," he murmured. "But there was something—a detachment, an oddness about William even as a baby. His sister Lisa was born a year later—a year younger—but streaks ahead of him in every way," John murmured, looking into the heart of the fire. "William's mother kept him at home with her as much as possible, but in the end, she had to let him go to school. Growing up was a lonely time for William. He rarely spoke to anybody except his mother and his sister. And as a teenager, he showed not the slightest interest in girls."

Doctor Coles frowned. "I think there was one girl—from the church group. But William became so obsessed with her that he frightened her away. That was the story of William's life, I'm afraid. He was obsessive about things and people. He didn't make many friends, and those he did have didn't stay around for long."

The doctor broke off. "Sorry, I'm rambling. I have so many memories of William and his sister Lisa from when they were growing up." He forced a smile on his lips. "I think nobody was more surprised than William himself when Margaret fell in love with him. It was the only time in his life I ever saw him really happy," he said wistfully.

Fergal shifted impatiently in his chair. "William's a grown man now. He's able to look about himself, but what about what the clergyman said about our grandchildren being in danger from him and from catching TB?"

John Coles tightened his jaw. *Damn Geoffrey Snodgrass. Hadn't he done enough damage already?* He wondered if the Furlongs would take the children now that they knew about the tuberculosis. He had promised their grandfather Samuel, who had been his old army comrade in the Battle of the Somme in 1916, that he would look after the welfare of his grandchildren. *If the Furlongs didn't take them and Aengus had William sectioned, George and Trisha will end up in Conney Burrow Children's Home,* he thought in despair.

A spark fell out onto the worn carpet and fizzled for a second in the silence of the room.

John Coles jumped up and gave the brass bell set in the wall a sharp pull. "Let me freshen your drinks—get you more tea."

The soft tap on the door broke the terse atmosphere. "I brought three cups, Doctor," Kathy smiled.

Damn tea! John Coles fumed. *What I need is a good stiff drink.*

"What is it, Kathy?" he said irritably as the waitress hovered at his elbow.

"Sorry, Doctor, but Granny says to tell you William Armstrong is taking the boat to England tonight."

John Coles' blood thundered in his ears. William was in no fit state to go anywhere—except as an involuntary patient for treatment at the psychiatric hospital.

"Who told your Granny that?" he barked.

Kathy's lip trembled. "Con Callahan, the postman, told Granny."

"Is Con in the Public Bar?"

Kathy shook her head. "He said he had a message to do, Doctor."

"The children, Trisha, George—is he taking them with him?" Maureen stuttered, grabbing at the waitress's arm.

Kathy backed towards the door. "I don't know. He didn't say."

Maureen cast breeching eyes at her husband and screamed as Fergal slipped from his chair and keeled over onto the floor.

Chapter 7

Despite his burning anger at his father, George felt a shiver of excitement. He could feel the ship's lazy throb as it lay within the shelter of the harbour wall. He crossed over to the other side and looked out at the murky, slushy waves that lapped at the bottom of the ship.

Sitting on the hard wooden seats, he looked at the dark sky and thought about Trisha alone in the farmhouse.

They were well out into the Irish Sea now. The navvies from the train were involved in a card school. George listened to their raucous laughter and coughing.

He went out on deck. The water looked dark and ominous. Waves rose up and battered the hull. The deck rolled and lurched beneath him. Steadying himself, he leaned as far as he dared over the rail. Sea spray clung to his hair and face, leaving a salty taste in his mouth. He felt scared and exhilarated at the same time.

"How's it feel to be headin' to England for the first time?"

George turned to see Sheamie Foy. He stood, his feet planted confidently on the rolling deck, his woolly knit berry pulled well down under the collar of his turned-up donkey jacket. His hands on the ship's rail looked brown like the fishermen George met on the road at home.

He's old, like Da, George thought. Leaning back over the rail, he spat into the oily-looking waters. His spittle got caught in the wind and blew back on him.

"I'd rather be going to school," he replied.

Sheamie laughed. "Aye? Not often a young lad says that. You like the books, then?"

"Mammy wants me to be an architect—design things—built hospitals."

Sheamie sucked at his teeth. "Aye, plenty of dreams and no money to make them real," he sighed. He watched the sea as it was whipped into peaks by the throb of the ship. "Ouch, schooling not for the likes of us?" he said, giving George's shoulder a squeeze.

"Mammy went to grammar school when she was young in Waterford. I won a scholarship to Mill House Grammar."

"Is that right? Your mother was from Co. Kerry? You go down there for your holidays?"

George shook his head. "Da says they're not our sort."

He has sad old eyes for a bit of a lad, Sheamie mused. *God help him when he gets a blast of the London Irish landladies. Skin ye for a ha'penny, the bitches,* he thought. "Was there nobody you could have stayed with while your da went across the water?"

George stared out over the water and shook his head.

"Mammy's parents wanted to take Trisha, but Da wouldn't let her go."

Sheamie considered this for a minute. "Why wouldn't he let her go?"

"We're not the same Church as them."

So that the way of it, Sheamie thought. *A mixed marriage or maybe a bit of turning o' the flag. He'll not be bothered with religion in England,* he thought.

"Here, I'm a nosy oul' bugger, so I am. What about a bottle of lemonade and a chip butty?" he offered, hearing George's stomach rumble with hunger. "We'll bring your da back something," Sheamie said as George looked over at is father.

William stared dully at George's retreating back. "Ah should get up and go with him, make sure he's all right," he muttered, watching the sea spray linger for a moment and then slide down the greasy windowpane of the deck like lost tears.

His body felt tense and heavy. He listened to the wind screeched and howling. The overhead lights flickered, bright, dim, and then bright again.

A woman screamed as a gull splattered against the window. "That's a sign of the dead or ghosts or something," she squealed.

"The dead will do you no harm," the passenger beside her snorted. "It's the living you need to worry about," she said, looking to where William sat, his lips moving, his head nodding every now and again as if he was having a two-way conversation with someone.

Blind to their stares, William mumbled on. "Don't be angry at me, Margaret. I know I promised…"

Another gust of wind shook the deck, sending the dishes and glasses crashing to the ground. The ship shook and bobbed. A baby howled as a tremendous clap of thunder, followed by a massive streak of forked lightning, lit up the interior of the cabin.

William hurled himself to the ground and waited for the Luftwaffe to strike.

Gradually, he became aware of voices around him. "Are you alright, sir?" Lying as flat as he could get to the floor, William tried to focus.

"It's just a bad electrical storm, sir—nothing to be worried about. Get back up on your seat, please. We'll soon be docking," the pursuer said.

It was only then that William realised that he was under the wooden seating. Clutching his old army kitbag, he rose shakily to his feet.

"That your bag, mate? You were with the 'Skins'?" A young soldier passing by paused to ask him. "My father was with the 'Foughs', The Royal Irish Fusiliers," the young recruit went on. "I'm following in my dad's footsteps," he said proudly. "Maybe you knew him." Pulling a dog-eared picture out of his breast pocket, he thrust it under William's nose.

"McCrystal" a voice thundered. "What the bloody hell do you think you are doing?"

"Sir, this man was in the 2nd Battalion, like my father. Look, sir, look at the number on his kitbag." The army officer looked with disdain at William's dishevelled state and unfocused eyes. "Get back to your company. I will deal with this."

"Have you forgotten how to act in the presence of an Officer of her Majesty's Armed Forces?" he snapped out to William.

William staggered to attention.

"You are behaving in a disgraceful manner," the officer snapped. "Pull yourself together, man. Show a bit of backbone." Taking a gold-,tipped pen from his uniform pocket he wrote something on a slip of paper and thrust it at William. "If you need help—which I very much doubt—they will give you a handout at this address; that should cure the problem," he said, tight-lipped.

Teeth chattering, George pulled his coat tightly around him as the last rays of sunrise faded and Heysham Docks loomed up in front of him.

He watched the harbour getting closer and closer. Excitement gripped him. Climbing onto the nearest seat, he scanned the throng of head. His father was sitting apart from the dismembered queue, which was swelling by the second.

He could see Sheamie Foy and the navvies forming a straggly line. *They look like a line of crows on the telegraph wires*, he thought, watching their black-buried heads bobbing along.

Crew called and shouted instructions as they operated the heavy machinery that opened the ship's doors. Impatient to be on their way to their final destinations, passengers complained and muttered at the delay. He could hear the cattle housed in the bowels of the ship lowing, knowing soon they'd soon be off the sea.

George, trying not to breathe in, burrowed into his coat. The smell of sick and stale breath was overpowering. Finally, the great door began to slide open and daylight filtered in over the heads of the passengers. Carried forward by the swell of crowd, George stumbled down the gangway.

He was in England.

He stared in amazement at the hordes of people making their way to the line of waiting trains. Others were forming a line to use the red telephone boxes across from him. His heart leapt. He would phone Ballet Post Office and tell the postmistress that Trisha was in the house by herself. The thought had hardly registered when he heard somebody shouting his name.

"Where you stayin'?" Sheamie Foy shouted, heaving his suitcases on his shoulders.

George looked expectantly at his father. William looked back at him and then down at his boots.

Sheamie screwed up his face and cursed. "Ah might know a place near Euston Station. It's not up to much. It'll do you for a night or two till you get better," he said fiercely, eyeballing William.

"Could I phone home first?" George asked.

"No time for phonin', young fella, if yer wants to get digs," Sheamie scowled, striding away.

Chapter 8

Con Callahan blew on his cold hands. *I'm getting too old for this lark,* he thought as the tyres of the post office bike crunched the hard ground, white with frost. "It's time I got the oul 'gold watch and bought meself a new fishin' rod," he said aloud, his breath making a mist in front of him.

A shape in the field next to the graveyard caught his eye. Was it a dog worrying the cattle? It didn't seem to be moving. Throwing the bike up against the stone ditch, he decided to take a closer look.

Closer up, it looked like the shape of a small child! His heart jerked in his chest. *Sweet Mother of God, it was William Armstrong's lass!* What was she doing in the middle of the graveyard field? She looked like she'd frozen to death. He ran out into the middle of the road, praying that Davy Dobbs hadn't passed with the early shift Belleek Factory workers.

"Is she livin' or dead?" Davy stuttered, afraid to touch her.

"What will we do? We can't leave her out here!" Con said, his heart beating like a handbell, his breath coming in short gasps from the shock.

"Take her to Erne Hospital!" a shocked passenger shouted from where the workers had piled out of the bus and were huddled together on the other side of the road.

"Dr Coles' house is nearer," another woman passenger shouted.

Davy kept his hand on the knocker until a light went on in the glass panel above Dr Coles' door.

"Where did you find her?"

"In the quarry field beside the graveyard. Is she livin' or dead?" Con quaked. "Ah think William has lost it altogether this time. Doctor, Ellen said ah should have sent a message to the Sergeant instead of you when William said he was leavin' her in the house on her own."

At the mention of police, Dr Coles drew the postman out of earshot of his son, Aengus. "Will you have to report finding her to Sergeant Campbell?"

Con sensed unease behind the doctor's question. He hesitated. He wasn't looking forward to being grilled by the new Sergeant, but he'd have to report finding her.

"Ah will, doctor."

John Coles drew his hand across his chin. "She's a farmer's daughter. She's used being out in all weathers. She'll be grand. I've given her a sedative. Aengus is bandaging her feet and hands. You did the right thing bringing her to me. I'll have a word with the Sergeant… and the postmistress," the doctor said, patting Con on the back.

"Will she need to go to hospital, doctor?"

John Coles took a deep breath. "I know it's a lot to ask and you have already done more than your share, Con…" He hesitated. "If she had somebody to look after her, she'll recover just as well at home. Would your wife Ellen be able look after her until her aunt Lisa comes…?"

Con shook his head vehemently. "No way. Ellen is afraid of bringing the TB into the house."

"Aengus and I will call every day—twice a day if need be," the doctor hurried on.

Con's shoulders slumped. "You can ask her, doctor. Don't be surprised if she turns you away at the door."

Chapter 9

Sheamie stopped at a house that looked to George as if nobody had lived there for a while. The peeling front door might have been brown at one time, but it was very difficult to tell now.

Sheamie put his mouth close to the letterbox and shouted, "It's me, Ma Higgins—Sheamie Foy." After a minute, the door opened a crack, and a pair of brown eyes looked out at them.

"Has Ma Higgins a room? Just for the night?" The door opened a little more, and George saw a girl who looked about the size of Trisha staring out at them.

"Shut that bloody door," a voice roared. George heard the clatter of something. The girl was thrust aside, and a pair of bloodshot eyes glared out at them.

"You blind?" Ma Higgins snarled, pointing to a faded sign in the window. "No Irish! More bother than they're worth," she barked, starting to close the door.

Sheamie stuck his big boot in the door opening. With a slow deliberate movement, he drew out a bottle of whiskey from his pocket and took a long, slow swallow. The woman's eyes fastened on the bottle. With a well-practised movement, Sheamie slid the bottle back into his pocket. Wiping his hand over his mouth, he smiled at the woman. "Forgot about that. It was only for the one night, but no harm done," he said, turning away.

"Only for one night?" Ma Higgins rasped, her eyes never leaving the bulge in Sheamie's pocket. "Stella,", she yelled. Like a ghost the girl materialised from the shadows in the hall.

"Keep your clothes on, your boots under the legs of the bed, and any money you have under the mattress you're sleeping on," Sheamie advised. "Here, give her this," he said, holding out the remains of the whiskey bottle. William recoiled as if he was offering him poison. "Give it 'ere," Stella said.

Sheamie shook his head. "Don't give it to her until you have everything you need for the room," he said, handing the bottle to George. He was about to go out the door when he turned and caught George's arm. "Only let your da pay for one night at a time," he hissed. "If you don't, you'll find your money drunk and your bed occupied by whoever gives her the money for more drink. Be ready early in the mornin' if you're lookin' for work," he said, brushing past William.

George tried to not breathe. The smell of damp and something that smelled like rotting turnips filled his nostrils. Groping his way, he followed the girl past several closed doors with dim chinks of light showing beneath them. She stopped at what looked like the ladder they used on the farm to get up to the hayloft.

"Stay close to the wall," Stella warned, starting up the ladder.

"Pay me now," the landlady demanded, coming down the hall.

George shot his father a warning look.

"You'll get your rent when we get the things we need," George said.

Ma Higgins blinked. "Another bloody lippy kid," she ground out.

"Make sure ye get the rent," Ma Higgins warned Stella.

William threw himself on the creaky bed and pulled the damp-smelling blankets around him. George sat down on his suitcase and looked in bewilderment at the room.

"How do you light the fire," he asked, his teeth chattering.

"Give it here and I'll show," Stella said, holding her hand out for the money.

"I'll do it—just you show me how," George said. After a few tries, the gas fire hissed and glowed orange, then red.

"Ere are you blankets and… fings." Stella mumbled. "Ya need a pan and a kettle," she said, backing out of the room again.

George knelt on the cold linoleum in front of the small gas fire and tried to get warm. He didn't know if his body was shaking from the cold or because he was scared. With a splutter, the gas fire went out again.

"Pan and pot," Stella said, setting them on the floor. She held out her hand. George took the money from his father and paid her rent for one night, handing over the whiskey.

Stella stared at him. "Ain't been in lodgings before, 'ave ya?"

George looked back mutely at her. She was as tall as Trisha but nearer his age, he realised. He could hear Ma Higgins yelling for her.

"Shop and chippy—end of street," Stella mouthed at him, slipping like a shadow down the ladder.

The attic room had no lock or bar. For what seemed like hours, George lay and listened to the strange noises of the house and the strange-sounding accents outside on the street. The smell of cooking wafted up to him, making his empty stomach rumble. He pulled the string beside the door, and a dim light filled the box room. He opened the thin plywood door and peered out into the darkness of the attic space. He could hear noises coming from behind one of the doors along the downstairs hall. He shook his father awake. "Da. There's a shop…What will I buy, Da?" he asked, his voice shaking.

Without answering, William fumbled out a handful of change and lay down again.

Holding the money in one hand and the dented tin kettle in the other, George went in search of the kitchen. All the doors in the hall were shut. Unsure which one might be the kitchen, he tried the one nearest to the bottom of the ladder.

"What's your game, mate?" a black man asked, leaping from his bed and towering over him.

The kettle rattled against the wall of the narrow hall.

"Kitchen," George stammered, trembling with fright.

"You Irish or Scottish?" the man asked, realising he was just a boy.

"From Northern Ireland," George stuttered. He wasn't sure himself. His father and Granda always said they were British, but his mother always said she was Irish.

"Water in bathroom—across there," The man nodded in the direction of the door straight across the hall. "Wait a bit. Ma Higgins has been in there. Whoa," he said laughing, waving his hand about as if to blow away the smell. "You just off the boat?" he said perceptively. George nodded.

"You hungry?" the man asked, noticing the way George's eyes lingered on the cooking pot. "Twenty-four-hour shop at end of the street," the man said, noticing the change clutched in George's hand. "Go to the shop—leave the kettle," he said, prising it out of George's hand. "I'll fill it, and you get it when you get back. Close the door behind you quietly, or Ma Higgins will not let you back in. I'll listen for your knock."

Out on the street, George wondered if the black man meant up or down when he nodded in the direction of the shop.

The lights of a passing car lit up the end of the street, and he caught a glimpse of a cigarette sign like the one outside Kielty's hotel. Breathlessly, with fear, he ran in the direction of the shop.

Not sure of the cost of things, he bought bread, milk, and cheese. His mouth watered at the sight of the cooked chicken and ham and the smell of chips coming from the chippy.

"Thank you for shopping with us," the man behind the counter, with the brown skin and crinkly smiling eyes, said. "You need change—for the gas fire?"

George shook his head. He had no money left.

"Kettle filled, boiled and ready," the black man said handing George the kettle and a dish covered with a cloth. "Curried noodles—enjoy. Return the dish later," he smiled.

"What kind of stuff is this?" William spat, pushing the bowl away. "You'll l need to look for a job at the price of things here," he grumbled when George said he's used up all the money he'd given him.

"What could we use to lock the door?" George said.

"Get in your bed. We have that's worth stealin'?"

George crawled into bed, staying as far away from his father as possible. *If we're not robbed or killed during the night*, he thought, *I'll be finding other digs.*

Chapter 10

The icy cold temperature in the room woke George. He looked at his father huddled under the blankets. *At least he didn't get up shouting from his nightmares in the middle of the night,* he thought.

"Da, I need more money for the gas fire," he said.

"I'm givin' you no more. That thing's eatin' the money," William muttered.

George recoiled when he went in the bathroom to wash the bowl before giving it back to the man across the hall. He stared at the peeling enamel on the big ugly bath. The toilet was even worse: a black ring of dirt surrounded it, both inside and out, and the big old-fashioned hand basin had mould growing around its taps. His stomach heaved.

There was no response to his knock on the door opposite. Tentatively, he pushed the door open, intending to leave the bowl on the table. The room was empty.

"He left early this morning—without payin' 'is rent," Stella's voice said from the dark shadowy hallway, making George jump. Backing away, he scurried back up the stair ladder.

"Da. The room below us is empty."

William grumbled petulantly, reluctant to leave the heat of the bed.

"It has two beds, Da. And it's nearer the kitchen and toilet, Da."

A hammering on the front door made them both jump.

"Yer Da ready?" Sheamie Foy bawled at George, meeting him coming down the attic ladder clutching his bag, with a kettle and saucepan under each armpit.

"Tell him to get a move on if he wants work the day. Ah thought farmers were supposed to be up with the sun."

George watched his father leave with a mixture of relief and apprehension. *What if something happened to him? What if he never came back?* He didn't know another living soul in England. Slipping the bar across the new bedroom, he lay down on the pile of clothes one of the single beds and sobbed with fright.

He jerked up when he heard voices.

"I ain't see 'im," Stella was saying.

"Stole everything f-king fing," Ma Higgins screeched, thundering down the attic ladder. "That what we get for lettin' them foreigners into the country," she shouted.

With a jolt, George realised she thought it was the black man who was in the attic room last night.

After a while, there was an insistent tapping on the bedroom door.

"It's me, Irish," Stella's voice whispered through the jamb of the door. "Let me in," she hissed. "You and your old man got me a slap," she said, pushing past George.

"I didn't mean to get you in bother. I just wanted to get this room before Ma Higgins gave it …"

"Drunken cow," Stella said disparagingly, seeing the stricken look on George's face. "Slap don't bother me none. It's nothing to what my mam and her sodden boyfriends used to give me."

George looked at her in confusion. "I thought Ma Higgins was your mother."

Stella turned her eyes to the ceiling. "You a cretin, Irish?" she sneered. "Ma found me, didn't she? Turnin' tricks, I was, in King's Cross Station when I was a kiddie…"

George wasn't sure he knew what "turning tricks" meant. "Why don't you live with your own mother?"

"You're such a baby—stupid too. You better wise up fast," Stella sneered.

"I'm a grammar schoolboy. I'm not stupid!"

"Not that kind of stupid. Stupid!" Standing up, Stella looked at him. "Ya need a different kind of education. You got money to buy your old man's dinner?"

George jingled the loose change in his pocket. "Not sure if I have enough. We… I lived on a farm. Not sure how much things cost," he admitted.

"Oh, poor little country boy comes to the big city," Stella mocked.

George's face flamed.

"Ma Higgins fancies cooked chicken for her dinner. She ain't got no money neither. Wear a coat that 'as deep pockets. We're goin shopping."

"How will we get food without money?" George asked as he followed Stella into an open food market. His eyes widened. He had never seen so much food or so many people in one place.

For a while, he forgot everything: his father, Ma Higgins, and even Trisha, as he listened, open-mouthed to stallholders yell out prices and watched customers haggled for the best bargains.

"Time to go, Irish," Stella said in his ear. George followed her, wondering if she'd forgotten about Ma Higgins' dinner.

Inside the front door of Birch ill Road, she stopped. "Want to see a magic trick?" she chortled. Pulling down the front of her dress, she pulled out two cooked chickens. George caught a glimpse of her breasts before turning away in embarrassment.

"Dinner for your da and Ma Higgins. That's what I mean about smart," she tittered.

George looked at her, dumfounded.

"Want to see what I have in the pockets of my frock?"

"Go on, put yer hand in—better than a lucky dip," Stella giggled. George's fingers brushed against her thigh and touched something soft. He jumped back as if he had been scalded.

Stella laughed. "Don't be such a baby. It's not what ya fink. It's only a few oul' ripe peaches I nicked from the fruit stall," she said, sniggering at the shocked look on George's face.

Chapter 11

"Seats are as scarce as hen's teeth," a passing woman scolded. Lisa wished she'd booked a berth. *Chance would be a fine thing,* she mused. Getting BJ to agree to her going home, and getting him to part with some of his horse winnings to help with the boat fare, had been no easy task.

Afraid to move in case she'd lose her spot, she stretched out beside her bag. Her thought went back to the heated argument she had with BJ. It had taken days, but finally, white with rage, he'd given in.

He'd squared his heavy-set shoulders. "And didnea come back wi' that bairn," he warned. "I'm no feedin' and clothin' another man's bairn. And mind ye get the boat fare from William," he'd shot at her as she pulled on her headscarf and checked for the hundredth time if she had her ticket for the boat.

Always careful to marshal her thought in case she spoke Scott Osbourne's name aloud without thinking, she'd buried her love for her teenage GI lover deep within her heart. *It was just a throwaway remark,* she told herself.

An audible gasp had gone up the first time the local girls had seen the American GIs at the dance in the Legion Hall.

"They look like film stars," her friend Mary Kielty had gasped.

Lisa had noticed Scott straight away. He looked so handsome in his dress uniform. She knew she looked good too, in her figure-hugging dress; her hair swept up to show off her long, slender neck. Daringly, she broke the rules, marching across the floor to ask him to dance.

"That was the beginning of my first love affair," she murmured.

Like flood gates swept away in a storm, a torrent of memories streamed back. The way Scott liked her to wear her high heels, showing off the nylons he gave her; and how he like the other GIs' admiring glances of her in her figure-hugging dresses. She smiled, remembering how much in love she had been with him. *I spend hours curling my hair just the way he liked it,* she mused.

A feeling of guilt dimmed her thoughts. She couldn't remember the last time she had fixed her hair or dressed up for her husband. "BJ never made me feel beautiful the way Scott did," she murmured.

A harsh laugh squeezed its way up her throat.

"But he was good enough to marry you when you found yourself up the duff, wasn't he," she reminded herself. Realising that she had spoken aloud, she glanced around but her words were drowned out by the announcement that they would soon be docking.

The case humped against Lisa's legs as she hurried along the platform at York Street station. She felt a frisson of excitement at being back in Northern Ireland, and home. *Funny how I still think of here as my home,* she thought.

Her step lighter now, she made her way up the steep stairs, across the iron overhead bridge, and down onto the far platform. The train for Fermanagh was already in. *Not a lot has changed since I've been away,* she thought, taking a quick look around her.

She cringed, remembering how she had scurried away from home all those years ago.

"Wait a while, daughter. Don't be in such a hurry to marry," her mother Sarah had advised.

"There'll be plenty of men—good men—when this war ends; you can have your pick of them. You were never short of admirers. Your father was always showing you off. I wish I had a penny for every time I heard you admired. Strangers would come up to me in the street and say, 'Look at her big brown eyes and that head of golden hair'."

Even now, fifteen years later, Lisa could still recall the astonishment she'd felt at her mother's compliments.

"Your mother's not one for gilding the lily. Take the compliment when she's givin' it," her father had laughed.

But her mother wasn't as complimentary the day she told her she was marrying BJ.

"He's asked you?"

Lisa shook her head. "I'm going to ask him."

Shocked, her mother had spun around, the small tight black bun she always wore bobbing on the nape of her neck, threatening to come undone. "Don't you dare, daughter! He'll think you're a wanton hussy," she'd breathed. "You're not even twenty-one yet. You have plenty of time to get a man. I didn't marry your father till I was in my thirties. There's plenty of time…"

"No, there's not."

"Aye, there is."

"No, mother, there's not."

Her mother's had face paled. "So that's what the new way of living does for you? Lowers yours morals and loosens your drawers," she'd said, her whole demeanour changing. "The Yank was well rewarded for the silk stockings," she added.

Lisa recoiled as if her mother had struck her. Only the tick of the old black-faced clock on the mantelpiece broke the terrible silence that had descended.

"We let the good Lord down," Sarah had said almost inaudibly.

Even now, trudging down the station platform, Lisa could feel the small hairs stand up on the back of her neck. She had never, ever witnessed her mother crying before.

"Mother," she'd said, reaching out a tentative hand. Her mother had flinched from her touch.

"William, "her mother had continued, "what does our William do? He announces he's secretly in love with a…a Roman Catholic—a papist. And he'll marry her in any church or no church. The pair of you has made us the laughing stock of the place."

The shrill of the guard's whistle brought Lisa's thoughts back to the present. Struggling in through the narrow door of the carriage, she heaved the suitcase on to the metal rack above her head and sank gratefully on to the worn upholstered seat.

"Pleasant enough day for travelling," the ticket collector said, noting the battered suitcase and the dishevelled look of the plump woman. Feeling his eyes sweep over her, Lisa patted down her hair that had blown into a frizz by the rough night sea crossing.

Stretching her tired body, she looked out at the landscape as it slid past. *The fields look like a patchwork quilt of dark greens and pale gold hemmed with the grey of the stone walls and hedges,* she thought. "Like the picture postcard William sent me," she murmured.

The train was crossing over the Fermanagh Lakes—the Lough Shore, Boa Island, and Lough Erne now. The water rippled and puffed up as the wind moved it. In the distance, Lisa spotted a small boat making its way into a small harbour.

It took her back to the days and nights she had met Scott, and they had sat and dabbled their bare feet in the cold water of the lakes like two children. "Oh, Scott," she said aloud. The feel of his name on her tongue saddened her and made her pulse quicken at the same time.

With his Texas accent and charming manners, he had been so different from the local boys.

"Our nights, sharing our secret love, were magical," she murmured. "I flirted with the local boys and BJ. But I only ever gave my love to you, Scott. I was a virgin the first time you made love to me," she murmured. Her eyes grew soft as she remembered how Scott had brushed the hair back from her face and told her he would love her forever.

Lisa could see the Donegal Hill in the distance and remembered their stolen trips across the Border. "I could get the call tomorrow, me darling Irish rose," Scott would say. "Some of the boys have already been shipped overseas. Hitler has to be stopped and we're the guys to do it," he'd boasted.

The train was slowing down as it approached Ballet station. She craned her neck to see if she could catch a glimpse of the old castle. She stilled. There it was, standing stubbornly with its back against the Atlantic Ocean, defiantly challenging the storms and gales to do their worst. Gathering her coat about her, she lifted down her case, hoping William was there to meet her.

The wind blowing along the platform was playing with the icicles that hung from the stationhouse guttering. The train gave its usual long low whistle as it rounded the bend. Passengers stepped cautiously over the gap between the train and the platform.

"No Lisa today either," Con grunted. This was his second day of meeting the trains.

"I might have known it would be blowing a gale," a plump woman said as she passed him. She stopped. "Con Callahan?" she said with just hint of a Scottish accent.

"Aye," Con said looking at her enquiringly.

"Have you seen William Armstrong? I was hoping he'd meet me off the train."

Perplexed, Con reached into his pocket and took out his glasses. "Lisa? Good God, I didn't know you. You're welcome back." He hesitated. "William's away… Ellen has a drop of tea ready," he said. "A'll tell you all about… William as we go."

Chapter 12

Lisa was reeling from the shock of what Con had told her on the way to his house. Doctor Aengus Coles was there, finishing his morning visit. Lisa stared down at her heavily sedated niece she had never met. She was struck by the resemblance to William and her own father, Samuel.

A terrible sadness filled her. She would never see her father again or hear him tell her about things on the farm or who he had met at the cattle mart. *I threw all that away,* she thought, *and for what?*

Dr Coles gave an impatient cough.

"I'm considering sending her to the Children's Hospital in Belfast. There will be questions asked," he said, linking his hands together and rocking slightly on balls of his feet.

"Why?" Lisa said.

Dr Coles gave her a cold stare.

"Why? Perhaps we might begin with why a young, motherless child was left abandoned without light, food or heat—left to wander outside in freezing temperatures," he snapped. "You do realise that we could have been dealing with another death here because of your brother's negligence."

Snapping his bag shut, he shot her another piercing glance. "Get some rest," he commanded. "This child has seen enough death and disease in her young life. She doesn't need any more."

Lisa's faced flamed. She felt she had stepped back in time. Once again, she was the young, foolish, trembling, white-faced girl sitting across the desk from old Dr Coles.

"Is your American boyfriend still stationed here?" he'd asked in a kindly voice.

Lisa had shaken her head.

"I'll see what can be done," he said, patting her hand in a fatherly gesture.

Lisa looked at the grim-faced of Aengus, Dr Coles' son. He was nothing like his kind-hearted father. Years of fighting for survival in the tenements of Glasgow came to her rescue.

"What do you mean by that?" she demanded.

"I have a surgery of patients waiting for me. Con will explain it," he said, buttoning up his grey woollen overcoat.

Lisa gripped the hot toddy Con had pushed into her cold hands. "Sit up beside the fire," he said, pushing her gently into the stuffed armchair.

"What did he mean…there'll be questions?" Lisa quaked.

"Ach, you know these young doctors…" Con soothed. "Old Doc Coles was a good friend o' your father's. Divil a word there'll be about it."

Lisa trembled with shock. She couldn't take it in that Margaret was dead and buried, that William had taken George out of school and left Trisha alone in the farmhouse. Guilt twisted her guts. *I should have come home when I got William's postcard,* she gulped.

Con gave himself a shake. "The postmistress will think I got lost," he said. Winding the warm muffler around his neck, he made for the door. "Stay beside the fire." He hesitated. "It's kind of… rough out at the farm. William hasn't bothered much since your father passed on. Stay wi' Ellen and me for a day or two—have an early night. Things will not look so bad then," he said, avoiding his wife's raised eyebrows.

Lisa slept fitfully, trying to decide the best way to break the news to BJ that it might be weeks before she came home. She wasn't looking forward to admitting to BJ what William had done. She got out of bed. She might as well phone him and get it over with. Then she'd go out to the farm.

Pulling the scarf over her hair and tightening the belt on her raincoat, she stepped out into the street. There'd be a pay phone in Kielty's Hotel.

She was just passing the Post Office in Castle Street as Annie Swanton, the postmistress, was opening.

"Lisa," she said, a broad smile creasing her plump face. "Con told me you were home. Come in, come in. I want to hear all about poor wee Trisha," she said.

"Well, I must say," she said, folding her flabby arms over her plump chest, "marriage suits you. And how many children did you say you have now?"

"Two," Lisa said shortly. "I was just on me way to Kielty's."

"It'll hardly be open this early. Were you going there… for any particular reason?"

"Just to make a phone call."

"Was it a local call… or an international call? Use the Post Office phone," she said, rushing over to the large black telephone sitting in a booth at the side of the counter "I'll put you through," she gushed, barely able to hide her excited anticipation of the juicy bit of gossip she was about to hear.

Hemmed in between the mailbags and parcels, Lisa fished out the number of the Nag's Head and handed it over. The phone rang and rang; its echo reverberating around the small Post Office.

Annie sighed in exasperation. Finally, a woman answered. Leaving a short message for BJ, Lisa turned to see the disappointed look etched on the postmistress's face.

Watching Lisa's retreating back, Annie wondered if she'd heard yet that the Yank was back and getting ready for a wedding.

For one wild, exhilarating moment, that's who I thought she was ringing, she muttered. "Now wouldn't that be a turn-up for the books," she said to the empty room.

Chapter 13

Sitting on the bus, Lisa could hardly curb her impatience. They had stopped at every crossroad since they'd left the town.

The biting cold December wind tugged at her she got off and started the two-mile walk to the farm. She could feel the roughness of the country road through the thin soles of her boots. Turning the familiar corner into the mouth of the lane to the house, she resisted the urge to run and skip as she did when coming home from school.

She turned and caught a glimpse of the lake where she and William had splashed about as children. Her eye travelled to where the border marked the division between Southern Ireland and Northern Ireland. "I'd forgotten how beautiful it all was," she said aloud. *Maybe you have to lose something to realise how precious it is to you,* she thought.

The raised latch made a clanking noise as it fell back into its position. The sight that met Lisa's eyes stuck her feet to the ground. A trail of peat mould lay scattered like mice droppings on the flagged floor of the kitchen. The black range, her mother's pride and joy, lay covered in white peat ash. The black iron kettle, its spout turned towards the wall, sat dejected and bereft.

An irrational feeling of betrayal rose up in Lisa's chest. This wasn't the kitchen she had pictured, dreamt of coming back to in her darkest days in the tenements. "I expected you would always be here, warm and welcoming like you always were," she whimpered to the cold silent kitchen. An image of her mother, short and stocky, grey patterned apron wrapped around her body, tied in a bow at her waist, standing beside the range, her finger pointing at her as it had done countless times before, stood looking at her. Lisa's heart contracted. Clear as a bell, she heard her mother's voice say. *Don't stand there, daughter, get that fire lit.*

Backing out of the kitchen door Lisa stood shaking in the yard. The silence, once welcoming, unnerved her now. *It feels as if the very birds are holding their breath,* she shivered.

Shaking, she sat down on the large stone flower pot her mother used to plant yellow daffodils in and fumbled for a cigarette.

Was it possible her mother had been waiting all these years for her to come home and take care of her kitchen?

It's just your imagination, she berated herself. Yet, the thought propelled her into action. Leaning a broken potato crib against the wall of the shed, she smashed her boot into it with practised ease. "Once a farmer's daughter always a farmer's daughter," she muttered, hurrying back into the kitchen. She pushed the thinnest shards of wood through the gaping bar of the grate. She needed paper to get the wood started.

"Da kept old bills and newspapers cutting in his wardrobe," she said. Getting the fire lit and her mother's range cleaned was now an all-consuming drive within her.

The wardrobe door in her parent's bedroom, swollen with damp, refused to open. Pull as hard as she might, it wouldn't budge. Agitated, she sat down on the end of the iron bedstead and gave the wardrobe an angry kick with her boot.

She heard a whooshing sound. The wardrobe door swung open and boxes of old newspapers and letters fell onto the bedroom floor. Grabbing an armful of the old newspapers, brown and crinkly with age, she ran downstairs to the kitchen.

Hoping she wasn't burning anything of importance, she tore at the damp pages. The fire struggled to light. Then, the thin shavings from the old wooden crate began to crackle in the grate.

Lisa grabbed up the iron kettle and made for the well.

Staring at her reflection in the dark sheen of the well's water, she rinsed and filled the kettle. Sitting back on her knees, she remembered her and William as children, flat on their bellies, floating sticks in the water, pretending they were ships sailing to America.

It was one of the few things my father ever beat me for, she reflected.

"Don't you ever let me catch you doing that again," her father Samuel had thundered, shaking her. "You could fall in and drown."

"That's enough, Samuel. William's the oldest. He should know better," her mother had scolded. Usually a mild-mannered man, her father had turned on her mother.

"You know as well as I do, he has nothing between his two ears," he'd bawled. "Lisa should have been watching him!"

"Poor wee Sarah did fall in" Lisa murmured.

The familiar rattle of a tractor and trailer coming up the lane broke her reverie.

"Faith Hamilton saw the smoke—heard you were home, so she sent me over with a few bags of dry turf and sticks for the fire. I'll put them in the shed," he smiled.

Robbie Black, my old dancing partner, Lisa thought, nodding her thanks. She hadn't seen him in years.

"She says you're to come over for a bite of dinner," Robbie smiled dusting his hands on the back of his jeans.

"That's very kind of Mrs Hamilton, but I need to get back," Lisa said. By now, everybody would have heard about what William had done. She didn't want to discuss it anymore.

"Tell you what, I'll call back in about half an hour. Have a bite to eat with your old neighbour and I'll drop you into town later."

Lisa put her hand to her bushy hair. *I must look a sight,* she thought.

"Yeah, OK. Thank you," she stammered, watching the easy way he swung up onto the driver's seat and deftly manoeuvred the tractor and trailer out of the yard.

Lisa resisted the temptation to run her finger around the plate and lick the gravy off her fingers like she did when she was a wee girl. "That was a really lovely dinner, but I do need to be getting back. Ellen and Con will think I'm taking advantage of their kindness."

"Robbie will take you," Faith Hamilton said, refilling Lisa's cup tea. "How's Trisha doing?"

"Dr Coles says it'll take a while for her to recover from the frostbite in her feet." Lisa hesitated. Faith was their nearest neighbour, and according to Margaret's letters, one of the few people in the village who hadn't shunned William when he'd married a Catholic.

"William shouldn't have left Trisha alone in the house. He should have waited until I got here," she said in a low voice. She held back in telling Faith that he had already known she was coming but that she wasn't taking Trisha back to Glasgow with her.

Faith sighed. "Poor William, losing Margaret was the last straw. He took it very bad." Faith glanced at her visitor. "William always needed somebody to look about him. Some people are like that."

Lisa's face tightened; she felt as if she was being blamed for not being there—blamed for William's actions.

"My mother made me promise to always be there for him," Lisa said. "I have my own family to think about now. I'm not taking his daughter to live with me in Glasgow."

Anger rose up in her. "My husband BJ says it's time William was made to face his own responsibilities and not always be depending on me."

"What will become of Trisha if you don't take her?" Faith said, sighing deeply.

Lisa trembled. She didn't know. But she knew if she took Trisha to live with her, there'd be no chance of taking a job to earn the extra money she needed to save to keep Andrew at school.

"I had kind of a vision in my mother's kitchen," Lisa said, changing the subject. "I had the strongest sensation my mother was in the kitchen with me and was ordering me to light the range," Lisa blurted out. "I don't think my mother's soul is at rest." Faith Hamilton was a churchgoing woman. She wondered what she'd make of it.

Faith shivered. Old Samuel had taken Margaret and her children into his dead wife's house against her dying wishes.

Faith drew in a deep breath. "After your mother died, it all got too much for your poor father. You were in Glasgow, and William was lost in action, thought to be dead… and Margaret came to live in the farmhouse," she said, her words petering out.

Sarah Armstrong will not rest, Annie Swanton had prophesised at a meeting of the ladies Committee. *You mark my words, the next thing will be, he'll be signing the farm over to her or her children.*

"My father and mother were happy enough to let me marry and live in Scotland," Lisa said, stung by Faith's implication she had abandoned her elderly parents.

Faith started to gather up the dinner plates. *I'm sure they were,* she thought. Even in wartime, being an unmarried woman with a child was still frowned upon.

She gazed over Lisa's head. "The war changed everything. It robbed Sarah, your mother, of the farmer's daughter she had her heart set on for her son. William might have eventually taken to farming if he hadn't been involved in the war effort: manning the soldier on the trains to make sure they didn't cross over the border into the South of Ireland, which was neutral. That's how he met Margaret." She put the dishes down and stood looking into the distance. She took a deep breath. "It robbed me of my sons—buried in a land I will never see, with—no gravestone to visit." She placed a caring hand on Lisa's. "There was a time when I hoped you would settle down, marry one of our sons—unite the two farms. But the war stole away your innocence," she said softly. "If the GIs hadn't been stationed here, you would never have met the Yank... or married your husband."

Lisa felt as if her heart was being wrung out. *How different my life would have turned out if that had happened,* she thought as she climbed into the jeep beside Robbie.

"Are you staying at the farm for a while?" Robbie asked, breaking the silence.

"I don't know. It all depends on Trisha getting better."

Lisa felt her tension beginning to melt away. "You still the best dancer in Ballet, Robbie?"

Robbie cast a sidelong glance and laughed. "It seems like another lifetime ago now, doesn't it."

A companionable silence fell between them. Lisa watched the headlights pick out the occasional frightened eyes of a rabbit as it scurried to safety across the potholed road.

"Thanks for the lift," she said.

Leaning over to open the door, Robbie's hand brushed against her knee.

"Maybe I'll see you again before you leave," he smiled.

Chapter 14

The smartly dressed receptionist pointed Lisa in the direction of the hotel telephone booths.

Lisa listened to the pub noises in the background at the Nag's Head as somebody roared out BJ's name.

"I dinnea want to hear how badly burnt her feet are," he stormed down the phone. "Ah want ye home here, wi' your own bairns. Am no sendin' you any more money," he shouted.

The sound of the phone being slammed down vibrated through Lisa's ear. She stood for a minute with the phone in her hand, hoping the receptionist hadn't heard BJ shouting. Embarrassed, she turned in the direction of the front door.

"Lisa," a voice called. "Lisa! I thought it was you," Robbie Black said, giving her his lopsided smile.

Lisa felt a red flush stain her cheeks. Had he heard the heated conversation?

"I hardly knew you without the peat dust in your hair," Robbie quipped. Remembering his kindness from the night he given her a lift back to Con's house, she bit back the sharp retort that rose to her lips. "Sit down beside the fire in the foyer, and I'll get us a drink."

Before she could refuse, he was away, striding into the bar. Sitting on the edge of the plush-covered seat, she took a good look at her surroundings. *It has changed a lot since Da used to bring me in on market day,* she mused. *Or when Scott used to sneak me in the back way and up to the complimentary rooms old Mac Kielty kept for the servicemen.*

"That fire is certainly doing its job," Robbie said at her elbow. "Your face is as bright as the rising sun." Lisa felt like a child caught with its hand in the sweetie jar. "My father used to bring me in here," she said to cover her thoughts about her and Scott in the hotel bedroom.

Putting a hot whiskey with cloves down in front of her, Robbie sat down and stretched his long jean-clad legs out towards the fire. Lisa could bet the money she didn't have that his jeans and his cashmere sweater he was wearing cost more than BJ gave her to keep the house for a month.

Feeling her eyes on him, Robbie gave her a long, slow smile. *He's used to woman admiring him,* she thought, *and I bet he doesn't often have drinks with women who have to borrow their neighbour's clothes.*

Taking a quick gulp of the whiskey, she felt it warm her all the way down to her toes. It had been a long time since she had sat alone with such a good-looking man. *Enjoy it while it lasts,* a small inner voice prompted.

"Is your drink alright?"

"It's lovely, but I feel a bit embarrassed about not buying you one back."

For a minute, Robbie looked deep into his own glass. "I hope you don't mind me saying, but I couldn't help overhearing your phone conversation."

Lisa felt mortified. Quickly, she started to close up her coat and gather her handbag. "Thanks for the drink, Robbie. I'll return it at another time."

"Don't go, Lisa. I'm sorry if I embarrassed you. I'm not known for my sensitivity. It's what comes of working with crusty old solicitors all day long," he apologised. "Sit down, please and let me buy you another drink—to make amends."

She watched him as he carried the drinks on a small tray and placed them on the table.

"It's not often I get an opportunity to drink in such a nice hotel," Lisa smiled. "Not that I drink much. It's usually a quick drink at Hogmanay or a special occasion," she added hastily.

"I'm not one for the drinking either," Robbie admitted. Lisa noticed that when he smiled, his eyes crinkled at the corners, giving him a boyish look. Her eyes traced the line of froth around his sensuous mouth.

"Did you know that they used to sell stuff from under the counter? Things you couldn't get during the war," Lisa babbled to cover her scrutiny of him. "I went to school with Mary Kielty, the owner's daughter. She used to bring sweets and biscuits to school. I wonder where she went."

"I think I heard Faith say she married after the war," Robbie said evasively, draining his glass. "Well, I suppose I better see you home since I got you tipsy," he joked.

Lisa smiled up into his eyes. *He's flirting with me,* she thought. "That would be nice but I'm only stopping up the street," she joked back.

Robbie held her coat and walked her to the hotel door. "Will you be out at the farm tomorrow?" he murmured, leaning close to her. For one wild, mind-boggling moment, Lisa was sure he was going to kiss her.

"I… don't know," she stammered, flustered by his closeness and attention. "But I would like to return your drink, even if it's only tea." She hesitated, unsure whether to shake his hand or just say goodbye. "Goodnight Robbie," she finally said, "I enjoyed your company."

"Me too," Robbie smiled. "Maybe I'll see you at the farm…"

Hurrying up the street, Lisa was amazed that her ability to flirt had resurfaced without any effort on her part.

Catch yourself on, Lisa, you're not twenty anymore, she chided herself. But still, she thought, it had been nice to be seen as a woman and not just a wife and mother for a change.

Chapter 15

Annie Swanton snipped the binding on the bundles of parcels and magazines. "It's going to be busy in the run-up to Christmas," she complained. "Empty the post box," she said to her fourteen-year-old granddaughter, Kathy, who was showing great interest in the pictures in some of the men's sporting magazines.

The bell tingled.

"Come in, come in, Gloria."

"Kathy, scoot over to the teashop and get a few of their freshly baked scone," Annie said. From the gleam in the pharmacist's eyes, she had a bit of gossip for her, just as the bell went again and Ellen Callahan came in.

Annie could hardly hide her annoyance. She'd hear nothing with her there.

"Were you looking for Con?" She said.

"No, no, just a few stamps for the Christmas cards."

"You didn't make it to the Armstrong funeral, Annie?" Ellen enquired.

"Far too busy," the postmistress said curtly.

"Father Ralph, the Catholic curate from Round Tower Chapel, wasn't there. Was he not invited?" Ellen asked.

Before the postmistress could answer, the door opened and a gust of wind blew Kathy's slight figure into the middle of the room.

"I did hear a man took ill after the funeral," Annie said quickly, changing the topic.

Her granddaughter struck a dramatic pose. "Granny, it was me that told you! I was there when he collapsed. Dr Coles ordered an ambulance, and he was taken the heart ward in the Royal Victoria Hospital in Belfast."

"Go and see to that tea, child," her granny interrupted her. Mac Kielty didn't like his young staff gossiping about what went on at the hotel.

"Was it brought up at the Church committee meeting about inviting Margaret's clergy to the funeral service?" Ellen persisted. She got her answer from the set of the other two women's faces. The postmistress drew herself up to her full five feet.

"Gloria and I have been members of the Women's Committee for years; we're both familiar with the rules regarding mixed marriages and Church services," she said imperiously.

"Was it discussed at the meeting?" Ellen said, standing her ground.

"Ellen, in all conscience, how could the Committee agree to let a Roman Catholic priest come into Rev Snodgrass' Church and take part in a funeral service?"

Sensing the rising tension between the two women, Gloria, bursting to share her titbits of gossip, said hurriedly, "Old Mac Kielty took the Furlongs into his own private quarters, and Mrs Furlong is staying there free of charge while her husband is in hospital in Belfast."

"He's a decent enough man—to be a papist—isn't that what you always say, Granny?" Kathy said.

Annie glowered at her granddaughter. "What about that tea?"

You really are a hard-nosed bigot, determined to keep us all in the last century, and you're making Kathy the same, Ellen thought, paying for her stamps.

"Did Lisa enjoy her drink in the hotel the other night with Robbie Black?" The postmistress shot at Ellen.

Ellen blinked. "What do you mean?"

"They were in Kielty's drinking. Didn't she mention it?" Annie's eyes glittered with the satisfaction of getting back at Ellen. "According to what I hear, he bought her drink all night. They were talking and laughing and carrying on like long-lost… friends."

Gloris sniffed. "Reverend Snodgrass doesn't hold with women going into public bars."

"He should tell his wife that," Kathy snorted as she handed round tea in her granny's best Coronation china teacups.

Annie spluttered tea into her saucer. It was common knowledge that Lily Snodgrass, the Reverend's wife, was too fond of the bottle. It was rumoured that Rev Snodgrass had asked Mac Kielty and the other publicans not to serve her.

"Here, child, take this bundle of magazines over to Gregg's paper shop. Tell them to keep them under the counter."

Kathy rolled her eyes. "Granny, who'll buy them if they're hidden under the counter?"

Annie sighed in exasperation. Then, noticing the close attention Kathy was paying to the front page of *Mr Universe,* she snatched up a fishing circular and planked it on top of the pile.

"Kathy Swanton—and you, the best attendee Rev Snodgrass has at his Sunday evening service," she scolded. "Straighten up, child. Remember, you're a Mill House Grammar pupil."

"They have got their work cut out for them there," Gloria murmured, gathering up her gloves in a huff.

Annie sighed. Any criticism of dear Geoffrey put Gloria into a bad mood for days.

Looking at Gloria's prim white blouse, fastened at the neck with its customary mother-of-pearl broach, Annie marvelled at Gloria in the role of *the other woman.* She allowed herself a moment to picture Gloria dressed up in some of the "playthings" she'd seen advertised in some of the smutty magazines. The image of straight-laced Gloria in fishnet stockings and black brassiere, whip in hand, gently thrashing poor old Geoffrey until he promised to be a good boy, made her chortle.

"Well, ladies, time's money," she tittered, getting back to the post.

Gloria marched up the main street, every inch the Sergeant Major she had been in the W.R.E.N.S. during the war. *It was only good manners and good training that kept me from telling Ellen Callahan a few homes truths about mixed marriages and their evils,* she fumed as she turned the key in the door of the pharmacy.

"That young man is still loitering about," she fumed as she turned the sign on the pharmacy door to Open. "He'll get a quick shift if he dares to show his face around here again. Condoms, indeed! What are the younger generation coming to? Look at that Kathy Swanton. Bit of square bashing would soon teach her to respect her betters," she muttered.

She flicked a feather duster over a counter display of Max Factor's new Pan-Stick range. "Geoffrey says cleanliness is next to godliness," she purred. The hand holding the duster stopped at the display of tonic wine. "That reminds me. I must fill Dr Coles' prescription for dear Geoffrey's wife. I'll be generous with its strength and quantity when I'm filling it," she murmured. "A few good glasses of the tonic wine, and she'll not be sober enough to attend the church supper tonight. I'll have the honour of sitting by Geoffrey's side," she said smugly.

Chapter 16

"Did you get your husband on the phone last night?" Ellen asked, putting the stamps beside the envelopes and writing paper.

Lisa nodded.

She started to laugh. "When I was out this morning, I called into the pharmacy. There was a young fella trying to persuade Gloria to sell him a French letter. There might be free love in America but not in Fermanagh," she chuckled.

Ellen busied herself filling the kettle. *She's not going to mention meeting Robbie. What has she got to hide?* she thought.

"It'll be one of those yobs from the new houses they've built in the Station Field."

Lisa looked in surprise at Ellen. It wasn't like her to be critical of people.

"Is it not better that he takes some kind of protection…?"

"Couldn't he wait till he married like everybody else?" Ellen snapped. "What happens if it doesn't work and some girl ends up pregnant? She'll be shipped off to England or end up in one of those Mother and Baby homes. Or shoved into marriage with some fool who thinks it's his child she's expecting." Too late, Ellen realised what she'd said.

"Oh, Lisa, I didn't mean…"

Lisa felt her face flush. "I'll go up and see about Trisha," she said, trying not to show the hurt that surged through her. *That's the kind of thinking that made me run away and marry BJ. Like Ellen said, I should have waited until my wedding night,* she thought.

She remembered the first time Scott had made love to her. She met him in the avenue of the old Castle, with its beautiful overhanging foliage and green fields that sloped gently down to the lakes. Since the GIs had arrived, it had been nicknamed *Lovers' Lane.*

She'd stood partially concealed behind a beech tree, listening to the creak of a squeaky bicycle coming down the avenue. The sight of Scott's tall, lanky frame hunched forward, his knees almost touching the handlebars of a girl's Raleigh bike, had made her lean up against a tree and laugh out loud. Scott had raised his hand in a wave, and wobbling perilously, landed in a bank of summer bluebells that carpeted the sheltered spots between the trees.

There was the sound of the front door opening and then shutting. Lisa heard Con's voice, then Ellen's angry tones and the occasional bang of a saucepan lid as Ellen made the dinner.

"Aunt Lisa, I'm fed up in bed. Everybody goes out in the morning and leaves me," Trisha moaned.

As if on cue, Con put his head around the bedroom door and winked at her, making Trisha laugh.

"Dr Coles borrowed a wheelchair from the old folk's home. Now, it's nothing grand, but it'll get madam here out for a bit of fresh air."

Trisha's face glowed. "Can I come down and sit in it now?" she begged.

"Here we go—Fireman's lift. Hold tight!" Con joked as he lifted Trisha's slight frame and pretended to throw her over his shoulder. Carrying her warm body downstairs, Con offered a prayer of thanks he had taken that route that particular morning and found her.

"Maybe you could try out the wheelchair after the dinner," Lisa suggested, looking at Ellen's stormy face.

"Well," Con asked as he settled back in his chair and lit a cigarette. "Well, what so important you couldn't tell me wi' Lisa here?"

Ellen took a deep breath. "I was in the Post Office for stamps, and Annie Swanton took great pleasure in telling me about Lisa's carry-on at Kielty's the other night…"

"Aw, pay too much attention to her. If there was a medal goin' for spreadin' gossip, she'd won first prize. The state you're in, I thought it was somethin' serious."

Ellen bristled. "It is serious! Out drinking all night with Robbie Black—making a show of herself! Is that serious enough for you?"

Con looked at his wife's flushed face. Ellen hackles were up. "Here, sit down, love. I'll make the tea. Tell me now, what exactly did Annie say?"

Ellen sighed when she'd finished. "We have to do something… before the tongues start wagging in earnest."

"It's not against the law to have a …"

"Listen to me, Con Callahan. We're keeping Lisa for free, and she's out spending money on drink!"

Con looked at his wife's angry face. It wasn't like her. Something else was bothering her.

"Did you and Lisa have a row?"

Ellen looked as if she was about to burst into tears. "No! But I had a few choice words with Annie and Gloria earlier about the Catholic curate not being there to help officiate at Margaret's funeral service," she sighed.

Con smiled at her. "That's one of the things ah admire about you, Ellen. You don't let yourself be browbeaten by the likes of them two wagging-tongue bigots."

He laid a gentle kiss on his wife's flushed cheek. Returning his kiss, Ellen thanked God for having such a good husband.

"What's Robbie Black's game?" Con asked as Ellen made a fresh pot of tea. "Lisa wouldn't be his type. He likes them well-heeled and fashionable," he mused.

He remembered old Samuel's dislike of Robbie. *Samuel was old, but he was an astute man,* Con thought. He'd never liked Robbie being around the farm. Now it appeared William was giving him free rein over the place.

"What do ye make of Robbie Black?"

Ellen shrugged. "He's been very attentive to Faith since her boys were killed in the war. They say he's very canny with his money," Ellen went on, "but then, it seems he likes a good time too—taking women to fancy restaurants and hotels."

"That's what I mean. Why would he spend money on the likes of Lisa?"

"I don't know but I think it's time Lisa spent more time at the farmhouse and took more responsibility for Trisha," Ellen said hoarsely.

Chapter 17

"We've been here four weeks. It'll soon be Christmas. Can we go home? I need to go back to school when the new term starts in January. I'll be way behind. Mammy said I wasn't to miss…"

"That was then—this is now," William growled, slinging his work bag across his shoulder. "Ah haven't got money for going home every turn around."

"II want it to go back to school. Mammy wanted me to carry on my education," George said determinately, as he heard his father slam of the front door behind him.

"He does that on purpose to wake Ma Higgins," George muttered. Sure enough, he heard her coughing and spluttering as she came down the hall. He waited for the tirade of abuse.

"Flamin' Iris—why did I listen to that silver-tongued navvy; one night, my arse," she ranted.

"This ain't a home for waifs and strays," she bawled. "I warned you about staying in during the day," she shouted, pounding on the bedroom door.

Leaving the digs, George walked up one street and down another, knocking on any door that had a notice in the window for rooms to let, like he'd been doing since they come to live at Ma Higgins. There were the usual signs: *No Irish, No Blacks, No dogs.*

He knocked on the door of a house that said 'Vacancies'. The woman looked him up and down suspiciously. "You Irish?"

"I'm from Northern Ireland, a Protestant, British," George explained.

"We don't want any of that religious crap here," the woman said, slamming the door in his face.

"You gave me the slip." Stella whispered from the shadow of the stairwell as George sneaked back into his room.

"I'm not going with you to steal," he whispered.

"It's not thieving. It's down the Irish Centre. They feed ya and don't ask questions."

George's stomach growled. *It would be nice to sit down and eat until I'm full,* he thought.

"It's a full Christmas dinner," Stella wheedled.

The Irish Centre was bright with Christmas decorations. The sound of Irish accents that sounded like his mother made George's heart ache for her and for Trisha.

Starving, he wolfed down his heaped plate of dinner and then another. Stella did the same, and then filled her pockets with lumps of thickly cut ham and slabs of turkey, nodding George to do the same for Ma Higgins' and his father's dinner.

George waited until his father had eaten the turkey and ham and the chips from the chippy at the end of the road before he mentioned going home for Christmas again.

William lay down in one of the narrow beds. Anger distorted William's face.

"We have no money to be wastin' going home for Christmas."

There was no money for the gas fire. George crawled into the other bed to keep warm, glad he didn't have to sleep with his father. I miss going to school and missed the heat of Trisha cuddling into my back, he thought, as he lay watching the shadows on the wall move and change as the light from the street lamp flickered through the worn curtains. He wanted to cry but was afraid his sobbing would anger his father. *I wish he had died in the war. Mammy and us were happy living with Granda,* he gulped, swallowing his tears.

He got up and started to clean up the pots and plates. "Da, you have to meet Sheamie Foy down at the pub," he said after a while.

William shifted in the bed but made no effort to get up.

"It's Friday night, Da. The gaffers will be picking the men for next week's work."

"Buying them drink to get work. No way of working that," William muttered.

"That's how it done, Da—you buy your round…"

William leapt out of the bed. "Take them rattlin' pots an' your naggin' and wash them in that thing thy call a kitchen," he roared.

Standing in the kitchen, George had an overwhelming desire to pile the dirty plates on top of the rest of the mouldy pile of dirty pots already cluttering the sink and run out into the night. But where he would go? he thought in desperation.

Ma Higgins came to the kitchen door and threw another bag of empty bottles into an already overflowing bin.

Leaving the pots, George went back into the room and shook his father awake. "Da, get up. Sheamie says…"

"That all I hear out from you, Sheamie says, Sheamie says." William balled his fists and beat them on the blankets. "It's bad enough having to listen to them all day with their bloody brogues and their holy medals pinned to their vests to keep them safe," he said disparagingly. "Ah don't want to go down to the pub at night listening to them singing about their dead heroes and how the British robbed them of their land," he bellowed.

"If you want to get work…" George leapt back as his father roared and raised himself up in the bed.

His heart pounded in his chest. He wondered if Higgins heard his father roaring and ranting. If she had, they'd find themselves sleeping under a bridge tonight. Racing back into the kitchen, he started to rattle the pots as loudly as he could.

Rage coiled like a living thing inside him against his father. Gradually, his breathing slowed. He was amazed to find that he had cleaned most of the mouldy pots. Swirling them under the freezing water tap, he left them to drain. His father had stopped shouting, but he could still hear him muttering and the sound of his feet knocking into things as he paced about the room.

George sat down the bin with its overflowing bottles. He remembered when he was in Scouts they had collected empty bottles and got a penny each for them. "Wonder do the pubs here pay for empty beer bottles," he mused.

"Forget the school. Have a job by the time ah get back from work today or Foy will get you something to do as a navvy," William scowled the next morning, pulling on his donkey jacket.

"Only if you write to Aunt Lisa and see if Trisha is all right," George shot back. William didn't answer him, but he gave the outside door an extra loud, resounding bang on the way out.

George pulled on his coat and waited for the landlady's stumbling steps in the hall.

"Bleedin' Irish would wake the dead of a mornin'."

"They're good payers, Ma," George heard Stella's voice say. "And Irish washed all the pots and pans in the kitchen."

Ma Higgins' cursing turned into a strangled chuckle. "Ain't been that clean since I chucked me old man out," she wheezed. "Did ya hear a racket last night?"

"Telly up too loud, I fink," Stella lied.

Stella tapped on the bedroom door. "Let me in Irish."

George buttoned his coat. "I'm not going shoplifting with you."

"Ma Higgins 'eard your old man ranting an' raving last night. Drunken old cow—told 'er it was the telly. Ya would be out in your ass if it weren't for me," she said, looking into George's stubborn face.

"Wear the coat that's too big for ya."

"Irish Centre first—Christmas party—we put our names down with Father Agnew last week, didn't I. Don't mention your old man," she warned as they queued to get into the community hall. "The priest finks ya live on the streets, like me."

George stared at her. "You live with Ma…" He stopped speaking as Stella gave him a sharp dig in the ribs. A man in a long black frock was making his way down the line, welcoming everybody.

"Ah, a new face," the priest smiled, shaking George's hand. "Enjoy the party and don't forget to call in and see us in the New Year," he said, moving on to the next person.

George reverently hoped Sheamie Foy wouldn't give his father any more work, and that he'd be home by the New Year.

"When're we going?" George asked, following Stella when the party was over.

"Into town—Christmas shopping."

George stared in amazement at the shops, decorated with masses of coloured lights and larger-than-life Santas in the windows.

Waiting to cross at the lights, George watched, fascinated as wave after wave of people rushed across the street like an army of busy ants.

Stella turned into a shop with huge plate-glass windows displaying an array of bags and coats with fur collars. A huge snowman in a snowy winter scene, looking so real like he was freshly built, took up a whole side window.

Christmas carols blasted out from every shop door.

"C&A," Stella said, pushing through the crowds that thronged the footpaths and into the clothes shop.

George trailed after Stella as she picked things up and put them down again before moving on. He relaxed—she didn't seem to be stealing anything.

"It's your turn, Irish," she mouthed at him.

George looked at her.

"Grab a handbag off some old crone who's too busy looking at fings to notice ya," Stella ordered, laughing at the look of horror on George's face. "Treat yourself to summit' nice for Christmas, like a new coat. Ya look like your old man in that getup," she laughed, disappearing into the hordes of shoppers.

His heart beating so fast he was sure every shop assistant in the place could hear it, George sidled up to a woman with a handbag hanging loosely from her arm.

Losing his nerve, he made his way into the Men's and Boys' department. Row after row of coats hung on rail after rail. Enthralled, he tried on coat after coat, forgetting he was supposed to be stealing one of them. Eventually, he found his size, and doing what Stella had told him, he took two and then three coats at a time into the curtained-off section.

The sales assistant watched him as the mountain of coats grew. *Don't run or do anything to make them suspicious,* Stella had warned. George kept trying on the coats and discarding them. Eventually, he went behind a rail, put a coat on under his Da's old coat, and buttoned it up. Passing through the store, he expected any minute to feel the tap on his shoulder, be taken to the manager's office, and have the police sent for.

Standing on the street corner waiting for Stella, he couldn't believe he had *actually* stolen a coat and got away without being caught. A great rush of adrenaline surged through his body. His feeling of guilt gave way to euphoria.

"Let's try another shop. Maybe I might steal a purse or wallet there," he babbled in excitement as Stella joined him.

Chapter 18

William eyed the new coat. "Where'd you get that?"

"Salvation Army," George said without hesitation, startling himself.

William made a snorting sound.

"Foy says he might be able to get you a job as a runner."

"I have to go to school, Da. It's what Mammy wanted. I'll find a part-time job," he said hastily, seeing William's face darkening with rage.

After his father went to bed, taking his courage in his hands, George knocked tentatively on Ma Higgins door. "It's me—Irish," he said, using the name Stella called him.

To his surprise, she opened the door. "I just wanted to know—what day they collect the rubbish," he stuttered. His voice began to waver as his courage deserted him.

"Thursday, I fink. Ask Stella. Kitchen's clean," she mumbled, shutting the door. George heard the rattle of the locks as she locked herself in.

He jumped in fright at Stella's muffled snigger. "Why are you always sneaking about?" George said furiously.

"You learn a lot when you're not seen," Stella said, following him into the kitchen. "My old woman's fancy man, Larry, 'ad a way of sneakin about. He'd walk about in 'is stocking feet. Like a stalker, 'e was, the mean bastard. The quieter he walked about, the meaner he got, and the worse he beat 'er up. One night he was beaten' on 'er so bad I thought he was going to kill 'er." Stella stopped talking.

George looked at her. "What happened?"

"I got the bread knife and stuck it in his leg," Stella shuddered. "He 'ad to go to 'ospital. I legged it before he got 'ome. I ain't been back since."

George listened in silence as he separated the bottles from the overflowing bin into groups.

"Da used to beat Trisha—my sister. I never told anybody that before," he said, ducking his head.

"Did the social fuckers put 'er in a foster home?"

George shook his head. "Mammy died in November. Da sent for my Aunt Lisa to come and take Trisha to live with her in Glasgow, and he brought me here with him." He focused on a damp spot spreading in the faded wallpaper spot above Stella's head. "I hope she's there safe with Aunt Lisa," he said, his lip trembling.

For a while, all that could be heard was the clinking of the bottles and the slurping of the cold water.

Stella slid down off the end of the sink and rummaged around. Finding a half-rotten potato, she deftly smashed it against the sink. "Makes a good stopper," she said, sticking it into the rusted plug hole. "Get more for them if they're clean," she said, filling up the sink and plunging the bottles into the water.

In silence, they washed the rotting food from the bottles and lined them up by size and shape.

"Why is your hair always greasy?" George blurted out.

Stella flung the bottle she was wiping into the filthy water.

"Cos I ain't had a decent wash or bath in ages," she shouted, running out of the kitchen.

In bed, George thought about Stella. *It's hard to explain,* he thought, *but when I'm close to her I want to touch her.* Standing close to her had given him a nice feeling. He'd sneaked a look at her breasts. He was sure they were bigger than the day she had whipped down her top and pulled out the cooked chicken she had stolen from the food market. He wondered what it would be like to touch them Shocked at the images that had floated unbidden into his mind, he quickly turned his back on his father and tried to sleep.

George heard a slap and then a yelp. Another lodger must have left without paying Stella the rent, he thought.

The imprint of Ma's fingers glowed on Stella's cheek. "She ain't got 'er sodden rent, but I got a few quid for me and you." Stella sniffed, a self-satisfied look creeping over her face. "He liked it too. Pity he's not a regular lodger," she gulped. She eyed George dressed in his old grammar school trousers and the shirt and shoes she had stolen for him as a Christmas present.

"You going someplace—all had done up fancy?"

George blushed. "I'm going to see if I can go to that school on the hill." What he wanted desperately to do was go home and back to school at Mill House Grammar. He wanted to wake up in his own bed, hear the cows lowing, and smell the farms smells.

Stella raised her eyebrows. "It ain't the kind of place where ya'll learn the kind of fings I can teach ya," she said.

"C'mon. Wear the coat with the deep pockets," she coaxed.

"I'm not going stealing with you."

Stella shrugged. "Be 'angry, then," she snapped.

George hesitated. "You know how to phone Ireland?" he asked.

"Yeah, 'course I do. Ya need the proper change and the code and number. You 'ave the number, don't ya?"

George shook his head. "Well, 'ow do ya expect to phone, you silly bugger?"

George's lip trembled. "It's the Post Office in Ballet. Mrs Swanton's the postmistress."

"That's alright, then. The flaming telephone operator be sure to know that number, won't she, you stupid bugger?" Stella scoffed.

A sense of relief flooded George. "Thanks, Stella. I'm sorry about what I said… about your hair," he apologised, his face reddening.

"C'mon, first you 'ave to 'elp me get Ma 'er dinner," Stella smirked but George could tell she was pleased he'd said he was sorry.

Kathy Swanton from his old school had answered the payphone in the Post Office. At the unexpected sound of her familiar, nosy tone, George clammed up.

"Who's speaking, please?" she kept repeating. He could hear her impatient breath in his ear and the sound of the operator asking him if he wanted to put in more money.

He'd held his breath, desperately hoping the postmistress would come on the phone, and he could find out if Trisha had gone to Scotland with his Aunt Lisa. Kathy had muttered something and slammed the phone down.

"I've no money left for the gas meter," he gulped, curling into a ball in his bed and watched the big blobs of icy December rain slid down the windowpane.

Angrily, he grabbed up the pies Stella had stolen and flung them at the wall.

"Da can starve to death, for all I care. Why should he live when Mammy is dead and maybe Trisha too?" he shouted the words reverberating around the room.

Chapter 19

Out at the house, Lisa lit the fire in the range. Going outside, she gazed with satisfaction at the grey plume of smoke from the chimney as the wind swirled it up into the sky. Shading her eyes against the unusually warm December sun, her eyes scanned the shortcut across the fields between their farm and Hamilton's. She wondered if Robbie had gone back to Belfast. "If he's still there, he'll see the smoke signals." She chuckled. "Lisa Mc Knight, remember you're a married woman and the mother of a teenager son and a half-grown daughter."

It had been three weeks and there hadn't been a letter or a phone call from William to ensure she had arrived and that Trisha was all right. He had tricked her, knowing full well she would come and have no choice but to take her niece back with her.

Holding her face up to the weak rays of the winter sun and the soft caress of the wind, she thought about how she'd lain in wait for the local boys who'd bullied William at school. Soon, it was the bullies who were afraid to walk home alone. "Now, William expects me to take his daughter and rear her for him! I'm not doing it," she muttered. The thought of going back to the already overcrowded tenement flat with another child was too much to even consider. "William can come back and take her to England with him. He's a grown man—he'll be forty in a year or so—middle-aged. He's not a schoolboy anymore," she muttered.

The upstairs curtains flutter out of the open windows and then retreat like shy maidens, only to show their face again at the command of another gust of wind. She had pushed the fear of tuberculosis to the back of her mind, stripped the beds of their dank clothes, and aired the mattresses.

Wiping a wet cloth over the kitchen window panes, her attention was caught by a moving figure in the far field. Her pulse quickened. Could it be Robbie, seeing to the cattle?

A feeling of disappointment washed over her when she realised it was Con Callahan and not Robbie. Gathering up the old tattered patchwork quilt from the privet hedge that acted as a boundary between the front footpath and what had been her mother's small rose garden, she started inside and left it to air near the range.

Con stood almost transfixed by the sight of the sheets and blankets blowing freely in the wind. He sat down on the stone ditch that bordered the field and pushed his cap back on his head. "There's always something about clothes blowing on a clothes line that reminds me of some place, but I can't put my finger on it," he murmured. He'd never known his mother, never mind his father. "All the oil biddies at Conneyburrow Home would tell me was that ah was 'handed in' when ah was four years of age. And nobody ever came back for me. Left like an unwanted parcel," he mused.

Giving himself a shake, he continued on down the side of the field and the shortcut into the farmyard.

Lisa took the packed lunch of chicken sandwiches and homemade apple tart out to outside to sit on the stone planter near the kitchen door. *It's not often we get a sunny summer's day in December,* she thought. There was a deep hole in the middle of the planter. She smiled. Mac Kielty used to tease her mother that it was part of an ancient rock priests used to say mass on years ago. "I'm surprised a good staunch member of the Ladies' Committee would have such a thing about her," he'd joke.

"It's a brave woman that would sit out on a fresh day like the day," Con remarked as he crossed over the yard. He noticed that it was as overgrown and dirty as ever. *Robbie Black is not doing much,* he thought. He grunted. What else would you expect from a city boy solicitor playing at be a gentleman farmer? he smirked.

"A mouthful of that tea would be grand, if there's any goin'," he said, smiling at Lisa. "But if it's all the same to you, after that trek over the fields, I'll take it in comfort at the kitchen table."

"It's looking much more like itself," he said, glancing appreciatively around the clean kitchen.

Sipping the hot sweet tea, he pulled a paper bag out of his pocket. "Ellen gave me these sulphur candles. She says light one of these upstairs and downstairs in a safe place before you leave the night, close all the windows tight but leave all the doors inside the house open when you're leavin'."

Lisa looked questioningly at the sulphur candles.

"They're supposed to kill any germs and… disease that's in the house," Con said.

"Thanks, Con. I don't know how what I'd have done without you and Ellen." She bit her lower lip. "William has let the place fall to bits," she said, a flush staining her cheeks. "He could have waited till I got here. There was no mention of him going to England in the postcard he sent. All he said was that Margaret was sick and he wanted Trisha to live with me. He never mentioned that Margaret had TB!"

Con saw the sheen of tears on her eyes. Pity stirred in him. Moving a little closer, he touched her hand. "It'll all work itself out in the end, lass," he said.

Without warning, Lisa leaned her head in against him.

Taken unawares, Con sat motionless. After a while, he moved to stand up. "Ellen was sayin' it might be good for Trisha to come out to—be amongst familiar things she knows," he stammered out.

Lisa dried her tears. "Dr Coles says her burns from the frostbite are healing."

She looked at him. "Your family are lucky to have a father like you to come back home to," she said, her face softening. "What I would give to have my father… and mother here now. Maybe you can be my 'father' from now on," she smiled, hugging him.

Plunging through the gap in the hedge, Con realised that his feelings at that moment in time were anything but fatherly as far as Lisa Armstrong was concerned.

The chill of an early dawn stirred Ellen from her sleep. She chuckled as she buttoned up her nightdress. It had been a while since Con had made love to her in the middle of the night. She lay watching the first rays of a new day creep across the bed. She thought of the lovemaking they had enjoyed when they were first married. The closeness they'd shared. *How did we end up almost become like two strangers sharing the same house, the same bed?* she thought.

Slipping out of bed, she pulled on her dressing gown and slippers and padded downstairs. A small glimmer of light still showed in the banked-up fire. Spooning tea into the china teapot she usually reserved for special occasions, she pulled back the curtain on the kitchen window.

"Maybe it's your own fault. When the boys and Hazel came along, Con was sort of pushed into the background," she admitted. Sipping the warm tea, she watched a chilly dawn break over Boa Island.

Now the nest was empty. It was just her and Con.

"Get involved with the Church or those new women's get-together things," people advised her. Ellen knew that would never be her way of filling her time.

"One trying to outdo the other with their snippets of gossip and tittle-tattling," she muttered. She'd joined the new art and craft class that was being started up by Mac Kielty's American granddaughter, Hannah.

"That's what I have always wanted to do—learn to paint," she said aloud now.

"Well, sure, whose stopping you?" Con's voice said out of the gloom.

Startled out of her reflections, Ellen felt her face flush. "Ouch, it's just something to fill the time."

She studied Con as he left half of his breakfast, which wasn't like him.

"You feeling out of sorts?" she asked him.

"I'm grand," he mumbled, reaching for his coat and muffler. "Didn't sleep well last night", he said, his face flushing.

Straightening the collar of his postman's coat, Ellen gave him a playful squeeze. For the first time in years, she kissed him on the lips. "Go on, the postmistress will be watching the clock. Maybe you'll have another restless night tonight again," she chuckled.

Chapter 20

"I don't know if I'm coming or going," the postmistress grumbled as Con started to load up the mail sacks.

" Know how you feel," Con responded, feelings of guilt and shame curling his stomach in knots.

Annie looked sharply at him. "You're looked at bit flushed."

"You're putting yourself and Ellen in danger of the TB, taking that child in? She could be carrying it." she barked, backing away watching two red spots in Con's face spread over his cheekbones.

Con wiped the falling snow off the seat of the bike and loaded the parcels into the huge basket in front. Before he could make his escape, Annie rapped on the small window that held the red letterbox and motioned for him to come back in.

"It has enough string on it to fly a kite from Breezy," Con said, referring to the local name for the mountains that sheltered around the bay. "What do you think it is?" He asked, looking at the odd shaped parcel she was holding.

"It's a Christmas cake," Annie said incredulously. Turning the brown paper parcel around in her hands, she read the return address. "Mary Kielty, sending an Irish-baked Christmas cake to her mother-in-law in Texas."

Con took off his cap and scratched his head. "Well," he commented with a wry laugh, "by the time it arrives in Texas, them cowboys won't need a knife to cut it. It'll be shook to bits." The postmistress gave him a frosty look and put the brown parcel aside.

Pedalling along trying to avoid the potholes, which he knew were covered in a thick, glassy layer of ice under the fall of snow, Con's thought turned to Mary Kielty. "A plain enough lass,—nothing to write home about," he mused. "Looks or not the Yank wed her," he mused. "Ah suppose her being left the farm and oul Kielty's business when old Mac goes helped," he mused. "It's a wonder Annie hasn't made it her business to tell Lisa yet," he mused.

He pulled the bike as close to the hedge as he could get when he heard the rumble of the bus. Davy Dobbs wasn't renowned for his careful driving. "And the snow and slippery conditions will add nothin' to that," Con reasoned, pulling the bike closer to him.

"Want a lift out to the border crossing?" Davy shouted.

"Thanks, Davy," Con said, grateful for the lift.

"It'll save me listenin' to the mother," Davy shouted above the noise of the engine and the rattling of the old bus.

"What's that?" Con said, moving further up the bus to hear what he was saying.

"Ah was saying—the mother is waiting on a seed catalogue from the Sunday paper, and she keeps asking me if there any sign of you comin' up our way," he shouted over his shoulder.

Con looked out the window as they passed the old buildings that had been built to train the RAF and bomber pilots to replace those shot down as they flew across the Atlantic. They passed close to the Armstrong farm. *If Lisa was going to live there, even for a short while, it needed cleaning up,* he thought. He wondered if Davy would be willing to do a bit of voluntary work.

Davy nodded his agreement. "Oul' Samuel and William, for all his faults, both did their bit during the two wars. It's the least the Legion members can do," he bawled, slowing to let a young woman driving a four-wheel drive fly past him.

"Would you look at that? The women will soon be lookin' to do my job," Davy grinned.

They couldn't do much worse; I'd be safer walking, Con thought.

"Will William be away long?" Benny, the conductor, asked, sitting down beside Con. Con was saved from answering as Davy slammed the brakes on again, and the bus slithered on the icy road. Benny got up and made his way to the front of the bus.

"Leave them off at the Northern Custom Post," Faith Hamilton instructed Benny, taking a goose from under each of her arms. "They're to be collected at the Border Post."

"Right ye are, missus," Benny smiled, tipping his cap.

"Some job this," he said, his double chins disappearing into his collar as he wedged the two geese behind the driver's partition. ". Yesterday it was an oul' woman with a load of clanking pots and pans and a wee oul' dog on a string she found on her travels," he laughed.

"This will do me," Con said as the bus neared the manned customs post that separated Northern Ireland from the Irish Republic.

Davy braked, realising he was closer to the border crossing than he realised.

"It would be a smoother journey if Davy would wear the glasses he has in his pocket," Benny observed in a low voice as the passengers were propelled into the back of the seat in front of them.

Shook from their place by the sudden stop, the geese slid along the damp floor in the direction of the bus door.

"Begod, they're going to walk into the Irish Republic under their own steam," Davy grunted as he opened the door of the bus to let Con and his bike out and let the uniformed customs officer in.

Chapter 21

Hearing voices, Lisa went out into the yard.

"Con Callahan sent us, Missis," Davy Dobbs said. "Where do ye want us to start?"

"And here's the wee lady herself," he crowed, looking past Lisa into the kitchen.

Trisha beamed at him. "Can I drive the tractor?" she asked, waddling out into the yard.

Benny and Davy laughed.

"George lets me," she said, a huffy look coming over her face.

"What about you sittin' in the back of the trailer and makin' sure we don't dump anything valuable," Davy smirked, taking in the rubbish and old rusting farm implements.

Turning back, Davy surveyed Lisa. "Didn't you marry the big Scotchman who worked out at the base with the Yanks in the 40s?"

Lisa nodded and went back into the house.

"You make a good cup o' tea," Benny said, rubbing the back of his hand over his mouth as he rose from the table. "Ah used to see you when the Yanks had the dances and the Christmas parties," he said, his face turning pink. "Ah was a lot thinner then," he laughed self-consciously, patting his protruding stomach.

"A'll take another cup o' that tea—if there's any more goin'," Davy said breaking into their conversation.

"Fancy yer chances there, did ye, Benny?" He laughed, dribbling tea on the clean table.

Lisa worked round him, clearing the table and mopping up the spilt tea. "You and the Yank and the Scotchman," Davy grinned, draining the last dregs in the cup. "Aye. You had a good thing goin' there, girl," he chortled. "The big Scotch navvy man one night and the Texan cattleman the next night," he laughed, giving Lisa a playful slap on her behind as she bent over the table.

Lisa could hardly believe what he had just done and the innuendos that were coming out of his mouth. Turning on him, she gave him a resounding slap across the face with the wet dishcloth.

Davy leapt out of his chair. "You bloody mad bitch! You've blinded me!" he yelped, holding his face.

"All your rolling with the Yank in Kielty's and in the trees in the castle grounds was all for nothin," he spat at her.

Lisa advanced on his again "Get out of this kitchen—unless you want more of the same," she said through clenched teeth.

"The lass who kept her drawers on got him in the end," Davy sneered, banging the kitchen door behind him.

Lisa's anger was beginning to subside when she heard raised voices in the yard. Not trusting herself to go outside in case she laid into Davy again, she crossed the gleaming quarry floor tiles she had vented her anger against Davy on. Robbie Black's jeep was parked in the yard. A heated argument was in full swing.

"Don't be comin' here telling me what I can and can't do. You're not in a court of law now. If ah knew as much as ah know now…" Davy was yelling glaring red-faced at Lisa, who watching him out of the kitchen window. "The place could run over with vermin for all ah care!"

"All I'm saving is that you should have asked or at least told me before you started dumping things." Robbie Black said, stomping off in the direction of the house.

"Fits you better if ye stuck to what you're supposed to know," Davy bawled at Robbie's retreating back.

Davy and benny turned as the familiar rattle of the postman's bike coming down the lane.

"He'll not take that Lord of the Manor attitude wi' me. He's only minding the place 'til William comes back," Davy stormed to Con. "The way he's goin' on, you'd think he owned the bloody place."

Con watched Robbie lift the kitchen latch without knocking as if he did own the place. Through the open kitchen window, he could see him talking to Lisa. A rush of jealousy caught him unaware as he watched Lisa's red hair and Robbie's piebald head bent close together.

Inside the house, Robbie whole demeanour changed. "Are you staying here tonight?" he asked, a soft note in his voice.

"I… don't know. Maybe…"

"Do you remember how to work the wick in the lamp?" he teased.

Lisa blinked. She kept forgetting that the farm had no electricity.

"It's OK. I got a new wick when I was in town," Robbie said, giving her his lopsided smile.

Chapter 22

Outside, the yard was inky black. "It's a good job Robbie put the new mantle in the lamp," she said to Trisha, opening the letter Con had brought her.

Taking it over nearer the lamp, to her surprise, several pound notes fell onto her lap. She ran her eyes over the single sheet of paper. *Well, one thing's for sure, Big Jim didn't write this,* she thought—probably her neighbour Madge.

She read it again:

Dear Lisa,

Sorry about the phone call the other night. I was tired after working and looking after the bairns. We all miss you, especially Isobel. It's getting nearer Christmas and there's nothing ready for Christmas morning for the bairns. I've enclosed some money. Come home soon.

Your loving husband
BJ

She put the letter aside. Listening to the clock ticking contently, she rested in the circle of the lamplight. The rattling of the kettle lid and the hissing sound it made as the hot water bubbled out onto the range woke her. For a minute, she sat there, her mind somewhere between sleep and wakefulness.

Walking on her stocking feet, she went up the stairs. She could hear Trisha huffing and puffing. "I want to sleep in Granda's bed, but the bed is all tossed!" Trisha pouted, pointing to the freshly washed sheets and aired blankets spread out across the foot of the bed.

"Don't sleep in Mammy's bed," she said to Lisa in a flat voice.

Lisa's heart jolted. It was the first time Trisha had mentioned her mother since the funeral.

"Why? What's wrong with your mammy's bed?" she asked carefully.

"George says Mammy coughed all over it when she was sick," Trisha said, no emotion in her voice.

Lisa felt a chill creep up her spine. Surely, only a few weeks after her mother's death, there should be tears?

"Let's get your Granda's bed made," Lisa said heavily.

Trisha looked up at her from beneath the curtain of black hair that fell over her eye. Bending down, she retrieved the doll she'd thrown under her Granda's bed and started to blow the dust out of its hair.

"I helped Granda make the bed when George was out bringing in the cows." Trisha said, dragging the bedclothes to the top of the bed.

"We'll both do it," Lisa said, spreading the clean sheet evenly over the bed and smoothing it down with her hands. "I helped your Granny make this sheet when I was a wee girl like you."

"I don't have a Granny. George and Sarah had a granny, but I never had a granny," Trisha said petulantly, sticking out her bottom lip.

"Of course you had a granny. It's just that she died before you were born. But she was still your granny," Lisa said, spreading the thick woollen blankets so that they hung level over both sides of the big bed.

"Where's Granda's quilt?"

"There are plenty of blankets on already. You don't need anything else," Lisa said, remembering to bring the old tattered quilt up later.

Without warning, Trisha flung herself on the bed and tore at the blankets.

"Granda always has the quilt on his bed. He tells me stories about the patches!" she screeched, beside herself with rage.

Lisa stepped back as Trisha dragged the clean blankets and sheets off the bed onto the floor.

"You'll make this bed again—yourself!" Lisa heard herself say in what sounded remarkably like her mother's tone of voice.

Trisha's screams followed her down the stairs and into the kitchen.

"What will I do if I have to take her back with me?" Lisa moaned as she pulled the kettle back onto the heat and poured the bubbling water over the tea leaves.

"I want Granda's quilt." Trisha's screamed from the top of the stairs. "It's been a long day. I wish I had something stronger," Lisa sighed.

The lights of a car lit up the yard outside as Robbie Black swung his jeep around and parked beside the barn to check on the cattle.

She smiled, thinking about the remark she had overheard Davy and Benny grumbling as they finished cleaning up the yard.

"Bloody gentlemen farmers give me the piss. Did ye ever see a farmer about these parts wear brown suede boots to bring in the cattle?" Davy had smirked.

"Aye, and that fancy sheep skin coat—it'll not be long before the cow dung makes a job of that! Just wait until he prods oul' Bessie; she splatters everywhere!" Laughing, the men had walked out of earshot. Lisa couldn't help giggling herself now as Robbie's tall figure clad in the tan suede three-quarter-length coat stepped into the light of the kitchen.

"Small present by way of apology for my heavy-handiness with Davy and Benny," he said, handing her a bottle of wine. Lisa felt the warm tingle of his fingers as they lingered on her hand.

Robbie's eyes moved up towards the ceiling as Trisha started wailing again. "She's throwing a strop," Lisa sighed.

"What does she want?" Robbie said, an irritated note creeping into his voice. It had been another hard day of standing in the middle of fields listening to farmers, with their hand stuck up cows, lamenting about the lack of government grants and the cost of farming. He could do without a screeching child just when he was about to relax.

"She wants the old torn quilt, behind you," Lisa said, nodding to where it lay across the back of the kitchen chair. "Her Granda had it on his bed and used to tell her stories about its patches."

Robbie sat down and stretched his corduroy-clad legs out in front of him.

"What about that glass of wine before both of us falls asleep from the heat of this fire?" he smiled.

"I'm not sure if there are any glasses," Lisa babbled, trying hard not to be as obvious as she inhaled the fresh smell of his aftershave.

"Give her the quilt," Robbie said, touching her arm lightly as she passed him. "It'll give us a chance to have a chat and enjoy the wine."

Robbie uncrossed his legs and moved back a little from the heat of the range. Learning forward, he clenched his hands loosely between his knees and gazed down at the floor.

"The boss asked me if I would be interested in heading up the new branch they're going to open in Dublin."

"That sounds like promotion," she said, smiling at him.

Robbie shrugged. He had no burning desire to take on any more work with farmers but it was good to be asked.

"Who will look after ours and Faith's farm?"

"Well, I'll certainly not be asking that clown Davy Dobbs to look after this for me," he growled.

Lisa looked appreciatively at him as she sipped the wine.

She studied his face in the glow of the fire. She noticed how his long, almost feminine lashes swept down over his cheekbones and his arched eyebrows rose slightly as he seemed to have a silent conversation with himself.

"It's not for a while yet, anyway." Robbie said, rising. "It's a shame to sit out here on these hard kitchen chairs when there's a good horsehair sofa and chairs in the sitting room down the hall," Robbie smiled.

Lisa looked towards the kitchen ceiling. Trisha had stopped screaming, and she could hear her telling her doll a story about the patches on her grandfather's old quilt.

She relaxed into the padded chair in the sitting room. "Why did you never marry?" she asked, her tongue loosened by her second glass of Chardonnay. Sitting in the old winged armchair that used to be her father's favourite spot, Robbie gave no response.

"Sorry, Robbie, it's really none of my business…"

"I don't really believe in marriage or families," Robbie said after a pause. "I was brought up by strangers in children's home." Startled at what he'd just revealed, his wine sloshed against the side of his glass. "Sorry, Lisa, I don't usually tell people that. It just seemed to slip out," he said.

Lisa glanced at him. It was obviously something that bothered him. Reaching over, she refilled his glass.

"Tell me," She said.

The simple request reminded her of her father. Sometimes he'd wait for her at the end of the lane after school. "How did it go today?" he'd say. He always knew when something was wrong. "Tell me everything and leave nothing out," he'd tease her as she linked her arm through his. Somehow, sharing her childish troubles with him had always made things seem better.

For a while, Robbie didn't speak. *Why did I tell her that,* he fumed? There was something about Lisa. She touched a chord deep within him that none of the fancy-executive type women he usually went out with ever did.

"Well, it's a very old story," he sighed. "My mother was only fourteen when I was born on the wrong side of the blanket in 1915," he said in a low voice. He stopped speaking and took a deep swig of his drink. "It was a family thing," he continued. "When it was discovered she was pregnant she was bundled off to England. Her father, my grandfather, was sent off to war and never returned."

Lisa reached over and stroked his arm. For a while, the only sound in the room was the gentle pop of the turf as it shifted in the grate. Lisa watched the warm orange flames lick the black inside of the old-fashioned fireplace and the way the leaping flames spread their shadows on the faded rose-patterned wallpaper.

"How did you come to be in Belfast?" she asked after a while.

Robbie rolled the wine glass between his palms. Lisa noticed how clean and well-kept his nails were. Not like BJ's, she mused—always dirty from emptying the rubbish from other people's lives.

"A woman named Maura worked at the Children's Home. She used to get permission to bring me to her family in Belfast for short holidays. When I left the Home, I had some sort of notion I'd look for my biological family, expecting them to welcome me." He gave a hollow laugh. "That was a big mistake. They didn't want secrets from the past cluttering up their nice, respectable lives."

Rising from the settee, Lisa put her arms around his stiff, tense body. For a while, neither of them moved. Then Robbie eased Lisa onto the rug in front of the fire until they their bodies were touching.

Her eyes heavy with sleep, the feel of Robbie's hands on her body in the morning jerked Lisa fully awake. Jumping out of bed, she swayed. She considered bending down to retrieve her clothes that lay scattered around the bedroom floor. But the best she could manage was to slip her arms into her dressing gown and push her feet into her slippers. She could hear Trisha in the next bedroom. "You have to go, Robbie. Trisha's awake," she whispered, gesturing wildly.

Chapter 23

Trisha sat at the kitchen table eating the porridge and toast Lisa had made for her. There was no sign of the terrible screaming temper tantrum she had subjected Lisa to the night before, but she had a faraway detached look in her eyes. Lisa wondered if she was thinking about her mother, the funeral, or her brother George not being here.

She reheated the pot and poured herself a mug of the strong tea. Shovelling in two heaped spoons of sugar, she sat down and took a good long look at her niece's small, pinched face. Reaching across the table, she stroked Trisha's hand, which was clutching the doll she had found upstairs.

"I used to have a doll like that when I was a wee girl. I called her Raggy. I gave her to your sister Sarah when she was a baby."

"She drowned in the well." Trisha said, taking a bite of the toast. Lisa felt her body tingle. Her gut tightened. She forced herself to keep calm. Unbidden, her eyes travelled over the field to the lip of the well. She didn't know if Trisha was talking about the doll or her sister.

"Who drowned in the well?" Even to her own ears, her voice sounded faint.

"Wee Sarah—and the doll," Trisha said. Positioning her doll on the table, she looked towards the well too. "Daddy said Sarah was his best girl, but she was bad, bad. She drowned my doll."

Lisa gripped the edge of the table, dumbfounded at the venom in her eight-year-old niece's voice. The drumbeat in her head from the wine the night before intensified.

"George told a lie," Trisha whimpered. "Sarah didn't fall in the well. She climbed in." There was a beat of silence. "Sarah stretched out, like this," Trisha went on, demonstrating by leaning over the table in an exaggerated stretch. "She did this with her hands," she said, opening her fingers and making a grabbing motion in the air. "She couldn't reach my doll. Then she made a big bubble," Trisha said, going back to eating her toast.

Shock waves shot through Lisa. Was Trisha describing what she had seen? Had she been there and watched her sister drown, or was she repeating what she had heard George and others say?

The image Trisha had described of Sarah's ten-year-old head disappearing below the dark waters of the deep well filled Lisa's mind. Putting her throbbing head in her hands, she shrieked silently at William. "You let one of your daughters drown, and now you're giving the other one away to me."

"There's something not right in your head. You need help. Your daughter needs help too," she moaned.

Chapter 24

Lisa picked a bunch of holly covered in rich red berries and put them on the family graves for Christmas, then waited for Rev Snodgrass outside Sunday school. It was too far for Trisha to walk to the graveyard, but Faith had taken her to see a Christmas nativity play at the school.

Reverend Snodgrass smiled his usual sardonic smile. "Well, well, Lisa Armstrong. Or should I say, Mrs McKnight? And what brings you to our little church hall?" he smiled.

"Visiting my family's graves." she'd said pointedly. The old clergyman looked at the dried muck and grass stains on Lisa boots. "Isn't the graveyard looking neat and tidy? One of our parishioners keeps the churchyard and the graveyard looking pristine," he smiled, avoiding her direct question.

"Why wasn't William's wife buried in the Armstrong plot?" she asked bluntly.

Gripping his Bible, the old rector went into a fit of coughing. "It was your mother's wish, child," he said, wiping his streaming eyes with a white hankie. "Walk up to the Manse with me. I'm not as young as I used to be, and it's always nice to be seen with a pretty girl," Geoffrey murmured smoothly.

"I can't believe that my mother, a churchgoing woman all her life, was so revengeful that she refused to have Margaret buried beside her daughter Sarah," Lisa burst out.

"You understand that to do so would have been to break a promise—a dying wish…" Reverend said in a shocked voice.

Lisa stopped walking and turned to face him. "So you'd let a woman who did everything she could for my father and kept the farm going, believing that William had died fighting for his country—you'd let her be buried in a pauper's grave because you thought to bury her beside her small daughter would have be some kind of treachery? What kind of man of God are you, Reverend

Snodgrass?" she said furiously. Realising that her voice had risen and that people were staring, she stalked away.

Chapter 25

"Trisha is doing much better now. She should soon be able to go home with you. I'm sure you're anxious to get home for Christmas."

Lisa braced herself. "I'm going home to my own bairns for Christmas, Doctor Coles, but I am not taking William's daughter with me. William can come back for her."

John rubbed his hand over his face. He had done it again. He had left it too late to act, and William was somewhere in England in charge of George. Short of getting the Salvation Army to try and locate him, he didn't know what else he could do. He had to make sure Lisa took Trisha.

"Where will she go if you don't take her? Surely you don't want your niece to be sent to the Children's Home in Enniskillen," he rebuffed her gently.

"What about her grandparents?"

Dr Coles sighed. "Fergal Furlong is ready to be discharged from hospital. But they feel they can't take Trisha now."

"Didn't they even want to see her before they went home?"

"They feel they're too old to take on a child now," John lied. They had been so overwhelmed at Fergal's collapse and all that they'd heard and seen that he simply couldn't burden them with a child to take care of on top of everything else.

Lisa's heart sank. The Furlongs had been her last hope. She could feel her control slipping. She was going to be forced into taking Trisha back to Scotland to live with her.

"My mother started all this by telling us all William's name was never to be mentioned again. If she had accepted Margaret and not disowned her own son—not cut him out of her will and her life because he married a Catholic—we wouldn't be in this... this situation now," she said angrily. "And you, Doctor. You convinced me I should marry BJ and not tell him the baby I was expecting wasn't his, and I was to go and live in Scotland with him—not come home for my mother's funeral, because my 'condition' would be obvious to everybody," she cried out.

"I can't take her. There's something… odd about her…like there was with William. I took care of William when we were growing up, but things are different now. I have two children of my own to take care of, and I'm living in a hovel of a tenement building. I can't cope with another child like William," she wailed.

The doctor felt the painful, shameful truth of her words. He placed a steadying hand on hers. "Trisha is like her father in some ways, but William was born like that. Trisha is like that because Margaret was never able to be a mother to her like she was to George and Sarah," he explained, clasping Lisa's hand between his.

"What was wrong William's wife that she couldn't look after her own daughter?" Lisa said defiantly.

Dr Coles' weary face folded in. "Margaret's father disowned her because she had married William, a Protestant, in a Protestant church. I often thought she was suffering from a broken heart. When she wasn't suffering from ill health or nerves, she spent her time trying to keep William on an even keel. All he had seen and had to do to survive at war had made him extremely volatile. Trisha suffered the brunt of his irrational rages. He believed that Trisha was… the reason everything was going wrong… going against him. Her granda and George saved her as best they could. But William *ii* her father…"

"Was Trisha there when Sarah drowned?" Lisa shot at him, remembering Trisha's description of the drowning.

Dr Coles shook visibly. "The day Sarah drowned, Lillian Snodgrass, the Sunday school teacher, came to the house and complained that Trisha and Sarah had shouted out during the service and acted disrespectfully. But the word of their bad behaviour was home before her," he sighed.

"William became incensed. He rarely beat Sarah. But as her punishment, he stood over her and made her beat three-year-old Trisha with a stick."

Lisa felt faint. "Where was my father?"

"Your father, Samuel, suffered a stroke," John said hoarsely. "He tried to make it to Hamilton's to get help to restrain William, but he only had it to the shortcut before he took the stroke."

The picture of his old veteran friend crying like a baby was still as vivid in his memory as if it were yesterday.

"You brought William into this world—a gift from the Almighty," Samuel had said through his garbled sobs. "I curse the day he was born," old Samuel had cried brokenly, gripping his limp arm with his good hand.

"Doctor Coles, are you all right?" Lisa asked, alarmed at the pallor of the old doctor's face and the terrible trembling of his body.

"Lock up this damned place, Lisa. Go home to your husband and children," John Coles croaked, stumbling to his feet.

As he shakily manoeuvred the old Ford with practice around the potholes, he glanced in the wing mirror at the silent Lisa and the chattering Trisha. "Where was Margaret the day Sarah drowned?"

"Sleeping," Dr Coles said gruffly.

"Lisa," Dr Coles said as they stopped at Con and Ellen's gate, "Take Trisha home with you. It's what your father would expect of you," he said almost inaudibly.

Watching them walk up the path, Dr Coles wiped the cold sweat off his brow. "Where was Trisha's mother, Margaret, the day her daughter drowned? Sleeping the sleep of the drugged—from heavy tablets which I prescribed," he muttered, guilt twisting his gut, as he put the car into gear and drove away.

Chapter 26

It was the New Year sales, and everybody and their mother seemed to be rushing about, laden down with parcels. *It'll be coming into the early lambing season soon,* George thought, as a woman with a large fluffy white dog crossed their path, reminding him of home.

"Try and remember where Sheamie Foy said he'd meet you, Da" George said, stopping in the middle Regent Street in the West End.

"It was something like 'the morning after'," William mumbled. A large black lady swept past him imperiously, giving him a dirty look as William's suitcase caught her a glancing blow on the shin.

"13 Birch Hill Road not good enough for you now?" Ma Higgins had grumbled as they were leaving.

"Too far from the new work," William retorted.

"Good lad you've got there,", Ma Higgins had said belligerently. "Let him go to school." George looked at her in surprise. Drunk or not she didn't miss much.

"Don't let 'im be like 'er," she said, jerking her head to where Stella stood, half-hidden in the shadows of the stairwell. "Thieving and whoring—that all she's fit for now."

George glanced at Stella. There was a dejected slump to her body. He wanted to explain that he hadn't known anything about moving until an hour ago. Anger rose in him. *Typical William,* he thought, *thinks of nobody but himself. Just like the day of Mammy's funeral: just pack up and be ready to move. No thought for Trisha or me,* George thought bitterly.

A second Christmas and New Year had passed without hearing if Trisha was with his Aunt Lisa in Scotland.

He looked daggers at his father. He couldn't even tell Stella where they were going. All his father would say was that, "Foy seein' to it."

Banging Ma Higgins' door behind him, George had the same intense feeling of hatred for his father he had felt the day they left home. "Only, this time it's stronger, and I intend to make him pay," he muttered.

William looked around him. The gaffer had said the pub was near a railway station. He cursed. London was full of railway stations. Which of them had Foy meant?

"Da, I'm not walking round in circles anymore," George said, sitting down on the bulging suitcases. Most of the clothes in it were stolen. He had got good at it since he'd stolen that first coat. Now it had become second nature to him.

"Asking directions is a waste of time," William moaned. "People are either tourists or foreigners."

"Here, I know this place—Paedar's Pub," William said, recognising a pub and eating place where the navvies went sometimes. "I know a woman who worked here."

He breathed a sigh of relief when he saw her behind the bar. "The pub's name has to do with a drink the morning after booze-up," he said, feeling foolish.

Rosie, the barmaid, laughed. "The 'air of the dog'," she said. "It's out Cricklewood way."

A blast of noise hit them as they pushed open the door of the pub. The air was thick with cigarette smoke and blue with swearing.

George had never seen so many navvies in one place. They stood in groups gathered around the bar and walls.

William looked around for Sheamie Foy. He was nowhere to be seen. Then, he saw Scotch Jock at a table, arm wrestling a man twice his size. Nodding for George to follow him, he threaded his way between the tables reserved for food. His lips curled in disgust. They were covered in dirty dishes, empty glasses, and overflowing ashtrays.

"Good ta see ye, me old mate," Jock roared, pushing over to make room for William on the already crowded seat. "Ah hear you're comin wi' us to do a job at Highbury?" he shouted.

William nodded. "Have you seen the gaffer?" he shouted back above the ear-splitting noise. "He's supposed to be gettin me and the lad digs."

"Playin' cards oot the back," Jock roared, nodding towards the back room of the pub.

William's heart sank. Foy was a sore loser. If he lost at the cards, he'd be in no mood to talk about digs or work.

Jock nodded to where a girl and an older man were tuning up a fiddle and a concertina.

At the first strains of the fiddle, lifted about the noise, a great cheer went up from a crowd at the bar.

"Clear the floor," someone shouted, as a young navvy threw off his coat, ceremoniously placing his bottle of Guinness on the bar and started to dance an Irish jig.

"I'll tell the gaffer you're here," Jock said as he drained his glass and headed in the direction of the back room.

"A lot of good that'll do me," William muttered. "The chances of getting him out of here before closing time are remote." He looked around for George. He didn't want some of his smart-aleck workmates putting one over on him and giving George drink. "Nothing would please them better," he muttered.

A hearty slap on the back almost knocked him off the end of the bench. William was relieved to see the gaffer was in good humour. The other navvies had nicknamed him Gael Foy because he was a native Irish speaker from the Gaeltacht in Donegal.

"How does lodging in Edgebury Road suit you?" Sheamie Foy asked.

"What about the job?"

"Aye, laying pipes for Murphy—Highbury Corner. Is that to your pleasing?" Sheamie said. "Play your cards right this time, Armstrong. Don't be pissin' the other men off with your oul' religious claptrap," he warned. "Here's your money and here's fiver—get a taxi for you and the young fella," he said, thrusting the money into William's fist. "I'll be a while here yet. The men still have to get their pay before they leave," he continued. "You're not staying yourself," he asked, knowing what the answer would be.

William looked around him at the men in Gael Foy's crew. It was the same old story. The end of another job, and Sheamie would get his rewards for hiring the men and making sure they stayed hired.

William looked over at Shay, the owner of the pub. A Co. Kerry hurler in his day, he stood head and shoulders above any man in the pub. *They'll be no arguing with him,* he mused. Shay and the gaffers had an arrangement. Shay gave the men food and drink on spec, and now it was time to square up their bills. *What they'll have left of their money will be easy carried,* William muttered as he took the address Sheamie proffered.

He ordered George away from a group of men singing and drinking at the corner of the bar.

Scowling, with a deliberate twist of his foot, George kicked the legs of a table full of drinks on his way past. Glasses scattered, and drink spilt in all directions.

"Armstrong, you're a bollocks!" Shay bawled.

Smirking with satisfaction, George headed for the door. He could hear the row gathering momentum as his father refused to buy a round of drinks for the table.

"It was an accident—the young fella… the bag…" William kept shouting.

"How many people live in this bloody digs?" William muttered, listening to the voices and footsteps as the large family of children, aunts, uncles, and Greek grandparents clattered up and down the stairs.

"I, Mrs Eufemia," the landlady had said the first morning. "Eat, eat," she encouraged George, pushing a plate of fried pancakes at him. "Plenty of honey—good for growing boy," she smiled, tweaking his cheek.

William muttered and pushed his plate of nuts and some odd-smelling stuff aside.

"You no' like?" the landlady demanded, grabbing up his plate and flinging it in the direction of the kitchen sink.

A brown-eyed girl sitting across the table from them said something in Greek to her mother. Throwing up her hands, she returned with a packet of cornflakes, which she planked in front of William.

"You speak English?" George asked the girl.

"I speak English at school. I don't get teased so much."

"I know how you feel," George said, thinking about the shop assistants who made fun of his Irish accent.

"Take this—good lunch—for digging holes," the landlady said, her earlier outburst against William forgotten as she thrust a huge carton of food at him.

"The smell of that stuff they're cooking down there would turn your stomach," William complained, turning over in the bed.

"If you give me money, I'll buy you dinners," George said.

William glared at his son. "We'll soon be moving anyway."

George swung around. "You have another row with Sheamie Foy? He warned you to stop preaching to the men."

William rolled into the bed and wrapped himself in the blanket. "Scotch Jock says there's plenty of work in Harlow."

The cream from the custard George was eating spilt down his shirt. "Harlow's miles away, Da. We have to stay in the one place. Aunt Lisa will never find us if we keep changing digs. And you said if I could get a part-time job, I could go back and do my O-Levels."

"Nobody's goin' to employ you at fifteen wi' no National Insurance card. Even Foy wouldn't do that."

"Oh! So you did remember it was my birthday? And I'm sixteen."

Tiredly, William looked at George. He had been six, and Sarah five when he came back in 1947. Everything had changed. Margaret had moved into the farmhouse, and his father Samuel had claimed his place as their father figure.

He had grown close to Sarah, but George remained apart from him and close to his grandfather and his mother. He had been close to his own mother—until she disowned him. Yet, some days, as a POW confined to pitch-black isolation cells, he felt his mother close to him. He stilled. He had no way of knowing then she was already dead and buried.

And then he had come back, and Trisha had been born… Bringing his mind back to the digs, he said, "Birthdays are for women and girls."

George licked the cream from the pastry from his fingers and gave a derisive snigger. "Yeah, Trisha is the only daughter you have, and you don't want her name mentioned. Do you, Da?"

Springing up in the bed, his face mottled with sudden rage, his father lunged at him.

Grabbing his coat, George flung himself down the three flights of stairs, a feeling of rage pervaded his every bone.

Walking blindly, he found himself at Marble Arch.

He listened half-heartedly to a man berating the government for not looking after the veterans of the First and Second World Wars.

"…Shell shocked… reliving the past, nightmares… mental hospitals," the speaker roared out.

Did his Da have war weariness? He began listening intently. *Could his father be admitted to a mental hospital?* He thought back to the night on the boat from Belfast to Haysham and William's suicide attempt.

"You missed your chance, Georgie boy," he said, imitating Sheamie Foy's Donegal accent. "I won't miss the next one," he said grimly, clapping loudly as the speaker finished his rant. Their bedsit was at the top of the old Victorian house; the stairs were steep and uncarpeted. *One of these nights with a bit of luck, his Da would be feeling suicidal again and with a bit of a push, fall down the stairs an, break his bloody neck,* he thought.

Turning up the collar of his coat, he headed for the pub where Sheamie drank.

"Can't you talk any sense into that father of yours?" Sheamie said as George slipped onto a stool at the bar beside him.

"What happened this time?" George asked.

Sheamie wiped the froth of the Guinness off his top lip George had bought him. "He's stopped eating with the men—sits by himself. The men are giving out about him being in their squad. Ah can't say ah blame them, son."

A feeling of anticipation buoyed George up. His father's nightmares followed a pattern. After another row with the men on the job, he'd become morose, and sure enough, his nightmares would come.

"Will you give him another change? He was in a POW in Poland. I think he must have those mental things old soldiers get," George said, pretending a concern he didn't feel. He needed time to get a chance to push him down the steep stairs and get a job where he could live in.

Chapter 27

The four-star Grand Hotel in Mayfair had a notice pinned to its menu board. *Waiter and dishwasher wanted—immediate start.*

"No paper sellers or ticket sellers," the snooty-faced woman behind the desk said, giving him a sharp appraising look.

"I'm here to apply for the job as a waiter," George said, using what he hoped was a manly English accent. His voice had started to break, and sometimes it came out deep and gravelly.

The receptionist stared at him, then picked up the telephone. "Someone at Reception to see Mr Swann," she smirked down the phone.

"Mr Swann will be with you directly," she said, her shoulders shaking. *The bitch is laughing at me!* George thought.

The door behind the desk opened, and a large, imposing man entered.

"I'm Mr Swann, Head Waiter," he said loftily.

George's heart was thumping so hard he could hardly get his words out. "I'm here to apply for the waiter's job."

Ike Swann ran a nervous hand around his sticky-up collar. He glanced at the sniggering receptionist. "Follow me," he commanded.

Once out of sight of the receptionist, he stopped. "What do you think you are playing at? You're not a waiter! You made me look a fool in front of that…woman," he spluttered. Taking a lily-white handkerchief from his breast pocket, he wiped it across his shiny, receding hairline.

"She's no woman. She's a bloody oul' slapper who needs a good shaggin'," George said, mimicking Ma Higgins' drunken voice.

A startled look came over the head waiter's face. Then he started to laugh. Bending over, he clasped his hands around the knees of his pristine trousers with their knife-edge crease and roared with laughter.

"What age are you?" he asked, mopping his eyes.

"Sixteen," George said.

Ike Swan rubbed his chin. It had been a while since he'd had a boy.

"You're hired," he said.

I did it! I did it! George kept telling himself. He had only got the dishwasher's job, but he didn't care. It paid money.

"It's part-time and only when we need you, remember that," the head waiter said as he got the hotel housekeeper, Agnes, to show George where he would sleep.

George looked around him. This was heaven compared to sharing digs with his crazy Da.

"Mickilo Martini, the chef, will feed you—if you keep on the right side of him," the head waiter said, glancing cautiously through the round porthole windows of the kitchen door before pushing it open.

"Some of the friggin' pots are heavier and bigger than him, so they are," the chef growled.

George stared at him.

"I know what you're thinking," the chef said as he carefully sliced steaks on the meat slab. "With a name like Mickilo Martini, you expect me to speak like the Mob and wear dark glasses, right?"

George nodded dumbly.

"Who do I sound like? Go on tell me!" the chef growled.

George looked at him, with his black hair tied back in a ponytail under his chef's tall hat and his hands red from the blood of the fresh meat.

"You sound like somebody from Belfast," George stammered out.

"That I am, and don't you forget it, wee lad. The Mob has nothin' on us Belfast boys."

"Why are you still standin' there with your gub hangin' open? Get over to that dishwasher and get started," Mickilo thundered.

"I'll give him a week," he said, turning back to Ike Swann. "If he even lasts that long."

Mickilo threw the head waiter a look. "He's just a child, an innocent Irish kid green as grass. He's not long off the boat. You keep your paws off him, if you want to eat," he growled.

"Marta," he roared at a slight-built girl who was chopping vegetables at another table. "Leave that for a while and get this… wain… started on the dishwasher."

"Yes, Chef," Marta said obediently.

"Mickilo's from Belfast?" George asked, nodding in the chef's direction.

"Always call him Chef. And don't bother him with questions," Marta said in a low voice. "He's very temperamental—especially when he's had a few too many drinks the night before," she whispered, giggling.

George stared in shock at the mountain of dishes. Trolleys stood three deep, their chrome faces swamped with dirty dinner dishes. No matter where he looked, he saw dishes and pots piled high. He gulped deep in his throat.

"Where will I start?" he asked.

"Scrape the leftovers into the slop buckets. Then, stack all the plates of the same size on top of each other until you get your first load into the dishwasher. You better put on this apron to keep the splashes of food off your clothes," she said, swirling him round and tying the long apron strings around his waist. "Fill the dishwasher with the scraped plates until the two wire trays are full. Push them in this end and take them out the other end. Oh, one other thing, make sure the plates are gleaming clean with no food bits stuck to them. Mr Swann will go ballistic if a guest complains. Talk to you later," Marta said, moving back to her own job.

"Will you be back?" a voice said as George straightened up from emptying yet another bucket of slop into the swill bin in the walled enclosure away from the kitchen.

He turned to see Mickilo Martini sitting smoking on top of several sacks of potatoes.

"I will," George said, a determined note in his voice.

"It'll not be so bad tomorrow. The girl who was on dishes left this morning. I think it was good timing from your end," Mickilo said.

"Oul' Swann take you on a day-to-day basis, then?"

George nodded.

Mickilo drew hard on his cigarette. "Slave labour—no stamps—no insurance," he snorted.

"I need the job," George said quickly, turning to go back into the kitchen.

"Take a break. You've been at it for hours, so you have. I'll send Marta out with something for you to eat."

"The dishes will pile up…"

Mickilo looked at him and laughed. "Don't worry; I'll put somebody else on dishes for a while. Here, have a smoke and content yourself," he said, throwing George a packet of John Players.

"The shape of your ass will be in the tatties if you sit there much longer," Marta's voice said.

George shot upright. "Sorry, I must have fallen asleep."

"Lucky for you, Chef seems to have taken a shine to you. Here, he said to give you this, and he has sorted it out with Mr Swann for you to come in on the early shift tomorrow," Marta said, holding out a parcel of food.

Taking another bite of the sirloin steak the chef had given him to take home with him, George offered the other steak to his father.

"I don't want other people's leftover," William scowled.

"Chef cooks it fresh for me."

"Why would he do that?"

George didn't bother explaining he didn't take his breaks when the hotel was busy, like now in the tourist season.

He waited his chance to broach the subject of going back to study again when the new term started. "Mr Swann says he'll put me on shifts at the weekend and after school," he said casually.

William looked at his son. He was nothing like the placid, childish boy who had come to London over two years ago. Working in the hotel had filled out his body and made him a lot less malleable.

Lately, he'd caught George watching him. It made him feel uneasy. The intuitive sense of danger and alertness he had developed to survive during in his time in the bombing of Malta stirred in him.

"As long as I'm paying the digs and keepin' us, I'll make the decisions around here. You're finished with learnin'."

Hearing raised voices, the landlady bustled into the small kitchen-cum-sitting room. She stood for minute, hands on her broad hips looking at them. The old grandmother, sitting beside the range, said something to her in Greek.

Turning, she began to rage at William, "You, you, bad man. Out. Out of my kitchen!" she said, waving her arms about. "You… make… air bad."

George smirked. His father knew better than to turn the word on Mrs Eufemia.

"What's so funny?" William scowled.

"She says you spoil the atmosphere," George laughed.

He wondered he had time for a shave before he met Marta at the Angel Cinema. He'd get a double seat for them. It gave him a chance to sit close to her.

Walking behind Marta on the carpeted walkway, he looked up to the balcony. "There's Mr Swann," he said, waving his hand. He was about to call out to him when Marta snapped his hand down.

"Not in front of all these punters," she hissed. "He's with his... male friend."

"What's wrong with that?" George said.

"Don't they have men like him in Ireland?" Marta giggled as she saw the look of disbelief dawn in George's eyes.

"Oh right," George said shocked. "I didn't know he was like that," he said.

"You're such a baby," Marts scoffed.

An unexpected feeling of loneliness swept over George. *That's what Stella used to say to me,* he mused. He hadn't given Stella or Ma Higgins much thought since he had started to work at the hotel.

"Here, young fella, you doing anything on the 15th of August?" Chef Mickilo called across the kitchen to George. "Need a pull-out. No money in it," he added, holding a spoonful of his speciality desert out for Marta to taste. "The craic is good, and the food is mighty," he laughed, waltzing the dish of banoffee pie around the kitchen.

"What's so special about the 15th of August?"

Mickilo gave him a look. "You're not Irish Catholic, then."

"I'm a protestant... and British, I think," George said. "Some days, I don't know who I am or what I am," he added in a low voice.

Mickilo stopped what he was doing. "What about a smoke?"

"Marta," he yelled. "Hold the fort."

"No problem, Chef." Marta shouted from the vegetable pantry.

Mickilo drew the cigarette smoke deep into his lungs and let it exhale slowly.

"Listen, son," he said, "once you cross the Irish Sea, it doesn't matter whether you're from the Protestant Shankill Road in Belfast or the Catholic Bogside in Derry, you're Irish. People here don't want to know," he said, tilting back his head as he swallowed a small glass of concentrated orange juice in one go. Screwing up his face at its bitter taste, he grinned.

"My head feels like there's a crowd of Belfast boys banging the lambeg drum in there—rough night last night. Well, what about the tea party on the 15th?"

George's brain clicked into gear. *Didn't the Catholic Church or some society belonging to them—St Vincent De Paul or something like that—help people? Maybe the priest could find out if Trisha was all right. Maybe he could bring Stella...*

"Can I bring a friend?"

The chef raised his eyebrows. "Female?"

George nodded.

Mickilo frowned. "Marta has had a few bum steers in her life. I wouldn't want you taking the piss, two-timing her with another bird," he warned.

"It's just Stella. I can see her another time, Chef. But won't the priest mind that I'm a Protestant?"

The chef laughed. "You're already in. I recommended you for washing the dishes."

George took one look at the fine bone china tea sets with their delicate embroidery of three-leaf shamrocks and tumbling roses, brought in by the ladies committee and backed away from the sink.

"Wise man," a voice chuckled behind him. "If ye broke one of those cups, you'd probably have to marry one of their daughters," Father Agnew laughed, shaking hands with George.

"It's good to see you again. I hear you have a wee job at the hotel now. Mickilo tells me you're a smart lad and a good, hard worker."

"I won a scholarship to Mill House Grammar School," George said.

The priest looked at him appreciatively. "That's no mean feat. I hear that you're thinking about going back to do your exams."

George nodded. "Mammy wanted me to be an architect."

Father Agnew pursued his lips. "I might be able to get you into St Stephen's. It's more of a 'college' than a school. Tough mind," he said. "It's nothing like your old grammar school," he warned.

Chapter 28

William knew if he tried to straighten up, the pain in his back would be excruciating. Sheamie had got him digging out ditches for McAlpine's out Brompton Railway way. Stupidly, he had complained that the men should take turns at it. The other men had sworn and cursed him. Nobody had come near him all week except Scotch Jock.

He gritted his teeth and straightened. Agonising pain shot up his back and down his arms. He lowered himself onto the mound of earth he'd just dug. He looked along the long line of navvies. Some smoked, others emptied buckets of cold water over their head and upper bodies to give them a short reprieve from the hot August sun.

A light breeze cooled the sweat on his body. Rubbing his hands together, he looked with disdain at the map of hardened welts and fresh open wounds that crisscrossed each other like the Piccadilly train lines.

The men along the ditches were rising to their feet, ready to start again. He heard brogues from: Kerry, Cork, Limerick, and a few Tyrone voices, and Scotch Jock, from Dundee. *An ex-veteran like me,* he thought.

"You never worked digging ditches before, Armstrong?" Scotch Jock asked, now giving him a pull up from the clay mound.

"Ah, think you know the answer to that already," William retorted.

"Come to the pub at finishing time—buy the gaffer a pint. The crew will curses your ignorance and call you a stupid fecker, but it'll be soon forgotten."

William shook his head. "Ah don't drink."

"Ye need to play the game," Jock insisted. "Don't cosy up to the gaffer on-site. Do it in the pub wi' a few pints."

William couldn't help laughing. Jock looked like a peeling tomato. "Feckin' heat wave—hotter than feckin' Spain," Jock grumbled as he tried to shade his white, almost translucent skin from the sun. "Right, back to the diggin'," he grunted. "See you at the pub later," he ordered, giving William the thumbs-up. "Play the game, play the game," he sang, walking away.

Trying to ignore the searing pain in his hands and body, William grasped the pickaxe handle and swung it into the solid earth of the ditch. He felt the tortured flesh of his hands stick to the pick handle. "When are you goin' to think before you open your big mouth?" he berated himself. "Never again will I be so shit stupid," he promised himself.

Foolishly, in his last job, he'd pointed out that if the men spent fewer nights in the pub, they'd be in better shape to work in the morning. "A fair day's work for a fair day's pay," he pointed out. "Some of the men are not fit to work, and the rest of us have to do their share," he grumbled.

Foy had been livid with him. "Do you have any brains between them two big stickin' out ears of yous?" he'd bawled. "Do ye not know when to speak and when to keep your bloody mouth shut? Most of them men live in digs where all the landlady wants off them is the rent. They go to the pub for company and a wee bit of the home they had to leave."

William understands homesickness and loneliness. The locals had treating him with contempt, and refused to serve Margaret in the shops. But he still missed the familiarity of life there. He even missed the farm.

He started to dig again, almost welcoming the hard grafting. The harder he worked, the less time he had to think about Margaret. Sometimes, he thought he caught a glimpse of her blond hair as a woman got on or off a train. His heart would leap with joy. He'd loitered about King's Cross station hoping to see the woman again, only to discover it wasn't his Margaret. The men on the site had a new nickname name for him now. They called him the "Pervy proddy".

Silent tears, mixed with sweat, fell into the hole he was digging. It was three years since she'd died. *Poor Margaret,* he thought. *Lying in a pauper's grave without even a flower or a plank of wood to mark your resting place.*

He startled as Scotch Jock shouted into his ear. "Whistle blew five minutes ago, man. Leave some work for the rest of us for another day."

William grabbed the hand Jock offered as he struggled out of the too-deep hole he had dug.

"Gaffer says you're to come to the pub. He'll be giving out the work for the next job." He held up his hand as William started to shake his head. "I know, you're not a drinkin' man but you eat, don't ye? Pub does good grub. Come on!

What have ye to go home for?" William realised he was right. George would out with the street gangs that he hung about with now.

Pulling his shirt over his burnt back, he grabbed his coat and followed Jock.

The surly looks on his workmates' faces turn to something resembling a smile as he passed the drinks he had just paid his hard-earned money for disappeared with various degrees of satisfaction down their dry throats.

He felt resentment grip the pit of his stomach. Sheamie and Jock were further down the bar, playfully boxing each other. Soon the mood would change to singing rebel songs about dead heroes.

Thinking about his past dead comrades, he'd fought alongside in the war, he curled his lip in contempt. "The real dead heroes are the men who fought for Queen and Country who lie in unmarked graves," he growled.

Scotch Jock caught William's eye, raised his glass and saluted him. William couldn't hear what he said but he guessed it was along the line of "Play the game, man. Play the game."

"Grab a couple of beers," he shouted.

"Am away to the digs to drop the sister a line," William lied. Jock raised his glass in a salute of acknowledgement and promptly joined in the singing of *Danny Boy*.

After the hot day, a rainy drizzle outside cooled the air. William's attention was caught by a young soldier and the blonde girl by his side. The soldier possessively laid his arm around her shoulders. The gesture instantly transporting William back to his last leave home before he had been shipped overseas.

Lisa had come to babysit George while he and Margaret had gone to the pictures. He had no recollection what film they had seen, but he remembered vividly their wild and wonderful love making in the old tumbledown bed that came with the old station house he had rented.

Those hours of our love was what kept me alive during my time in Leros when the German Luftwaffe were bombing us. Shell after shell rained down on us relentlessly.

"Ah expected to die every day," he mused, watching the soldier and his girlfriend move up along the line for the cinema. "I'd hear the drone of the planes and curl up with the pictures of Margaret and George, expecting never to see them again," he muttered, following the soldier and his girlfriend into the cinema. Seated behind them, the girl's golden hair tumbled down over the back of her seat, almost coming to rest on William's knee.

Margaret's hair had been like that—soft, long and wavy. After their night of love, it had lain in wet tendrils on her bare breasts. He'd brushed it out until it framed her face. Turning to him, she wound her legs around his body. This time their lovemaking was tender and gentle.

"That's when wee Sarah was started," he murmured.

The usherette's light caught him as he stroked the girl's hair…

Chapter 29

George walked aimlessly down Oxford Street. It was Halloween break from school. Father Agnew had been right. It was nothing like his old grammar school. It was full of misfits and thugs no other school would take. He scuffed the toe of his shoe against the sludgy ground and felt the water seep into his sock.

Oxford Circus was thronged with businessmen armed with briefcases, using black umbrellas like battering rams to clear the way as they rushed for the trains. Traffic with hardly a hand's stretch between them, revved their engines and honked their horns. At the first sign of a traffic light changing, engines got ready to race down the street like racing drivers.

The novelty of the sights and sounds of London still amazed him, but he wished he could go back to his D's new digs and crawl into bed. It was odd, but dirty as Ma Higgins' house had been, he missed it—missed Stella. His stomach growled with hunger. He had no work in the hotel this week, and he missed the chef feeding him. He noticed a group of boys smoking, the cigarette hidden in their cupped, half-closed hands. He tuned in to the sound of the cockney accents. He'd started to hang about with street gangs since starting St Stephen's. He earned their company by stealing food and drink for Knuckles, the gang leader.

Lost in his own thoughts, he took no notice of a man who sat down on a bench beside him.

"Hello, George."

He startled. He had been in London for almost three year, and it was the first time anybody had ever spoken his name outside of the hotel.

"Father Agnew?" he said, surprised. Dressed in a pair of old jeans and a woollen jumper, the priest looked more like of the down-and-outs that slept rough on the park benches.

Father Agnew laughed at the expression on George's face. "We're allowed to dress whatever way we like—within reason—on our day off," he smiled. "Not at the hotel today?" he said, taking in George's hangdog expression and the swelling around his cheekbone. Thrusting his hands deeper into his pockets, George lowered his eyes and stared at the ground.

The priest stretched out his legs and settled back into the damp seat. He watched the school group clowning about.

"How are you finding the new school?"

"It's nothing like my last school."

"Lookit, call in anytime to the Irish Centre. It'll soon be Christmas panto time. Come and bring your friend… what's her name, Marta. We promise not to try and make you into a Catholic," the priest joked, walking away.

"Yeah," George muttered. "It's nearly Christmas. That's what started the row this morning."

"It'll soon be Christmas again, Da. You said you'd write to Aunt Lisa. Trisha will think we've forgotten all about her," he said as he packed his father's work lunch box.

William's fist had shot out and hit him on the side of the head. "You might be nearly 18 now and think you're tough running with that gang, but don't think you're goin' to tell me what to do. She brought nothin' but bad luck and misery to your mother and me."

George had felt something snap inside him. Grabbing the heavy canvas workbag, he flung it at his father head and grabbed a knife from the table. "That's the last time you'll ever hit me," he'd shouted. "Next time I'll stab you with this," he screamed, brandishing the knife.

He stood under a bus shelter, his face and head aching from his father's blow, his cheek beginning to swell. The adrenalin rush he had gotten from the look of fear and disbelief on his father's face ebbed away. Now he had to go back and face him.

"You getting on or not, mate?" the clippie called to him, breaking his thoughts. George shook his head. Preoccupied with his own thoughts, he didn't see the woman on the bike or the small dog on the lead that trotted along beside her.

The woman cowered on the ground, clutching the yapping dog in her arms. "Don't take my dog!" she quacked. Her hand trembled as she thrust a small backpack at him.

George stared down at her incredulously. She thought he had knocked her off her bike to mug her and steal her dog. That was the kind of things Knuckles and his gang did. They thought George was weak. He'd show them, he thought. Reaching for the bike, he started to pedal.

After a while, his anger died and he stopped and searched the backpack she thrust at him. He ate the cheese and ham sandwiches and pocketed the money he found in the backpack. He turned the keys he'd found in the zipped pocket over in his hands. What should he do with them? Maybe he should try and find the girl, apologise, give her back her bike and the keys to her house.

Knuckles' sneering face jumped into his mind. They'd mock him if he told them he'd stolen a bike and then went looking for the owner because he was worried she'd be locked out of her flat.

Helpless exasperation rose up in him. A knuckle was right. *I needed to toughen up.* He raised his hand, ready to fling the keys into the shrubbery. On second thoughts, he dropped them back into the bag and retrieved the bike. He'd take it back to the digs—give it to the gang—tell them he'd stolen it. *It might give him some street cred.*

His father stood inside their digs, stony-faced, beside his packed suitcases. They stared at each other, open hostility on both their faces. Finally, William turned away. "Pack your stuff. We're moving."

The angry voice of the landlady followed them out the door and down the front steps. George caught the word "Paddy wagon." He guessed the woman was shouting they were lucky she wasn't sending for the police. He turned his face full on so his father could get a good look at his handiwork.

William stared impassively back at him.

What I'd give to give him a piece of what he has been handing out to Trisha and now to me, George muttered.

Knuckles' face rose before him. *He's my age, but no way would he let anybody smash a fist into his face,* George thought.

His anger mounted against his father at the shake of the landladies' heads.

Eventually, they found a number for a room to rent scrawled on the wall of a telephone box. Barely noticing its condition, George dumped the cases and, without a word to his father, slammed out the room door and went in search of Knuckles and the gang.

Chapter 30

"Get a move on," Lisa called in exasperation as the giggling in Isobel's room grew louder. BJ would soon be in for him dinner, and she had to be ready for her part-time evening job in the cinema when he came in.

Trisha concentrated on her image in the mirror. Aunt Lisa was using her as a clothes horse to try on the dresses she had to adjust for the customers from the shop. She arched her eyebrows and looked with satisfaction at their new shape. Lisa would go mad if she knew she had bribed Isobel to pluck them. She'd promised she'd go into Woolworth's in town, to get her photo taken at the photo booth to send to her favourite pop idol. Turning sideways, she pulled her school shirt taunt over her breasts. With a thrill, she noticed that today their peaks could be seen pressing against the thin material. She pouted her lips and glanced seductively from beneath her long dark eyelashes.

"Stuart Moss will be pleased;" she murmured to her image.

"What are you doin' in there?" Lisa's irritated voice jerked her out of her fantasy of Mr Faber, their exchange French student teacher. Taking one last lingering look at her body, she scrambled into her clothes.

"If you're not out in five minutes, you can stay in and tidy that room of yours," Lisa scolded, sticking her head around the girls bedroom door. BJ had built in a set of narrow wooden bunks in the small room. It left little room for furniture except an old lean-to mirror and a chest of drawers.

The scowl on Lisa's face turned into a grin as she looked at the two of them, happy as two peas in a pod in the makeshift space. Isobel, as usual, had her head stuck in a pop magazine of her teenage pop idolism and at twelve, Trisha was checking out what she was wearing and the make-up she wasn't supposed to wear.

Made up, Isobel still looked her age, but Trisha looked like a teenager.

Moving to the window, Lisa watched them cross the street arm in arm; Trisha, long-legged and stills limping slightly from the scarred skins on her feet, her long ebony-black straight hair bouncing as she walked; Isobel's short, round figure hurrying to keep up, her wiry mop of unruly auburn curls defiant as they stuck out from her ears.

It still amazed her that Isobel's and BJ's protests about Trisha living with them had literally disappeared. She crossed the kitchen to tidy up the girls' room before BJ came in. The mirror was jammed at a rakish angle between the back of the door and the foot of Trisha's bed. They had obviously been trying on a combination of clothes.

"It's odd, but having to share and be so close together in such a small space brought Isobel and Trisha closer," she mused. *And with Trisha for company, it took Isobel off my back and let me concentrate on getting Andrew educated,* Lisa thought. He was just waiting to enlist as a RAF cadet.

She heard BJ whistling as he came up the stairs. He had got used to the idea of her going out two evenings to the Embassy and two mornings a week to "Stitch in Time."

He salvaged his pride by boasting that his woman worked in an office and did sewing for folk to 'lazy to de their own. "A wee bit o' pin money wi' the extra bairn," he explained it away.

"Any Christmas cards or a letter from the absent father?" BJ asked, "This'll be her fifth Christmas and Hogmanay wi' us and no' a word from that William bugger," he muttered, glancing at the calendar where the girls had the days marked off for the New Year street party to bring in 1963.

"Has he ne feelin' for the wee lass?" BJ growled as he washed his hands at the sink.

Lisa shrugged resignedly. "I wrote back to the address on the one and only letter he sent me, but he never wrote back."

BJ swallowed a mouthful of dinner. "She's a bonny wee thing. She'll be a looker." He chuckled. "She reminds me o' you—the way she acts and goes on 'til she gets what she's efter."

Lisa snorted. She was glad she was going to work. BJ was in one of his romantic reminiscing moods, and she knew well where that would end.

"Ah think Isobel feels it." BJ went on. "She'll no' get a look in wi' the lads when Trisha's abut, wi 'that crow-black hair and them big dark eyes she has." BJ shifted in his chair. "Your William's a bastard, leavin' her orphan wi' ne mother or fether. What wud he heve dun if we couldnea heve given her a hame?"

"Her granny and granda live in Co. Kerry. They might have taken her if her granda didn't have a heart attack." Lisa said defensively.

"Am no blamin' you or the lass. William wasnea in his right mind efter Margaret's burial, but he knew what he wus at. He knew you'd come and take her—sort out his problem, like ye always did."

"Awk, Lisa," BJ said, his face brightening. "She's done well. When ah saw the state o' her feet and hands, scalded from the frost, ah thought she'd be marred for life."

Lisa nodded. The train and boat journey from Larne to Stranraer had been a nightmare. She'd had to half carry, half drag Trisha along with the cases. Trisha's hands had healed well, but the soles of her feet and her toes on both feet were puckered and wrinkled like an old woman's.

"Make sure they both do their homework when they come back from the club. And don't let them soft-soap you with the old tale that they did it in school or when they came home."

BJ snorted. "A'll no' be much help if they start eskin' me for the answers."

Lisa laughed. "You'll do all right. You have plenty of practice writing and doing sums at the bookies."

She struggled into her coat, careful not to admire herself in the mirror above the fireplace. BJ fancied she met men there. Most of the time was spent walking up and down, flicking the ushers light over roaming hands and panting bodies in the back row.

"I'll not be late," she promised, air kissing the back of BJ's head for effect.

Walking past the plate-glass windows of the Jiffy Cleaners, she admired her new purple heather-coloured coat with its sixties-styled low-slung belt that hugged her hips. It was out of Madge Gamble's Great Universal catalogue. She was paying half a crown a week for it, but it was worth every penny. She turned its black velvet collar up and enjoyed it luxurious feel against her cheek. She'd buy black knee-length boot and black leather gloves to match it as soon as she had enough paid off the coat.

Chapter 31

Getting off the earlier school bus, Trisha saw Stuart Mosley and his pal rush out of the newsagents, chased by the elderly Indian man who ran it. Laughing, they ran up the nearest close, calling out racist obscenities.

Trisha followed them. She could hear the angry shouts of women as Stuart and Colly ran headlong into the lines of freshly washed clothes that ran the length of the greens.

"Stealing again?" she asked, coming up behind them where they lay laughing on the rubbish-strewn ground of what the Corporation called the park.

"Want a smoke?" Stuart asked. "Well, you're no' getting any. Steal your ean."

Trisha threw her school bag on the grass and sat on it. Opening her blazer, she leaned back on her elbows.

"You loss a button fea yer bloose?" Colly said, inching closer to her. Trisha nodded without taking her eyes of Stuart.

"You tryin' to touch up my woman?" Stuart said.

Colly started thumbing through the pages of the magazine he'd stolen from the shop. He sucked air in through his missing front teeth and stared at the picture of a topless model wearing bikini bottoms and holding her large bare breasts in her hands.

"See this, Stu, see this," he said excitedly.

Stuart's eyes moved from the gaping hole in Trisha's blouse to the model, who gazed out from the page as if she was looking straight into his eyes. A stream of obscenities rolled off his tongue.

Trisha's heart thumped. The model looked fantastic. Sometimes, when Lisa was pinning and adjusting the short mini dresses on her, she imagined walking down the catwalk, giving the audience her sexy, sultry look.

If she had the picture of the model in the magazine, she could practice looking and acting like a real model.

"Tits and ass," Stuart drawled, watching Trisha's eyes ravage the picture. "Didnea knows ye liked the lassies," he smirked.

"You have a dirty mind, Stuart Mosley," Trisha said, aiming a kick at his shin.

"The peelers will be round asking if anybody knows who was stealing. I'll not tell if you give me the magazine," she coaxed.

Stuart stared hard at her and smirked. "Aye? Is that right, you'll no' tell it was Colly and me?"

Trisha nodded.

Stuart grinned, "Ah might—if ah can feel your tit."

Trisha drew in her breath. "I'm not kind of girl, Stuart Mosley."

"Aye? Is that right? What abut the other night? You were dyin' fer it," Stuart chortled, looking at Colly and laughing.

Trisha thought back to the night she'd let him kiss her. All the girls in school boasted about how they let boys kiss them. She didn't want to admit she'd never kissed a boy.

"It's great, makes ye feel all funny," the girls giggled in the showers after PE.

Trisha hated PE. She hated the way the other girls stared at her feet. Two of her toes had fused together with frostbite, making her feet look as if she had only four toes.

Stuart had stuck his tongue down her throat, almost choking her. He had smelled of boiled cabbage and sweaty feet. It had been disgusting and had made her want to throw up, but she was able to say she had kissed a boy.

"You're not touching me," she shouted, swinging her bag at Stuart's head. "I'll tell Uncle Billy, and he'll half kill you."

"Ah'll give it to ye if ye just let me have a quick feel?"

Colly jumped to his feet. "Och, Stu, yer no' going to give her the pictures. There's plenty o' lassies wantin' to show ye."

"Git away hame te your own hoose, Colly, and look at your Maggie's arse," Stuart growled, feeling Trisha's resolve weakening.

"That's enough," Trisha said, pushing a panting Stuart aside. Grabbing up her blazer, she buttoned up her blouse and fled up the street clutching the magazine. Breathlessly, she raced up the tenement stairs, hoping that the flat would be empty for once.

A note on the kitchen table said Lisa was away to deliver some clothes to the shop and would be back later. Flinging her school bag aside, she quickly stripped down to her pants and stood in front of the mirror. The scarred glass on the dressing table distorted and blurred her image. Gathering up her clothes, she rushed into Andrew's room. Propping the picture from the magazine on the chest of drawers, she tried out the poses of the model. Gradually, she began to get the hang of it. Rolling her pants down into a thin bikini line, she cupped her breasts and imitated the sultry smile on the model's face.

Something—a sound—made her turn towards the door. Andrew stood staring at her, open-mouthed, as if he had never seen her before.

"Get out of my room!" she screamed, grabbing for the bedcover.

"This is my room," Andrew said, his voice high-pitched and strangled.

Chapter 32

Hatred and venom spewed out of George. "I wish he had died in the war," he said vehemently.

Knuckles cracked his knuckles one by one. "Ya want us ta help ya? Want your old man done over?" Knuckles said, a rush of savage excitement coursing through his veins.

"We can 'ave a bit of slap and tickle with 'im," the gang member with a dragon tattoo boy covering his face and neck said, grinning at Knuckles.

George shook his head. "I can do it myself—pay him back for that he's done to my sister."

The other gang members sniggered. "Mummy's boy, ya ain't got the balls for it."

George swung to face them. "I robbed the woman and stole her bike, didn't I?"

Knuckles grinned. "How ya going to do it, Baby Face?" he said, a mocking smile on his face.

George gritted his teeth. He hated the way they put him down all the time. He'd show them. "I'm going to pitch him down three bloody flights of stairs and break his bloody neck."

Knuckles shook his head and laughed. "No fun in that for us, Baby Face," he smirked. "I 'ave a 'fun' plan."

Fear knotted George's stomach. The gang's 'fun' plan involved kicking some unsuspecting person to a pulp.

"Your old man goes drinking of a night?"

George shrugged. "Friday nights he goes to the 'Hair of Dog' pub in Croydon. That's when the navvy gaffers give out the work. Or he goes walkabout in the nearest park and sits on the benches with the hobos," George said disparagingly.

Knuckles hadn't mentioned about the gang duffing his father up again—until tonight. George decided that, for all his hard-man talk Knuckles knew better than to tangle with the Irish navvies. He'd been wrong, he thought, watching as the paramedics stopped working on the still bloodied body.

He shook violently and shrank further back into the shadow of the bushes. A bag of empties rattled at his feet. Knuckles stiffened and slid the knife he always carried up his sleeve down into the palm of his hand.

"Is he a goner?" a woman walking her dog called to the paramedics, stretching the body into the ambulance. The paramedic sighed. "He's still breathing, but he'll maybe not make it to the morning."

"Go on, get out of here—shows' over," a policewoman growled to the watching crowd that had gathered.

The heavy knuckle duster in his hand red with the old man's blood, George followed Knuckles out of the park.

"Wasn't much fun as I'd thought, Baby Face. The old guy didn't put up much of a fight," Knuckles muttered disappointed.

Then he laughed and thumped George's shaking shoulders.

George leaned into the grass and threw up. "I've passed the 'test'?"

"You ain't a paid-up member yet, Baby Face. Ya still 'ave to go 'ome and toss your old man down the bloody stairs likeya said ya had the balls for."

Ashen-faced, George stared at him. "That wasn't him! Who was he?" he choked out.

Knuckles shrugged. "Just some old hobo," he chortled.

"Don't worry. Yak has the knack for it—but not the stomach—yet," Knuckled joked as George heaved his guts up again.

Horror at what he'd just done swept over George. He needed to get away from Knuckles... He had put all his years of hatred of his father into the attack. Once he had started, he didn't want to stop.

It was what he had thought about—no, dreamt about—getting his revenge on his father. Instead, he had beaten up a helpless, harmless old tramp—somebody else's father—*who never did me any harm,* he moaned. Knuckles would want him to do more of the same. Stumbling along with the swaggering, buoyed-up street gang, he prayed reverently. *Please God, if there is a God, don't let the old hobo die.*

Chapter 33

Her arms tired from carrying the heavy bundle of clothes from Stitch in Time, Lisa puffed her way up the three flights of tenement stairs. She hoped BJ was in a good mood. It was going to take a while to get through this lot.

"Somebody else is movin' out down there," BJ complained. "We couldnae piy the high rents in them fancy hooses the Corporation is building."

Lisa didn't bother to tell him she had already put her name down for one of the new houses in a new development right on the edge of the country.

"We might, if you stopped backing horses and throwing your money across the bar," she retorted.

"I'm no movin'! What was good enough for Nan is good enough for me," BJ growled, shaking out the paper and turning to the racing section.

Lisa drank her tea and remembered the first day she had come to live in the flat. Coming in the street door and climbing up the stairs, the smell of stale cooking and voices coming out from behind the doors on each landing they passed. Finally, dragging the cases into Granny Mac's flat.

"Did she bring the hoose wi' her?" had been BJ's granny's first greeting, as she took me in from head to feet, Lisa thought.

No wedding day welcoming cup of tea in a nice cup and saucer like Mother would have ready, Lisa thought.

On the second day, Granny Mc Knight pushed a sheet of paper at her. "Washday, mind ye keep to the time on there," she said, thrusting a pillowcase full of dirty washing into Lisa's arms.

Lisa had carried the dirty clothes into the bedroom and hurled them at BJ, refusing to wash his granny's clothes.

Putting her backside against the sink, Lisa turned to face BJ. She wanted to see the look on his face when she told him that Miss Thomas from the fancy designer shop in town had offered her work.

"She said she might be able to use the girls for off-the-peg garments sometimes." She knew it was a white lie, but BJ didn't know that.

"Whose gonnae look efter the bairns? No sense o' havin' bairns if your no' here to look abut them. Ye need ta keep an eye on growin' lassies," BJ stormed.

Lisa sighed. The boys were already noticing Trisha. Miss Thomas' business partner had noticed too. *"What have we here,"* he'd purred, circling thirteen-year-old Trisha like a tiger stalking his prey. Trisha had preened and given him a dazzling smile.

"It means working with designer clothes and the model—getting their designer cast-offs for the girls," she said, knowing BJ's heart and eye was on Isobel and Trisha.

"It might mean they'd get a job in a nice dress shop when they leave school. They'd have a head start on other girls."

BJ opened his tobacco tin and rolled a cigarette.

"Would you like te work in a fancy shop that sells clethes when ye leave school?" he asked, ruffling Isobel's hair of frizzy curls.

Isobel looked down at her plump body. "Lassies who work in posh clethes shops look like Trisha," she said quietly.

"There's yer answer," BJ said triumphantly.

"What abut you, darlin'?" he asked Trisha.

"Oh, Uncle Billy," Trisha said, snaking her arms around BJ's bulky middle. "It's my dream to be a model."

Lisa watched BJ melt like butter in a summer heatwave.

"You're as beautiful as any of them toffee-nosed lassies that oul' bag of bones Miss Thomas has parading up an' dun on them stages," he smiled, cupping Trisha's face between his hands.

"Catwalks, Uncle Billy," Trisha twinkled back at him. *Maybe Miss Thomas might take me to London when I'm older, and then I could try and find George and my father,* she thought, crossing her fingers behind her back.

Chapter 34

William threw his dole card on the desk.

"Working on the buses or labouring is all that is available," the desk clerk said. She fixed him with a stare. "The buses wouldn't suit you. They like them pleasant," she added imperiously. "Whimpey's are looking for labourers."

William hadn't worked for three weeks, and the bit of money he had saved was almost used up.

"It'll have to do," he mumbled. "Am sure they'll not be a lot o' difference there than wi' Foy. The men will spend their wages in the pub, back horses and play cards," he grumbled, picking up the docket the girl proffered.

"Best summer we've had for years, but it's goin' to be a bad winter," the dumper driver shouted over to him, scraping the bucket along the ground and dumping a mountain of clay beside William.

Getting down, he came over beside William. "Jayson, man, take it a bit easier. They'll be no work for the rest of us if ye keep working at the rate you goin' the last couple a days. You on the lump?" he asked.

William nodded. "Cash in hand," he said briefly.

"Kind of an uncertain way to work, isn't it?"

"Suits me," William grunted. He didn't bother to tell him he was lucky the gaffer had taken him on.

"Armstrong! I thought it was you," a familiar voice shouted.

William looked in astonishment at the small stocky figure of Scotch Jock.

"I though the squad was in Harlow?"

"Aye, yer right, but Coyle here and me," he laughed, giving the black man with him a resounding thump on the arm, "had a wee bit of business to do in Camden Town, didn't we, Whitey?" he said.

"Good to meet you, mucker," the man said, nodding at William.

William glared at him.

Jock laughed. "He's no' mockin' your mucky wellies. That's what the men call themselves where he comes from—your part of the world."

"Good to hear my own accent for a change instead of all these culchie brogues," Whitey grinned.

"Here, Armstrong, use the shovel like this. Let yer shoulders do the work. Lean your knee into it like this," he said, digging into the mountain of brown soil as if he had been born to it.

The whistle shrilled.

"C'mon Armstrong, a bite to eat. Its Friday—pay day," Jock said laughing.

William looked down at his mud-splattered boots.

"It's not a feckin' dinner party you're goin' to," Jock said, knowing William was about to back out. "It's only your money they're interested in," he jibed.

The place was mobbed with men dressed in black donkey jackets and mud-caked boots. Jock seemed to know everybody. "Hello, Rosie, darlin'," he said, patting a waitress on the bum as she wiped the table with a dishcloth.

"If you put your hand on my ass again, you'll be goin' without your dinner," the woman said, whirling around. "Ouch, it's only you, Jock Scott," she said. "I might have known."

"'Ere, you're never Irish," she joked, hearing Whitey's accent as she took his order.

Whitey grinned. "Me Ma was from the Bogside in Derry. Me Da came from God knows where."

"It weren't the Emerald Isle, for sure;," Rosie chortled, turning her attention to William.

"I'm a Protestant from Fermanagh and proud of it," William joked just as a lull came over the noise in the pub.

His new gaffer, eating at the next table, turned around and cursed.

William pretended to read the menu. He could feel the gaffer's eyes burning into him. Somehow, he knew he'd be getting the shit jobs on the site from now on.

"Don't mind him," Jock said, shovelling a huge piece of meat pie into his mouth. "I'll back you up. We oul' army men need to stick the gether. Isn't that right, mucker?" he shouted, thumping Whitey on the arm with his fist.

Funny thing, William mused as he walked back to the digs. *Ah don't know why I said that in the pub. It just seemed to come out.* He moaned. *I'm turning into my mother,* he thought in astonishment.

An image flashed into his mind of his mother rising up out of her sick bed and slapping him hard across the face. It was the day after he'd married Margaret. "Get out of this house and don't ever put your foot in it again," she'd screamed at him. "If there's righteous God, he will strike you and her and any children you have," she finished, falling back in the bed.

He pushed the past away and thought about Rosie, the waitress. He wondered if she was married. He thought he remembered seeing a ring on her finger. For some reason, it filled him with a sense of disappointment.

He thought about what Jock had told him about his new gaffer.

"Don't cross him." he said in a stage whisper as he zipped his fly coming out of the gents'. "He'd make a bad enemy. If he takes spite at ye, move on," he said "But don't forget am on your side. Us oul' veterans have to look out for one another," he laughed, thumping his gammy leg.

If it came to it, ah know the way Jock would jump, William mused, feeding money into the meter for the gas fire and striking a match. *The gaffers are still putting work Jock's way,* he mused. *It's more than they're doing for me,* he thought.

A sense of homesickness came over him. He wondered how Robbie Black was getting on with the farm and if Mrs Hamilton was still looking after Margaret's grave. On impulse, he sat down and wrote a short letter to Faith.

"Here, proddy, did they not teach you to count in that school you went to on the Shankill Road in Belfast?" the gaffer's voice roared behind him. Straightening up, William looked at him blankly.

"I never went to school on…"

"Ouch, well, I can see that," the gaffer said, cutting across him. "Get away from that cement mixer or this feckin' school will be fallin' down round the teachers' ears. Three shovels of sand to one cement," he roared. "And enough water to mix it," he shouted, cursing profusely.

"Put him back in the loader, gaffer," a voice rang out. "Give him plenty o' oul' Lizzy's clay te shovel all day long and see how he likes that!"

"Did ye get your sub for yesterday?" the gaffer asked, sensing a row brewing. William shook his head.

"What sub?" he asked.

"Call up to the office and they'll sort you out. Armstrong," the gaffer called after him, "tell them to give you your cards while you're there."

Trudging out of the worksite, with the jibes of the crew stabbing into his back, it was a minute before the rumbling of the trains made William realise he was only a short way from Brompton Train Station. He stood for a minute, savouring the sights and sounds of the station. Much bigger than the little country station at Ballet, it reminded him of the Belfast Station at York Road. A longing for familiar faces and things washed over him.

Making his way to the ticket window, he asked about train times that would leave him near the Euston Station.

"Downstairs—Underground—Just missed the 12.05," the ticket box man said. "Time for a cuppa before the next train, mate."

William checked his pay packet. In his haste to get him off the site, the gaffer hadn't waited for him to pick up his lunch box. He'd have to use some of his meagre pay. *I'll have to get another job right away,* he thought.

"A word to the wise," the ticket collector said, viewing William's mud-splattered jersey and boots. "Her indoors likes a clean floor. If I were you, mate, I'd visit the washroom before having that tea!" He winked at William as he drew the glass window closed.

William was glad he had taken the ticket clerk's advice as the grumpy-looking woman in a blue overall dumped his cup of tea down, openly surveying his boots.

He'd washed off as much of the muck as he could from his hands and arms and gingerly washed his muddy Wellingtons in the toilet by thrusting his foot in and flushing again and again. Hurriedly, he flattened his hair with his hands and rushed outside before a cleaner or somebody else arrived and challenged him about the state he'd left the place in.

Deep in thought, he didn't notice the woman stop beside him.

"'Ello, stranger."

William looked up to see Rosie from the pub, smiling down at him.

"I ain't seen ya since the night you were in the pub with Jock Scott and that black Irish lad."

William squirmed. "Sorry about that," he mumbled, taking a sip of the tea to hide his embarrassment. "Jock can be a right… rough."

Rosie laughed. "Don't worry, I know 'im from coming in the pub," she said, sitting down uninvited.

"Well, that as maybe," William said stubbornly. "But he can be too free with his hands sometimes."

Rosie smiled. "A lot of the men do it. Some even feel they can run their hand up your leg—dirt beggars. Finished early today?"

William looked down at his hands. "Gaffer fired me," he said, trying to keep the despondent note out of his voice.

"What about a refill?" Rosie offered, her fingers brushing William's hand as she picked up his empty cup.

He watched her as she made her way to the tea counter. Her short, greying hair had a light wave to it. He caught a glimpse of a neat skirt and blouse under the open swing coat as she sat down again. He wasn't good at guessing women's ages, but he thought Rosie was in her forties.

"Florrie will bring it across," she said. William noticed that the woman behind the counter was all smiles now. *Rosie was obviously a regular,* he thought, as he bit into the chunky chicken sandwich.

"Ever fink about working in the factories out Edgewater way? I hear they're looking for men in the Engineering Works," she said, looking enquiringly at William.

William shook his head.

"This couple comes in to the pub to 'ave a bite to eat sometimes. Have a few little kiddies—looking for steady bloke that doesn't roll in drunk on a Saturday night." Her light brown eyes studied William. "Thought the digs might suit you and the lad. It was just a thought," Rosie said when William didn't respond.

A silence fell between them. *Say something, man,* an inner voice prompted William.

"What brings you out this way?" he blurted out.

Rosie's face grew sombre. "I was on my way to the cemetery to put fresh flowers on me husband's grave."

Tongue-tied, William looked back at her.

"He was an air raid warden—killed one night when the shelter roof collapsed. It's a long time ago. My two boys are all grown up now."

"My wife Margaret died a few years ago," William blurted out.

Rosie gave him a sympathetic look. "Sorry to 'ear that. It can be tough in the beginning, especially if it's sudden like," she said, beginning to gather up her bag.

"Pity you have to go." William drew in his breath in surprise as the words fell from his lips and hung between them. His hands shook as he fiddled with the teaspoon.

"What time's your train?" Rosie asked.

William glanced at the clock above their heads. "Missed it again," he said ruefully.

Rosie considered for a moment. "Why don't I show you around the old Brompton Cemetery? It was badly damaged during the Blitz, but it's still a nice place to stroll around."

William's courage deserted him. "Some other time. Ah need to look for work," he stammered out. He saw Rosie's face cloud over.

"Yeah, some other time," Rosie murmured as she went out the door. "He's a quiet sort of bloke. I could 'ave sworn he liked me. Bit like my old man was, in a way. He needs a bit of lookin' after, an' all," she murmured.

On impulse, she turned back into the station café and bumped into William rushing out. They both started talking at once.

"Ah don't like graveyards, but Ah'll come to your husband's grave. Put on the flowers," he panted. "If you don't mind bein' seen wi' a navvy." He stopped and looked down at his half-washed boots.

Rosie laughed. "I fink you need a good woman to keep you on the right path, Will Armstrong. I was just comin' back in to give you directions to the engineering works and the address of the lodgings in Edgewater."

William walked away from the engineering works with a lighter step. The manager had enquired if he had any references. William had balked at the question. He could feel the old trembling starting in the pit of his stomach.

"Do ye mean since I came over the water or since ah was demobbed?" he asked.

The manager got up from behind the desk and stuck out his hand.

"Any man who could face the Luftwaffe deserves a job," he announced, shaking William's hand. "C'mon, one of the lads will show you your bench and explain what you'll be doing."

William followed him, willing his legs to stop shaking.

"We're a light engineering works," the manager explained. "Your job for now will be to make sure to keep the men supplied with whatever they need. Work hard, and you can maybe train with the tool makers later on."

Fumbling his thanks, William hurried out to the fresh air. He had a good feeling about this job.

Sitting on the train, he thought he'd stop off and tell Rosie his good news.

"What about a night at the flicks?" she offered as they parted at the Tube Station. "There's a good one showing at—Saturday night," she dimpled up at him.

Chapter 35

"Stop lifting up his eyelids. He's sleeping," seven-year-old Anne scolded, trying to balance a tray and pull her brother off the top of William's bed at the same time.

William tried to keep his face straight. The tray wobbled precariously. "Happy birthday," Anne smiled, proffering the tray. "Mammy made the tea, but I made the toast myself," she said, sticking her tongue in between the gap in her front teeth.

"I duttered it," Andrew lisped. William looked at the soggy toast swimming on the tray. "Eat it," Andrew ordered. "It's your birfty."

"Ah, I think I hear your mammy shouting you for your breakfast," William smiled.

"Can we come back when you light your gas fire?" Anne asked shyly.

They both turned at the sound of their father opening the bedroom out. "Right, out you two—downstairs," Andy, William's landlord, ordered.

"You should chase the pair of them, waking you out of a good warm sleep on a Sunday morning," he said.

"Anne brought me tea and toast," William smiled, indicating the tray.

"Oh, aye, that's right, it's your birthday, me old mucker," Andy laughed, lifting the tray off Williams knees. "Here, don't forget about the cricket match after the dinner," he said.

William heard Regina, Andy's wife, with her light step on the stairs and then her soft tap as the door.

"A good Ulster fry for a good Ulster man, like us, on his birthday," she smiled.

William reddened at the thought of his landlady seeing him unshaven and in his vest.

"We're off to do a bit of praying," she smiled. "We might try the Methodists this Sunday. We've tried them all. Even that open-air preacher at Speaker's

Corner, in Hyde Park," she laughed. "Any Sunday you feel like coming with us, you know you'd be welcome."

"Ah was never much of a prayer," William admitted. "If they'd just forget about religion and left Margaret and me to get on with our lives…" he murmured.

"You should have done what Andy and me did and got out," Regina advised. "It wasn't an easy decision to leave all our family and friends," she said, arranging the tray. "They weren't all against us, you know. Some even dared to say openly it was alright for us to have a mixed marriage and start a family."

She hesitated for a minute, then went on. "I hope you don't mind the children. They miss having a granny and granda like they had in Derry."

Wiping the last piece of the egg yolk with the final slice of bread, William lay back against the soft, clean pillows. He could hear a church bell pealing in the distance. Could be St Paul's Cathedral, he mused. He had told Regina bits and pieces about him and Margaret. But he still found it difficult to repeat the ugly things his mother had said and the contempt the locals had held him and Margaret in after they were married.

She's right. Like them, we should have crossed the water or emigrated, he mused.

He savoured the feeling of contentment and peacefulness that seemed to fill every room in his new lodgings. The Cuddys had taken to him and treated him like family. *When one door closes, another opens,* a quiet voice inside him murmured. William nodded his assent. It certainly had.

Life had settled into a routine of going to work at the engineering factory, seeing Rosie, and helping Andy down at the Seamen's Mission.

"Some sorry sights there," he mused. Some of the men had been deployed at Dieppe. Some, like his father, Samuel, had been in the Great War. "Whoever named it that needs their head examined," he muttered. "There's nothing great about war, any war," he emphasised.

Padding into the bathroom, he thought about the obvious love between Regina and Andy and their youngsters. The hand holding the shaving brush stilled, and he stared at his reflection in the mirror. *Ah wish George and me…* He let the thought drift away. These days George rarely came home. When he did, he was demeaning and threatening.

Finished shaving, William decided to go out and get the Sunday papers and some sweets and biscuits for Annie and Andrew. He knew they'd be up peeping around the door as soon as they got back.

"Light the fire," Andrew would say, throwing himself on the rug in front of the gas fire. William was happy to do it.

Having no grandparents to help them was something he had never thought about before. It made him wonder how Margaret had managed to work the farm and still look after George, Sarah, and his father when he was a POW. Guiltily, he pushed the thought away that the Furlongs could have helped. "If Ah had let Margaret have contact wi' them or let her write to them after ah came back," he murmured.

Putting his key in the door, he knew from the charged atmosphere in the house that George was back.

"Playing the benevolent Granda," George goaded him when he saw the kiddie sweets. "Fit you better if you found out how your own daughter is doing. Or even where she is," he shouted. "Instead of playing granda to your landlord's mongrel kids," he yelled, his face contorted and ugly with rage. William's skin crawled with embarrassment. He hoped the Cuddys hadn't heard George.

"What's going on here?" Andy's voice boomed from the open bedroom doorway. "What did you just call our children?" he said, squaring up to George. "Nobody, nobody, calls my kids mongrels and gets away with it." His lips white with age, Andy stepped closer.

George held up his hands in a gesture of surrender. "It's just a word. I've been called it often enough myself. I'm sorry. Your kids are…"

"Don't you use that fake cockney accent on me, mucker. You're from the Northern Ireland, just like Reina and me, and just like Andrew and Annie—you're half Prod, half Catholic."

"Yeah, that I am, mucker," George smirked. Making for the door, he met Regina face to face.

Enraged, she whacked him hard, leaving a trace of her fingers on his face.

"I left Derry, left my family and friends so my children could walk the streets without being called filthy name by foul-mouthed bigots like you," she raged.

She whirled around. "See these scars on my neck and head? They're from being tied to a pole, tarred and feathered, and left there for people to spit at me because I married Andy—a Protestant from the Waterside," she said, livid with rage.

"Our children are not half breeds. Don't you ever put your foot inside my door ever again. If you do, I'll not be responsible for what happens to you, you wee shite," Regina said, storming out of the room, followed by Andy.

George threw William a self-satisfied smile. "Looks like we'll be moving again, Da," he sniggered.

"Ah think you should stay in the hotel for a while—let this blow over," William muttered.

George shrugged. "Suits me. I'm planning to go and see my sister, your daughter, in Scotland."

William looked at him in surprise. "What about your job at the hotel and that school or college or whatever it is you had to get going to?"

George smirked. "I'm finished with that hole." *It's more like an open-air borstal,* he thought.

A sense of relief pervaded his father's mind. With George not around, the Cuddys would let him keep on renting.

The sound of Andrew's feet coming up the stairs propelled William out onto the landing.

"Mammy fays dinner is fetting cold," he lisped.

"Tell her ah not hungry," William said in a low voice, conscious of George listening to every word.

"C'mon," Andrew said, reaching for William by the hand. "I fink you should eat your dinner. Mammy's fery fery mad," he advised, tugging William towards the stairs.

After a while, the red angry heat left Regina's cheeks. "How did you and your wife live in Fermanagh and put up with the like of that?" she asked.

William chewed the Sunday roast and thought how the railway workers and boys he had gone to school with crossed the street rather than pass him. But worst of all had been the foul names shouted after Margaret when she walked George in his pram.

What had he done about it?

Nothing.

"The rows started before we even got as far as the weddin'," he said hesitantly.

Regina snorted. "Church or Chapel minister or priest—am I right?"

William nodded. "And everybody from Con Callahan, the postman, to the clergy had advice on which it should be."

"What did you go for in the end?"

The colour crept up William's neck. "Ah said Ah'd marry Margaret in church or chapel, but Ah couldn't do it—ah couldn't marry in the Catholic church when it came down to it," he admitted, shamefaced.

He gazed down at the table. "We got married in a Presbyterian church where nobody knew us. We told the minister Ah was soon to be shipped out. He didn't ask any questions. Margaret was a devout Catholic. She cried at the altar. Ah could feel her tremblin' when she took her vows."

Rising abruptly, William headed for the stairs. "Tell Andy Ah'll not bother wi' the cricket today."

George stopped in the hall and straightened his short leather bomber jacket. He smiled at his refection in the hall mirror.

"Be sure to ask your lodger what he did to his own daughter—same age as yours," George snarled. "Then we'll see if you're so bloody fond of having him in your house playing granda to your kids."

A rush of satisfaction filled George. With a bit of luck, the landlord would toss his Da out on the street. *Let him live in one of the rough men's hostel. He'll not be so pampered there,* he smirked.

Chapter 36

George headed for the underground, a buzz in his belly at the thought of his date with Marta. They were careful to hide their get-together's. Agnes, the hotel housekeeper, hadn't been impressed to find him trying to sneak into the female staff rooms. To cover their relationship, their trips to the cinema had been fewer, but it didn't stop them snatching time together when Agnes went to see her sister, who lived in Whitechapel.

He was surprised at Marta's choice of place for them to meet. It was the pub where Sheamie Foy and the navvies usually drank. His heart did a little jump. He hoped Shay, the pub's owner, didn't remember when he'd deliberately knock over a table and his da had been thrown out. Spilling blood from fistfights was one thing, but to spill the navvies drink was another thing altogether.

He glanced in the mirror behind the bar and smiled at his reflection.

"In the snug," the barman said, giving him a wry smile.

George was surprised to find Mickilo Martini deep in conversation with a red-eyed, blubbering Marta. He looked at Marta's and the chef's heads close together, and he was reminded of the night they had sat like that at the guest tea at the Irish Centre.

"Well, ye didn't listen to what I told you, did you, young bucko?" Mickilo said straightaway.

George felt his stomach tighten. He looked at Marta. She was wearing that little girl look she used when she wanted things to go her way.

"What do you mean?" he asked cautiously, remembering the chef's volatile temper.

"I fink I'm up the duff," Marta gulped.

Mickilo's lip curled. Protectively, he put his arms around her. Marta leaned in against him.

George's blood rushed to his feet. No way! He wasn't getting tied down with a kid.

"You can't be. I... we were careful," George said. He wanted to ask if it was his, but he didn't dare with Mickilo glaring angrily inches from his face.

"Night we was at the Pallie," Marta gulped.

Mickilo turned angry eyes on her.

"I was drunk, wasn't I?" Marta snivelled.

The veins stood out on Mickilo's neck. "You got her drunk first! You dirty wee bastard," he bellowed, glaring at George.

"No! It was Marta who had the vodka. She got it off Ricky—the barman," George retorted.

"He gave it to me for me friggin' birthday," Marta bleated. "But it was you who wanted sex!"

George shrank back as Mickilo's eyes narrowed into slits. He knew it was pointless to argue, but he tried anyway.

"You're a liar. It was my first time to drink and have sex. But it wasn't yours," George said through gritted teeth. "Don't be putting all the blame on me."

"Randy wee bastard," Mickilo spat at him.

"She wanted it. She did things to me you wouldn't belie—"

Like a wounded animal, Mickilo let out a roar. Lunging at George, he clamped his hands around George's windpipe and squeezed.

George smelled Mickilo's whiskey-laden breath on his face, saw his staring eyes, and heard Marta scream before the floor rose up and swallowed him.

"What the fuck is goin' on in here?" Sheamie Foy asked. "Here, you're alright, son; that mad half-breed of a chef and his side... Shay put them out to fuck," he said, pawing awkwardly at George's arm.

George inhaled and gagged. Ricky was holding something foul-smelling under his nose.

"Jesus, you're goin' to kill him altogether," Sheamie swore. "Get him a half and a pint. That bugger Mickilo nearly choked the life out of him."

George sipped the strong whiskey and gagged again.

"Throw it down yer gob," a voice from the bar shouted. "If you can bed a cow like yer woman, you can down a glass of the golden stuff."

A great roar of assent went up from the crowded bar.

"Drink, that's what got me into the bother I'm in, in the first place," George gasped out as the whiskey raced over his tonsils.

"Give him another drink. Put it on the sheet for his Da. He should be here bloody lookin' after him," Sheamie growled at the barman.

"Not a bother. Gael Foy," Ricky, the barman, said cheerfully. It was turning out to be a bit of a good night's craic. A bit of a lovers' fallout—makes a change from the oul emigrants crying in their beer for the old country, he thought, setting the drink in front of George.

"Sow yer oats while ye can. It soon passes," a maudlin drunk advised him.

"Have another," somebody near him advised. "Did ye hear the story about the man who took the bull to the mare…?"

"Best of order now; keep it clean," Shay's voice bawled.

The drink kept coming. George drank whatever was put down in front of him. Why not? His da would have to pay for it.

He had a vague recollection of leaving the pub with the navvies and somebody bringing him back to the hotel.

It was still dark when he woke. He sat up. The room shifted. He lay down carefully. His throat felt like he'd been chewing razor blades.

Somebody was in the bed with him. "Fuck off, Marta," he slurred, feeling hands on him. His hand went to his throat. Mickilo's grip had been like a vice.

A hand crept between his legs. Marta. Bitch! He didn't want to be a father. He was sure it wasn't his. Marta and Mickilo… he thought as he shifted to the edge of the bed.

The movement made him want to vomit. The hand moved with him and snaked over his buttocks and around his genitals.

"Get off me. You're a bloody lying bitch. It's not mine," he grated, his hand beating at the arm that encircled him.

He froze.

The arm was hairy!

His mind jumped about. Who had brought him home last night? Was this another of Knuckles' 'tests' because he'd failed to push his Da down three flights of stairs before they got thrown out of their lodgings?

He gasped at the feel of an aroused man pressed into him.

Fear, cold and terrifying, made him jerk his hand under the edge of the mattress. His fingers curled around the sharp paring knife he had stolen from Mickilo's kitchen.

Abruptly, the knife was in his fist, and he was thrusting it again and again deep into a soft body.

Ike Swann, the head waiter, made a gurgling sound and then lay still as death.

Chapter 37

"Faces as soft and unwrinkled as a newborns baby's bottom," Lisa grumbled jealously, looking at Trisha and Isobel examine their flawless young faces. What have they to worry about with their clear skin as smooth as alabaster? She watched the girls as they examined each pore for blackheads.

It was hard to believe that Isobel was the eldest of the two. Trisha, tall and reed-thin with a woman's figure already showing in her hips and breasts, looked sixteen instead of her thirteen years. Isobel, small and round, still held her rolls of baby fat and looked more like twelve instead of sixteen.

"Two buddin' beauties," BJ said half admiringly, following Lisa's stare.

"Easy seeing; they don't have to worry about keeping the house clean or doing the shopping with very little money in their purse," Lisa said tartly. "I was hoping to go to the Festival as well as the rest of you." Getting up, she shook out the newly washed sheets.

Glancing in the mirror that hung beside the sink, she examined the crow's feet around her eyes and the small lines at the side of her lips that gave her mouth a turned-down look.

"There's Postie," Isobel squealed. Throwing open the window, she waved and shouted at the postman before flying out the door and racing down the stairs.

"Letter for ye, Ma," Isobel said. Trisha looked at the postmark and William's spidery handwriting. "Not much for the writing, our William, unless he wants something," she muttered.

"Even worse at piyin' for her keep," BJ said, jerking his head in Trisha's direction.

Trisha gave BJ one of her doe-eyed hurt looks.

"Ouch, you know Ah didnea mean it, wee flower," he said laughing. "Your da disnea know the great lass ye are, or he'd be knockin' in the door to see ye," he soothed.

"Some hope of that," Lisa sniffed.

In the six years she had lived here, he hasn't even asked how she was getting on. *He probably wouldn't recognise her if he met her in the street,* she thought.

Trisha pouted her lips and gave BJ the smouldering look Lisa had caught her and Isobel practising in the mirror in Andrew's wardrobe.

"Stop doing that! It makes you look like a tart," Lisa exploded.

"It's from Paul McCartney's fan club," Isobel squealed, clasping the envelope to her heart. Lisa had persuaded BJ to let Isobel write to pen pals and join pop idol's fan clubs. Now the walls of her room and even the ceiling were plastered with pin-ups of the Beatles, Donavon, and the Rolling Stones.

"Stop that bloody jumpin' and swannin' about! Ouch, for Christ's sake, will ye talk some sense into that daughter of yours?" BJ said, glaring at Lisa as he watched Isobel bobbing up and down on the sofa. "It's bad enough havin' to listen to you goin' on about havin' ne money. Now ah have te look at her kissin' a bloody cardboard picture of some boy in a band." BJ stopped to draw breath. "Get in and get that room of your tidied," he roared at the girls.

Lisa looked at him in surprise. "What eating you? What's wrong?"

"Why should anythin' be wrang? Can't a man hey a bad day now and then or is that only for women?"

Lisa let the dig pass. She knew that lately she had been crabby and impatient with everybody.

"Maybe if I had a bit more help and a bit more money around here, I'd be in a better mood," she snapped.

BJ shifted angrily on his seat. "It's no' my fault the work is on short time."

"Oh, Aye, I forgot," Lisa said. "Pity the wee bit of money we do have is spent in the Nags Head. You can bet your life the landlord is not worrying where the money is coming from for his next dinner," she shouted, grabbing up the wet washing to hang on the outside line.

It's not fair me shouting at BJ. Lisa thought. "He's not like some around here who'd rather take the government's money than work," she muttered as she spread the sheets out on the long lines. "I'll answer William's letter and find out where he's staying and take Trisha to him," she mused. "It would be one less mouth to feed."

"They say when you talk to yerself, ye have money in the bank," a voice cackled behind her.

Lisa startled.

"Sorry, hen, I didnea mean to mak ye jump," Madge chuckled.

Lisa sighed. Madge was a kind old soul and had pulled them out of a tight spot many a time, but she was in no form for listening to her today.

She pushed down her irritation. "Here, give me that bath of wet clothes and I'll hang them up for you," she said. "Didn't I tell you to say to BJ when he's out for the paper if you had a load to hang out, and I'd send the girls down to do it for you?"

Madge sank thankfully on to the bench and rubbed her swollen knees. "Ouch, so ye did, hen, but its Miss Smyth's washin' am doin' the day. The Captain o' the Girls' Brigade and ah didnea want the lassies to see her corsets and big drawers and them fol-de-dals she wears under that smart-lookin' uniform o' hers."

In spite of her bad mood, Lisa laughed. "I'm not surprised she never got a man," she laughed as she secured the corset with an extra peg. "By the time he'd get that off her, the notion would be off him!"

"Ouch, ye have to laugh, hen," Madge said, pulling out the packet of Woodbine. Sitting down beside the old woman, Lisa was grateful for the cool dampness coming off the seat as another rush of heat starting in her chest.

"Ye no 'keepin' well these days, hen?"

"I'm well enough," Lisa lied. She knew that once Madge started to blether about ailments, she'd be there all day.

"Your big man still on short time then?"

Lisa nodded. "He sits watching the bloody horses on that television. If it's not him, it's the girls watching Top of the Pops," Lisa burst out. Mortified, she felt a tear slide down her cheek.

Madge considered her for a while as she drew on her Woodbine. "Any money for the lassie's keep from that brether o' yours?"

Lisa shook her head. "He says the work is scarce in England too."

Madge made a dismissive snorting noise.

"She is growin' up fast. She'll start the curse early. You mark my words. That's when the bother starts," Madge warned. "Mind, they learn all about it at school nowadays. Ah don't think it's right learnin' bairns those things."

Lisa hid a smile. "Will I see you down at the Centre for Summer Festival?" Lisa asked, rising to her feet.

Madge shook her head. "Gordon no' keepin' that well. Ah'll see how it goes."

Lisa was still thinking about Madge as she passed some of the empty flats on the stairs. There were three families living on a landing. Now a lot of the flats lay empty. The families had moved out into the new housing estates dotted around Glasgow.

She could hear BJ shouting at the girls. "What's wrong now?" she asked, peeved. "I can hear the bawls of you half ways down the stairs!" BJ's face was thunderous but it had sickly pallor to it.

"I've seen whole families flit quicker than it takes them two te wash themselves." BJ snarled, pounding on the toilet door.

Lisa could hear giggling as the bar on the toilet door was pulled back, and Isobel ran out with a towel wrapped around her head, closely followed by a giggling Trisha.

Lisa whipped the towel from Isobel's head.

"It'll wash oot, Ma. It'll wash oot," Isobel squealed.

Lisa drew in her breath. BJ still thought of Isobel a wee girl. He'd go ballistic when he saw her mousey brown hair dyed sloe black.

"Ah want to look like Trisha. Da loves her black hair," Isobel sobbed. Hands on hips, Lisa stared in frustration at the pair of them.

It was true. BJ had taken to Trisha as if she was his own. "She cud be your lass, except for that black hair."

Trisha had her mother Margaret's delicate bone structure, shapely body, and long legs, but she has her granny Sarah's doggedness, William's oddness, and my sneakiness, she admitted.

"She looks like a bloody gollywog," BJ growled. "Can you no' keep a closer eye on them?" he said, turning to Lisa.

"If you hadn't been so busy watching the racing, you might have noticed what they were doing. I was down hanging out the washing. Remember!"

"You're no' goin' to the summer Fair looking like that," BJ barked at Isobel. "Trisha can go wi' Andrew."

BJ has blinkers on as far as Trisha is concerned, Lisa mused. She could bet the hair-dyeing had been Trisha's idea. *She streaks ahead in her thinking than Isobel, she thoughts. And she can twist BJ around her wee finger,* she fumed. *Just like you could your father,* an inner voice mocked her.

Andrew stirred from where he was arranging the pieces of a kit in the right order. At seventeen, he stood head and shoulders above both Lisa and BJ. He scowled at them. "Ouch, Da, I'm meetin' the boys from the Cadets. Trisha could go wi' Stuart Moss from the next close," he said, looking over to where Trisha was trying to comb the knots out of Isobel's hair.

"What do ye mean?" BJ stormed. "Isn't he the lad who got chased oot o' school for giving the lassies drink and taking them up the back o' the close?"

"You friends wi' the likes o' him?" BJ demanded.

Trisha pouted and folded her arms in a huff.

"Ah'll soon put a stop to his gallop," BJ growled, reaching for his coat.

"Young girls take a fancy to all kinds of fellas. Don't be going out to get yourself in trouble, BJ. She'll have a fancy for somebody else next month."

"She's a bairn! And he's a wee perv!" BJ shouted, banging the door behind him loudly.

Chapter 38

Lisa couldn't resist taking the bank book out of her handbag. "Nice wee nest egg fer a rainy day," a woman said, staring over Lisa's shoulder as she sat on the bus. Lisa pushed the book to the bottom of her shopping bag and pointedly ignored the nosy woman, who was ready for blether.

Lisa didn't want to talk. She wanted to bask in the glory of having received a cheque for the very first time in her life. "And for my own creation," she marvelled.

When the formidable Miss Thomas said she wanted to see her, Lisa's stomach had fluttered in trepidation. She had been doing remodelling for the designer shop for a while. She wondered if one of the prominent Glasgow middle-class wives of doctors and solicitors had complained about the renovation she had done on one of their outfits.

"Miss Thomas will see you now," a PA said haughtily. Lisa felt as if she was expected to courtesy when she was ushered into the office. A gaunt woman sat ramrod straight behind a very masculine-looking desk. From the length of her upper, body Lisa guessed she was taller than the average woman. What surprised her most was the woman's appearance. Greying hair scraped so severely back from her face that the skin looked stretched. She was plain, almost to the point of being ugly. She didn't acknowledge Lisa's presence.

Despite being ignored, Lisa felt that she was being scrutinised intensely.

"You are an accomplished seamstress," Miss Thomas said without raising her eyes from the silk two-piece she held as tenderly in her hands as a newborn baby.

"Thank you."

"Miss Thomas," the other woman said. "All my employees address me as Miss Thomas."

Lisa's heart thudded against her ribs. "I'm not really in your employment. I just remodel the occasional garment," she said.

"You will be if you can salvage this contour silk."

Quaking inside, Lisa reached a shaking hand towards the garment. With a practised eye, she examined where the raw silk had been ravaged as someone had attempted to modify the design.

"If you can redesign it so that it can be sold…"

Lisa picked up her shabby bag. "This is a job for someone who has worked with raw silk in the past. I have never had that opportunity. I don't think I could do it justice," she said. "Thank you for thinking I could."

Cold black eyes swept over her.

"Two things," Miss Thomas said icily. "Never again cut me off in mid-sentence. And don't ever tell me what to think," she said. "I believe you can do it. If you do it well, you will have more work in the same calibre, and you will be paid handsomely for your craft." As if the matter was now closed, Miss Thomas went back to the paperwork on her desk, and Lisa was left to carefully gather the folds of the silk material into its tissue-filled box and take it with her.

It took the best part of the following week to unpick the silk suit. Lisa's eyes burred, and her back ached. Finally, it lay on the makeshift workbench.

Lisa delved her hands into its luxurious folds. "Like dipping your fingers in liquid gold," she murmured, letting the material cascade over her hands. Breathing in its smell, she wondered what it would be like to wear raw silk and expensive perfume. "If Scott had taken me to Texas, I would have known how it felt to be like the well-heeled woman who shops in places Like the Elegant Dresser," she murmured, rubbing in the new hand cream she had treated herself to soften her hands before she would start working on the raw silk.

She sat back on her heels and scrutinised the pattern of the material—a pair of white love doves imprisoned in a gilded cage. She suspected the suit had been commissioned especially for an engagement or a wedding gift.

For once, Lisa was glad of the many hours her mother had insisted she laboriously pick garments apart stitch by stitch using small pincer scissors. "Mother was a hard taskmaster but a good teacher," she murmured, remembering how the unpicked material would be carefully washed in soft Persil suds and rinsed out in clean rain water from the water tub. The final rinse always got a measure of rose water and glycerine to give it fragrance and softness.

She could hear Trisha and Isobel arguing about who would peel the potatoes and who would hang out the washing. Maybe if she pays me well, I could buy one of those new twin-tub washing machines and a new cooker, she mused. "In the meantime, I better get BJ dinner," she muttered resentfully. "If he comes back from work to a half-dead fire, no hot water, and the kitchen full of wet clothes…" Too late, she heard BJ's voice on the stairs. Reaching for her purse, she decided to send the girls to the chippy.

"Ah could have bought that bloody bit o' thing meself for all the money it has cost me on fish suppers." BJ growled. "That's the third time this week ah hev come home to greasy cod and half-raw tatties fer me dinner."

Lisa clamped her lips together. She wanted to point out she still had to go to work at the Embassy and Stitch in Time, as well as work on the silk suit during the day.

"It's no' just the fish an' chips. It's sendin' the washin 'out to the Co-op. Since when do the likes o' us send clethes te the laundry? That's alright for the likes o' people who can shop in Miss Thomas and waste money on tattle like that," he grumbled.

"It's only for now. I'll make it up to you when I get the extra money," Lisa promised.

Rushing into her clothes for her work at the cinema, Lisa glanced at the girls attempting to hang the wet clothes on the lines behind the tenements. Trisha' body had a gracefully movement to it. "Maybe her idea of being a model should be encouraged—for the time being," she mused. *It would be one way of getting her to stand still while I use her to redesign the silk suit,* she thought. But first she needed a design.

Taking the early bus into Glasgow the next day, she began her search. Most of the dress shops had the same fashion: shift dresses and hippy-styled floating skirts. But she was looking for something that had that extra touch—something that would show off the exquisite lovebird pattern and the luxurious quality of the fabric.

She almost balked at the entrance to the House of Nazerier, with its gleaming marble entrance guarded by a liveried doorman. And its tall plate-glass windows adorned with glittering mannequins dressed in haute couture dresses.

It breathed, "You need money to shop here."

"And money is the one thing I don't have," Lisa gulped. But there in the window was the creation of her fantasy dreams.

It was perfect for the silk suit remodelling.

I'll change a few things, she thought. *My design won't have real diamonds sewn into the lapel of the small exquisite bolero.* "It doesn't need it," she murmured to herself. "The love birds can carry it off without it."

"It's not... in your size," the sales assistant said, looking down her long nose at Lisa as if were was a bad smell.

"I just want to see it."

The assistant looked away. "It's not your style. I don't think you can afford it," she sniped, casting a haughty look at Lisa.

Lisa was about to argue when she sensed a frizzle of excitement pervade the shop as the doors swept open and two black-suited men wearing sunglasses entered.

"The First Lady," the assistant breathed.

Lisa's mouth fell open. It couldn't be, could it?

Rather abruptly, Lisa found herself concealed in a mirrored changing room presided over by another snooty-nosed shop girl who informed her that the garment she wanted to see would be brought to her directly if she stayed out of sight.

For the next half hour, Lisa enjoyed the luxury of being ignored. Up close, it was too showy but she'd get what she wanted—the basic cut of the garment.

She now knew exactly how she would redesign the silk material.

Carefully, she copied down the cut and the intricate detail of the suit on the back of her shopping list.

"Will ye stop cutting up me paper and wrapping it around the bairn's arms and legs?" BJ shouted.

"I have to get the pattern right." Lisa mumbled, her mouth full of pins. Finally, she let Trisha step down from the upturned wooden crate that was used to hold the potatoes and vegetables.

Pulling on her cardigan, she made for the door.

"Where ye goin' now?" BJ called in frustration as the door closed behind Lisa.

The spotty boy in the chippy looked doubtfully at her. "Ye jist want the brown paper? Ye dinny want it wrapped around a tasty bit o' fish an' chips?"

Lisa shook her head. "Could you give me as much you can?"

He scratched himself somewhere below her line of vision. *I'm glad I'm not getting chips tonight,* Lisa thought.

"A'll need to check with the boss," he said doubtfully. "Ochs, bugger it. Yer a steady customer," he said. Reaching under the counter, he drew out an unopened ream of brown paper. "Tak what ye need—bring it back when the boss no 'abut," he said, thrusting it into Lisa's arms.

"Thank you," Trisha said gratefully.

"You look like a scarecrow," Isobel giggled as Trisha stood on the vegetable crate, arms extended.

"I'm going to be a model. All you're going to be is a factory girl," Trisha said cattily. She let out a yelp as Lisa dabbed her with a pin.

"Don't be so bitchy. Stay still," Lisa ordered.

Painstakingly, she adjusted the brown paper pattern. Getting it right now had become much more than the opportunity to earn money. Somehow, the silk dove material had become the project that would help her escape from the tenements.

She cast a glance at BJ: shirt sleeves rolled up, paper spread at his feet. *He's content with his lot in life and nothing I say or do is going to change that,* she thought. Her mind flashed back to the conversation she'd had with him last night in bed.

"Life is passing us by," she'd said.

BJ had shifted and lit a roll-up. "Ye want to move to them new houses they're building out in the country?" he asked incredulously.

"The close is different now that some of the families have moved out," Lisa argued. "The police were here again this week asking Madge and the older neighbours if they were having any bother with the squatters in some of the empty flats."

"The polis!" BJ snorted. "Upstarts, the bloody lot o' them. Ye forget I was brought up here. Ah remember when it was rough."

"It's worse now, BJ," Lisa argued. "The people who live in the flats are different. In Granny Mac's day, everybody knew everybody else and helped each other out. Now, the people come from the city, and they move in and out…"

BJ turned his back and thumped his pillow, signalling the end of the conversation.

"What about the couple and that crowd that has taken over the flat at the end of the next close?" Lisa persisted.

"They're just hippies," BJ yawned.

"Isobel and Trisha are at an age where they could be easily impressed with that kind of living," Lisa retorted.

"They're jist bairns."

Lisa felt her frustration rising. "They're both teenagers… they're young and impressionable. And the flats themselves are becoming more and more rundown. The stairs are dirty, and somebody has started to empty rubbish on some of the landings."

BJ lay down but got up almost immediately again as he took a fit of coughing. "Did ye get me that bottle from the chemist?" he asked when he could get his breath.

"It's in the cabinet in the kitchen. I'll get it," she said resignedly. "Doctor says he's not giving you any more until you come down and see him. He's says he told you to get a chest X-ray."

BJ snorted. "I haveny time te sit about half of the day while they poke and prod at me. A'd heve to work twice as hard if we moved to a them new hooses on that fancy Orchard Road ye heve your mind set on," he coughed.

"I bring money into this house too, remember," Lisa huffed.

"Aye, ye do, and most o' it goes on Andrew and that notion he has o' being a RAF pilot," BJ muttered.

"People have to have dreams, BJ," Lisa murmured, shifting to the other side of the bed.

Lisa eyes gleamed with satisfaction. The silk material clung to Trisha's body like a caress. The skirt floated over her slim hips and ended in a fluted edge just above her knees. The tiny bolero skimmed her soft breasts. The broad cummerbund of the shirt hugged her waist into a small band of shimmering blue.

Trisha turned as she heard BJ draw in his breath. "You're beautiful, lass" he said. Then, feeling Isobel's sullen eyes on him, he hastily went back to his paper.

Miss Thomas tapped her foot impatiently as Lisa withdrew the creation from its bed of tissue paper. The light caught the flutter of the white dove wings against the gold bars of the cage. Miss Thomas drew it towards her like a long-lost lover.

"Trisha will model it," Lisa said.

Miss Thomas ignored her. "Bring me a mannequin," she instructed her assistant.

"A lifeless stand will not do it justice," Lisa heard herself saying. Her heart throbbed in her throat. This woman, who Lisa suspected had never unpicked a garment or worn remodelled clothes in her life, was not going to get away with simply putting her creation on an inflexible piece of plastic and wire.

Something in Lisa's stance must have penetrated, because with a curt nod, Miss Thomas granted her request.

Trisha was dressed, stripped, and dressed again as a range of foundation undergarments were used and discarded, only to be replaced by something else. Finally, Miss Thomas stood back and smiled her tight smile. "Shoes, stockings, suspenders," she commanded. "Hat, gloves, bag," she instructed.

Lisa sat down weakly. She wished BJ was here to see this waif of a child he had been dead set about not having in his home turn into this vision of elegance and beauty. It wasn't simply the clothes or the accessories. There was something ethanol about Trisha that Lisa knew instinctively hadn't come from either Margaret or William.

Soft hand clapping made her turn around.

"Very beautiful," a voice with a slight foreign burr to it said.

Lisa watched the small, sallow-skinned man hold out his hands as he walked towards Miss Thomas. "You have surpassed yourself, my cherie," he said, kissing her lightly on the cheek.

Turning, he bent over Lisa. Taking her hand he held it to his lips. "And you are the talented artiste who created such a divine creation," he breathed.

"My signature piece," Lisa quaked. But he had already turned away and was focusing on Trisha.

Lisa had never held a cheque before. The staggering amount swam before her eyes.

"Sign here," Miss Thomas said smoothly as she slid an official-looking form across the desk to Lisa. Getting up from his seat on the soft leather sofa, where he had been sitting beside Trisha, the sallow-skinned man stood behind Miss Thomas' chair, gently massaging her long neck.

"You must bring me the paper design. You understand it is now my property," Miss Thomas said, smiling her tight smile.

Lisa thought about the brown chip paper with its crossed-out lines and multitude of alternations. She nodded in agreement.

"You can't," Trisha's voice said confidently from the depths of the leather sofa. Three pairs of eyes turned in her direction.

"Uncle Billy lit the fire with it this morning," she said.

Miss Thomas drew in her breath in shocked disbelief. For a minute, Lisa had the feeling she was about to snatch the cheque back.

"It's okay. It was a one-off, anyway," Lisa said hastily, pocketing the cheque.

The sallow-skinned man frowned and then laughed. "You will make a good business associate," he said. "A one-off—that is it. No one in the fashion world will ever have a creation exactly the same as this one. It's priceless."

"And you, my little minx," he said, turning back to Trisha, "you will come to the London fashion Show with me as a good luck charm."

The hairs prickled on the back of Lisa's neck.

Trisha preened.

"She can't," Lisa stated, rising to her feet.

"Aunt Lisa," Trisha wailed. "I want to be a model!"

"And so you shall, my little good luck charm. But first…"

"She can't go to London."

"Why not?" the man asked, a petulant pout coming over his mouth.

Lisa said the first thing that came into her head, "Because we're going to Ireland for the summer."

Chapter 39

Robbie felt the other traders' eyes on him as he searched the Farmer's Market for Faith Hamilton. "Well, how did you get on for your first day as a stallholder?" He asked, locating her near the back.

Faith glowed. "They loved my homemade jams and chutneys. And I have taken orders for more next month," she beamed. "It was worth my while coming."

"How do you think you did, profit-wise?" Robbie said.

Faith didn't answer right away. *Everything has to have a balance sheet before it suits Robbie,* she mused. To her, having a stall in the Farmer's Market was as much about seeing old friends and meeting new people. She missed having the Armstrongs as neighbours. It made her lonely to look across the fields and see no smoke coming out of the chimney. "Even after paying the money for the stall, I think I still made a small profit. It's all about building up your trade," she said staunchly.

"You tryin' to show the rest o' us up?" a voice joked. Robbie felt his jaw tighten. He knew Con was giving him a dig about the cashmere sweater flung casually over his arm and his well-pressed flannel slacks.

"That the finest bit o' lamb's wool I've seen in here for many a long day," Con scoffed. Robbie didn't bother to correct him. *I wouldn't expect someone like him to recognise quality clothing when he sees it,* he huffed, taking in Con's baggy-kneed corduroys and well-worn shirt with its rolled-up sleeves.

"Any letters from William or Lisa these days?" Con asked casually, watching Robbie. *He's making a mint out of that farm and not putting a lot back, judging by the state o' the yard and the house,* Con thought.

"I had a letter from him a while back. He wanted to know if anybody had seen to Margaret's grave," Faith said.

"Am sure William would be willin' to spend a wee bit o' the profit from the cattle to put the odd bunch o' flowers on his wife's grave now and then," Con said, glancing at Robbie.

"I had a letter from Lisa. She's thinking maybe she'd get home for a wee break. She's hoping to get one of the new houses they're building as part of clearing the Glasgow slums. Her husband hadn't been well with his chest."

"Pack up, Faith," Robbie ordered impatiently. Once Faith got talking, she'd tell Con line for line what was in Lisa's letter. He couldn't get it through to her that telling Con was like taking out a gossip column in *The Enniskillen Chronicle.* He'd tell Annie Swanton, and she'd relay it in exchange for other gossip from customers coming into the post office.

"Ready?"

Faith looked around, satisfied Robbie had left nothing behind.

"I suppose the Ladies' Committee will be waiting on an invitation to the 12th ceremony and celebrations?" Con enquired.

Faith nodded. "It's being held in Enniskillen this year, but it's not the same without my husband, God be good to him—and my boys."

Con gave her a comforting pat on the arm. Both of Faith's sons, like a lot of other local lads, had never come home from France and the Normandy landings. *And oul' slippery Robbie wasn't long taking advantage of the situation,* he thought. Annie Swanton hadn't been able to find out if there was a family connection.

But what Annie found out was that Robbie was receiving letters with a Scottish postmark, addressed to his solicitor's office. If Robbie was writing to Lisa, he was keeping it very close to his chest.

"Will ye be gracin' us with your presence on the Walk to the Field with the brethren, Robbie? Ah hear there are bands from all over Scotland and from Canada. There's talk some of the American servicemen who served here—the GIs—returning to join in the celebration," Faith enthused.

An angry flush crept up from under Robbie's open-necked shirt.

"I have better things to do than be marching on a sweltering day like today behind a man thumping a Lambeg drum, supposedly celebrating a battle between a Catholic and a Protestant king in 1690," Robbie raged, all pretence of civility gone.

Faith shot him a shocked look. "Robbie, keep your voice down. People…clients of yours are listening," she scolded, glancing around at the other stallholders and the farmers milling about.

"Will you make it yourself, Con?" Faith asked.

Con shifted uneasily. He and Ellen usually just went put to the corner of the street and watched as the bands with their bright vibrant colours and banners denoting the name of their lodge and their communities, marched past. He fiddled with the pot of gooseberry jam.

"Just take the bloody pot of jam and let us get home," Robbie snapped from the back of the jeep as he searched for a safe place to put a carton of unsold duck eggs.

Con winked at Faith. "He'll soon be ordering you off the farm and takin' it over, lock, stock, and barrel," he chuckled as he pocketed the pot jam and walked away.

Faith watched him go. "Who else am I going to leave it to?" she murmured. Her eyes swept the surrounding hills and the distant cemetery. "Everybody else belonging to me is lying up there beneath six feet of clay, or in an unmarked grave in France, in a place whose name I can hardly pronounce," she moaned.

Chapter 40

As the taxi driver dropped them off, Lisa's heart warmed to see the smoke curling out of the chimney of her old home.

Faith Hamilton had been as good as her word, and despite the summer sunshine, a small fire glowed welcomingly in the grate.

The kitchen looked clean and welcoming. She noticed that someone had installed a bottled gas cooker. Robbie had a key to the house. Her heartbeat quickened, remembering how the last time she'd been home, a small touch and an endearing kiss had turned into hot, hungry sex on the rug in front of the sitting room fire and then, later, in her father and mother's bed.

Trisha and Isobel ran upstairs to pick their room. Lisa went out into the yard and savoured the silence. Her gaze travelled over the rich green and gold of the fertile fields, trimmed with the loose stone walls and the purple and yellow mix of gorse and heather.

"More beautiful than the colours in a hand painted shawl," she murmured aloud. On impulse, she squeezed through a gap in the hedge and took the well-remembered shortcut.

A slight breeze lifted the hair off the nape of her neck, and she felt a freedom of spirit she hadn't experienced for a long time.

Panting a little with the exertion of climbing the hill field, she stopped on what her father had called the "Fairy Mound." He'd never farmed this part of the field.

"No," he'd say decisively. "It's bad luck to disturb the 'wee folk'. They can be very spiteful if you disturb them."

"Robbie Black is obviously not superstitious," she murmured, sitting on the edge of the crop of yellow maize that adorned the mound and the surrounding field.

As she climbed into the upper field, the sweet, cloying smell of the wild whin bushes filled her nostrils. *They call them broom in Scotland,* she thought. Sitting on a boulder unearthed in the ploughing, she pulled out a cigarette. She had a good view of the countryside from up here. She could see walkers on the mountain track just across the border in Donegal.

In her letters Faith Hamilton had told her that American and German tourists had started to come to the area for the salmon fishing and the mountain climbing. Lisa's gaze fell on the lakes and beyond, where the wild buttercup and foxgloves grew in abundance among the thistles and wild grasses.

"Tomorrow I'll get Trisha and Isobel to pick an armful, and we'll visit Margaret's and my mother and father's graves," she smiled.

She threw the butt of her cigarette into the wild grass and then quickly retrieved it. "You've become a townie," she chided herself. That's what her father used to call the weekend visitors who arrived with their pet dogs, shop-bought hawthorn walking sticks, and Barbour rainwear.

"Many a gorse fire was started by the flick of a discarded fag," Lisa said aloud.

She picked her way amongst the cow pat. "Summer sandals bought in Glasgow—not much use on the land," she chuckled.

"But at least unlike the last time I was home, they're not borrowed; they're my own," she said to the curious moon-faced cows that were watching her. "The money from redesigning the silk suit let me spend a little on new clothes for us all. And I'll be able to afford to give Andrew some extra money during his training with the RAF."

Struggling back through the gap into the yard, she stopped. Trisha and Isobel were walking in the direction of the farm well. She wondered if Trisha had told Isobel about wee Sarah drowning in it. Trisha had never mentioned it again from the day she had accused Sarah of drowning her doll.

"Isobel, Trisha," she called out. "Don't go too near the edge of the well." Too far away to hear what she was saying, they just waved and walked on.

Lisa carried her case upstairs and checked out the sleeping arrangements. Trisha and Isobel's cases lay open on the bedroom floor of her father and mother's room. Next door was Williams's room when he was growing up and next to that was her room.

Curiously, she poked around. Comic books, bits of sketches, and bits of model kits lay at the bottom of one of the drawers. "Must have been George's room too, before they went to England," Lisa murmured. Opening the huge barrel-fronted wardrobe, she gazed at George's school uniform with its Mill

Grammar distinctive badge on the pocket of the blazer. How proud Margaret had been when he'd won the full scholarship.

The shelf of the wardrobe still held old cardboard boxes and a pile of old newspapers, brown with age, that she had shoved in as she'd washed and cleaned the house when she'd come to bring Trisha back years before. "I'll have time to go through them right this time," she murmured. On impulse, she pulled over the wooden chair beside the bed and wrestled one of the boxes to the floor. A cloud of dust rose up, making her sneeze.

Old papers cuttings of men in uniform; faded photos of people she didn't know. A picture of William's christening. She gazed at her mother, dressed in the style of the 1920s—low-waist dress and Mary Jane laced brogues; her father dressed in his army uniform. Both were obviously delighted with their new son.

She delved into the box again, hoping to find a photograph of their wedding day. She found a photograph of herself when she was in the Girls' Brigade, a later one of her as a Land girl, and a school group phot William, standing slightly apart from the rest of the children.

Taking the photo to the window, she studied the sea of faces. There she was, second row, front, with her arch-enemy, Lillian Snodgrass, tall and awkward-looking, standing head and shoulders above the other children, looking almost as unhappy as William.

"Bean pole Lily," she murmured, instantly remembering the nickname they'd had for the rector's daughter. "Probably a Sunday school outing to the seaside in Portrush," she mused, turning the photo over in her hand.

She had bullied Lillian. "I was jealous of her because she was the teacher's pet—and I wanted a red case like she carried to school." Lisa smiled ruefully. "Have you any idea how many times I got the cane because of you," she said, jabbing her finger at the surly-looking Lillian. She could still hear the whoosh of the cane as it snaked through the air and the Master's voice saying, "Lisa Armstrong. You're a disgrace to your poor mother. Good-living woman that she is."

Lost in her memories, gazing out the upstairs window, she saw Isobel, followed by Trisha, clamber over the barred gate into the field where her father used to keep the bull.

Turning back to the, box she dug deeper, hoping to find a photograph of her mother and father's wedding. A medal, its face dulled and tarnished, fell out of the box and on the floor.

Lisa stilled. Her quiet unassuming father had been decorated for his bravery at the Battle of Somme. She decided to carry the box downstairs and see what else was in it.

Sitting on the stone flower planter outside the back door, she held her face up to the July sun. "It's so peaceful just sitting here, listening to the lowing of the cows and the distant ringing of the Town Hall clock," she murmured. Watching the grey cigarette smoke spiral up into the air, she wondered why she'd never seen the beauty and peace of her home place before.

"It took me to live in the cramped poverty and noise of the Glasgow tenements to make me see what I had taken for granted all those years," she mused.

"Right, Lisa," she chided herself, "Get up and finish the unpacking," she said aloud just as she saw Trisha, Isobel, and Faith crossing the field to the house.

"I didn't recognise Trisha. How proud her Granda Samuel would be to see you all in the home place," Faith said, holding back a tear. Lisa brewed up a nice pot of tea and had a slice of Faith's freshly baked scone bread, which she'd left on the kitchen table covered with damp clothes to keep the crust soft.

"I was wondering, once you get settled in, if the girls and you would like a wee trip to the seaside?"

"Yes please," Isobel and Trisha chorused in unison.

"Would next Saturday suit?"

"Thanks, Faith, that would be lovely." Lisa smiled.

The girls excitedly raced up the stairs to see what they would wear on their day trip out with her the following week.

Faith fiddled with her grey hair. Then, nervously, she dropped her hand to fiddle with the small pendant nestling in the open neck of her white blouse.

"Do you still think about the Yank?" she asked quietly.

Lisa drew in a quick breath. "Sometimes," she lied.

Faith wondered if Lisa knew the GI was here with his family. Should she mention it or leave the past in the past?

Chapter 41

After Faith left, Lisa heated up the teapot and went back to the old box.

"My father kept everything," she smiled. The old newspapers and envelopes were brown and crinkled with age. There were papers dated 1912, with both Samuel and Sarah's signature on them, where they both had signed the Ulster Covenant against Home Rule in Ireland. Looking closer, Lisa saw that the copies were different. Her mother's copy, signed in her maiden name, Sarah Smythe, was against Home Rule, while her father's, though he against it, was prepared to recognise the rights of Catholics.

"That was always the way it was in our house," she murmured. "There was no way my mother was ever going to accept Margaret as her daughter-in-law," she said aloud, folding the old papers and slipping them back into the tattered envelope.

She heard the hum of a car engine. The driver waved to her as he dropped off his passengers. Picking up their cases, two men started up the lane.

"Lisa," the older man said, "What are you doing here?"

"William!" Lisa stammered. She stared open-mouthed at him. When she thought of William, she still thought about him like he was when he married Margaret. This man was middle-aged. "I can't believe it's really you. It must be eighteen years since I saw you last," she stuttered. "You've changed a lot. I could have passed you in the street and not recognised you," she said, looking at the muscles that rippled under the light shirt he wore.

William snorted. "There's nothin' like digging ditches to put muscles on you," he shrugged.

Dragging her eyes away from William, she looked at the younger man and couldn't stop herself from gasping. He was the picture of Margaret.

"I'm George," he said.

Lisa was rendered speechless. "You were just a baby the last time I saw you," she finally managed to say.

"I'll put the cases in my room," George said, heading for the stairs.

Lisa brain clicked into action. "Hold on. You'll have to share with your father. The girls are sleeping in Granda's old room, and I'm sleeping in the front bedroom."

"What girls?" William said.

"My daughter, Isobel and your daughter, Trisha."

George's eyes widened. "Trisha's here! My sister Trisha is here! I've been looking for her for years," he said, a delighted smile spreading across his face.

Lisa nodded. "They're out …"

William's face contorted. Cutting off Lisa's words, he banged past her and up the stairs.

"How long are you staying?" William asked, coming back down.

"A few weeks—maybe over the summer holidays—depends if BJ keeps well enough to look after himself."

"What about you and George?" Lisa asked, pushing a mug of tea towards him.

William shrugged his shoulders. *Not much change there,* Lisa thought. *My brother is still a man of few words.* William picked up another piece of scone bread but didn't answer her question. He wasn't sure. Something serious had happened, but George wouldn't tell him what. When it all came out, he'd probably have no place to live when he went back.

An awkward silence fell between them.

Sitting across from him, Lisa watched the sullen look she knew so well come over his face. She had been his buddy, his big sister, his protector when they were youngsters. Now, they sat like two strangers in the house where they'd both been born.

"It's been a long time since we sat at this table together," she said, trying to rekindle some of their old closeness.

William stared around the kitchen. "Were you searching for something?" he asked, nodding to the box of old letters and photographs. "You're away a long time. You should have asked first."

Lisa held a rein on her temper. She didn't want to have a full-blown row with William after not seeing him for so long.

"Do you want me to go in with the girls and let you have Mother's room?" she asked, changing the subject.

"No." William barked. The last thing he wanted was to sleep in his mother's room. He always imagined he could still feel her presence there.

Lisa waited for him to ask about Trisha. Madame Thomas had sent her some of the photos she'd had taken of Trisha wearing the silk suit. Maybe William would like to see them.

"I want to go over to Hamilton's to see Robbie Black," William said, rising.

"Why don't you have a rest and we can go through the old letters and things together later?"

William stared at her, then turned and headed back upstairs. She heard the bedsprings creak and then silence.

"Did you make any dinner?"

"Bottom shelf in the cooker," Lisa said absently. William didn't move from where he was standing.

"Surely, after looking after yourself in London for years, you know how to get a warm dinner out of the oven," Lisa said, rising from her chair.

William pushed a heaped forkful of potatoes and turnips into his mouth. He wasn't about to tell Lisa that unless George or the landlady cooked, he ate in the café or bought pub grub.

A strained silence fell between them. They listened to the shuffling in the other room.

"George decided he'd put up the old camp bed in the wee room where mother used to do the sewing." Lisa said, going back to look at old photographs.

William stiffened. "That's the room his mother died in."

Lisa put down the photos and looked at him. "It's okay. Con Callahan helped me to burn the old bed and mattress that was in there. I burned sulphur candles—fumigated the whole place. Didn't you notice the freshly washed blankets and quilt on your bed?" she teased him.

"When did you do all that?"

"When you went to England and I came over to find Trisha."

At the mention of Trisha's name William clenched his fists.

"You're taking her back with you. She's not coming to live with me."

Lisa lit a cigarette and inhaled. She knew Trisha could be self-centred and a bit of a drama queen. She resented, was even jealous of, the way she could twist BJ round her little finger but she couldn't understand William's attitude.

"She's your daughter, William. She's lived with me long enough."

William made as if to rise from his chair.

"No! Listen to me, William. I took her because she had nowhere else to go. I figured once you got over Margaret's death and got yourself straightened out, you'd come for her. You haven't sent one cold penny for her keep…"

"You try livin' in London! By the time I paid for the digs and fed George and me, there's nothing left. And George was no help. Instead of getting a job and helping me, what did he do? Go back to school," William growled.

Lisa couldn't believe what she was hearing. "That's where he should be. George was doing great at his grammar school here before you dragged him off to England?" She lit up another cigarette. In a more measured tone, she started to tell him about the night Trisha had nearly died. "She was lucky Con Callahan came along when he did," she said.

"Con Callahan," William sneered. "He always was an interfering, nosy oul' bastard." The venom in William's voice startled Lisa.

"If it hadn't been for Con, you might have been in trouble with the authorities for leaving Trisha alone without food or light. You knew I wasn't taking her back with me. I told you in my letter."

William smirked. "Oul' Dr Coles would have sorted things out. It wouldn't be the first time," he said, giving a mirthless laugh.

"What things?"

William threw her a mocking glance. "Your quick marriage to big Jim, for one. Our good-livin' Christian mother wanted to get rid of what was in your belly. She called it 'the devil's seed.' But for once, Dr Coles wouldn't do it. He got Da to marry you off to big Jim."

Lisa's heart thumped so fast she thought it would jump up her throat.

"Andrew is BJ's son!" Even to her own ears, Lisa's voice sounded high-pitched.

"Is that what the stupid big sod believes? Wonder what he'd say if he knew the truth?"

Lisa jumped up. "Don't push your luck, William! Andrew is training to be a RAF pilot…"

"Like father, like son," William retorted.

"You'll be keeping her, and I'll not be payin'," William said vehemently.

Grabbing her cigarettes Lisa headed out into the yard. "What would BJ say if he thought he had been deceived all these years?" she moaned.

Chapter 42

"Any breakfast?" William mumbled.

Lisa stared at him. After threatening her and blackmailing her into taking care of Trisha, he still expected her to cook for him!

"You know where the press is. Get your own breakfast."

William hesitated. "Ah have to go into Belfast this mornin' to see Robbie Black in his solicitor's office. Will you… come wi' me, Lisa?"

Lisa busied herself, clearing away the girls' breakfast things. She knew asking her to go with him was his way of apologising for the row. It was time her brother accepted responsibility for what he said and did.

"I have to see to Trisha and Isobel," she said, tight-lipped.

"Faith Hamilton will keep an eye to them."

Lisa swung around. "That's right. I forgot. Push them onto to somebody else to take care of them!" Refilling her cup, she pushed past him and went upstairs, remembering she had to tell Trisha that her father and George were there. William had been in bed when the girls came back, and George hadn't been in all night. She went back down and out to the milking shed.

Trisha's eyes grew round. "George and Daddy are here?"

Lisa nodded. "Come in when you're finished. And don't forget to use boiling water to rinse out the milking buckets," she called over her shoulder.

William glared at Isobel as she stood holding two cans of steaming milk. "Who are you?"

"Daddy," a voice said hesitantly behind him. Whirling around, William found himself looking into Trisha's anxious face. For a minute, they stared mutely at each other. Then, taking a tentative step, Trisha made as if to give him a hug. William jumped back, making the cup and plates on the dresser shake precariously as if they might clatter to the rough tile floor any minute.

Trisha followed him, gripping his arm an started to cry. "I thought you had forgotten about me," she sobbed, burying her face in his chest.

William stood as if turned to stone. Only his face, contorted with sudden rage, showed any sign of emotion. Shoving her aside, his hand went to his belt buckle.

Isobel squealed in fright and dropped the cans of milk. "Ma, Ma, quick, quick, he's goin' to belt Trisha!" she bawled.

"He was taking off his belt to thrash…"

"Stop that screeching, Isobel, and get something to clean up the milk," Lisa ordered, watching the fresh milk spread over the quarry-tiled floor. "Upstairs and tidy that room," she ordered a white-faced, trembling Trisha.

William stared after her. The tall teenager that fled past him bore no resemblance to the snivelling youngster he remembered.

"I wasn't goin' to take me belt to her," he said in an appeasing voice. "She… took me by surprise, that's all," he said. "Is that other one yours?"

"Yes, that's your niece Isobel. It doesn't surprise me that you didn't recognise your own daughter. Its years since you've seen her," Lisa snapped, stooping to mop up the pools of milk.

"Maybe if you'd used your belt less and not listened to oul' twisted bitches like Lillian Snodgrass sprouting religious claptrap, you still might have had two daughters," Lisa said, viciously swiping at the milky mess.

William's face turned puce. "You blame me for Sarah fallin' in the well and drowning?"

For a minute, Lisa didn't speak. "If you hadn't forced wee Sarah to beat Trisha, she might not have felt she had to climb into the well to rescue Trisha's bloody rag doll to make up to her wee sister."

William gave a mirthless laugh. "Mother swore on her deathbed that we'd pay for what we did. Margaret has already paid. She got TB and died, and Sarah drowned," he said, his voice shaking.

"You'll pay too," he spat out, "and so will that bitch upstairs."

Lisa looked at him incredulously. *Some holiday this is turning out to be,* she thought. It might have been safer to let Trisha go to the London Fashion Show with that creep and Miss Thomas.

Chapter 43

"Hey! Hold on there," George laughed as a girl with long black hair flung herself into his arms.

"Oh, George, George," Trisha sobbed. "I thought I'd never see you again."

George stared open-mouthed at the girl. "Trisha?" he breathed, hardly daring to believe it was really her. Gathering her into his arms, he rocked her like a baby. After a while, he untangled himself from her tight grip and stood her back to get a good look at her.

"You look so... different. All grown up," he said giving her another hug. "Still expected you to be like you were when I went to England."

Trisha stiffened. "Don't leave me again."

Lisa caught the fleeting expression that crossed George's face. Moving away from Trisha, he turned to Isobel. "And who would this good-looking girl be?" he smiled.

"Your cousin Isobel—she wants to be called Izzy," Lisa said, rolling her eyes.

"Please to meet you, cousin Izzy," George said, leaning over and planting a quick peck on her cheek. A deep crimson blush spread over Isobel's cheeks, and she giggled.

"Is Da here?" George asked.

"Upstairs. Why didn't you come home last night?" Lisa asked.

"I need to see my father," George said evasively, taking the stairs two at a time. Lisa put a restraining hand out as Trisha made to follow him.

"Can we go swimming in the lake, Ma?" Isobel asked.

"I'm not going. I want to stay with George."

"You'll have plenty of time to see him and talk to him."

Lisa watched Trisha's lower lip began to wobble. Moving closer, she tucked a stray hair behind Trisha's ear. "Dry your eyes. You don't want George to think you're still a baby," she admonished gently. For a brief moment, Trisha leaned her head into Lisa's chest. In spite of her frustration, Lisa felt a rush of pity for her. "Tell you what, I'll send him down to the lake as soon as he comes downstairs. Keep near the edge of the lake—it can be very deep in parts," she called after them.

Coming downstairs again, George took a comb out of his back pocket and studied his reflection in the small mirror beside the dresser.

Looking at George, Lisa couldn't reconcile the image of the toddler she remembered with the young man before her. With his drainpipe trousers and fake leather bomber jacket, he looked nothing like she had imagined him to be. *He looked more like the boys that hang around the street corners in Glasgow,* she thought.

"Where's Trisha?" George asked, sneezing from the mouldy dust coming off the old box of letters Lisa was emptying onto the table. "What are you doing?" George asked.

"I'm sorting out the old boxes of stuff that have been at the back of your granny and Granda's old wardrobe for years."

"I remember my Granda, but not my granny," George said. "Yeah, we were happy living on the farm with Granda. Things changed when Da came back," George sneered.

He might have a baby face and a ready smile, but there is something about him that gives me the creeps, Lisa thought.

"Did you know my mother?"

"I did. You look very like her," Lisa said, forcing a smile on her face. "She was a nurse in the Royal Victoria Hospital in Belfast before you were born. She used to write to me when you and… your sister Sarah were young. How do you like London?" she asked.

"It would be alright if Da didn't keep on falling out with the gaffers and getting sacked."

"Your Da was never the best at getting along with people, even when he was at school," Lisa laughed, trying to make light of it.

"He couldn't wait to get rid of Trisha after Mammy died," George said abruptly.

"Your mother was the only person your father ever truly loved. When she died so unexpectedly, he… couldn't cope, and Trisha was…hard to manage."

George gave a bitter laugh. "Is that what he told you? He forced Mammy into having Trisha. Then mammy got sick> and Da hated Trisha. He was the big returning decorated war hero in the village. But at home, he was like a madman—houting and raving and walking about all night waiting for bombs to fall on us all."

Lisa's gut tightened in fright. George's baby face, filled with hatred had turned menacing.

"Why don't you go down and meet the girls coming from the lake," she said. "You and your sister can take a walk over to your mother's grave—spend time together," she suggested. "Tell Isobel I need her here, to help me sort out this lot," Lisa said, looking at the growing bundle of papers, brown with age.

Watching Trisha paddle in the small enclave of shallow water that lapped on to the small pebbled beach, George had a sudden flashback of his sister Sarah on her seventh birthday, paddling and splashing about like Trisha, her dress tucked into her knickers to keep it from getting wet.

"Mammy says you're too big to be showing your pants now," he'd shouted playfully, flinging a handful of stones at her, making the water splash up around her. "What'll you do if Robbie Black comes on the tractor and sees your bare legs?" he'd called.

Sarah had splashed the water at him and laughed. "I'll tell him it's my birthday. He might give me a present," she'd giggled.

Sitting down on a stump of a broken post, Trisha started to put her socks and shoes back on.

"Where did you get those scars? I don't remember your toes like that. What happened to them?" George asked.

"They got like that from the frostbite. 'Mermaid toes,' that's what the kids at Isobel's school nicknamed me."

George looked at her questioningly.

Tears welled up in Trisha's eyes. "I went out to search for Mammy's grave. I wanted to find flowers for her grave."

Trisha looked down at the thin white line that ran down her thumb and halfway across her wrist. She glanced up at George through her thick eyelashes. "The knife slipped when I was trying to cut the hard bread in the morning…"

Shocked, George realised Trisha was talking about the time her father had left her alone in the house after their mother's funeral.

"Right, let's gather wildflowers for Mammy's grave," he said, the intense hatred he had for his father for leaving his sister alone in the house growing.

Trisha gingerly parted the thorny thistles and stretched her open palm through the tall yellow dandelions as she tried to reach the purple wild flowers that grew in abundance along the graveyard path.

A thorny bush grasped her long hair and wouldn't let go.

"Stop squirming," George ordered as he painstakingly separated each strand from its jagged grip.

"How will we know which one it is?" she asked, gazing around at the tall, forbidding-looking crosses standing erect and aloof above the graves. She shivered in spite of the warm sun.

"I don't think it's in this part," George said.

"Da still doesn't like me, does he?" Trisha mumbled as they climbed up to the upper part of the graveyard. Ever since that first day, her father had avoided her.

George plucked a long blade of grass and ran it through his teeth. "I don't think he even likes himself," he said.

Trisha scuffed the ground with the toe of her shoe. "Mammy didn't love me either—not like she loved you and Sarah," she said.

George gave her a little nudge. "She did so. She tried her best to protect you... from Da," he murmured, putting his arms around her and tucking her like he used to when she was small.

"Mammy was very sick," he went on. "She wasn't able to look after you. But me, Granda... and Sarah... always took good care of you," he said, looking intensely into her face.

Trisha shook her head. "She let Daddy put me out in the dark shed. And she let him light the fire with the wooden dolly Granda made for me with his penknife," she said, shifting away from him. "Mammy was only pretending to be sick. I sneaked in and hid in the wardrobe. Daddy combed her hair and kissed her. She wasn't sick then, was she?" Silent tears rolled down her cheeks. How she had wished and wished her father would brush her hair and be gentle with her, but he never was.

George whirled her around to face him. "I told you to stop sneaking into their bedroom."

They walked in silence, each lost in their own memories.

"What age was I when Granda Samuel died?" Trash asked after a while.

George shrugged. "I don't know, four or five."

"I still remember him," Trisha said.

"He spoilt you," George said, pretending to tweak her ear.

Trisha smiled. "I loved sleeping in his big bed. He'd tell me stories about quilt with all the different squares. He said he thought when I grew up, I'd make clothes for people to wear." She paused, "I can't make clothes, but I can model them for Miss Thomas," she said proudly.

"You still making up stories?" George said scowling at her.

"No. Aunt Lisa works for Miss Thomas. I modelled a silk suit, and her creepy old boyfriend wanted to take me to London to a fashion show."

George looked at her. *She is pretty classy-looking—even if she is my baby sister,* he thought.

"Come on, let's leave the grave to another day," George said, tossing the flowers into a weed-infested mound. "Why don't we go back by the lake again? You can show me how good your mermaid feet are at paddling," he said heavily.

Chapter 44

William slapped the brown manila envelope on the farmhouse table. "Our father's last will and testimony," he growled.

A frisson of excited expectation rose in Lisa. William had never shown any interest in the farm. *I was always my father's helper on the land,* she thought. Her hand shook as she cleared a space on to the table.

"That one," William said, tapping a folded document. "Look at the date," William growled.

Lisa noticed it had been drawn up and signed the year their father had died. She felt a stab of guilt. William had written and told her Margaret had been hospitalised after the shock of Sarah's drowning. "And Da's no use on the farm after his stroke," he'd written "Come home and help me."

How could I? she thought. Granny Mac was getting old, and BJ wouldn't hear of her going to an old people's home. "Nan remembers the days of the poorhouses;. She'll die in her ean bed, in her ean hoose," BJ had insisted.

William's voice broke into her thoughts. "Never even left me a pot to piss in," he shouted, slamming his hand on the table. "He left the whole lot to Margaret, and after her, to George and Trisha."

Lisa startled. "It was me who worked about the farm—went to the cattle marts." Her voice trailed off in confusion. "I always thought that…"

"He would leave it all to you?" William sneered. "You, Father's favourite! And Mother's competition!"

Disappointment rose like bile in Lisa's throat. She didn't know whether she was more hurt at her father robbing her of her birthright, or the realisation that he had been happy to let the hill farmers tweak her cheeks or put their hands sweaty on her long hair so he got a better price for his cattle.

She shivered. "And bought me off with a bag of sweets and a bottle of McDavid's lemonade," she muttered.

William was watching her, a look of satisfaction on his face. "Da wasn't the good churchgoing man you took him for when it came to making money, was he?" he smirked, as if privy to her thoughts.

Tears blocked Lisa's throat, but she wouldn't give William the satisfaction of seeing her cry. Her hands shook as she lit up a cigarette.

"Look at the clauses," William shot at her.

"He left me some of the land," she breathed.

William smirked. "Aye, the useless bit the Nissan huts sit on."

Lisa's face flamed. The Nissan huts—the place where she'd first given her virginity to Scott. Her father was paying her back, punishing her by leaving her land that was useless to farm on.

She took a deep breath. "At least the farm will still keep the Armstrong name," she mumbled. "Trisha will marry but the farm will still be in George's name. What's so funny?" she asked as William laughed derisively.

William didn't often smile, never mind laugh. "The farm will be in Catholic hands," William said mockingly.

Lisa shot him a hard look. "Da would never let that happen."

"George is Catholic. You and Margaret saw to that," he retorted.

"George is not Catholic!" Lisa ground out. "You named him for the king." Then, a memory surfaced of Reverend Snodgrass refusing to let Margaret's baby into his church, of another church, and Margaret holding the baby dressed in the christening gown her mother had sent from Waterford. The priest, Margaret's nursing curate, stood at the door with his christening stole around his neck, saying, "I have everything ready. We will first read George into the Church." She remembered thinking that the priest was too good-looking not to be allowed a wife.

Lisa eyes scanned a short letter attached to her father's will.

To Whom It May Concern

I, Sarah Jane Armstrong, leave my farm and all my land and belongings to my husband Samuel on the grounds that William, his wife Margaret, or any children they may have never set foot on my farm.

In the event of my husband Samuel's death, the farm and all it entails will be divided between the Church, my daughter Lisa, and any children she may have at the time of his death.

Signed, Sarah Armstrong

"What's this?"

"An earlier will," William grunted, "dated the year mother died."

Lisa felt completely confused. "But my children are benefactors in Mother's will. How could my father, leave everything to Margaret and her children? He broke the clauses in Mother's will. Margaret and her children *lived* on the farm, lived in her house," she said, perplexed.

"Father made out a new will."

Clenching the end of the table, Lisa stared incredulously at William. "Father made out a new will after you were found as a POW!"

William was enjoying Lisa's ravings. He wondered if he should tell her he had his suspicions about his father and Margaret after he returned home in 1946. It was obvious they'd thought he was dead. He decided against it. She'd probably tell him he was imagining things again, like she had when he confided in her that he thought Trisha was the reborn spirit of a Donegal comrade who had died unnecessarily, after he'd told him of a foolproof plan to escape from the prisoner-of-war camp in Poland.

A pause fell between them. "Do Trisha and George know that they have been left the farm?"

William shrugged. "George just joined up for three years with the Inniskilling Fusiliers. It'll be a few years before he's back."

Lisa wasn't listening. She was checking the date on the most recent will. "Was father… mentally affected by his stroke?" she asked carefully.

William glared at her. "If you're thinking he wasn't the full shilling when he signed that," he said, jabbing his finger at the will, "forget it. He kept a tight rein on everything—including how ah chastised Trish," he said vehemently.

"Did he not discuss it with you—talk about the farm…"

William started to pace the kitchen floor. "Father never broke breath to me after… wee Sarah drowned," William muttered. "Ah talked to him about you lying down with the GI like a mongrel bitch."

Lisa gasped. She felt faint. Her whole world was crumpling around her. Her father had literally written her and her children out of her birthright. She could see it all clearly now. He'd put her out of his life when he married her off to Big Jim. He had washed his hands of her, given another man the responsibility for her.

Now, the brother whose battles she had fought all her life was bad mouthing her. "You think I'm a trollop?" she gasped.

Aware that William was quoting some biblical scripture or other at her, she put her hands over her ears and slumped down in the chair.

It was a while before she realised that loud-screaming sounds were coming from her. She gazed around her. She wanted to go home to Big Jim and her rundown flat with its worn furniture and makeshift kitchen. *This house is no longer my home. I have no family here. Maybe I never had. Maybe you can be born an orphan,* she thought, a sob catching in her throat. But she was going to see Robbie Black about the wills before she went back to Scotland.

Chapter 45

"What did you want to see me about?" Robbie asked. "I'm very busy," he said curtly.

"I wanted you to have a look at these and tell me what you think," she said, pushing a thick brown envelope across the table. "Then maybe we could go somewhere nice for a bite to eat," she smiled. "I haven't seen you since I came back for the summer," she smiled.

Robbie glanced surreptitiously at Lisa. Against his better judgement, his eyes strayed to where she nervously fingered a small teardrop pendant that hung in the hollow of her throat.

He was beginning to regret keeping in contact with her—or confiding in her about his life when he was young. A lot of things had changed since the last time she'd been home to Fermanagh. He now was in a relationship with the daughter of his elderly partner, who wanted her married off. No way would he ever let it slip to her about his sordid birth details.

His lips thinned into a narrow line. Out of the blue, his birth mother had decided to contact him, and now he was having trouble getting rid of her. He snorted. As far as my future father-in-law-to-be is concerned, I'm Faith Hamilton's distant relative and in line to inherit the Hamilton land.

He gave Lisa a brief smile. Perhaps he could turn her visit to his advantage. She had been keen enough the last time she was home, he smirked. He might be able to wangle the Armstrong place too, he thought as his phone buzzed again and again.

A smell of mothballs wafted up his nose as he withdrew the crackly, brown-edged papers from the envelope.

"Letts go to the public offices in Wellington Street. It's just around the corner," he said as the phone rang again.

Lisa felt frazzled. Robbie was acting pig-ignorant. It was obvious he wanted nothing more than get her out of his office as soon as possible, she thought, following him in through the double glass doors of the Public Records Office.

Robbie headed for a small secluded table at the back. Quickly, he separated the documents and held one up.

"This is an old will be drawn up by the people who left your mother, Sarah, the farm."

Lisa looked puzzled.

Robbie exhaled impatiently. "Your mother was hired out when she was a girl to an old couple who had no family. When they died, they left the farm to Sarah," Robbie said impatiently, as if he was explaining something to a child. He held up his hand as Lisa started to ask a question.

"This newer will was the one your mother had drawn up just before she died." He leaned back and steepled his fingers. "Your father had her will rescinded," He held up his hand again as Lisa started to interrupt "Your father successfully contested your mother's will on the grounds that she wasn't in her right mind when she signed the document."

"Father declared Mother insane so he could change her will!" she gasped, looking in utter disbelief at him. "When we were growing up he never turned the word on her... She made all the decisions. Father just went along... most of the time." Lisa felt her body slump.

Robbie looked pointedly at his watch. "It happens. Families contest wills about property and farmland all the time. It's what keeps solicitors in business," he said coolly.

Something stirred in the back of Lisa's mind. She racked her brain. There had been a connection between the different wills; something to do with who had witnessed them. How did Father prove that Moth...?

"He did what he always did," Robbie said with a mirthless chuckle. "He got Dr Cole, his old army mate and Lodge colleague, to say that Sarah's mind was unbalanced because of her illness."

Her head was whirling. Lisa drew in a deep breath and let it out slowly. "What reason would Father have to do such a thing," she asked, her mind searched around for reasons for her father's behaviour. William had been reported dead, missing in action. *Father must have been trying to make sure that Margaret had a home if anything should happen to him,* she thought. *And that the farm would pass down to George and Trisha. It would still remain in the*

Armstrong line. That must be it. It was the most logical explanation she could come up with.

"Mother had included me in her will before father changed it," she said, rapping her knuckles on the folder documents lying between them on the desk. "Why should William's son and daughter get everything now just because Father took Margaret in to live with him?" She watched as the professional mask slipped over Robbie's features.

"If it could be proven that Dr Cole falsified the state of my mother's mind at the time of her death…"

Robbie ran his fingers around the collar of his shirt. Suddenly, a sense of foreboding and apprehension gripped him. It would only take a whisper of underhand dealings in a small rural farming community like this to break the trust farming families had in him and his office.

"This is a valid will that states your father left the farm to George and Trisha," Robbie said, gathering up the documents and pushing them back into the envelope with an air of dismissal.

Lisa stood up. "What if it could be proven Old Dr Cole had been wrong and my mother's will was valid?" She knew it was a longshot. John Coles had been her father's secret keeper, confidant, problem solver, and family friend for years. It would be almost impossible to prove he had lied. "You have no objections if I get another firm of solicitors in Scotland to look at all these documents," she said, feeling she had just been dismissed like a stupid schoolgirl.

Robbie stilled. It had been him who had signed off the present will. "Why don't we get that bite to eat, and we can talk it over a bit more—to put your mind at ease," Robbie smiled.

For the first time, Lisa noticed something about Robbie she had not noticed the night he'd made love to her out at the house. His smile never reached his eyes.

"Let's go somewhere nice," she said, tucking her arm through his. She felt him stiffen, but she didn't withdraw her hand. *He wasn't so reticent the night the night he undressed me in the firelight,* she thought. Hiding her anger, she looked up at him. "After all, when I go back to Scotland, we'll probably not meet again for years." she said.

She guessed from Robbie's expression that was good news for him.

"Did you know that I am now Trisha's guardian?" Lisa said as the traffic whizzed past them in Royal Avenue. She knew she was stretching the truth, but Robbie didn't know that.

Robbie felt his irritation fade a little. He looked down at Lisa. Their lovemaking the night he had disclosed his upbringing to her had been spontaneous, but making love to her in the cold light of morning had been a deliberate act of revenge. *Old Samuel never liked me,* he mused. *It had felt good to be having sex with his bloody daughter in his bed. But it wouldn't happen again. Unless... William doesn't sell me the land,* he thought.

He glanced down at her bare legs and shoddy sandals. His lips flattened. Where in the city could he take her, dressed like a charity case? Their firm had an account at the Hilton Quay Hotel. Staffs there were used to barristers turning up with oddly dressed and strange-looking clients.

Lisa couldn't help fingering the thick, embossed damask napkins. "This is something else, Robbie," she breathed as the smiling waiter swished the tail of his black coat behind him before pulling her seat out with a flourish.

Robbie frowned, and she quickly stopped fingering the napkin and hid her work-worn hands under the table. "Do you come here often?" Despite Robbie's obvious disinterest in her, with their knees literally touching under the table, she couldn't keep her heart from beating faster, sitting so close to him.

"From time to time," he said curtly. He pulled down his eyebrows. "Slow down on the wine. It's pretty potent," he growled as Lisa drained her glass and held it out for a refill.

"It's out of this world." Lisa breathed. The thought of her father's will faded into the recesses of her mind as she let the welcoming effect of the wine sooth her frayed nerves.

"Explain to me again why Father's will is valid and Mother's isn't," she said, lifting the wine glass to her lips. Robbie rubbed his hand over his face. "Because," he said, an exasperated note in his voice, "your father had Sarah's will rescinded." He held up his hand again as Lisa opened her mouth to speak.

"Look! I see someone I need to speak to," Robbie said. "Don't drink anymore wine and be ready when I come back." Watching his stiff, retreating back, Lisa slipped off her sandals and let her aching feet sink into the deep luxurious piled carpet. It was heaven. She emptied the remainder of the wine into her glass and, for a moment, held the empty bottle afloat.

"Will madam require anything else," the waiter asked. Lisa focused on him. He seemed a kindly soul despite his stiff collar and black tie with its little bits dangling down. "Could I have another bottle of this?" she said, trying to put on a posh accent. The waiter glided away just as Robbie came back and stood, waiting for her to rise. "Maybe you should go to the ladies' before you go out into the street," he growled, eyeing her flushed face.

"I think I'm tipsy." Lisa hiccupped just as the waiter placed the uncorked bottle of wine in the centre of the table. Colour stained Robbie's grim features.

"Robert? I thought it was you," a female voice trilled.

Lisa gazed at the small, petite, perfectly formed, beautifully dressed blond, forty something woman, smiling at Robbie.

"Roselyn, I… left a message. I got caught up in… business."

"And this would be…?"

"Pro bono client," Robbie blustered, watching his girlfriend stare at Lisa's bare feet peeping out from beneath the table.

Lisa tried to hold in the hiccup, but it slipped out, bringing a fit of giggling with it. "Gets me sloshed—has his way wi' me. Only way I can pay the kind o' money your boyfriend charges," Lisa said recklessly, in a good imitation of Old Madge's broad Glasgow accent.

"It's not like that at all," Robbie said, horrified. "Don't take any notice of what she says. She suffers from anxiety exacerbated by drink," he spluttered.

Giving him a contemptuous look, Roselyn stalked away. For a minute, Robbie stood dumbfounded. Then, giving Lisa a dark look, he rushed after the woman. Lisa glanced around, aware that they had drawn the attention of some of the other diners.

She felt tired, deflated. Robbie had been ashamed of her. *Trying to pass me off as a drunken neurotic charity case,* she fumed, thinking back to his attitude in the office when she'd produced the wills. *He deserves all dear Roselyn is going to give him,* she murmured, watching the two of them obviously having a full-blown row.

"Would madam like a strong cup of tea?" the quiet voice of a waitress asked. Sipping the sweet tea, Lisa slipped her feet back into her sandals as discreetly as she could. She glanced down at her ankles, which were beginning to swell up like two overinflated balloons.

"I'll have to spend the money on a taxi," she murmured as she drained the last dregs of the tea. She jumped when a voice spoke behind her.

"Would you like Reception to book you a taxi?" the woman asked, glancing to where Robbie and his girlfriend were holding hands, now partially hidden by a large palm plant.

Lisa sighed. "Thank you, that's very kind of you."

Bending down to pick up a stray napkin, the young woman gazed at Lisa's swollen feet. "Did madam know there is a foot massage and shoe boutique on the first floor? Well worth a visit. I'll tell the taxi driver to collect you there in an hour," she smiled. "Oh, and don't forget to take this," she said, handing her the bottle of wine in a beautiful appointed bag. "If you see anything you fancy, you will find the account details you need in there as well," she smiled.

Lisa's eyes rounded. Robbie had an account here where you could shop as well as eat!

Glancing again in the direction of the petite blond, the woman gave Lisa a knowing smile. "Lovely shoes she's wearing. I expect she'll pay another visit to the shoe boutique before she leaves today," she said in a low voice.

Stepping into the plush lift, Lisa fought with herself whether or not to visit the shoe boutique. It would be lovely to get a foot massage, she thought, looking down at her feet encased in the rapidly disappearing straps of her sandals. Quickly, before she could change her mind, she stepped out of the lift and headed for shoe boutique. Carefully, she picked up a black patent pump. The leather felt soft as creamy butter.

"Italian leather, handmade," the sales assistant, a middle-aged woman, said at her elbow. "Aren't they beautiful? Would you like to try them on?" Looking down at her feet, Lisa shook her head.

The sales assistant nodded gravely. Guiding Lisa by the elbow she steered her to a small door discreetly hidden by a velvet curtain. "It's not the regular, but you can't walk home with your feet in that state, so you can't," she said, dropping her posh shop accent.

Before Lisa could tell her that a taxi was coming to pick her up, the woman pushed the door open and showed her into a small room. Picking up the receiver of a black telephone, she twirled its silver dial around twice.

Sitting in the back of the taxi, Lisa couldn't believe she had spent so much of Robbie Black's money. During the foot massage, she had found herself telling the woman about Robbie.

"Don't talk to me about solicitors! Skin you for a ha'penny, so they would," the woman snorted. "Now, that's better," she said, a satisfied gleam in her eye as she stood looking down at Lisa's feet. Lisa could hardly believe it. A slight swelling was still showing around her ankles, but they rest was gone.

"How much do I owe you?" she asked, praying she had enough money in her purse. The woman, back in sales assistant mode again, pursed her lips and took stock of Lisa.

"Let's try on those soft black leather patent pumps you were looking at earlier," she said. Guiding Lisa to a secluded cubicle, she began to carry in a range of shoes for Lisa to try on, starting with the black leather pumps.

"It was like winning the Pools," Lisa murmured. She glanced at the boxes beside her on the back seat of the taxi. She had bought the black leather patent pair—and the matching handbag; a pair of warm winter boots, and pair of black leather brogues for Big Jim.

She ran her hand over the box holding BJ's new boots. "For all your faults, you're a decent man," she murmured. "It took me a long time for me to see it, but I do now," she whispered to the picture of the brogue boot staring up at her from the fancy shopping bag the saleswoman had put them in.

"Nearly there now," the taxi man said, watching her in the mirror as he turned into York Street and the railway station.

Struggling up the steps and over the overhead bridge, she noticed that the last train for Fermanagh was in and people were already boarding. Awkwardly, she tried to run, but the boxes that the shoes were in made it almost impossible. She wished now she had taken the saleswoman's advice and left the boxes, but somehow, she had wanted to keep them. *They'll be useful to store stuff in at home,* she had told the woman.

"Here, give them to me," a young red-haired man said. Lisa hesitated.

"It's alright. I'm a porter," he said, dumping the shoes and bags inside a carriage door and helping her in after them, just as the guard blew his whistle for the last time.

Chapter 46

The train was packed, but finally, after bumping her bags and shoeboxes into other passengers' legs and shins, Lisa found an empty seat and eased herself into it, nursing her parcels.

By the time they reached Ballet Station, Lisa could feel the start of a headache behind her eyes. Standing shoulder to shoulder, packed in as tightly as sardines in a tin, the passengers queued to get off. Lisa tried to hold her breath, hoping those behind and in front of her couldn't smell the wine on her breath. Staring idly at the couple in front of her, she noticed a difference in their ages and wondered if they were father and daughter. Apparently not, she thought, as the man's pudgy hand felt the girl's bum.

"Damn ridiculous way to run a commuter service," she heard the man complain loudly to the beleaguered porter as he got off the train. *An American,* Lisa thought. *Maybe George was right. Maybe Ballet was becoming a tourist spot for anglers,* she mused. She looked at the man's back as he swaggered out of the station exit. "Somehow, I don't think he's here for the fishing," she mused. Passing by him on the steps of the exit, she could still hear him ranting. "...Wouldn't happen in my country," he was saying, jabbing his finger at the station master.

The pain behind her eye was moving across her forehead. "Better go and buy some aspirin or something before I go home," she muttered, hoping it was late-night opening. Rounding the corner into Main Street, she sighed in relief.

The bell tinkled, but it was lost in the irate conversation that was going on between the pharmacist and the woman she was serving.

"It's not advisable to take too many of these... if you take... alcohol," Gloria was saying. Lisa could feel her head really throbbing now. She wondered if Gloria would mind if she opened the tablets she had just picked up and swallowed one or two of them while she waited to pay. She studied the customer's reflection in the mirror behind Gloria's head. Lisa noticed the woman's gaze on her. Quickly, she averted her eyes.

"Mary Kielty!" Lisa said before she realised she had spoken out loud. The woman in front turned around to face her. "I'm sorry! Do I know you?" she said, giving Lisa a maudlin look. "That's the worst thing about coming home on holiday to a small place like this. Everybody knows you!" she said, spreading her hands dramatically. "People have nothing better to do than mind other people's business and give advice nobody wants," she said, glaring at the pharmacist.

Lisa caught the distinct smell of brandy on the woman's breath as she brushed past her. "Excuse me! I have to meet my husband off the Belfast train."

"I think you may have just missed him," Lisa retorted, collecting her change from Gloria. "The train has already arrived." The woman stopped with her hand on the handle of the door. A startled, frightened looked flitted across her face and then was gone.

"Sorry, Lisa, sorry Mary, I'm just closing up now," Gloria said, barely able to contain her excitement. *Wait until Annie Swanton hears this bit of juicy gossip,* she thought, almost breathless with the exertion of appearing calm. *Mary Kielty and Lisa Armstrong face to face in my shop, and they hardly recognised each other.*

"Lisa? Lisa? William Armstrong's sister!" Edging her way around the now-beaming Mary, Lisa nodded and began to walk in the direction of Back Street and the one and only taxi man in Ballet. *I hope he's sitting in his usual spot, watching the world go by and chewing on the end of his Sweet Afton cigarette,* she thought.

"Lisa, Lisa! Wait, wait. I haven't seen you since we were in school," Mary called. "Come and meet my husband," she panted, trying to keep up with Lisa's hurried strides. Lisa walked on.

"I'll meet him at the dance in the marquee on Monday night," she said. The smell of drink on Mary's breath was making her feel nauseous. "I've been in Belfast shopping all day. I need to get home and see if the girls and George are—"

"George? You mean Cockney George. How do you know him?" Mary asked, a note of possessiveness creeping into her voice.

Lisa stopped. "How do you know George?" she asked, putting her bags down on the pavement. Mary tossed her head and giggled like she used to do when they discussed boys at school. "How do you think I know him?" she giggled. "You'd better not… what did we use to say? You better not try and wipe my eye. He's mine; I saw him first," she chortled.

Lisa stared at her.

"You're old enough to be his mother," she snapped.

"I am not! How dare you say that to me?" Mary said, her eyes flashing.

"Mary, darlin'. Oh, I'm so glad to get back to my beautiful Irish Coleen," a man's voice said as a pair of flabby arms swung Mary around, giving her a resounding smack on her bum. Mary, all smiles again, wrapped her arms around the man.

"Sorry I wasn't there to meet you off the train, darling," she jabbered. "That stupid woman in the pharmacy… You wouldn't believe how far behind the times they still are here."

"All right, all right, calm down. I'm sure you handled her with kid gloves," the man joked. "Introduce me to your friend, Mary," he said, turning to face Lisa.

"You might already know her. You knew so many women from here when you were stationed here in '42," Mary slurred, winking at Lisa.

Turning, Lisa came face to face with the man who had been doing all the complaining on the train.

"Darling," Mary babbled. "Meet my old school pal, Lisa Armstrong. Lisa this is my husband, Scott Osborne."

Lisa saw the double door of the entrance to the hotel behind Scott Osborne's head begin to tilt and spin. "Here, steady on there," she heard him say as he steadied her swaying body. Just for a second, she felt the feel of his arms around her before Mary started to shout hysterically, Without having any real recollection of how she got there, she found herself sitting in the coolness of the hotel foyer, and somebody was talking about sending for Dr Cole.

"I'm fine, I'm fine," she stammered, struggling to sit in a more upright position.

"Jeez, Lisa, you scared the bejesus out of me," Scott exclaimed.

"Right folks, show's over," Mac Kielty's voice boomed over the top of the excited babble of voices around Lisa.

"You all right, Mrs McKnight?" Mac asked.

"Thanks Mac. I'm fine now," she heard her own voice say as she fought down the feeling she was going to be sick.

"Drink that down, and you'll feel better," Mac Kielty said, pushing a glass of brandy into her shaking hands. Lisa watched the golden liquid slosh against the glass. Shakily, she stretched out her hand and placed it on the table.

"Mac, could you get me a taxi? I need to go home. Isobel and Trisha are by themselves…"

"Sit there till you come to yourself. I saw the girls in the queue for the pictures a while ago. Bring Mrs Mc Knight a good strong cup of tea and put plenty of sugar in it," he called to a passing waitress.

"I don't see you for… what—twenty years? And the first time we meet again, you nearly give me a heart attack," Scott Osbourne chuckled, leaning across the table and covering her hand with his.

Paralysed with shock, Lisa stared at the man sitting opposite her. She couldn't take in that this middle-aged, balding man with a sweat line on his upper lip and a ring of fat pushing down the waistband of his trousers was Scott!

"You look… so… different," she blurted out.

He looked at her with a bemused expression on his face. "Do I?" he said, running his hand over the crown of his head where he had combed the longer strands of hair in a diagonal sweep.

"Sorry, that sounded very rude," she said. "It's just when I thought about you… I always imagined you as you were when you guarded the camp where the sea planes landed," she whispered helplessly. Untangling her hand, she reached out and clasped the brandy glass between her clammy palms.

"A lot of things have changed since then," he sighed. "I have married, had children—lost my hair," he said jokingly. "But one thing hasn't changed: I never stopped thinking about you, Lisa. I never stopped thinking about you and the fun and good times we had."

Lisa gulped down the remains of the brandy. She could feel it burning her throat on the way down.

"Your tea, Mrs McKnight," the waitress smiled, placing a clean napkin on the table and putting a white china cup and saucer on top of it.

"Thank you."

"Oh, and the boss says he has your taxi ordered, but it might be a while because it's away with a crowd to a dance in The Mecca in Enniskillen."

"One-horse town and one taxi," Scott quipped. "That's why I keep my own car for use while I'm here. I'll be glad to take you home."

Lisa's teacup clattered into the saucer, slopping the tea onto the clean napkin. She wanted to pinch herself. *Was it a dream or the effects of too much wine she drank earlier in the day? Was she sitting in Kielty's with Scott Osborne like they had done in the past?*

As if he had read her mind, Scott slipped his hand over hers again. "Remember when Mac used to let us slip up the back stairs," he said, rubbing his thumb over her wrist.

"I see you two are catching up on old times," Mary said, startling them both.

Scott hastily withdrew his hand and, leaning towards his wife, gave her a kiss.

"Isn't he a handsome devil?" Mary hiccupped as she linked her arm possessively through Scott's. "He loves the ladies, but he always comes back to me," she chorused, reaching out for her glass. Lisa felt a stab of unreasonable jealously shoot through her at the sight of Mary's drunken hand caressing Scott's chest.

"Can you believe little mousey Mary Kielty married her real life American war hero?" Mary gloated.

Lisa shook her head. She couldn't take it in.

"I must go. I'm fine now. The walk will clear my head," she mumbled.

"No, no, don't go yet. I'm sorry if I have embarrassed you. I'm always doing that and... nobody likes me... just like it was when I was at school," Mary blubbered drunkenly as Lisa pushed back her chair and made to get up.

"Time for bed, my little four-leaf shamrock, before we make a fool of ourselves and feel bad about it tomorrow," Scott chided.

"Just one more drink! Lisa, will you have one more... what is it they say here? One for the road," Mary giggled.

"It's as well you're not a sea liner, or you'd float all by yourself on dry land," Scott laughed, helping his swaying wife to her feet.

"Wait for me," Scott signalled to Lisa as he put his arm protectively around Mary and led her between the tables to the back of the room and the back stairs.

Lisa sat back in her chair. She felt punch-drunk. She closed her eyes and swallowed hard. One part of her wanted to gather up her parcels and race out into the darkening street, but another part of her wanted to wait for Scott.

Wait for me. How she'd longed to hear him say those words when she was twenty and he was a piece of glamour and excitement from another place. Turning, Lisa noticed Scott making his way back to the table.

"Dad," a voice called. "Dad," the voice called again as Scott eased himself into the chair opposite her.

"Darling," he crowed, scrambling out of his chair again and giving a slim, fair-haired girl a bear hug.

"Jay and Kathy are here as well," the girl babbled, nodding behind her in the direction of the bar.

"Come on, Lisa. Come and meet my family," Scott beamed, swelling with pride.

"Sorry, what's your name?" Lisa stuttered out.

"My name is Hannah. I was called after my great granny Kielty—my granddad's mother," she said with quiet dignity.

Lisa's heart stilled and then started to drum in her chest. Her soft voice and direct blue-eyed gaze was uncannily like Andrew's.

"I'll pick you up tomorrow," Scott murmured to Lisa as his family crossed the foyer to them.

Lisa hesitated, but not for long. *He didn't look like the old Scott, but maybe he's the same inside,* she told herself. *Maybe we could be that young couple again—if only for a short while,* she thought, her excitement beginning to build.

Chapter 47

The young American girl behind the bar eyeballed George.

"My father arrived on the evening train last night." Hannah Osbourne said in a low voice, placing his drink down in front of him. "Drink that and get out."

Shit, George thought; *she knows about me and her ma.* "It would have been good to have it to say I bedded mother and daughter," he smirked, heading for the Station Bar. He sank his pint and moved on to the Station Bar.

The Station Bar was full of revellers over from Scotland for the 12th of July celebration. They were downing drinks as if they were water.

The music blared, and the bandsmen kept drinking and playing cards. They reminded him of the Irish navvies and Sheamie Foy.

Before he knew it, he was embroiled with them in a poker school.

"You'd rather have the lassies than the cards," a big, burly guy wearing a kilt and sporting an elaborate sporran on a leather belt said as George's eyes wandered to a tableful of women laughing and drinking at the far end of the lounge.

"I'm Jimmy, the drum major." he went on.

George grinned. "Could be that," he admitted.

"I think he fancies yer lassie, Jimmy," a voice roared above the ear-splitting din in the packed bar. The drummer's eyes narrowed, and he closed his fist.

"I'm out. Time for home and a bit of grub," George said, tossing in his cards. He didn't want another beating over another woman.

"Where is Aunt Lis?" he asked, coming into the house.

"Belfast—she went on the early train this morning," Trisha said.

"What's wrong with you, Izzy?" George asked as a glum-looking Isobel came into the kitchen and sat down at the far end of the table.

Isobel's lip trembled.

"What's wrong with you?" George persisted.

Trisha rolled her eyes. "Auntie Lisa says we might be going home and she's going to miss seeing her boyfriend Trevor banging the Lambeg drums."

Isobel hiccupped.

"Fancy going to the pictures tonight? I hear some heart throb is in it," he said, teasing Isobel.

"He's far too old!" Isobel said between hiccups.

George turned on her. "Shut up your whining and snivelling. Ah don't like what's on in the pictures. The actors are too old," he snarled, mimicking her voice.

Trisha laughed. "You like them old, George. We saw you drinking with an old woman," she giggled.

George's lips flattened. He'd wanted Mary to borrow her father's car and drive over the Irish border into Donegal, but she'd refused.

"Why pay for a hotel bed when we have a perfectly good bed in my father's hotel here?"

That was just the point, George thought irritably. *It was her father's bloody place.*

The image of Ike Swann, the head waiter, flashed into his mind. *If oul' Kielty finds me bedding Mary in his hotel, the knife might be sticking out of my belly this time,* he thought.

"She was legless. Trevor said she was a… alkie…"

"What's all the shoutin' about?" William's voice said, coming into the kitchen.

"Nothin' that concerns you," George retorted.

"You asked them to go the pictures and now you're going back on your word?" William said, noticing the nerve twitching in George's clenched jaw.

George snorted. "You'd know all about breaking promises, wouldn't you, Da?"

Keeping control of the hatred for his father that was bubbling just below the surface. George looked his father in the eye. "You got a good fat price for the livestock, then?" he said, throwing out a feeler.

He knew his instincts had been right when he saw William's hand still before he unhooked his coat from the hook behind the kitchen door.

William stopped in his step but didn't turn around. He wondered if George had heard rumours in the village about his granda leaving the farm to him and Trisha.

"That money should come to me, Da!"

"Why do you think that?" William asked carefully.

"Because it was Granda and me… and Mammy who worked to keep this farm going," George said, squaring up to him.

William breathed easier. So, he didn't know about inheriting the farm yet. It would give him time to bargain about the price of the land he was thinking about selling. George would never agree to him selling his granda's land to Robbie Black.

"Mac Kielty is looking to buy land to start up a new craft business for that American granddaughter of his," William said, testing the waters.

"And why would that be of any concern to me?" George sneered. *Snooty wee bitch,* he thought. *Ordered me out of the bar and threatened me with her big war hero da,* he fumed.

William took a pound note from is pocket and threw it on the kitchen table. "They're on holiday. Take them two to the pictures," he said gruffly.

"I'll be looking for more than that before I follow in your and Granda's footsteps when I report for my basic training in St Lucia's Barracks in Omagh."

"When have ye to go?"

"As soon as the 12th weekend celebrations are over, Father," George sneered, pocketing the money. "If I don't see you before I go, I'll look you up when they send us across to do our combat and weapons training in Aldershot," he smirked.

William felt fear's tight grip on the pit of his stomach. For some reason, the old hobo man who had been beaten almost to the point of death jumped into his mind. Whatever his son's rush to join up, it was more than following in his and his grandfather's military service footsteps.

After George and the girls left for the cinema, William thought about his conversation with Rosie on the phone earlier in the day.

"Not safe to sleep in your own bed now," she rattled on.

William had been only half listening. It had taken a few goes to get the hang of putting the money in the phone box's slots after he was connected. "Haven't ya heard about the bloke found stabbed in his bed in that hotel George's works in?" Rosie said.

"Hold on, Rosie. Bloody contraption of a thing," he'd muttered as the phone box swallowed his coins and begin to bleep for more almost immediately.

"…ain't that a turn-up for the books?" Rosie was saying when he finally got more money in the slot.

"What was that?" William asked.

"Jock—remember Scotch Jock? He used to arm wrestle everybody—well, blimey, you could have knocked me down with a feather duster when Sheamie Foy…" The pips went again, and he hurriedly pushed more money into the slot.

"What about Jock?" he asked.

Old Jock had been a good friend to him, and he hoped nothing bad had happened to him.

"The Old Bill arrested 'im this morning; something to do with the stabbing." The noise from the bar swelled in the background.

"What stabbing? Speak up, Rosie, I can hardly hear for that din behind you," William said loudly.

"Sheamie Foy said Jock was arrested this morning by the peelers. He is helping police with their enquiries," Rosie's voice said irritably.

William had held the phone away from his ear and stared at it.

"Why would Jock be arrested?"

"He was friendly-like with the old geezer who got stabbed at the hotel. Him and the old geezer were found in bed together," she said in a loud stage whisper. Her voice faded as she turned away to speak to somebody.

"Listen, darlin', I 'ave to go—I'll tell you all about it when I see ya."

Somebody had left a paper behind them in the foyer. Furtively, as if he was doing something wrong, he turned the pages. The story of the stabbing was on page five. It said the man who had been attacked had been an employee of the hotel for many years and was considered a valued member of staff who had given loyal service to the hotel and its patrons.

William's eyes had fixated on the name of the hotel. It was the same name as the name on the side of the cartons of food George used to bring home. *Getting mixed up with that street gang changed George,* he thought. *But surely he wouldn't stab a man in his own bed!*

Chapter 48

His feeling of apprehension about George made him restless, William went out into the yard. There was a dead heat and a heavy, oppressive stillness in the air.

"Like the calm before the skies open and there's thunder and lightning storm," he mused, thinking back to his childhood and the forked lighting and roar of the thunder.

Crossing over the fields now that bordered onto the lakes, William looked to where several small cruisers and fishing boats were moored. The last of the day's sun glinted off the white of the small cruisers, giving them a look like he'd seen in the holiday advertisements Rosie was always stopping to look at.

Maybe I might take her on a holiday, he thought. He patted his breast pocket to check on his money and remembered he had left what he'd got for the sale of the cattle away safely in Samuel's old army overcoat. His fingers curled around his and his father's war medals Lisa had found in the box of old papers.

He turned through a gap in the hedge out onto the road and headed for the old Nissan huts. His thoughts went back to the meeting he'd had with Robbie Black in his plush city centre office earlier in the week. Robbie had mentioned he might be interested in taking the ground the Nissan old huts sat on off William's hands.

"Father left that bit of land to Lisa," William had pointed out. Robbie had leaned back in his swivel chair and twirled a pencil between his fingers.

"You can sell it. You have power of attorney until George is twenty-five," he stated. Peering in through the windows thick with dirt and cobwebs, he wondered how many soldiers and airmen had slept there and how many of them had died and were buried in some place their families could hardly pronounce the name of.

Sitting on the broken stone wall that separated the road from the fields, he studied the drawings the Land Registry Office had given him. He didn't understand it, but the man had carefully pencilled in the important parts in red ink.

"Nice bit of land there," he said, tapping it with a pencil he had chewed the end off. "Given the interest in development and holiday resorts in that area, you could be onto something here," he said, a faint smile creasing his serious face. William nodded his appreciation and pocketed the map.

It was beginning to dawn on him why Robbie Black wanted to buy this particular stretch of land. "I hope this doesn't bring back painful memories, but is the well where your daughter drowned on that same piece of land?" Robbie enquired, knowing full well it was.

William flinched, the question catching him off guard. He nodded.

"Right! The very first thing I would do is fill it in so no other child or animal could fall into it," Robbie said, throwing William a mock sympathetic look. Instinct told William Robbie was trying to put one over on him.

"I don't think it's a good idea to break up the farm," he said tersely. Memories assailed him. His mother, in an old pair of green wellies, a woollen hat pulled down over her ears, slipping and sliding as she herded the cattle down the steep hilly field for milking. The swish of the cow's tail across her arms as she sat on a low stool, milking; his father, sitting on a turned-up bucket, his head dropping wearily from time to time as he watched and waited for a calf to be born. And the picture in his mind's eye of his father gently cleaning the mother and the newborn calf with clean straw.

Robbie narrowed his eyes. "I have been farming the land for you for years now; I'm not sure I have the time to continue doing that in the future."

William shifted in his chair. It occurred to him that having Robbie as a renter for the farm and as his solicitor wasn't a good idea. "What kind of money are you talking about for the land the oul' huts are sitting on?" he'd asked.

Robbie rubbed his freshly shaven chin. Rising, he began to walk up and down the office. "Well, you know yourself, William; it's mainly scrub land—lot of whin bushes and rough ground. Not much good for growing anything. But I'm sure we could reach a price that would suit us both," Robbie said, putting his hand lightly on William's shoulder. "Why don't I get Sam Weir, the auctioneer, to take a look at it, see how much land there is exactly, and then we can agree a price," he smiled, sitting down again behind his heavy oak desk.

"Was there something else?" he asked, looking at his watch.

William had eyeballed him. "Aye. I was in the Land Registry Office before I come to see you. The man there gave me this," he said, pulling a piece of crumpled paper out of the pocket of his coat. "He thinks its prime land for development and should fetch a good price."

Catching up a stick from the hedgerow, William's thought about when Robbie had broached the subject of the well; he had been wearing his kindly concerned neighbour's face.

"If he thought he could make me feel anymore guilty than ah do already, he's wrong," William sighed. "Ah have no interest in the land—never did. All ah want is to get back to London, see Rosie," he sighed now, looking around him. "But if he's interested in the land with the huts on it, he can pay a good price for it," William growled.

He stepped back over the stone wall into the field where the well was. Low and ominous, thunder rumbled overhead. The dark hedges and foliage that surrounded the open well cast dark shadows on its smooth surface. Staring into its dark depth, every instinct in William urged him to get away. But his feet dragged him to its edge.

An irrational, faint hope stirred deep in him. *Maybe, maybe, if he stared long enough into the well's depth, he would see Sarah's smiling reflection? See the image of her dancing around the kitchen in one of Margaret's dresses; hear her call, "Look at me, Daddy. Look at me, daddy. I'm on stage. I'm a star."*

He hadn't cried when, months too late, Dr Cole's letter had reached him when he was in a gun post defending Malta, telling him his mother was dying. Or when Sarah's small coffin and later his father's coffin were laid beside hers in the Armstrong plot.

A shudder passed over him. *Reverend Snodgrass had considered it 'a Christian, act,' given the inclement weather, to break his promise to my mother and allow Margaret's corpse and me across the threshold of his church so he could conduct the funeral service inside!* William thought. *But because we had a mixed marriage, his Christian faith would not permit him, a man of God, to bury my Margaret in our family plot.*

He hadn't cried. Red-hot burning rage had saved him when they put Margaret's coffin into the pauper's grave in the frozen ground.

He lay flat on his belly, racking, tears dripping into the well's still dark water, the last words Sarah's had cried out filling his head. "Don't beat Trisha, Daddy. Beat me. I was bad too, Daddy. I was bad too."

"Och, my wee Sarah," William choked out to the gathering dusk. "You were never bad. You were never bad."

He felt his heart crack and splinter like the thick ice on the puddle holes on a winter's morning when a booted foot slammed into it. He shook uncontrollably; tears ran in torrents down his face, smothering him.

He sobbed for all the things Sarah would never see or do. He sobbed for forcing Margaret to give birth to a daughter she didn't want to have. "She should never have been born," he shouted out.

All the pain and rejection of his past caught up with him as another avalanche of tears assaulted him. He banged his head against the rocky, hard, unyielding ground. Incoherent words poured out of him. "Why am I alive? Why, why?" he roared. "Better men than me never came home from fightin'. Why me?"

Cattle in a nearby field startled and stared; their black-and-white faces loomed eerily over the hedge in the falling dusk.

A tentative moon flittered across the black water of the well. William searched for wee Sarah's face, but all he saw were the events of the day of she drowned flash by as if on a cinema reel:

Lillian Snodgrass enraged at Trisha and Sarah's behaviour in Sunday school, Sarah and Trisha's mouths open, their screams mingling together as Sarah beat Trisha—her punishment for disrespecting the Bible lesson.

And his father's face twisted, his arm dangling at a funny angle; Trisha reaching out for the rag doll clutched in Sarah's arms, George trying to breathe life back into Sarah after he pulled her from the well.

William felt himself sway, tip forward; felt his grip loosen on the edge of the well, saw the lighting streaking across the face of the well like a thousand shooting stars…

Chapter 49

Lisa wished she could have left Isobel and Trisha at home, but Faith Hamilton wouldn't have kept them if she'd known the day's outing was with Scott. And William was nowhere to be seen.

"Hope you brought your buckets and spades," Scott teased the girls. Turning back to Lisa, he gave her an appreciative look and winked at her. Lisa blushed and nervously patted her hair, remembering how Scott used to like her to look nice.

She checked her lipstick in the wing mirror. Trisha's surly face loomed up behind her. "Why can't Isobel and I wear lipstick?" she grumbled.

Scott laughed. "Little Miss sassy," he joked.

Lisa's heart lifted. She had wrestled with her conscience half the night, wondering if she was doing the right thing or not. *What can happen with Isobel and Trisha watching our every move?* she reasoned.

"I've brought a picnic, a bottle of wine, and a nice warm tartan rug," Scott murmured, laying his hand briefly on her knee. "Think I'd know my way into the Irish Republic in daylight?" he laughed as they neared the border crossing. "Most of the time I was stationed here, I sneaked over at night on a borrowed Raleigh bicycle," he chuckled.

Scott slowed the car. "The lakes are still beautiful," he murmured. "This was one of the places I held in my memory when the Japs were bombing the hell out of us," he mused.

Lisa thought the landscape never looked more beautiful.

"Did you know Aunty Lisa when she was young?" Trisha asked innocently.

"Did you know me Da?" Isobel asked, not to be outdone.

Trisha snorted. "Your Da wasn't in the army. My father was. So, if he knows anybody, he probably knows him best."

"My Da helped to build the army camps for the soldiers." Isobel retorted.

Scott grinned at them both in the mirror. "I met lots of soldiers… and civilian workers," he added hastily, "All brave men—ready to do their bit for their country."

The girls nudged one another and giggled. "You sound just like Elvis Presley," Isobel giggled.

Scott glanced at the ruins of an old castle perched on the top of a hill. "Did you know that monks used to live up there? They built it high and round so they could see their enemies approaching. They used to ring the tower bell to warn that strangers were about," he said over his shoulder to the girls.

"Granda said the lakes had magical powers," Trisha said. Lisa turned to look at her. She wondered if seeing George again had stirred up old memories.

"It's true, Aunt Lisa," she said defensively, mistaking Lisa's look for one of disapproval. "He did say that."

"I know, Trisha; he used to tell me stories like that too when I was small," she said.

"Tell me! Tell me! I didn't hear the stories," Isobel begged. "I never even saw me Granda," she huffed.

Scott glanced across at Lisa. "You never brought her to Fermanagh to meet her grandfather?"

Lisa's face flushed. "It's a long story."

"She never brought Andrew, me brether, either, and he's older than me," Isobel moaned.

"You have a son?" Scott said, a note of something she couldn't quite fathom in his voice. She could feel the panic starting to rise. *How to tell him about Andrew had been one of the things that had kept her awake last night.* But she couldn't just blurt it out. Not with Isobel and Trisha sitting with their ears pinned back.

"There was a well along this road," Scott said. "One night, the old man who owned it forgot to put the lid back on the well. During the night, the water rose and spread over the farmer's fields. In the morning, there was this lake we are driving past now!"

Trisha snorted. "That's a stupid story. Somebody made it up."

Isobel giggled. "Faith told us about how two giants who had a fight. They threw rocks at each other and made the giant steps at Potrush."

Scott laughed. "You smartass girls don't believe in folktales. But I know lakes have magical powers," he said, glancing out the car window at the blue of the cloudless sky reflected on the lakes surface.

Lisa thought of the nights they'd sat looking into its depths. It had seemed to have an almost alluring romantic quality as the moon shone down on it and Scott's arms held her close. She wished she could walk arm and arm with him now and recapture the magic.

Blowing the car horn loudly, Scott made the cattle look up from their grazing. The girls cheered and waved madly at an elderly farmer leaning on a gatepost, looking into a field.

A sign for Castle Archdale pointed right. "Why don't we do a bit of a detour and show the girls where the sea planes took off from during the war?" Scott said.

Lisa listened to Scott telling stories about his adventures when he was stationed in Enniskillen during the war. The girls leaned forward against the back of his seat, their faces alight with interest.

Scott always has that effect on women, she mused. *And who can blame them? Even in an overweight way, he still has the charm and charisma he always had. That was one of the things I always loved about him,* she thought.

"This road is as familiar to me as my own front porch," Scott murmured. "I've been down it many, many times in my memory and visualised the seaplanes flying out over the Atlantic to guard the convoys from the German submarines," he murmured, his good humour subdued by the memory.

"When we were overseas, lying in the mud, waiting for the Japanese to attack, I'd think about the happy times we'd spent here watching the tall water birds—herons, standing graceful and still in the water. Or remember lying in my bunk listening to the sound of the water as it lapped in between small rocks that stretched out along the shore like a contented cat on a sunny day."

"Weren't you scared sleeping in the haunted castle?" Isobel asked. Getting out of the car, Scott linked his arm in hers and was off again, telling her all about the place he had been billeted in and the great parties the GIs had for the children when they were stationed there.

"You even had your own cinemas and everything inside where you stayed," Isobel said in awe.

"Yep, we sure did."

"Well, what you think?" he asked, tickling Trisha.

She wriggled around until she was facing him. "I don't believe in ghosts. That only for children, and I'm not a child anymore," she said, batting her eyelashes at him. "I'd rather get to the seaside and try on my new swimsuit," she said coyly, gazing up into his eyes.

Scott chuckled. "She reminds me of you—sassy and up for it."

"She's William's daughter."

Scott frowned. "Wasn't there something? I remember Mary's mother writing to her?"

"He married, Margaret—a Catholic. She died from TB," Lisa said succulently, not wanting to go into it.

The border customs officer glanced casually into the car as Scott slid to a stop beside the peaked-capped customs official. "Anything to declare?" he asked, smiling in at the two girls, who were busily licking two large ice cream cones.

Getting out of the car, Scott struck up a conversation with him. Through the open window, Lisa could hear him reminiscing about the days of the smugglers when he was a young raw recruit.

"Oh, yes, it still goes on," the official was saying. "Instead of smuggling tea, sugar, and the likes, they're smuggling cigarettes and cattle now, as well as the odd shipment of guns," he said nonchalantly.

Lisa smiled at the remark. Thinking about gun running made Lisa think of Mary Kielty. Sergeant Swanton and her father always talked in low tones about Catholics and the IRA. Her mother always gave the badge on his cap a good shine with the sleeve of her cardigan.

"For Queen and Country," she'd smile, looking up at the picture of the Coronation of Queen Elizabeth in 1951, which took pride of place above the fireplace.

Lisa smiled, remembering how she used to study Mary in class. She was the only Catholic she knew. And she didn't look like she'd be out at night smuggling guns off boats coming into the bay, she used to think.

"Where did you tell Mary you were going?" she heard herself ask Scott as he started up the engine. He didn't answer her question. It was obvious Scott didn't want to discuss it any further. *Well, he's going to have to… if things work out between us,* she mused.

They were on a mountain road. She wondered if Scott had taken a wrong turn somewhere as they passed a guide and a group of tourists preparing to tackle the short walk up the foothills.

Scott pulled over to the side and went back to ask directions from the guide.

"Fancy climbing the mountain? The guy says there's a lake at the top and breathtaking scenery. It's more a walk than a hike," he added, leaning in the car window.

Lisa looked down at her new black leather patent shoes. She didn't want to climb a mountain in them.

"We just passed a pub. We can have a drink," she smiled, moving her body towards him. Time dropped away, and she was flirting with him again. *Where did that come from?* she wondered as she saw Scott's eyes widen and a pleased smile light up his face. *I haven't flirted with BJ or any other man for years,* she thought in amazement; *yet it had just come back to me—like second nature.* Scott gave her the lopsided little boy grin she remembered so well and hurried back to the guide. "The guy says the girls can join them, and he'll keep a lookout for them," he said, "and we can go and have that drink," he grinned.

"Good day to you," a small, dapper man dressed in a black suit and waistcoat shouted above the sound of a football match on a transistor radio a customer had at the bar.

Hearing Scott's American accent, the man immediately found a table for them and waved Scott towards the bar. "Shelia, will get you anything you want," he said his eyes sweeping over Lisa. "What'll it will be for the lady?," he asked glancing at her legs. "We serve the best of Guinness."

"Tea, just tea… please," Lisa said firmly. *My stomach still hasn't recovered from all the wine I drank that day in Belfast,* she mused.

She watched the barmaid giving Scott the benefit of her full cleavage— smiling and leaning in close to hear what he was saying. A frizzle of jealousy shot through her. "Don't mind Shelia," the man's voice said at her elbow as he put a pot of tea, a plate of scones, and a pot of strawberry jam on the table. "She's a married woman." Lisa laughed. "Aren't we all?" she said. She can smile and thrust her breasts at him all she wants but she'll not get him. He's mine. I'm not letting another woman take him from me again; I'll fight Mary Kielty for him if I have to, she assured herself, smiling grimly.

"What are you smiling about? Thinking of me?" Scott grinned as he pressed her knee under the table. "I thought you might be jealous of the very helpful barmaid," he laughed.

"Did you… think about me when we were… apart?" she asked, blushing like a schoolgirl. Scott's response was lost in the loud cheer that rose; the favourite Gaelic football team had won. "Time for the darts match," the man in the waistcoat said as he refilled Lisa's teapot.

Scott downed his bottle of Guinness. "Haven't played darts in a pub in years," he said, rubbing his hands together like an excited youngster. Lisa felt peeved. She had hoped Scott would take her for a quiet, secluded walk before the girls came back again. "He hasn't changed that much," she mused. "Yeah, he had lost the slim, athletic figure of his youth and his hair… but he still had that self-assured, confident way with him that suggested the world and everything in it was there for the taking," she thought as she watched him lined up to take his throw of the darts.

"Tactics and strategies is what won the war, and they will win this game," he declared as he took careful aim. The locals chuckled good-naturedly. Lisa's eyes swung to Shelia, the barmaid, who was running her hands over her figure. She'd moved to stand at the end of the bar waiting for Scott to notice her—just like Mary Kielty used to do when they GIs were drinking in the bar in her father's hotel. Lisa recalled that the servicemen, Scott amongst them, had spent a lot of time and money drinking and eating in Mac Kielty's. There had been whispers that Mac Kielty's brought in "Belfast beauties" to help the servicemen to relax.

She gazed at Scott as he walked back through the fog of cigarette smoke like a hero returning from battle. Suddenly, she wanted him to make wild, passionate love to her like before. Startled at the ferocity of her own feeling, she fled towards the door just as it swung open and the girls came in, bringing a rush of hot July air with them into the dim interior of the pub.

"Time to move on, ladies," Scott asserted, seemingly unaware of Lisa's flushed face and twitching hands as he focused on buying the girls crisps and lemonade. "Whoa, hold on there, gals," Scott ordered as he pulled into the parking lot beside the seaside fairground. Doors already open, Trisha and Isobel were out of the car before it completely stopped.

"You're gonna need some greenbacks like these," he said, waving two-pound notes in his hand. "Don't spend it all in the one shop," he laughed in a fake country Irish accent.

"Chips first or the Big Wheel first?" Isobel squealed excitedly to Trisha.

"Big Wheel first," Lisa said firmly visions of them being sick on the people below.

"Stay together… and don't talk to any strangers," Lisa ordered.

"Ma! We're no' bairns," Isobel moaned.

Chapter 50

Scott grabbed Lisa's hand and pulled her down the grassy, sandy incline that led past the seafront. Soon, they had left most of the families on the beach behind, and all that could be heard was the cry of the seagulls as they circled overhead. Lisa had dreamt about being alone with Scott for years. Now it was happening, she felt tongue-tied and awkward, shaken by the force of her urge for him in the pub.

"The cliff walk looks secluded," Scott said, pointing to where a couple were walking, arms entwined. Lisa hesitated and looked down at her new black patent shoes. She could see wet grass and water stains on the soft leather. *Why didn't I just wear my summer sandals*? she berated herself.

The cliff path looked very narrow. After a while, the path narrowed even further until they were forced to walk in single file. They were well above sea level now. Doe-eyed sheep gazed curiously at them as if wondering what they there doing there.

Lisa's inner voice was asking the same question. She had never been unfaithful to BJ. As if he'd read her thoughts, Scott placed a hand on each side of her face and run his thumb along the inside of her earlobe.

"You trust me, don't you, Lisa?" he asked, tracing her jawline. *This is Scott,* she reminded herself. *The only man I have ever loved.* of course she trusted him. The trouble was, she didn't trust herself.

Scott grabbed her hand and helped her through a gap in the wire fence, which had been trampled down by other couples.

"Maybe I should take off my shoes and walk in my bare feet," she murmured. Then, remembering she was wearing nylons, she decided against it.

"Let's sit for a while," Scott suggested, mopping his face with a large white hankie. Sitting down in the long grass overlooking the Atlantic Ocean, Lisa could feel herself shaking. Well below them, people walked their dogs on the beach, and children shouted in excitement as they flew colourful kites high in the air.

"Have you missed me, Lisa?" Scott asked.

In a blink of an eye, Lisa's reticence left her. This was the moment she had dreamt about when she had no money, had to put up living with old Granny Mac's demands, and BJ's gambling and drinking. *This is where they picked up where we left off twenty years ago—maybe even be the beginning of a whole new life,* she thought.

She looked into Scott's eyes. "I missed you every minute of every day. I've never stopped loving you, thinking about you, Scott" she babbled. "I have something to tell you…"

Scott's kiss cut off her words as his arms encircled her, drawing her down onto the soft grass.

"How much you have missed me?" Scott murmured.

Lisa could feel the heat of his body and his hands as they caressed her.

"I missed you every minute of every day," she breathed. "Thinking about you is what kept me from going mad," she said, wriggling her feet out of her shoes.

Scott kissed her until she thought she would lose her breath.

"I missed you too, honey. I used to think about us… like this. Lying together, the way we did when we first."

Lisa's heart soared. Scott had never stopped loving her. There had been times when she'd look in the mirror and think, *Scott wouldn't love me if he could see me now.* But despite the extra pounds and the shoddy, borrowed, unfashionable clothes she wore, Scott still loved her, she thought.

"You meant so much to me," Scott breathed as his hands moved in little tingling circles on her back.

Lisa's heart was beating so hard it was making her breathless. She wished Scott would stop talking and kiss her again, and again, long and passionate.

"I was your first lover," Scott murmured. "I will always have first claim on your love," he said hoarsely. "It'll always be that way. We were meant to be together…"

Lisa felt her heart soar. *There*, he'd said it. *We were always meant to be together.* Any guilt she had harboured about cheating on BJ melted away. There was no need to feel guilty. Scott was her soulmate, and she was his. They had been born for each other.

"You're still fantastic… your breasts, full and smooth," Scott moaned, fumbling with her bra. "Oh, how I've missed holding them, stroking them," he murmured.

As his palms worked their magic, Lisa could hear the distant muted sound of waves, feel the cool grass against her hips, and heard the soft whoosh of nylons as Scott's fingers released first one and then the other of her stockings from her suspender belt.

Waiting was agony. She began to wriggle on top. Scott used to like it that way. Then, she felt him stiffen and draw away abruptly.

Jolted out of her ecstatic state, Lisa raised her head. A small dog was staring hard into her face. Startled, she stared back.

Scott let out a string of curses. Sensing Scott's hostility, the dog began to bark furiously just as a man came around the headland and whistled for it to follow him.

Mortified, Lisa scrambled to a kneeling position and frantically searched the long grass for her bra.

"Why don't you keep that damn mutt of yours under control?" Scott bellowed at the man's retreating back.

"Bloody peeping Tom pervert," Scott screamed.

Lisa stared at Scott. His face was contorted with rage. His fly was open. His penis hung flat and wrinkled like an old, rumpled, deflated bag. She had an almost uncontrollable urge to laugh.

"He's gone now," she soothed, trying to ease him down beside her again.

"Yeah, he's gone. But him and his bloody mongrel have to come back this way," Scott retorted furiously. "I'll damn well wait for the bastard and damn well show him what happens in the States to peeping Toms like him."

"It's alright. We'll have plenty of time to be together," Lisa said, attempting to massage his back.

"Oh yeah? When the fuck would that be now?" Scott snarled, putting on a fake Irish accent. "You're going home in a few days' time, and I'm going be stuck in this godforsaken place with my bloody alcoholic of a wife and her bloody father watching my every move," Scott growled into her face.

Lisa recoiled as if he'd struck her. She had never seen Scott behave like this. Gathering up her tights, she stuffed them into the pocket of her cardigan.

"I'll wait for you at the car park," she said.

Shocked, tears blinded her as she stumbled and lurched on bare feet over the uneven ground. She glanced back up the path. Scott was nowhere to be seen. He was waiting for the man and his dog to come back.

Sick to the pit of her stomach with disappointment and mortified at being caught making love like a lovelorn teenager, she stumbled on.

Nothing had changed from an hour ago—the sun still shone and families' still picnicked on the beach, and yet everything had changed. She felt as if the world had turned on its axle.

Scott had acted like a violent stranger she didn't recognise. He'd scared her. The waves battered the rock face.

She shivered, suddenly cold despite the hot July day, remembering the scared look that had filtered across Mary's face when she realised she'd be late to meet Scott off the train.

She hoped the man with the dog had another way down and didn't have to pass Scott, who was obviously waiting to confront him.

Chapter 51

The dance floor of the marquee was jam packed with all the revellers from the parades earlier in the day.

Lisa waited for Scott to apologise or explain what had come over him on their day trip, acting so pig-ignorant towards her.

All the way home from the trip, Scott hadn't uttered a single word, yet now he was acting as if the disastrous cliff walk meltdown had never happened. Her heart ached, as if the life was being squeezed out of it. She didn't know what to think or how to think. Had Scott meant what he'd said—that he loved her. Had she meant it when she told him she was his soulmate and he hers?

"Drink, ladies?" Scott said, giving Isobel and Trisha a mock bow.

"They're too young for drinking," Lisa said, aware that some of the locals were watching their meeting with undisguised interest.

"Oh, Mama tiger defending her cubs," Scott drawled, turning to the crowd gathered around the edge of the dance floor as if inviting them to agree with him.

"When did you become so dammed motherly? The way I remember it, you weren't always so all-fire prissy," he sniggered.

"We'll have to be going soon, girls," Lisa said, holding hard to her self-control. "We still have some packing to do."

Scott pretended to pout. "Mama tiger, please let the pretty girls spend some time in the company of a real live decorated war hero," he slurred.

"He's just a drunk old man," Trisha whispered behind Scott's back, seeing the look on Lisa's face. "We're getting lemonade."

Secured in a small alcove where she could get a good view of all that was going on, Annie Swanton nudged Gloria. "Doesn't look like the Yank and Lisa are having a very happy reunion, does it?" she murmured, watching the meeting between Scott and Lisa.

Gloria wasn't listening. "What is Mary Kielty wearing? It's disgraceful to see a woman of her age dressed like that."

"It's a mini dress. Our Kathy has one," Annie said.

"Your Kathy is only a teenager. And she has a good pair of legs," Gloria asserted. "Mary Kielty must be forty if she's a day! Geoffrey doesn't approve…"

Anne chuckled. "Oh, I think Geoffrey has enough to be worrying about tonight," she said as the clergyman's wife made a beeline for the bar.

Ellen, sitting beside them, sipped her sherry and watched the dancers. The good Reverend's wife was just back from being treated for "nervous depression" at an addiction centre in Dublin.

"Weren't the bands lovely with all their coloured banners," Gloria enthused, plastering a big smile on her face as Reverend Snodgrass swung his wife away from the bar and onto the dance floor, dancing cheek-to-cheek with her. *It's no fun being the other woman at gatherings like these,* Gloria thought.

"How's Kathy getting on with the studying at university?" Ellen asked, expecting to get the head snapped off her. Annie could be touchy about her granddaughter.

The postmistress sipped her sherry before answering. "She's talking about getting engaged to Jay and going back to the States with him… if they marry. But who know what will happen in the future," she added evasively.

Ellen was so startled she nearly fell off the chair.

Kathy was going to get engaged to a Catholic and might marry him? She glanced at the postmistress, wondering if Annie was tipsy. It wasn't like her to disclose personal information like that.

"I suppose Jay is only half Catholic, anyway," Ellen said hurriedly. "Mary hasn't been a practising Catholic since she married Scott."

"Geoffrey doesn't approve of mixed marriages," Gloria huffed. "He says it can only lead to trouble later on."

The postmistress gulped at her drink. Ellen waited for the explosion.

"Times are changing, Gloria. And we have to change with them or lose our grandchildren from our lives," Annie finally murmured.

Flabbergasted, Ellen reached out for her glass. *If she hadn't heard it with her own ears, she wouldn't have believed it*—Annie Swanton agreeing that it was alright to have a mixed marriage. *She had had been one of the agitators that turned the shopkeepers against serving William when he married Margaret,* she thought.

Two red spots had risen on Gloria's face. "I don't agree. If we start… diluting our religion, it'll be no time before Rome and the Catholic Church is telling us what to do. What happens when farms and property that has been in Protestant hands for generations has to be passed down to a mixed-marriage generation! It's… inconceivable, Annie," Gloria spluttered, glaring at the postmistress.

Annie ignored her and waved at a passing waiter.

"Make mine a large double," Annie said to the surprised waiter.

"Let me buy you ladies a drink," a male voice said at Annie's elbow.

"That's very good of you," Annie said, turning around. "Oh, it's you William… I didn't know… I thought… you didn't drink," she said in confusion, staring at the foolish grin on William's face.

"Holidays nearly over now, William," Ellen said, making room for him beside them when he returned with their drinks. "When do you have to go back? Or maybe you're staying and taking on your own farm again?"

William wiped the froth of the pint off his top lip.

"Goin' on tomorrow night's boat—be on me own."

Annie raised her eyebrows. "Isn't George going back with you?"

"He's joined the army."

"Good training and discipline for him," Gloria said approvingly.

William took a deep drink of his beer.

"I suppose Lisa's holiday is nearly coming to an end too?" Ellen asked casually. With Lisa out of the way, she thought, Con would go back to his old placid, plodding self and not be poking and prodding her at night.

William nodded, taking another swig out of his almost empty glass. "Aye, she goin' too, and taking Trisha wi' her."

Annie glanced at Gloria. There was no mistaking the relief in William's voice.

"Thank you for the drinks," Annie said as he rose to leave.

"No bother, Mrs Swanton. You were good to me mother and father," William stuttered out before turning away.

"Sarah Armstrong will rise up in her grave," Gloria gasped as they watched William make his way unsteadily back to the bar. "He wasn't long getting the hang of the drinking," Gloria scowled. "Look at him! Holding up the bar with that Davy Dobbs. He'll be none the better for his company," she grumbled. "He's more familiar with the bar stool than the church pew," she admonished.

The house was in darkness and Lisa and the girls were asleep when William got home. Sitting down beside the fire, he decided he'd wait for George. He'd had a long talk with Davy at the bar about the flashbacks and his near miss at the well.

Maybe he could make George understand the effect fighting a war had on men, on families after they returned.

He'd shake George's hand. Wish him well. *Not part on bad terms like me and Mother did,* he murmured, settling into the chair beside the fire.

He woke with a shudder. The fire had died, and the kitchen was icy cold. He heard the rooster clear its throat. It must be near morning, he thought. His throat felt like sandpaper and his head thumped. George hadn't come home. His bed was empty, but his suitcase was still there.

"Might as well start the packing," he muttered.

He felt in the pocket of Samuel's old greatcoat for the money Robbie Black had given him from the sale of the cattle. It wasn't there.

The empty wooden coat hangers clanged together as he agitatedly searched and re-searched every coat pocket in the wardrobe. He needed that money for getting back to London and to pay for the kneeling plate he had ordered for Margaret's grave.

He threw open George's case. It was empty. His old army kitbag was gone.

Chapter 52

George whistled cheerfully as he slammed the door of the door of the bandsmen's van shut, saluted the driver, and headed off down the street after getting street directions for Smithfield Markets.

He had been in Belfast's Smithfield Market once before when he had been very young. He remembered it as an enchanted place. His Granda Samuel had bought him a huge bread roll filled with an even bigger sausage and a big bag of sweets for the train journey home.

With the old kitbag swinging off his shoulders, he felt on top of the world as he walked up and down the narrow-cobbled walkways between the stalls. He stopped and fingered some of the goods for sale on the stalls, but the stallholder was focusing on something behind him. Jerking around, George saw a copper looking his way. His mind jumped to Ike Swann. Had the old head waiter died, and were the London police already looking for him?

"I hope the basic training is short and they send me overseas right away," he'd mumbled and shot around the corner into the next row of stalls.

A tug brought him out of his reverie. His eyes widened. "Where did you come from?" he grinned, squatting down beside a small monkey busily trying to undo his shoelaces. The monkey jerked away from his outstretched hand and set up a racket, squealing and wailing.

"She doesn't like being handled," a voice said from behind the counter. George looked to where a sunburnt, red-haired man was sitting on a chair cleaning an air rifle.

"Good job she's not a woman, then," George laughed.

"Easy seen you've never met the wife," the man grumbled.

George moved on. Further up, a man was selling mice and dead-eyed gerbils. He kept moving and stopped beside a stallholder who was twisting a snake around his body.

"Here's a young bucko who'll not be afeard to give it a try," the snake charmer shouted at him.

George ignored him.

"C'mon, lad, you've faced worst things than a pissin' snake, so you have."

George stared at him. Then it hit him. The man was looking at the kitbag. He thought he was a soldier home on leave. George was just about to say he hadn't done his basic training when it dawned on him that if the copper came asking questions about him from the stallholders they wouldn't be looking for a soldier.

"Fancy watch you have there for a young lad," a stall holder observed. George quickly withdrew his arm from the counter where he had been admiring a tray of knuckle dusters like Knuckles wore. The watch was the one thing he had stolen that he had kept.

"Present—from me girlfriend," he said in his fake London accent.

"Is that right, wee lad? She must have a good wee bit of money about her, so she must. Here, don't run away," he said as George made to move away from his searching eyes. "Did you want to see them rings you wus lookin' at?" Swiftly, the stallholder withdrew the tray from under the glass display cabinet. "There's more of them bigger Teddy Boys' knuckle dusters under the counter, so there is," he said, smelling a sale. George caught the glint of a diamond from the gold ring the man was wearing on the little finger of his left hand. It looked worth stealing.

George tried on a few of the rings.

"Might come in useful… if you got into a tight corner," the stallholder coaxed. "Here let me show ye, how they work," he said. George watched as he slipped the gold ring from his finger and laid it on the glass-topped counter. George felt the adrenalin start to pump as he watched the man demonstrate the knuckle duster rings. The diamond on the ring on the counter glittered in the bright overhead light, "Could I see… the ones you have under the counter?" he asked.

Sure of a sale now, the stallholder bent down and searched around for the tray George had pointed at. Quickly, George pocketed the gold ring. Picking two of the biggest rings at random, he quickly slipped them on his fingers.

"I'll take these two," he said, holding out the money.

Remembering Stella's instructions never to run, he walked casually on to the next stall before quickly slipping behind the market stalls and up a side street.

"Better get something to eat and a B&B for the night," he mused. "Get a few quid for that," he murmured, feeling the ring in his pocket. He wondered if he should try and flog it to one of the local pawn shops.

His hand involuntarily slipped over the bulge in his zipped fake leather jacket. His father's wallet was there in his inside pocket. He smirked softly. *Da will be in a right oul' flap by this stage,* he mused to himself. "Served the bastard right for not sharing the profits from the farm with me," he muttered as he headed for the city centre.

Standing on the corner of Royal Avenue, he watched the late-night shoppers mingle with the early pub-goers. Trisha would be mad at him when she discovered he'd gone away without saying goodbye. *I'll write to her at Lisa's,* he mused.

The smell of food wafted from restaurants, and noise and music spilt out from the bars. George's stomach grumbled, and he realised he was ravenously hungry. Going down a side street, he caught the smell of fish and chips.

A group of teenagers loitered around the café door, chewing gum and smoking. They looked him up and down but didn't speak or offer to move. Slipping one of the knuckle duster rings on to the hand that held the kitbag on his shoulder, he pushed through them and made his way to a table at the back.

The waitress continued to chew gum as her eyes washed over him.

"Fish, peas, and chips looks good," George smiled. Shaking a liberal amount of vinegar and a good sprinkling of salt on the chips, he began to eat. He motioned to the waitress again.

"Large glass of milk," he mumbled, his mouth full of fish.

"Didn't your Ma teach you not to speak with your mouth full?" the waitress smiled cheekily. When she left, George carefully slipped some money from his father's wallet. He considered counting the money but thought better of it, seeing a group of men eyeing him.

Slipping a ten-shilling note into his pocket, he got ready to pay. *What was keeping the girl with the milk?* He wondered.

"Sorry for keeping you," the waitress apologised. "But we're very busy… Bank Holiday weekend. Would you like a big slab of homemade apple tart to go with that milk?" she asked, seeing George had cleaned his plate.

George nodded. He watched the sway of her hips as she went in behind the counter. *Would be nice if she could put me up for the night,* he mused. He laughed into himself. *You're in Belfast, Georgie boy. It might be 1964, and the Beatles might be singin' 'Love, Love Me Do,' but free love ain't spread to here yet,* he mumbled, biting into the huge slice of apple tart. Still, he mused, *maybe I'll wait a while. Have a wee chat with her. Maybe flash the cash a little. Might be my lucky night,* he mused.

Gradually, the feeling of the warm café and the humid atmosphere on a full stomach lulled him into a state of tired relaxation. He was just deciding he'd chat up the waitress when a voice spoke beside him.

"Think you have something that belongs to me, so you do, wee lad," the market trader he'd stolen the ring said threateningly, a mutinous look on his face. "You thieving wee bag of sh—"

"No need for that; leave him to us." It was only then George noticed there were two men in cop uniforms.

"Need a word with you at the station, young fella," the shorter of the two men growled.

Chapter 53

Happy is the corpse the rain falls on. Isn't that what they say? William thought. *You must be very happy, Margaret,* he murmured. He remembered the straggling mourners, rain soaking into them as they carried the coffin from Reverend's Snodgrass' church—the same church they'd forbidden her to enter when she was alive.

Why didn't you take her to her own church like she begged you? a small voice nagged at him.

He came to his mother and father's family plot. It was weed-free but barren of flowers except for a small remembrance wreath of fresh red poppies. His heart ached as he gazed at his mother's name carved into the stone. He traced the carved letters with his finger. *Sarah Armstrong 1880-1943.* She had refused to see him before he was shipped out to a gunship in the Mediterranean. *And she died while ah was a POW in Poland, not knowin' if ah was alive or dead,* he muttered.

The name of his grandparents, long-dead relatives, and his father, *William Armstrong 1886-1952,* were also carved into the stone. Wee Sarah's name had not been carved in, he noticed. *She'll not be remembered as a true Armstrong because of me and Margaret's mixed marriage,* he murmured. He picked a bunch of wildflowers and placed them against the headstone.

Turning away, he started to climb, making his way into the older part of the graveyard where paupers and people of no consequence were buried. He stopped at a mass grave known as the Tramp's Grave. The man who had been found dead along the railway line had been buried without being identified. Church records simply named him *the beggar man* and buried him along with other unknown or nameless people. The graves in this part of the cemetery haphazardly backed onto or crisscrossed over the top and bottom of other graves, as if the gravediggers had simple picked a spot and dug a hole in the ground.

He was high above the road now, and it afforded him a clear view of the town and the surrounding countryside. Breathless with the exertion of the steady climb, he stopped to draw breathe. *Had I passed Margaret's grave? Should I go back?*

He wished now he had asked Lisa to come with him, but she was packing to go and still wasn't speaking to him.

I remember thinking that if Margaret's head was slightly tilted, she'd be able to see the lakes below, he muttered. Then, he noticed a grave laid out on a slope where the grass had been tramped down, which had fresh flowers on it among the weeds. Carefully stepping between the overlapping graves, he stopped at what he hoped was the foot of Margaret's grave.

No small cross or marker bore her name. *It could be anybody in there,* he thought. *It's as if oul' Reverend Snodgrass and the loyal locals hoped once she was dead and buried her existence could be wiped out—forgotten about,* he growled.

He felt awkward just standing there. Should he pray… or just talk? He hadn't prayed much since he had been at Sunday school. *Expect when the ground shook and buildings fell down when Italian bombers were blasting all around me to hell, when I was stationed in Valletta, my hands grippin' a gun stickin' out of a concrete bunker. Ah prayed then alright! Ah prayed that the God Father promised would be on my side and bring me home safe to Margaret,* he mused.

He sat down on the edge of the weed covered grave. "Hello Margaret," he said, feeling foolish. Sitting there, he told Margaret all about the navvies, the drinking, and the terrible digs where he and George had stayed. He stopped talking. He couldn't tell her the son she had loved so much—had such great plans for—was part of a violent street gang, or his growing fear that George might have stabbed a man.

He got up and started to clear the tall weeds and dead leaves from the grave. The sun burnt his back through his shirt. *At least I'll have something to show for my work here,* he muttered, thinking about the days he worked with Sheamie Foy and the navvies in Brompton cemetery. *You can see the lakes and the road, now,* he murmured. *You called it the road to your childhood home, Margaret.*

Why did I not let you go there—see your mother and father—take the youngsters to visit them? he moaned.

Sitting back on his heels, he wiped the sweat off his face with his forearm, wishing he'd brought something to drink with him.

"Must be a water tap about this place," he muttered, shading his eyes. A stone wall skirted around the graveyard, separating it from the low-lying area of the nearby mountain.

"They'll be a stream there," he muttered.

Getting nearer, he saw that some of the wall was crumbling, and wild rose brambles and moss from the mountain were keeping the old wall standing. Thorny bushes caught at his arms as he swung himself up and dropped down on the other side where a mountain stream trickled over stones.

Cupping his hands, William drank thirstily from where a shallow well had been formed between the rocks and boulders that littered the ground. Straightening up, he caught the glint of the sun flashing on something. It was the spokes of a bike as somebody pedalled along the road below. The figure on the bike left the road and began pushing the bike on the steep mountainous path to the graveyard.

William looked around him. There were plenty of stones. He could make a makeshift surround for Margaret's grave. Stripping off his shirt, he piled as many similar-sized boulders as he could find near the cemetery wall.

He recognised the man pushing the bike. It was Con Callachan. "Why didn't you leave the bike at the bottom?"

Con took a minute to get his breath back before answering.

Sitting down on a boulder, he lit up a John Player's. "The village is getting like everywhere else now. There's some would steal the cross of a donkey," he wheezed. "What are ye doin?" he asked, eyeing the growing pile of stones.

He waited for William to say sarcastically, "Still carryin' the gossip, Con?"

"Fixing up a makeshift surround around Margaret's grave." He glanced to where a bulky parcel tied to the carrier on Con's bike.

Con untied the mouth of the brown hessian sack and withdrew a stone angel.

William drew in his breath. He knew nothing about art or statues, but even he knew the sculpture was exquisite.

"It's a beautiful thing," he said to Con's surprise.

Con nodded. "It is. Hannah, Mac Kielty's granddaughter, makes them. My wee girl is buried somewhere alongside the wall there," Con said, thrashing down the weeds and placing the stone angel in the shelter of a wild white rose bush in full bloom.

"There ye go, darlin," he said softly. Bending forward, he placed a kiss on the angel's head. He wondered how many more years he could climb the mountain on the day his daughter was born and died.

"Why isn't she buried in your family grave?" William asked.

Con sighed deeply. "Church rules. Only babby's who have been baptised can be buried on consecrated ground. So, Ah brought her up the mountain and buried her as close to the consecrated ground of the graveyard wall and blessed ground as ah could get."

William felt as if he were intruding on something very private as Con stood knee-deep in wild bracken and fern, his shoulders bowed in supplication to a cruel god for a daughter he had never known.

"Did she have a name?" William asked hesitantly.

Con looked at him in surprise. It wasn't like William to show much interest. "Rose Ellen. She was the reason Ellen agreed to marry me," Con mumbled.

For a while, the only sound was the distant hum of traffic.

"Here, you start carrying the boulders over to Margaret's grave and I'll throw the rest of these over the wall," Con offered.

Con watched William laboriously construct a makeshift surround around the perimeter of his wife's grave. He remembered the day he delivered the letter from the War Office to Margaret telling her William was missing in action, presumed dead. "Life has a strange way of turning and twisting things," he mused. "Who would have thought William would survive a German prisoner-of-war camp and poor Margaret would die?" he murmured, heaving more boulders over the wall.

The sun was fading as William put the last stone in place around the grave. "Rest in peace—until ah can do better for you, Margaret," he murmured.

The squeak of the front wheel of Con's bike kept them company as they tiredly trailed down the steep incline.

"Do you think Mac Kielty's granddaughter would engrave wee Sarah's name on the Armstrong headstone?" William asked.

"With a heart and a hand," Con assured him. "Kielty's girl will do whatever you need done."

William nodded. *If George hadn't stolen his money, I could have used some of that,* he thought.

Chapter 54

Dropping his air of arrogance, George put on his baby face and let his lower lip tremble. "I'm sorry. It was a stupid thing to do," he mumbled, letting his head drop onto his chest. He withdrew the gold ring and placed it on the table, careful not to let his watch be seen.

The policeman picked it up and examined it. "Nice piece of kit. Must be money to be made in the market stalls," he said, slipping the ring into the breast pocket of his coat. "What did you intend to do with that?" he said, pointing to the huge threatening-looking knuckle ring with its serrated edges.

"Nothing I just… liked it," George mumbled. "They're like… fashion," he stuttered.

Wrenching off his coat, the policeman flung it across a chair.

George reared back as the copper reached across the desk and jerked George's jacket open.

"Well, well, well, what do we have here?" he said. "A wallet stuffed to the gills with money. You rob a bank or something?" he exclaimed as he started to thumb through the money.

George's stomach lurched. He could feel the fish and chips threatening to explode from his throat. "I didn't steal it. My father… gave it to me." He could see a vein throbbing in the cop's neck.

"Stole it, didn't you? Or maybe you're into selling the uppers and downers?"

George stared at him. "No! I'd never do anything like that."

"Don't play the innocent with me, young fella. I've seen it all. It comes through that door every night—a shitload of it!"

Kicking the leg of George's chair, he pulled the kitbag into full view and wrote down the number stencilled on it. For a long moment, he just sat there and stared at it.

George's stomach went into spasm. *Why did I take the bloody bag? And why was I unlucky enough to meet an old bastard like my da, who thinks he's a war hero just because he fought Hitler?* he fumed.

"I'm going to be sick," George lamented.

"The brave man that had that rank and number hadn't time to be sick. He was too busy fighting a war. Not like you young shithead these days, running round carving people up with knives and knuckle dusters. The brave soldier who owned that bag is probably lying buried on some unmarked grave somewhere," PC Brown went on.

Sweat trickled down between George's shoulder blades. *I wish my bloody father had died in the war and his bones rotted away.*

PC Brown watched him closely. *He looks innocent enough,* he thought. *And this might be nothing but an opportunist theft, but my instinct tells me otherwise. And what's that fake cockney accent about?* He had a contact in the Met keeping her ear to the ground, now that the terrorists were taking their fight for Irish freedom to the mainland. *She'd done well for a country girl from Fermanagh,* he mused. He'd get her to throw a check on this lad, see if he anything to do with an IRA cell or an Irish gang operating across the water, he thought, looking at the bulging envelope stuffed with money.

He drew the black telephone on his desk towards him and twirled the silver dial just as the door opened and Det Maloney limped in the interview room.

"OK if I sit in on this interview?" he asked.

PC Brown shrugged. "Be my guest. I'll be back shortly," he said, rising.

Detective Tomas Maloney slid into a chair and pulled a sheaf of papers towards him. "Name—and no bullshitting me," he said quietly.

George could feel the greasy bile rising up his throat. This one wasn't bawling at him, but somehow, he felt he was more of a threat.

"You got a name or not?"

George spine prickled. *The way the cop sounds like my mother.*

The door of the interview room opened, and PC Brown came back in. He frowned.

"You ever lived in London?" he shot at George.

"I've just signed up in Omagh. I'm a new recruit from Enniskillen heading for basic training," George said, sidestepping his question. "My grandfather and my father were in the army. I'm very sorry about the ring. It was a stupid thing to do, but I don't want it to ruin my career in the army," he pleaded. "I want to follow in my father and grandfather's footsteps."

"Who did the kitbag belongs to—your granda or father?"

"Bought it off some oul' guy who wanted money for booze," George lied. They'd check out the number, but it was the 12th holiday fortnight in Northern Ireland. He'd be long gone before some civil servant got off their ass to send them the information that the kitbag was his da's.

Detective Maloney pulled his right leg into a sitting position. "Gammy leg, old war wound," he said to the unspoken question in George's eyes. Leaning back, he thrust his thumbs into the waistband of his trousers. Surreptitiously, he watched George fidget and shift in his chair. There was an air of tension about him that was more than about stealing a ring, money, or even an old soldier's prized kitbag.

Taking a small tin out of his pocket, he started to roll a cigarette. "When do you have to report to your unit?" he asked.

"Thursday," George said, every nerve in his body screaming with tension.

The detective licked the edges of the cigarette paper. The sight of his pink tongue darting in and out over the gummed paper made George want to vomit.

Striking a match, Tomas Maloney carefully puffed the cigarette into life and inhaled deeply. *He looks familiar. Should I know him?* he thought, trying to pin down where he had seen him before.

"Thursday? A bit early, aren't you? Good-looking chap like you must be leaving a girlfriend or two behind."

George smirked. "Girlfriend's old man back home for the marching season—thought it wiser to leave early." *At least that's half true,* George thought.

"Not easy leaving the family, is it?" Det Maloney said as the door closed behind PC Brown again.

In the absence of the arresting copper, George allowed himself to relax a little. This cop was a bit friendlier. *Maybe it would work out after all.*

"How many brothers and sisters did you say you had?"

George looked down at his feet. "One sister, now," he mumbled.

Wonder what happened to the other one, Det Maloney mused, but he let it pass for the time being.

"Good to see young fellas like you still joining up. Came up North meself to join up. The Inniskilling Fusiliers," he said, nodding at the kitbag. He gave a small chuckle. "Yeah, I came up from Wexford to join a regiment with 'Irish' in its name when I wasn't much older than you. What age did you say you were?"

"Eighteen," George replied, realising the cop was from Co. Kerry—that was why he thought he sounded like his mother.

"What's date your birthday on?"

"Fourteenth January."

"And the year you were born?"

"1942."

"Didn't go down too well at home, me joining the British Army," Tomas went on, writing down the information George was giving him.

George shifted uneasily on the chair. He wasn't bloody interested in the copper's life story, but he didn't want to get on the wrong side of him either.

"How did you come to be a cop… policeman in Belfast?" he asked, feigning interest.

"Sure, they didn't want me below in Waterford. I was considered a traitor for fighting for the Brits." He looked over George's head and into the distance of the gathering dusk outside the window. "Truth be told, I came North because of a woman," he said inaudibly. "Right, back to business," he said, snapping out of his reverie. "Empty the kitbag," he directed. He cursed when he saw the contents spill out onto the floor. "You any idea how much paperwork there is in that lot, son?" he sighed. "If you'd stolen that bloody ring half an hour later, it would be somebody else's headache, and I'd be home with the wife and family now," he grumbled, reaching over and answering the shrill of the black phone.

"Be back in a minute," he said, limping towards the door.

George stole another look at his watch. *Must be a bloody Irish minute,* he thought, sliding it back behind his cuff.

Finally, the door opened and then slammed shut again behind the two coppers. As soon as he saw the expressions on their faces, he knew the game was up.

"Why are the Metropolitan Police looking to question you in connection with a stabbing, George?" Detective Maloney said, emphasising his name.

George stared out of the small window of the plane. They had kept him for three night and days in a stinking holding cell at Townsend Street Station. He had kept saying over and over, *It was an accident. I didn't mean to stab him.*

"You stabbed an old, defenceless waiter with a kitchen knife. How many times did you 'accidentally' stab him?" Det Maloney asked him repeatedly.

George shivered. He didn't know. He could only remember the paring knife sinking into the soft, fleshy belly of the man.

Chapter 55

"Hold the placard and look straight ahead," the police photographer instructed.

"Am I being charged?" George asked as he followed a constable back down the long corridor. Keys jangled as doors were unlocked to let them through and then locked after them again.

"All I know, mate, is that you're up before the magistrate—10 o'clock Monday morning," the guard said, opening the door to his cell.

George curled into a ball under the single blanket on the hard wooden bed and lay rigid, listening to the click of the key in the cell door. His first night in Ma Higgins, he had been afraid to sleep because the door had no lock. Well, it had now.

"Armstrong—visitor for you," a guard shouted. George leapt off the bed. The Belfast cop, Det Maloney, who had escorted him and handed him over to the MET coppers, said he'd get word to his father. George waited impatiently for the cell door to be opened.

"Here, what's your rush? Hands against the wall, legs apart," the guard growled, kicking at George's feet.

"What are you doing?"

"Stupid Irish git, you 'ave to be searched every bloody time you go to the visitor's room," a voice shouted from the cell opposite. "You never been in gaol before?" He gave a mirthless laugh.

"No worries. He'll soon be a repeater like the rest of you," the officer yelled back. "This place is like a revolving door for drunks and thieves," he growled, shoving George in front of him up the corridor and into the interview room.

A man wearing heavy-framed glasses that seemed too heavy for his thin nose to hold up indicated George should sit in the chair across the desk from him.

"My name is Goldsmith. I have been appointed as your solicitor."

George stared past the thin-jawed bespectacled man to where his father William stood, with his back against the wall where a sign said 'Visitors'.

"I have been appointed by her Majesty's Armed Forces to represent you," his solicitor stated.

George smiled sardonically.

"You find this amusing?"

George shook his head. "It's your name—Goldsmith. If it hadn't been for a gold ring, I wouldn't be in this hole of a place," he said petulantly.

"If only that were all," the solicitor murmured. "There's the serious matter of the stabbing of an elderly gentleman, and I believe there may be some… issue with a young lady," he said baldly. George flinched. *They couldn't hold making love to Marta against him. Marta had practically raped him!*

"There are other matters to consider also," Mr Goldsmith went on. "According to your father and the arresting officer's report, you had a substantial amount of money on your person, which you said your father gave you," the solicitor said, glancing at William.

William shifted from one foot to the other. He had barely gotten off the boat and settle into his new lodgings before the police had arrived asking for him.

His new landlady had stood her hand on her chest, taking deep breaths. "I hope it's not… political," she'd whispered.

William looked at her in confusion.

"You and your son are Irish, aren't you?" she squeaked. It was a minute before William grasped her meaning. "No, no. it's nothing like that," he said. "My son has no interest in politics." He could see that she didn't believe him.

"You better find new lodgings," she'd said, backing away from him.

"Well, sir, did you give your son the money or not?" the solicitor asked.

William's skin chilled under the intent scrutiny of the solicitor. "He took… borrowed my wallet. The money was in it."

Mr Goldsmith stood up and adjusted his glasses. "There will be a brief hearing in a magistrate's court…" The solicitor hesitated.

"You know if your son is sentenced, his career with her Majesty's Armed Forces will be over before it has even begun," he said, picking up his briefcase.

George heard his father draw in a sharp breath. A sense of jubilant excitement filled him. He might not have got a chance to push his da down the stairs and break his bloody neck, but his son's dishonourable discharge from the army would bring shame on him, the decorated war hero.

"Will you be here for the court hearing?" his solicitor asked, turning back to William.

William fumbled his hands out of his pockets and shook his head. "Ah have to look for new digs because of him," he said.

Filled with hate, George lunged at him. "If you'd stayed home and let me stay at grammar school, I wouldn't be in this stinking place!" he screamed as the guard wrestled him to the floor.

"Too busy bedding bloody Rosie to bother about me!" George yelled bitterly at his father's retreating back. "I'll soon put her right about you, Da, the first chance I get," he promised.

"On your feet, Paddy, show's over."

"I thought Irish families were supposed to be close—look out for each other. Not much love lost between you and your old man," the officer scoffed as he marched George down the corridor and stopped beside the door of a holding cell.

"This isn't where you took me from," George said in alarm.

The guard threw a quick check up and down the corridor. "Shut it, Paddy. There's a real treat in store for ya. You get to spend the night with an old mate," he gaffed, thrusting George into the cell and slamming the door shut. "Night, Paddy," he sang out, laughing. "Sleep tight."

"Hello, Baby Face." Knuckles grinned, swinging his body down from the upper bunk. Staring into Knuckle's leering face, George blanched, the seriousness of his situation sinking in.

Chapter 56

William looked around the court. A Catholic priest was the first to give evidence. William stared at him. He didn't know George even knew a priest. The priest talked about George's charity work at the Irish Centre and his determination to return to his studies.

George's new headmaster, Mr Watkins, was next. He spoilt the image of George as a young, motherless immigrant that the priest had tried to create, by giving evidence of his aggressive behaviour at St Stephen's and his membership of a violent street gang, who the police suspected had almost battered an old homeless man to death.

Agnes, the, hotel housekeeper, was next to be called to the stand.

"Do you know of any reason why George Armstrong would want to stab Ike Swann, his head waiter? The man who gave him gainful employment when he needed it?"

Agnes shook her head. "George was a good, hard worker and never had any rows with Mr Swann. They got on well together."

"Come, madam! Speak the truth. Ike Swann had more than a work-related interest in my client, George Armstrong," Mr Goldsmith retorted.

Agnes face flushed red. "Mr Swann… sort of took George under his wing, so to speak," she stammered out.

George's solicitor smirked as she stumbled from the witness stand.

"Yes, indeed it would appear that way," he murmured loud enough for the judge to frown at him.

Then, it had been Marta, George's ex-girlfriend's turn. Every eye in the packed court swung to her. With her slight frame, small tear-stained face, and her demure suit with its white Peter Pan collar, she looked innocent as a child. Tears coursed down her face as she recounted how George had got her drunk and practically raped her.

"When I told him I was up the duff—pregnant—he put all the blame on me," she sobbed. From the mutterings and ferocious looks on the women's faces in the public gallery, they would have happily lynched George there and then themselves.

"I didn't rape her," George shouted out. "She wanted it as much as me, more even."

"And I suppose an old, vulnerable man wanted to be stabbed while he slept in his bed," Ike Swann's barrister sneered.

Mr Goldsmith placed a restraining hand on George's arm, but it was too late.

"He wasn't in his own bed. He was in my bed," George yelled. Gasps of horror emanated from the courtroom.

William's body shook uncontrollably. By the time all the witnesses were called, he hardly recognised the person they were talking about as his son.

George began to sweat profusely as the steely eyes of the judge fastened on him.

"In sentencing you, I have taken into consideration the circumstances of the situation you found yourself in. Mr Swann has given an account of how he came to be in your bed that night and accepts his culpability in the matter," he intoned, looking over his glasses at George. He stopped and scanned the courtroom. "I believe your father is in court," he said with a mixture of pity and disapproval.

William could hear his heart hammering against his ribs. *If ah hadn't brought George over here... all to be rid Trisha,* he thought.

It's her fault, he muttered, barely able to hold his anger in check.

"You are young," the judge was saying, "but you have the making of a very dangerous man. The public need to be protected from you. I am sentencing you to five years in prison."

As the prison van swept out through the courthouse's gate, the flash of photographers' cameras lit up its dark interior, and people banged on its side in outrage, swearing vengeance. George put his hands over his ears to try and block out the hammering, and the baying, and screaming of the crowd outside the van, like hounds after a fox.

Chapter 57

"Hurry up, or we'll miss the train," Lisa said irritably, looking at the array of clothes on the bed that Trisha had tried on and discarded. "Wear something decent. Don't be giving the prison guards an eyeful," she said, looking at sixteen-year-old Trisha standing in her bra and knickers.

Trisha rounded on her. "Why do you always look at me as if I'm a trollop?" she yelled, slamming the door shut in Lisa's face.

"You're a sight for some eyes," BJ wheezed. "Watch yourself in the Big Smoke with all them long-haired teddy boys," he said, searching around his bed for his inhaler.

"It's here, Uncle Billy," Trisha said, picking it up from the old armchair beside the bed. It was the only thing of Granny Mac's that Lisa had allowed BJ to bring to the new house from their old tenement flat.

BJ patted the side of the bed. "Sit down a minute, lass. Ye nivir seem te have a minute these days, the way Lisa harps on at you about trying on dresses or walkin' wi' a book on yer heed to mak ye walk straight," he grumbled. "Ah wanted to tell you somethin'."

Trisha laughed and pretended to balance her handbag on her head.

A fit of coughing caught BJ as he laughed at her antics. He clasped her hands.

"When your Aunt Lisa mentioned you comin' te live wi' us, ah wasne for it. Ah didnea want you here" He stopped and looked her in the eye. "Ah hear her throwing it te ye sometimes when she thinks I'm taking your side o' the argument. But ah didn't know what a great lass you'd be," he said.

Trisha shushed him, seeing he was getting agitated and out of breath.

"You'll no hold it against me, will ye?" he pleaded. "Am fair proud o' you, lass. Fair proud."

Feeling the tears coming, Trisha hugged him. "I'll make you a nice warm cup of tea before we go," she croaked.

Spooning tea into the pot, she switched on Lisa's latest kitchen gadget—the new electric kettle. Her eye caught the letter standing to attention on the windowsill behind the potted plant. She picked it up and read it again. BJ wasn't going to get better, but he refused to go away to a sanatorium.

She gazed out at the row after row of houses exactly like Lisa's. Three-bedroom houses with a bit of a back garden, tin bins, and a shed that held coal.

Her uncle Billy hated it. His old friends and neighbours had been scattered to new housing developments just like this one.

Trisha felt his loneliness. It filled the house like a living, feeling thing. She had suggested to BJ that he should get an allotment like their new neighbours. He'd sat down on the tin dustbin—like the ones used to carry effortlessly on his shoulder down three flights of stairs—trying to get his breath back after the short journey from the living room sofa to the backyard.

"Wish I had the wind for it," he'd gasped.

Hearing Lisa's hurried step, she quickly poured BJ's tea and carried it upstairs.

"Am only a bloody useless nuisance," he wheezed. "Ah be better going to that hospital."

"Trisha!" Lisa's voice carried up the stairs.

"You goin' te visit that brother o' yours in jail?" BJ wheezed.

Trisha nodded as she checked her hair in the dressing table mirror.

"Jails are more like holiday camps nowadays. It's ne wonder most of them end up back in again," BJ grumbled, pressing the clothes down agitatedly.

"George won't be back in again."

BJ grunted. "Who will give a jailbird like him a job, lass? You know what they say—if he's no good, he's no good. Ah know he's your blood and ye want to see him. But be careful, lass. That's all am sayin'."

"I'll bring you a new book from stationary shop at the station," Trisha said, quickly turning away.

Sitting in the train, she thought about George. When she'd asked why he'd left without saying goodbye the year they'd been in Ireland, Lisa told her he had to go early to start his basic training in the army.

It was only after she'd found a letter that her father had written to Lisa, complaining about George being jailed for stabbing a man, that she learned the truth.

It had surprised her that her Aunt Lisa was willing to take the time and pay the train fare from Glasgow to London. Shifting into a more comfortable position, she settled down for the long journey. *One day when I'm a famous model I'll have a car and a driver,* she mused pulling a copy of *Vogue* out of her bag.

"Wait for me in front of the prison," Lisa instructed. "Don't be making promises to him about coming to live with us when he gets out," she hissed. "We don't have the space."

"You could turn your sewing room back into a bedroom," Trisha huffed.

"That's for Andrew when he comes home on leave."

"Andrew can sleep on the sofa."

"Your brother is not coming to live with us. And what will happen if Miss Thomas finds out you have a brother in jail for almost stabbing an old man to death?"

Trisha stilled. Miss Thomas was her ticket to living and modelling in London. And not even for her brother George would she give up a chance to be a model.

She checked her hair in the grimy window of the prison reception area and smoothed her hands over her red mini dress. She knew its slashed neckline and dropped waist showed off her figure to its best. Her knee-length white boots—a present from old octopus-hands Gashcyoin, Miss Thomas' side kick, for her not her letting on to Miss Thomas where his hands strayed during a fitting—set her outfit off.

Picking up her matching bag, she glanced at herself again, pursued her lips, and gave her hair a final rake with the wide-toothed comb so that her long black hair bounced and rippled as she walked.

The male prison guard smiled at her. She gave him a flutter of her eyelashes and a small shake of her hips.

"Empty your pockets and leave all personal belongings here," a busty female searcher with hands like a navvy intoned as the line of visitors edged their way forward. Rummaging through the spilt contents of the bag, she fingered the expensive free make-up samples Miss Thomas' models had given Trisha.

"Somebody has a sugar daddy," she smirked to the female prison officer who was waiting to frisk down the women.

"Fancies herself as another Twiggy," her colleague retorted.

Trisha gave her the haughty look Miss Thomas cast at other designers. For her insolence, the female searcher probed deeper and longer than she needed to.

"Move on," she finally said, satisfied that she'd made Trisha feel embarrassed and uncomfortable.

"Trisha Armstrong—door three," a voice boomed out.

An official-looking man rose from behind a desk and shook her hand, gesturing that she should sit down. Trisha's stomach lurched. Was she in trouble for snubbing the guard? Or had something happened to George?

"I'm Bruce Weatherman, the prison Governor, and this is Detective Tomas Maloney from the Royal Ulster Constabulary in Belfast," he said, a note of irritation in his voice.

Trisha elegantly crossed her legs and straightened her back. She could hear Miss Thomas's voice inside her head saying, *Decorum and demeanour, everywhere, everyplace—even in the Ladies,* she'd rasp in her cultivated highbrow tone.

Trisha noticed that the curve of her thigh revealed by her mini dress wasn't lost on the Governor.

"Well, to business," he said, straightening his tie. "You're probably wondering why I called you in here and why I am taking up your allocated visiting time with your brother," he said.

Trisha waited unsure how to respond.

"You'll have your visit, don't worry about that. Detective Maloney here has something to ask you. Until recently, he was the only visitor your brother has had since he has been with us. I thought it would be useful for you two to meet."

"Has.my father not been to see my brother?" Trisha asked surprised.

The Governor opened a file in front of him and flicked back some pages. He shook his head. "He came once, or twice in the first phase of George's incarceration, but not lately, I'm afraid."

Trisha glanced at the other man. He hadn't moved or said anything since she'd come in. He'd just sat there, watching her. In an open-necked shirt and summer slacks, he looked like the usual type of visitor she saw in the visitor's room. She wondered why a detective would be visiting George.

"Do you have contact with your father?" the detective asked.

Lisa shook her head. "I've lived with my Aunt Lisa since my mother died." She tried to keep the quiver out of her voice but didn't quite make it.

"You take it from here," Governor Weatherman said, standing up.

"A pot of tea and some nice cream buns from the canteen would be good," Det Maloney said.

Trisha saw the Governor's back stiffen. "This is the last bite of the cherry, Maloney. You've already got more than your fair share," he growled.

Lisa could sense the tension between the two men.

The new knee-length boots were chaffing the back of her knees. She smoothed down the short skirt of the mini dress. *Could you be arrested for showing too much flesh?* she wondered. *Wise up,* she berated herself. *You see worse on the street. Girls my age, sashaying about in hot pants with their boobs hanging out,* she thought. She gave a short snort. *Dear Aunt Lisa would never allow me to dress so provocatively,* she thought.

"Let's sit over here," Tomas said, nodding to a table with a chair on either side of it.

A curt rap on the door made Trisha jump. "Your tea, sir," the female searcher Trisha had seen earlier said sourly. "Close the door after you on the way out," Tomas said curtly.

He filled their cups and bit into a cream finger before he spoke again. "Your brother George has requested to be considered for early parole," he said, brushing the crumbs from the front of his shirt. "This is the third time in as many years. I want you to talk to him. He needs to stop saying it was an accident, show some remorse, and stop claiming he was defending himself," the detective said.

"It was an accident," Trisha said defensively. "George told me, and I believe him. That old guy got into George's bed… and touched him!"

The detective held her gaze. "Ike Swann has held up his hands and accepted his part in it. He gave a statement to that effect." The detective licked his finger before continuing. "Without it, George would have been given a much longer stretch for attempted murder. It was a very, brutal sustained vicious attack," he finished.

Trisha gulped. George wasn't a killer. A flashback hit her without warning— George, shoving her under the blackcurrant bushes, warning her not to come out until he came back for her.

"Are you all right?" Tomas Maloney said, taking the cup and saucer out of her trembling hand.

Trisha didn't realise she was crying until a tear dripped down her chin and left a wet circle on her dress. "George looked after me—saved me when Da beat me," she sobbed.

"Here, here, dry your eyes. If the Governor comes back in and sees you like this, he'll have my guts for garters," Tomas said, handing her a big white hankie.

"Sorry, I didn't mean to cry. It's just that George is the only brother—the only family I have."

"Shush now, I didn't mean to upset you. If your brother's parole appeal fails again I want you to help me to get him out of this place and transferred to Northern Ireland to finish out his sentence," he asked.

As she waited for Lisa, she wondered why a detective like Tomas Maloney would have such an intense interest in George.

Tomas Malone walked around Piccadilly Circus. His supervisor hadn't been as understanding about him coming to London this time.

"You a special interest in the lad's case or what, Maloney?" he'd asked.

"He's one of our own. Just making sure the lad gets fair play across the water. It's not a great place to be Irish there these days. His father doesn't seem too concerned about him."

He stopped and took a photograph from his wallet. The small photograph of a girl was faded with handling and grainy with age. It had been snapped on Sandy Mount Strand with a black-and-white Kodak camera. It was the one he had carried in his breast pocket all the time he had been away at war. His hand strayed to his wallet again. Her letter was in there too. *I think he's your son, Margaret. I'll do my best for him,* he murmured. *But it's not looking good for the transfer to the North,* he sighed, pressing the photo back into his wallet.

Chapter 58

Ken, William's new landlord opened the boot of his blue Cortina and threw in his and William's wellies. William glanced back at the house, hardly able to believe his luck. A tall, three-storey, old Victorian-type house, it stood smartly beside its neighbour, its bay window bright with potted plants.

Babs, Ken's wife, had given him the top attic room. It was as far removed from the room he and George had slept in at Ma Higgins' attic room as you could get.

"Good day for the job," Ken announced, turning into the allotment. William breathed in the smell of the countryside. After the hot, stifling atmosphere of the engineering tool room, it was great to breathe in clean air. They were only two miles from King's Cross Railway Station, but they could have been in a different world. Other allotment users waved and saluted them as they passed. Ken's plot snaked up to an embankment and the forest beyond. Strands of barbed wire marked the boundary, but over time the wire had flattened to allow access to the forest.

A sense of wellbeing spread through him as he helped Ken turn the soil and lay out the ground for cabbage, carrots, potatoes, and spring onions. He scrutinised the ground, measuring with his eye, making sure the cabbage wouldn't shadow the spring onions as they grew and spread out.

His sense of contentment pushed the worry about George to the back of his mind.

Straightening his back, he stood and tracked the line of the ground as far as the barbed wire fence with his eye. He stepped it out and made his decision. Marking the width of each drill by kicking a shallow track at each end with the heel of his boot, he tied an old hessian sack around his waist. Walking in a straight line, he began to drop in the seed potatoes at even intervals.

"You can take the land from the farmer, but you can't take the farmer from the land," Ken smiled, proffering a mug of tea. "Three sugars—just the way you like it," he said. William looked at him. Ken laughed. "Rosie told Babs. These woman of our have us all figured out," he chortled.

"Ever think about going back and reclaiming that farm of land of yours on the shores of Loch Erne?" Ken asked.

William sipped the sweet tea. "Ah wasn't much of a farmer. Lisa, the sister, she should have been the farmer."

Ken surveyed the well-laid-out ground. "People change. Sometimes things get in the way of what we should be doing when we're younger. Maybe you should give it another go, see how you get on."

William shrugged. "Rosie wouldn't leave her home and her sons."

"You ever ask her?"

William shook his head.

The smell of burning drifted across. The men were finishing up and lighting the brazier against the cool of the evening. The flames leaping in the old barrel, and the men grouped around it, reminded him of the nights he'd helped Andy, his last landlord, in the Seamen's mission. They'd go out into the night with soup and sandwiches, sometimes blankets, and try to help the homeless who slept rough. William suspected many of them weren't old seafaring men, but that never stopped Andy from offering what help he could. *George spoilt all that,* he thought. Andy had asked him to get other lodgings. For a while, he had been like the men at the mission, sleeping rough where he could get it.

"A'll be back shortly." William said, wiping the empty cup on the end of his jumper. When the men finish working on their plots, they gather in a clearing for a bottle of beer. That was William's cue to walk deeper in the plantation.

"Is that how George will end up? Homeless, when they let him out of jail." he murmured. Rosie refused to even talk about him, let alone let George come and live with them.

A companionable silence fell between him and Ken on the drive back.

"Will you move with the engineering firm?" Ken asked.

William considered the question. The factory was closing down its works in Edgewater and moving to Glasgow.

"Ah don't know."

"It would be nearer to your sister."

William tightened his lips. *And nearer Trisha,* he thought. *Ah don't want her causin' trouble between Rosie and me. George makin' a good enough job of that as it is,* he thought.

Ken glanced covertly at William and cleared his throat. "Babs mention the good news?"

William shook his head.

"We've been accepted to adopt another baby. Well, she's not a baby. She's an older child. Alice was only an infant when we adopted her."

"Ah didn't know Alice wasn't yours," William couldn't keep the surprise out of his voice.

"She is ours. She just wasn't born to us," Ken retorted.

"Ah didn't mean she's not yours…" Confused, William stopped talking.

"No harm done, mate. It's a common enough response," Ken grinned. "It's just we'll need extra space." It was a moment before William understood he was talking about him having to move out.

"Will you need me to go before the cabbages and stuff comes up?"

Ken didn't answer for a minute as he waited at a level crossing. Releasing the handbrake, he started up again as the train thundered past.

"Did you think about what we talked about, contacting the British Legions Veteran's Association?"

William grunted. "The last thing ah want to do is parade around glorifyin' killin' in the name of war," he said.

Ken grinned. "They do other things, like supporting people, help you get over things." Ken hesitated. "Babs and I hear you at night." Ken plunged on. "No, no, it's not that you disturb us," he rushed on. "It's just we're worried what'll happen when you move to new digs."

William sat, clutching the handle of the door.

"There's help out there for people who have witnessed what no person should ever have to see or remember," Ken went on.

"It's doesn't happen as much since Rosie and me…" William's voice petered out. He wondered if Rosie had told Ken about George being in prison. Was that the reason he wanted him to move out?

"Move in with Rosie." Ken knew he was nagging like an old mother hen, but he couldn't stop. In his job with the homeless, he saw men like William every night, begging for a handout or curled up in a doorway covered with a cardboard box. "You know it makes sense, mate," he said, giving William's knee an encouraging pat. "You spend most of your time there anyway."

William pulled the crumpled letter from his pocket, written on official prison notepaper, and handed it to Rosie. "George needs a place to live after he's released."

Rosie's shook her head. "You livin' 'ere—that's OK, but not 'im. He ain't comin' to live 'ere, Will."

"It'll only be for an address after he's released. He'll not want to be hangin' around me or you for long."

Rosie gave a mirthless laugh. "Oh, I know what 'e finks about me… and you. It was all in that letter what he wrote from prison. 'Shacking up with a barmaid'—I think was his talk. Meals made for ya and all the comforts of home day and night. Not to mention the 'air-raisin' things he accused ya of." Rosie snorted.

"Maybe, maybe you'd think about it," William pleaded.

Rosie untied the strings of her apron and took her time folding it. "Didn't your sister mention she'd moved into a bigger 'ouse, in the last letter you 'ad from her? She can give 'im an address."

William shuffled his feet. "I never answered it. And anyway, that was the Christmas before last."

Rosie raised her eyes to the ceiling and reached for her coat. "All I know, darlin', is that I ain't 'avin' him livin' in this 'ouse," she said resolutely. Shaking out her scarf, she fashioned it around her neck. "We've been happy goin' out of a night. We don't need 'im here messing things up, do we, lovey? You want summit fetched back after I finish work?"

"Do Sheamie Foy and the navvies still come in?"

Rosie stopped in her step. "Things at the works not goin' well?" she asked perceptively.

"There's talk they're moving to Scotland. Some of the workers are already up there training."

Rosie stared at him. "You kept that close to your chest. When is all this supposed to 'appen?"

William shrugged. "If it closes down altogether, and I decide to go wi' them, would you move up there with me?"

Rosie stared at him in disbelief. "Have you lost your bleedin' mind? I'm a Londoner! 'Ardly been out of the sound of Bow Bells since the day I was born! What about this 'ouse and the boys?"

"Your 'boys' are men—left home years ago!"

"They're still my boys. All I have left of their father—killed in that air raid shelter trying to be a good citizen," Rosie said. "I know you never took to them."

"They don't like me either."

"That's true enough. The feeling is mutual. Anyways, it's a daft idea to fink I'd move up north. I'd never see the grandkiddies."

William snorted. "You don't see much of them now. Your sons only come when they want to borrow money or want you to look after their spoilt brats while they have a week away in Blackpool."

Rosie's face flushed. "Reggie comes on Sundays…"

"Aye, to get bloody fed," William said, gritting his teeth.

The door shuddered as Rosie banged it behind her.

Chapter 59

"Ma, the peelers are comin' in here," Isobel's voice called. "Stop gawking out through the curtains, Isobel. There's enough of nosy bisims in this place without you starting."

"Mrs McKnight?" the serious-faced policeman asked.

Lisa's heart began to thud. Something had happened to Andrew. He'd been away on a "duty," as he called it.

"No point in asking where I'm being sent, Ma," he'd chide her when she pressed him for some more information.

"Is it Andrew?" she asked, her voice quivering.

The policeman stared. "Andrew? No. It's your daughter."

Lisa's heartbeat slowed, relieved it wasn't Andrew, and then sped up again when she saw Trisha trip over her own feet as she got out of the police car.

"Steady there," the young copper said, tightening his grip on her arm as he helped her.

Trisha staggered up the footpath and leaned against the jamb of the door.

"Drinking behind the shops wi' Stuart Moss again," Isobel said, disgusted.

"It's a bit more serious than that, I'm afraid. Drunk driving around the estate," the older copper said.

Trisha glared belligerently at him. "I wasn't driving. I don't have my licence yet. I'm going to be sick," she mumbled, leaning over the low hedge that separated them from their neighbour's house.

Lisa looked in despair at a drunken Trisha in hot pants, a boob tube and thigh-length boots.

"Thank you for bringing her home. I'll try and see that she doesn't keep company like that in the future," Lisa said, hoping to appeal to the officer's good nature.

The policeman surveyed Lisa. "Car riding at high speed, especially where drink is involved…" He hesitated. "That a good-looking daughter you have there. Haven't I seen her picture in the paper?"

"Niece, she's my niece," Lisa interjected, stepping back into the hall.

Trisha slouched in the direction of the upstairs. "Don't go up there. Your uncle BJ has enough to worry about without seeing you looking like a drunken street walker."

Trisha hiccupped drunkenly. "Oh, pity I'm not like perfect Miss Isobel. Or golden boy Andrew. Well, let me tell you, dear Aunt Lisa, golden boy is not as goody-goody as you think," Trisha said, giving a drunken giggle. "There are things about him you don't know, and I do."

Lisa's hand itched. She wanted to smack the drunken smirk off Trisha's face. "Isobel may work in a factory, but she doesn't dress like a street walker," she retorted.

"At least they get paid for lying on their back. What did you get the night you lay naked beside Robbie Black in Granny's bed in Ireland?"

Lisa leapt at her. "Shut your filthy mouth. You don't know what you're saying."

Trisha's stomach heaved, and she vomited over her own and Lisa's feet.

"I want to go and live with my father," she snivelled, wiping her mouth with her sleeve.

"Your father can't…" Lisa stopped. She had been about to say that her father couldn't stand the sight of her, but the look in Trisha's eyes, she knew that.

Trisha slumped down onto the floor and tugged at her knee-length boots. Without the boots, and sitting there in the middle of her own vomit, she looked like a lost, vulnerable child, Lisa thought, her anger ebbed away. *I'm not able for this anymore*, she moaned, sinking into a chair. *I'm tired. Tired of attending to BJ and tired of having no love in my life.*

"Clean yourself up and call good night to your uncle Billy before you go to bed. He's been waiting to see you all day." She sighed, watching Trisha's wobbly ascent up the stairs.

Halfway up, Trisha stopped. "Did Miss Thomas phone?"

"She did. But don't think that you are getting to go to London to that fashion show after the showing up you've just given me in front of old nosy bag next door," Lisa retorted.

Chapter 60

Loud, angry words poured from Arianna, the Italian model's throat. With a guttural stream of words, she flounced out, shouting what Trisha was sure were obscenities at Miss Thomas.

"I heard that there are some film directors, model agency bosses, and even high-profile music stars on the guest list," Lara, the model who was sharing an apartment with Trisha for the show, whispered under cover of Miss Thomas' screeching.

"The House of T'ASS is ruined, ruined. And all because of that bitch!" Esther Thomas was screeching.

Trisha's stomach churned. When Miss Thomas was like this, she picked on the lowest, newest, least important model. *That's me,* Trisha thought, trying to take in calming gulps of air.

"Tonight, the House of T'ASS should be showing the world's fashion gurus and editors the new autumn and winter collection. It cannot happen now. We are ruined, ruined!" Esther Thomas wailed.

"Breathe, breath, my cherub," Gashcyoin soothed, kneading Miss Thomas' tense shoulders.

Trisha stifled a nervous giggle. She always wanted to laugh when Gashcyoin called Miss Thomas that. Standing six feet three in her stocking feet and taller than Gashcyoin or any of the models or photographers, she was the least cherub-looking creature you could ever imagine. Ramrod straight and reed-thin, legs up to her armpits and clad in black leggings and a black leotard, she looked more like a demented Russian ballerina than the boss of a top-notch fashion house.

"You, girl," she hissed. Even in the chaotic noise and fevered activity, Trisha could hear the ice in her voice.

"She means you," Lara mouthed, giving Trisha a frantic nudge.

"Is she deaf or stupid?" Esther Thomas bawled.

Gashcyoin snapped his fingers, indicating Trisha should come at once.

Esther Thomas studied her as if she was a piece of meat. "She is about the same height," Gashcyoin soothed. "She'll do for rehearsal…"

"She is big… up here."

Trisha stood stock still as Miss Thomas prodded her breasts. She yelped as fingers dug into her buttocks.

"She is skinny, child. Arianna… she is curvy… like a woman. The gown needs curves," Miss Thomas wailed, tears pouring down her hollow cheeks.

"No, my cherub," Gashcyoin soothed. "She is the perfect balance. Young, firm breasts and a sexy bottom," he said, stretching the elastic on Trisha's nylon briefs. "The men… and the photographers will love her," he said, kissing Esther Thomas' hand. "And she will have been your discovery."

Trisha cupped her breasts with her hands. She didn't think Gashcyoin would paw her with Miss Thomas watching. But she was taking no chances.

"It is only rehearsal. Arianna will be back in time for the big finale," he soothed.

"People are starting to arrive and there's a long queue outside. And there's an army of photographers!" Lara squealed, peeping out from backstage.

"And no Arianna!" Esther Thomas howled, throwing her hands up in the air. Then, flattening her lips, she turned. Gathering Trisha's long, glossy curtain of hair in her thin hands, she twisted it up into a knot on top of her head. "Gown, accessories?" she shrieked.

"Flowing gown, virgin seductress," Gashcyoin puffed, demonstrating with his hands.

Miss Thomas scrutinised Trisha. *It might work.* The gown was pure silk. It would show off her young body, her vulnerability, and her high breasts. She frowned. *Gashcyoin was wrong. This girl was no virgin. She's known a man. She's already spoilt.* She glanced at the bulge beginning to appear in his pants. *She would not tell him. Not yet.*

Esther nodded at the dresser.

"Wait!" Gashcyoin panted. He gathered Esther's hands in his. "She mustn't wear anything that will impede the flow of the gown."

Silence fell over the models. Miss Thomas drew herself up to her full height. She knew exactly what Gashcyoin was asking. He had worked hard to produce the guest list. As "production manager", he was entitled to his perks. But what if it threatened her reputation or her couture collection?

A war raged within her. Other fashion houses were becoming more daring, more adventurous. Some of their models were even wearing topless swimwear. *Would it be a step too far or a brave step into the future?*

Trisha stood motionless before her. Her heart thudded. *This was the break I've been waiting for since I modelled the silk suit when I was thirteen.* But would she dare to wear nothing beneath the gown? She had seen Arianna model it backstage. Its sheer silk fabric fell in folds, accentuating her curvy body, leaving little to the imagination. *But if I didn't do it, I might never get the chance again.*

She visualised how it would shimmer and glow under the lights of the catwalk.

Miss Thomas had hinted that *Vogue* and *Glamour* scout photographers would be there tonight. And some of the girls had whispered that the Editor of the newest fashion magazine, *Chic Glitz,* would be there as well.

I'd sell my soul to be on the front page of Chic Glitz—just once.

The buzz on the front stage and in the auditorium was clearly audible now.

Time was running out. It was time to decide.

Miss Thomas reached a decision. *This is no business for the faint-hearted.* She snapped her fingers. A dresser materialised, and stripping away Trisha's bra and briefs, slipped a light body stocking over her naked body. There was an audible gasp from the assembled models.

Trisha felt her throat close over with excitement and trepidation. *I'm really going to do it. I'm going to walk down the runway wearing a couture gown. Not one that Lisa had remodelled from somebody else's design but a gown designed by a top fashion designer.*

Her knees trembled and sweat gathered between her breasts. She was afraid to lift her eyes to the mirrors propped around the room. An image of BJ came to her. *He'd be shocked. No, he'd be beyond shocked. But he doesn't understand what you have to do to make it,* she reasoned, pushing down her misgivings. *I'll do this. I'll do it as good as Arianna,* she promised herself.

"The theatre is full," Lara whispered in awe. "But I don't see anybody... Oh, yes, I do. I see..."

"Enough," Miss Thomas hissed as she watched the emotions wash across Trisha's face and body.

"You are very beautiful. You have the black raven beauty of the Celtic race. A beauty inherited from a proud and gallant people. Make your forefathers, and me, proud when you step on that runway," Esther commanded, towering over

Trisha. "I will make sure the lights are caressing, not too revealing…" She stepped so close to Trisha that she could feel the intense heat coming off Miss Thomas. "You know what your body can do for you. Use it tonight," she said, laying a bejewelled hand on Trisha's.

Trisha nodded, stiff with nerves.

"You are such a clever woman, my cherub," Gashcyoin gushed as he watched Trisha prepare her hair and take her appointed place. "She is a natural. And such poise for one so young," he gushed.

Esther smiled. *I've seen the hunger in Trisha's eyes. This little scrap of humanity, this little nobody could be my passport to bigger and greater things,* she gloated. She glanced at Gashcyoin. *If it works, I'll need protection, at least for the time being. If it doesn't work and the fashion press berates the young novice model for her wickedness… so be it.* She shrugged. *Gashcyoin will find other work for a model willing to sell her soul. No doubt, there will be a few directors and producers in the audience who would be willing to use her beauty and her talent in other ways,* she mused.

A hush had fallen over the auditorium. Esther took up her position out of sight and scrutinised the seated guests. As usual, the most prominent and prestigious fashion house editors, handpicked celebrities, and their entourage were seated in the front rows alongside the buyers. The photographers were strategically placed at the end of the catwalk to get the best shots of the models as they sashayed towards them.

Then Trisha was on the catwalk.

Flashbulbs popped again and again. Esther noticed that most of them were for Trisha.

Clothes were changed, and make-up and hair refreshed in a flash. Esther's eyes misted over. The colours were fabulous; the fabrics breathtaking. The models, stunningly beautiful, showed what clothes could do for a woman.

Esther knew that tonight she was not competing directly with the new mass-production markets off Kings Road and Carnaby Street. But fashion was like shifting sand. The small boutiques and new department stores were a thriving business. She knew that some of the garments in her collection would be made up in cheaper, more accessible fabrics and styles, but for tonight she revelled in her creations and her models.

The night was going well. She could sense it in her bones. She gritted her teeth. She'd deal with Arianna later. Her coveted trip to Paris was definitely off.

Trisha was too inexperience yet for the older, more established fashion houses. But there were plenty more ready to fill Arianna shoes, she thought.

Trisha's heart thudded like a drum as she heard her music cue and made her entrance for the second time. Now that her chance to make it big was here, she was terrified. What if her high stiletto heel caught on the hem of the long, sweeping tail of the gown? What if they didn't like her? Or, she forgot the routine she was supposed to follow? Placing one foot in front of the other in a swaying movement, she sashayed across under the lights and against the backdrop of staged images that accentuated the style and glamour of the collection. Her palms felt slick with sweat, and she could feel small rivulets of it gather between her thighs. Every sinew in her body was tensed.

It was impossible to see anything or anybody over the footlights, but she could hear the applause and see the photographers' bulbs flash.

A lull fell as she started out on her last walk, wearing Arianna's gown. More confident now, she remembered Miss Thomas' murmured words. *You know what your body can do for you. Use it tonight.* This was perhaps her only chance. At nearly eighteen, she was still young but younger, more twiggy-like models were coming up fast behind. She knew how to use her body. It had got her through school and saved her from the girls who called her names and mocked her Irish accent. Wearing the school's hottest guy on her arm gave her advantages. Then, there was Stu. He was crazy out of control, but he had the drink and the ability to make her forget for a while that her father didn't love her and that her brother was in jail.

She wondered who was in the audience. Lara said that sometimes they'd get asked to parties afterwards. "Or some photographer might take a fancy to you and date you for a while," she'd giggled. Caught up in the excitement and wonder of it all, Trisha felt her nipples begin to harden and push against the flimsy translucent material.

She glided to the end of the catwalk and slowly pivoted as the bulbs flashed and the back light illuminated her figure under the gown.

An audible gasp went up from the audience.

"She's not wearing any underwear," somebody said in a loud stage whisper. Then... silence.

A slow hand clap and a faint chant started at the front of the catwalk and slowly gathered momentum; a crescendo of sound filled the theatre and bounced off the walls. Trisha quivered under the onslaught of sound and the fevered flashing of the cameras. Momentarily stunned, she was unsure whether to keep to the routine or stand still. The house lights went up, and she glided backstage to the gleeful ogling of Gashcyoin and the baleful glare of the other models.

The clapping stopped. The sound died away. For a moment, nobody moved. The flashbulbs were curbed.

Then a man leapt up onto the catwalk.

"Let's raise our glasses to the most breathtakingly display of fashion and beauty in true art form I have ever witnessed," he asserted. "Madame Thomas, and the House of T'ASS, I congratulate you. Such beauty and fashion to grace a runway! Magnificent! Your Celtic, dark-eyed beauty? She will go far," he declared in an accented voice. "May we see her beauty one more time?"

Gashcyoin nudged Trisha on stage. She stood there for a minute, smiling. With the stage lights dimmed, she could see the audience. She was flabbergasted at the crowd and the waves and smiles. The flashbulbs crackled again. She gave a slight bow and walked backstage into the glaring face of Arianna.

"You little slut bitch, you stole my dress and my audience," she spat, hatred blazing from red-hot eyes.

Chapter 61

Trisha hugged herself to keep warm. "Even in summer, this place is like an icebox," she muttered. Pulling the red and gold shawl Lisa had made her off the sofa bed, she wrapped it around her kimono-style.

When she told people she lived in Knightsbridge, they raised their eyebrows as if to say, "Aren't you posh." It wasn't like that at all. Miss Thomas kept old loft studios that had once been owned by some famous music producer who had to flee the country; she used them as bedsits for junior models like herself and Lara. They place still had the arty, uncomfortable, low-slung sofas and floor cushions as seats.

The front door banged, and Lara's feet pounded up the stairs. "Trisha, Trisha," she shouted, banging both her fists on the door.

"You're never going to believe this!" She squealed, almost tripping over Trisha in her headlong rush into the room. "We're in *Chic Glitz*!"

As if it were a piece of valuable art, Lara placed the fashion magazine on the coffee table. They stared at it in stunned silence.

"Oh my God, it is us, at the fashion show," Trisha gasped, her legs beginning to wobble.

The fan mail that had come for her after the show had been from women's libbers berating her for allowing her body to be used as a sex object by the fashion industry.

"Listen to this," Lara breathed. "It says… new young hip models… Oh, it doesn't mention me by name, but it mentions you… Says you look exotic and sensuous… like sex on legs," Lara giggled.

Her whole body shaking, Trisha looked closer at the photo. She was looking straight into the lens of the camera. Her eyes seemed luminous; the lashes long and sweeping. She drew in a shuddering breath. She looked beautiful. The long silk gown seems to melt into her body, revealing the curve of her thighs and the upward sweep of her breasts. Her face flamed. The photograph exposed the shape of her hard, erect nipples as they push against the silken fabric. She felt a leap of excitement and, yes, pure pleasure, but when Lisa saw this, that would be the end of her modelling career.

Miss Thomas hadn't been mistaken when she said she knew how to use my body, she thought. *The only difference is that it seemed to do it of its own accord.*

An image came back to her of the day she had agreed to let Stu Moss feel her breast in exchange for the magazine he had stolen.

"That was the start," she murmured. She had practised posing in front of the dressing table mirror until she could pose like the model did in the magazine.

"Let's go up the King's Road and try on all the kaftans and beads in the shops," Lara said, clapping her hands in excitement.

"What about that private showing Miss Thomas said she might need us for?"

"Eeh, she didn't say for sure."

Trisha giggled. Lara was from Darlington, and when she got excited, her northern accent came back again.

"Come on, we'll be back before she misses us," Lara coaxed.

Trisha pulled on the new skin-tight jeans she had badgered Lisa into buying her. "Now I'll not have to get in a cold bath to get them to shrink to fit," she giggled as she donned a paisley-patterned blouse.

The pipes rattled a tune as she splashed water on her face. Applying a light coat of lipstick, she glanced at her reflection in the mirror. Apart from the long lashes—now without their lashings of black mascara and eyeliner—she could see little resemblance to the photo in magazine. She scraped her hair into a high ponytail and tied it with a bright yellow scarf. "You look more like a schoolgirl than a House of T'ASS model," she murmured to her reflection. "Let's hope the ticket collector on the London to Glasgow overnight train thinks so too," she mused. As soon as she got the private showing over, she was going home to Glasgow to see her uncle Billy.

"Ready," she called, pulling on her favourite high heels and slinging the handbag she had bought in the flea market in Petticoat Lane over her shoulder.

"Let's go to Carnaby Street and try on all the clothes there."

"We haven't got time. Miss Thomas…"

"We have time," Lara retorted.

Music blared from the small clothes shops squeezed in between greengrocers, butchers, and barbers, selling everything from kaftans to knickers.

Trisha's eyed widened. Clothes of all colours—bright reds and oranges in big swirling patterns, and blues and greens; blouses and skirts seem to come in every colour imaginable.

Further on, a street trader was shouting, "Not thirty, not twenty, but ten smackers for a top of the range radio. 'Ere, tune it in to… one of them rock 'n' roll stations," he shouted to a young boy who was helping him.

Laughing, the girls moved on as an old couple begin to dance to the music. "Eeh, look at that."

Inside, the haberdashery shop was like an Aladdin's cave. Material of all kinds and colours was draped over bamboo poles. Some of the more exquisite fabrics had been made into tapestries.

"It's like a magical place," Trisha said, her eyes shining. "My auntie Lisa would love this shop. When I have money, I'm coming back to buy some material for her to make me a shift dress," she vowed.

The turban swathed shop owner bowed. "Pretty lady always welcome in my shop," he said, giving her a wink.

They moved on to a dress shop heaving with women in different stages of dressing and undressing.

"I thought behind stage was crazy, but this is manic," Trisha giggled.

"Let's try something on," Lara said, reaching out for a red mini dress with broad diagonal white stripes.

Trisha grabbed a pair of electric blue hot pants. Then she spied a pair of long white cowboy boots that would go perfect with them.

The queue for the changing snaked its ways almost to the front door.

"Try them on here," Lara's muffled voice said from behind a rail of dresses as she dragged her top over her head and pulled on a blue and white paisley jumpsuit.

Trisha wriggled out of her jeans, shook her hair free from the restraints of the ponytail, and, trying on a pair of short shorts, pouted her lips in a mock kiss, striking up pose.

Her eyes scrutinised her legs. She seemed to be getting taller, but in the short, saucy shorts her legs looked toned and curvy. She sighed with relief. At five foot ten, she didn't want to grow anymore.

Just as she was undoing the button just above her crotch, she heard the voice.

"Welcome to clobber, Soho style," a man's voice sniggered.

Trisha froze, half naked, one hand tugging at the white cowboy boot.

Lara's unzipped maxi dress fell around her ankles.

Flash bulbs popped. "Not what you're used to, is it, my beauties," the photographer chortled as the camera snapped and flashed.

"Run for it." Lara bleated. Then, realising she was standing in her bra and baggy knickers, she scrabbled around for her jeans and top.

"Get out of 'ere, before I ram that camera where the sun doesn't shine," a woman bellowed.

"Just goin', darlin'. It's not every day you get House of T'ASS models shopping in your shop, is it? You should be paying me for the publicity I'm going to bring ya," the photographer laughed, still snapping away.

Panting breathlessly, they dodged into a noisy, crowded café.

"Eeh, that shop manageress didn't half look chuffed when she realised who we were. I got a dress, and you got a pair of boots, for free," Lara laughed.

She sniffed the air like a bloodhound. "Beefburgers," she sighed.

"We can't eat. We have a show tonight."

"Just a 7-UP… and we'll share a bag of chips," Lara pleaded.

"Oh, go on, it'll not show that quick. We'll probably work it off running out of other photographers' way now that we're famous," Lara giggled.

Trisha slid further into her seat. A woman across from her was feeding her handbag. Trisha watched as a ball of white fur popped its head out, took the offering of food and disappeared back into the bag.

"By, this looks good," Lara said, plonking a tray with two beefburgers and two 7-UPs on the table.

Trisha's flat stomach growled in appreciation at the sight of the food, but she knew as soon as she ate the burger, it would swell up.

"We're showing tunic tops and shift dresses tonight," Lara said, catching Trisha's hesitation. "Eat up," she said, licking her tongue around the tasty sauce that was oozing from her burger.

Trisha wrapped her burger in a clean napkin and placed it carefully in her bag. "I'll eat it after the show tonight," she muttered, ignoring Lara's hungry eyes on it.

"Maybe we'll get lucky and get asked to a party with food," Lara sighed.

"Miss Thomas will kill both of us if our picture is in some sleazy magazine next week," Trisha groaned.

Lara glanced at her. It was common knowledge amongst the older, more experienced models that girls as hell-bent on making it, like Trisha, could be used and abused by both the fashion houses and the photographers.

"You'll be OK. She sees something in you," she said caustically.

"Eeh, look at that! John Lennon," Lara said, stopping in front of a shop window where most of the televisions for sale were tuned into the Beatles singing, *Love, love is all ya need.*

"Fat lot of good love is to the poor buggers fighting in Vietnam," a man growled, pushing past them.

Lara was still humming the Beatles song as they pushed open the outside door of the flats and started up the stairs past the broken lift.

"The hippy squatters who live in the flat below us are always pushing the buttons," Trisha grumbled.

"They've asked us to a party Saturday night."

Trisha stopped. "Did you say we'd go?"

"Eeh… I said I'd think about it, and I did, and we're going."

Chapter 62

"Is that a letter from the lass to say she'll be here to bring in the New Year?" BJ said, puffing as he pulled on his boots.

"No," Lisa said shortly, "It's a wedding invitation and an invite to a 'hen' party for Cathy Swanton's upcoming wedding."

There was a letter from Andrew. He'd written to say he was back in Wiltshire and was volunteering to be part of an elite team who parachuted behind enemy lines.

Sipping her tea, she slit open a brown window envelope. "Probably another rent increase," she muttered. She glanced around her comfortable, airy kitchen with its tiled floor and gas central heating They had been offered it after the hospital consultant had written a stern letter to Glasgow Cooperation, stating that given BJ "serious health problems," he needed a house with a downstairs bedroom and toilet. They had been delighted to get the last house on a terrace of ten; new and modern, it was right on the edge of the countryside. Better still, it was away from the estate and the rowdies Trisha used to run with, she mused, and BJ was able to get out for short walks.

Her eyes scanned the letter. It was from a solicitor.

Dear Mrs McKnight,

You wrote some time ago regarding a will Mr Samuel Armstrong (deceased) had drawn up at the offices of Simms & Simms, Old town Road, Belfast. I would respectfully request you contact this office at your earliest connivance.

Respectfully Yours,
Fredrick Edwards

"What do you make of that?" She said, handing BJ the letter.

BJ read the letter and chucked it in the direction of the dog's bed. "There's no money to be got out o' that. It would just be throwin' good money efter bad. Am away up the road wi' the dog. She has more sense than some o' the women in this hoose," BJ grumbled.

"Does that include your darling Trisha?" Lisa retorted. She moved to the window and watched BJ throw a stick for the dog. As old Gordon says, she mused, "a feather could knock him down."

The ringing of the phone startled her. "Hello Mum," Andrew's familiar voice said. "Happy New Year te you and Da."

Lisa's heart swelled with pride. "You never forget, do you, son!"

"I was hoping to get back in time for the celebrations… but it's not looking like it now." Lisa thought she detected a note of something in his voice.

"Maybe you'll get some leave soon. Nothin' much goin' on here, anyway," she lied. "Hogmanay's not the same since we left the tenements," she said, trying to make light of what she knew would be a nice evening with her new neighbours.

"Think old Gordon and Madge will be your 'first footers' tonight for 1968?" Andrew asked.

"Hope they are, Andrew. New friends are nice, but old friends are like family," she said almost to herself. "Gordon always asks about you."

Andrew laughed. "It was a bit of luck him getting rehoused down the road from you and Da. How's Da and Isobel?" He paused. "Did Trisha do anything exciting for her eighteenth? Some of the lads have pictures of her pinned up in their lockers; is she still in London with Miss Thomas?"

Lisa sighed. "She doesn't come home much anymore. She and Isobel had a row… about the scanty clothes she wears for modelling."

"There were shots of her in the local Chronicle, and there was even one in a magazine," Andrew commented. He didn't mention Trisha's picture had been in *Playboy*.

There was silence for a few seconds. "Do you know where you're going next?"

"Don't know… yet. I've finished the… special course. Could be Cyprus or Northern Ireland. Your old home ground, Ma."

Lisa heart stilled. She had heard about the rising unrest over civil rights.

"Watch yourself, son. I'll be thinking about you." she choked out, preparing to hang up the phone before he heard her blubbering.

"Ma, I wanted to ask you. How long were you and Da married before I was born?"

Lisa let out a small gasp.

"Never mind; the money has run out—I'll talk to you about it when I get home on leave," Andrew said. Lisa heard the pips go, and he was gone.

She sat down heavily on the chair. She knew the day would come when she'd have to tell him.

Maybe she'd take Mary Kielty up on her invitation go up to London. It was time to tell Mary her husband, Scott, had another son—his firstborn son, Andrew.

Trisha. She spotted Lisa walking towards the barrier.

"How is Uncle Billy?" she asked as they made their way out into the street. Lisa bit back the retort that if she was that worried, she'd come home and see for herself. "He misses you coming home."

Trisha thought she sensed a feeling of anxiety in her aunt. "Stop rushing for a minute, Trisha, I'm not as young as I used to be. We'll stop for a cuppa."

Trisha looked at her. She looks less from the 'sticks'. Classier, she thought, taking in the nice two-piece costume suit with its fur collar and the nice leather shoes and handbag. Her hair was the only thing that spoilt the effect. She still wore it in a ponytail; its bushy frizz bounced up and down as she walked.

"Here's a pub does food," Lisa said.

"You wouldn't find Seymour dead in a place like this," Trisha said under her breath, reaching for the menu. Lisa had a way of wrinkling things out of her, and she didn't want to share Seymour with anybody. She thought of Lara. Lara loathed Seymour. *She's just jealous,* she thought.

"Ready ta order?" a rotund woman with permed, brown greying hair asked. Trisha scanned all the name of the dishes. *Ugh, fat and more fat,* she thought, curling her lip.

"We'll have chips, fish, and peas," Lisa said.

"Green salad and iced tea," Trisha instructed the waitress. The woman sucked the end of her pencil. "Sorry, darlin', not much demand for salad, green tea, or any other colour 'ere," she smiled.

"How many nights are we staying?" Trisha asked Lisa.

"It depends—one, two days maybe," she murmured. She had to have the conversation with Scott about meeting Andrew, his firstborn son. And despite how demeaning he had been with her in Ireland and ignoring her since, she still held fast to the dream that Scott had meant it when he said he loved her—always had and always would.

"Who will look after Uncle Billy?" Trisha said sharply, bringing Lisa back to the café.

"I need a break," Lisa said defensively, looked into Trisha's dark accusing eyes. *She reminded me so much of William,* she thought, *and so bloody self-centred.* "If you came home once in a while, it would help. Looking after your Uncle Billy tires me out and ties me to the house. I need a bit of fun in my life too," she snapped.

A frisson of guilt assailed her. Moving out of old Granny Mac's tenement flat had turned BJ into a lost soul. He depended on her for everything. If she mentioned going out, he became more helpless.

Trisha had tuned out to Lisa's moaning and went back to thinking about Seymour.

That first night as the private viewing ended, Seymour had materialised from the shadows, dismissed the other models and said, "Can you stay and have a drink with me?" She'd broken Miss Thomas's rule and stayed behind when the others, including Lara, left.

"…Why don't you come," Lisa was saying, bringing Trisha out of her daydreaming about her new boyfriend.

"Go where with you?" she said, surprised.

"Mary Kielty Osbourne," Lisa with a posh mock flourish of her hand, "is having a bridal shower for Kathy Swanton in the Mayfair Hotel. Come with me. At least I'll have something to boast about too," she said, looking at the tasteful way Trisha was dressed and her manicured nails and make-up.

Trisha shook her head. "I have a date," she said smugly.

Chapter 63

George's solicitor coughed discreetly. "I'm afraid your father isn't able to have you to live with him," he informed George. "You cannot be released until you have an address where your probation officer can visit you," he explained.

"What about my aunt Lisa? I could stay with her. She has a three-bedroom house!"

Stefan Goldsmith rustled some papers in his briefcase before clearing his throat. "It seems she has been responsible for your sister Trisha for some considerable years. She believes she has done her bit for the family."

George swore under his breath. The warden shifted his position and rattled his keys.

George smiled a knowing smile. "Maybe I know a few home truths her old man might be interested in hearing that might change her mind."

Stefan Goldsmith rose to his feet. "I hardly think blackmailing your aunt is a good start to your release, Mr Armstrong. Anyway, I have done all I can. I'm afraid you will remain here at her Majesty's Pleasure unless you can secure an initial release address."

George knew that the news that he wasn't being released because none of his family wanted him to live with them would be back on the cell block before him.

Sure enough, the jibes started as soon as the warden turned the heavy key and the first door clanged shut behind him.

"Ouch, poor wee orphan," a prisoner shouted.

"Nobody wants him," another voice shouted out. Somebody on the floor above started to roar out the words about no mother's arms to hold him when he cried.

George gritted his teeth and balled his fists. It had been a long time since he'd cried for his mother.

Knuckles, his old gang leader and first cellmate, had been in and out of boys' homes and remand schools all his life. He was tough, wild, and volatile. "Never show weakness. Not to the screws and not to any prisoner. Watch and learn, Baby Face," he'd advised.

The cell door banged shut behind George. But it held no terror for him now. Not like it had the first days and weeks when he'd been on remand, where one whispered lie by another prisoner meant a cell search where the guards overturned beds and withdrew privileges.

Throwing himself on his bunk, his thoughts went back to Knuckles. George soon noticed that the prison gang leaders like Knuckles kept the other prisoners in check and meted out discipline—until he was ambushed in the showers and ritually humiliated. Holding him down, his head and his genitals were shaved. Following his shameful demise, the guards would come and wrestle him to the ground, throw his bedding on the floor searching for weapons that he could use in a revenge attack. The first time it had happened, George had tried to help him.

"We're just doin' our job, Paddy. Butt out," a fat, burly guard hissed, clamping George's arms and legs in a grip like a vice and hurling him face down on the floor. The smell of sweat and bodily fluids had filled his nostrils. Knuckles had thrown the slop bucket over the guards. Face down on the cell floor, he listened to the terrifying roaring and shouting and banging from the other prisoners.

"You have a visitor, Paddy," Tobin, the prison guard, said, breaking his reverie. "Turning into a right party, ain't it? I spend more t time escorting you out and frisking ya down these days than I do anything else," he chortled.

George steeled himself for the body search.

"You know ye love it, sweet pea," a prisoner called from one of the cells. "Mind ya keep yer hands to yourself, Tobin. He's mine!"

A manic laugh followed the threat. George recognised the voice as that of Grudger, 'lifer' prisoner who was kingpin now. Even the guards feared him.

The other prisoners nicknamed him Grudger because if he took a grudge against you, he'd take his revenge. Now the crazy bastard had taken a grudge against him because he was being paroled. George hoped he'd get out or transferred before the guards turned a blind eye and let Grudger at him.

"Who's the visitor?" George asked.

The guard smirked. "A looker, too good for scum like you, Paddy."

It must be Trisha, George thought as he waited for the guard to unlock and relock the cell block doors. He'd noticed the guards couldn't take their eyes off Trisha during her visits.

Looking at her, he could hardly believe she was his sister. The way she sat straight as an arrow and the way she carried her body when she walked; her long, gloss hair falling down her back like a black velvet curtain.

"Make it short. You're used up your extra privileges," Tobin grunted.

"Stella," George said in surprise. Then, shamefaced, he looked down at his clothes. "How did you know…?"

"Oh, you're still such a baby, ain't ya? It's in all the papers about ya getting let out—but no place to live. You're a regular mass murder now," she laughed. "You're never out of the news."

She looked him up and down. "You're still 'andsome, ain't ya—tougher, like." she chuckled. "'Ere," Stella giggled. "Your mug plastered over all the dailies, like you were a film star or sommit."

George shrugged. "You have to be tough to survive in this hellhole." He thought about what he'd had to do to be in Grudger's gang. He wasn't proud of it. *But without the pact I made, I'd never have survived,* he consoled himself.

"I suppose you were scared shitless… in the beginning?"

George gave a rueful laugh. "You could say that, darlin'," he said, imitating her cockney accent.

George's thoughts began to wander as Stella prattled on. He'd approached Grudger, naked, in the showers—a surefire death wish if the rumours were wrong.

Grudger portrayed himself as all male, but George had heard a sniggered whisper to the contrary. He didn't put him right when Grudger sneered, "You lonely without yer oul' waiter, mate, Baby Face? Need a little company to while away the lonely times?"

He wondered how many other people thought he and Ike Swann had been lovers. But it had worked in his favour. Grudger had kept him safe from the other prisoners.

Stella was right—up to a point—he still looked the same, but prison life had changed him forever. He'd never again be that innocent boy who had come to jail handcuffed to Detective Tomas Maloney.

"You still living with Ma Higgins or has the booze killed her since the last time I saw her?" he asked, dragging his mind back to the present.

Stella shifted in her chair. "I ain't livin' with her no more. When I told 'er about ya needing a place to kip, she booted me down 'ere to fetch ya back. You can 'ave the attic room if you clean up the place for her," she said.

George laughed out loud. "That's what she sent you four hundred miles to tell me? I could have the stinking attic room?"

"She always had a soft spot for ya. Even your old misery guts father and his screeching of a night didn't tempt her to kick ya out. Anyways, this ain't no Buckingham Palace, neither;" she sniffed, wrinkling her nose. "And you'd be free from all that slopping out, wouldn't ya?"

George thought about Grudger waiting for his chance. He wouldn't let him walk out unscathed.

George shuddered. He had to get out fast. *But living in Ma Higgins'! If the vermin didn't get him, the bloody freezing cold would. But I have a few scores to settle. I can't do that from in here,* he thought.

"She'll get paid for 'ousing an ex-con," Stella said in a wheedling voice.

George laughed. It was so long since he had laughed—really laughed. It felt good and reminded him how Stella had taught him the skills to survive in the jungle of London. "So that's it. She's after the money for the booze."

Stella nodded.

"You've always looked out for me," George said, leaning closer to her.

"No touching," the guard barked.

"Oh, give over, little fart—all blab and no balls. If you didn't 'ave that uniform... I've seen your kind..."

"Tell Ma Higgins if the governor agrees, I'll come and clean the place up for her, but I want a room downstairs," George said hurriedly before Stella got locked up too.

Chapter 64

George stepped out through the door out into the weak January sun, grasping the kitbag and a brown paper bag. "We'll take the Tube. It the handiest way to get to Croydon," Detective Tomas Maloney said.

"Whatever you say," George said, surprised to find that the volume of traffic, the screeching of speeding fire engines, and police sirens were making his nerves jangle. He hadn't expected to feel threatened by getting back into the rush and bustle of things again.

A bus whizzed past, inches from him.

"It takes a bit of getting used to again. Why don't we go and get something decent to eat and watch the world go by for a while?" the detective suggested.

Tomas looked at George as he waited for their food to arrive. Prison had changed him. He still had that baby face, but a cold, hostile, fearless toughness emanated from him. Whatever he learned inside, it wasn't for the better. Tomas sighed.

"Things have changed since you went inside," he began.

George sneered. "Yeah, I know. The Brits and the Americans are fighting in Vietnam, and flower power and the Beatles are here."

Tomas looked into George's cold eyes. "That and a whole lot more. You have a record now. Finding a job and somewhere decent to live, given that you're Irish, is not going to be easy."

George wanted rid of him. He'd been useful while he'd been inside, but he had no use for a minder now.

"I'm British, not Irish," he snapped.

"He still mouthing that same oul' shite?" a voice said.

Nearby, choking on the steak, George looked into the face of Mickilo Martini.

Mickilo laughed, extending his hand. "Over here, mate; they don't give a fiddler's," Mickilo said, sitting down opposite George at the table.

George balled his fists as he looked at the chef sitting there in his whites, a tea towel tucked into the waistband of his trousers.

"I was keeping this till you got settled with Ma Higgins," Detective Maloney cut in hastily. "But this is as good a time as any," he hurried on. "Mickilo has a job going… if you want it…" He stopped speaking. The incredulous look on George's face said *no bloody way, mate.*

"You not worried I might knife the punters?" George sneered. A feeling of satisfaction ran through him when Mickilo had the grace to look ashamed.

"You're not interested, then?" the chef said, relieved.

His conscience is not going to be that easily wiped clean, George thought. "What's the job?"

"The pub restaurant here is not as fancy as the Mayfair Hotel. But if you're interested, it's £2.50 a week, board if you want it, and all you can eat. Oh, and one other thing: You start on dishes in the kitchen."

George's head shot up. That had been his job when he first started in the hotel, and it had been the job he'd been made do in prison. He was finished with washing the arse of other people's pots.

Mickilo laughed. "Settle down, wee lad, I'm takin' the piss. You start here in the bar, serving the food. Shift work—early mornings, midday to evening, and when I need you."

George laughed manically as he left the restaurant. There was a God after all, and he'd just handed him the solution to completing his first piece of "business."

He'd use Sheamie Foy's old trick. He'd keep Ma Higgins well drunk with whiskey. She was going to be his alibi when he took his revenge on Mickilo Martini.

He'd even get paid while he planned how to do it.

Chapter 65

Sheamie nodded to Rosie to set up another round of drinks. Wiping down the bar, Rosie laid out a clean beer mat and placed a fresh pint in front of him. He took a long swallow before he turned and called, "Mickilo, me old mate."

Rosie grew cautious. It was always wise to be careful when Sheamie Foy talked in that soft, lilting Donegal brogue. Rosie knew he bore Mickilo a grudge. The Bible was sacrosanct to them; they didn't take kindly to Mickilo swearing lies on it. These rough, tough, hard-hitting, hardworking men had great respect for their religion.

"You still bedding that lying bitch with the crocodile tears," Sheamie asked, his voice rising.

Quickly, Rosie cleared the empty glasses and bottles off the bar.

"Young Armstrong stole the bloom off the rose; beat ye to it there, so he did," Sheamie sniggered.

"Sheamie," Rosie cautioned. "You know the house rules. Starting a fight…"

"Ouch, come on, Rosie!" Sheamie shouted. "I was only saying…"

"And you'd be right. We live and learn, so we do," Mickilo agreed, lifting his pint in a salute to Sheamie. Expect some of us never learn, he thought, already regretting listening to his conscious and giving George Armstrong the waiter's job.

"Women!" Sheamie said, his anger temporarily mollified.

Rosie kept her guard up. Mickilo Martin had a fiery temper that went with his half-Irish, half-Italian genes. She wondered what he was doing here tonight.

"The boss in tonight, Rosie?" he asked. "He usually gives us a few bottles of sherry for the Christmas Bazaar ticket draw. Maybe you'd mention it to him?"

Rosie nodded, keeping her eye on Sheamie, who was making his way down the bar closer to Mickilo.

"A drink for this man," he said, draping his arm around Mickilo's shoulders. "I have it on good authority that he's one of the best chefs in London and he's very good to Father Agnew. Isn't that right, young Martini? Isn't it the truth I'm saying?" he said, slapping Mickilo on the back. "Sorry for my remarks earlier. Me mouth ran away wi' me... again."

Mickilo shrugged. "If I'd known as much about that bitch Marta then as I know now, I'd have kept my trap shut," Mickilo admitted.

Sheamie took a slug of his beer. "That's good enough for me. Mind, you'll have to sort out the lying on—what is it your proddy fella, William, calls it, Rosie? The Good Book, with Father Agnew," Sheamie warned, looking first at Rosie and then at Mickilo.

"Already done," Mickilo lied. "I've went one better, me old mate. I've given young Armstrong a job," he said triumphantly.

"Well then, there only one thing left to do. Have one for the road with me," Sheamie hiccupped.

Relieved, Rosie began to clear up as the two men shared grievances over their beer.

"No digs or work or any bloody thing arranged for when he got here. Dragging that poor lad to England the very day his poor mother was put in the ground; took him away from a posh grammar school! Is it any wonder the lad went buck crazy and stabbed oul' Swann? If bloody Rosie only knew the half of it, she'd chuck him out on his arse!"

Hearing Sheamie mention her name, Rosie stopped washing up the dirty glasses to listen.

"George told Marta... No, wait till you hear," Mickilo was saying in a conspiratorial whisper as Sheamie straightened up, clenching his fists at the mention of Marta's name. "George told her that his Da beat the youngest girl with his belt or anything he could get his hands on," Mickilo said, stopping to take a deep drink from his glass. "The mother died from TB." Mickilo continued, "Armstrong couldn't bloody stand the sight of her—left her by herself for his sister—in a farmhouse in the arsehole of Donegal."

Will never mentioned any of that, Rosie thought. She was beginning to realise she knew very little about Will.

"Lousy northern proddy bastard," Sheamie was saying, bringing Rosie out of her reverie. "He better not show his bloody face about here looking for work," he spluttered, wiping a big calloused hand over his mouth.

Chapter 66

The Hair O' the Dog pub was crowded and noisy. The singing and raucous laughter were ear-splitting. William ignored the catcalling and drunken roaring and elbowed his way to where Foy was at the bar. Sheamie was shouting something at him. *Maybe I'm in luck for a start,* he thought.

A sense of relief washed over him. The engineering works had all but moved to Scotland now. Some days he regretted that he hadn't moved to Glasgow with them. "No point in cryin' over spilt milk," he muttered as he pushed in beside Sheamie.

Without warning, Sheamie's first shot out and caught him a thunderous blow along the side of the head. William staggered backwards over a table. He could hear men swearing and roaring profanities about their spilt drinks. The next blow lifted him off his feet. He felt a whoosh as a blow connected with his nose. He flayed wildly with his arms, but he was no boxer. He felt the crunch of bones. His ears were ringing and his eyes dazed as blow after blow rained down on him. Others had joined the fight now. A boot caught him in his gut, doubling him in two. Defeated, he crumpled. His head bounced off the iron rungs of the bar stools on his way down. A boot caught him a glancing blow between his legs. "That's enough," he heard Shay's voice roaring.

"That'll be little to what you'll get if it's ever heard you're beatin' that wee daughter o' yours again," Sheamie bellowed in William's face.

A haze of pain filled his mind. His instinct for survival gave William's legs the strength to make for the head for the door. Out in the street, he caught a glimpse of his bloodied face and clothes in a shop window before his legs folded under him.

The flashing ambulance sped past the bus stop with its siren blaring. "That sound always reminds me of the night my hubby was killed during the Blitz," Rosie murmured, climbing onto the bus. She'd had a nice time looking at the shops all done up for Christmas and listening to the lovely carol singing by the Salvation Army.

She glanced at the paper somebody had left behind them. British Rail was looking for clippies, male and female. "A cheery personality and be prepared to do shift work and weekends." She pursued her lips. "Maybe it's not for Will, but I might 'ave a go—sick of cleaning up and listening to drunks like Sheamie Foy," she muttered as she got off the bus and headed for home.

The doorbell chimed. *That'll be Will now,* she thought. "Forget your key… again." Her voice trailed off when she saw the two serious-faced police constables standing on the step.

"Mrs Kitchenn?" the tall, skinny one said, taking off his peaked cap and tucking it under his arm.

Rosie nodded.

"Does William Strong live here?"

Rosie shook her head.

The policeman looked perplexed. "You sure, dear?" he asked.

"I fink I'd knows who live 'ere," Rosie said.

"It's just that a man was taken to St Christopher's Hospital earlier today, and he gave your name and this address to the ambulance crew," the WPC with him said.

The nurse busied herself with the bag of blood and the monitor beside the bed.

Choking back her tears, Rosie looked down on the battered, unconscious face of William.

"Is he hurt badly?"

"The doctor will be able to explain it all to you. What relation did you say you were to the patient?"

"I'm not a relation."

"Oh, in that case I'm afraid…"

"He's been livin' wi' me," Rosie said, her face going pink.

"I'll let the doctor know you're here," the nurse said, giving Rosie a surprised look. *Probably thinks love is only for fresh young things like 'er,* Rosie thought.

William winced in pain and pulled a face as he tried to shuffle himself up on the pillows. "The doctor says I'll not be able to work for a while," he moaned.

"We'll manage," Rosie said, curling her fingers around his hand. "There are some things more important than money. I knew that the night I watched you struggling to draw breath," she said softly.

"I'll make it up to you, Rosie," William said, squeezing her hand.

Trisha's letter crackled in Rosie's coat pocket. She wanted to come and see her father. The letter had been stiff and distant. She had asked if she could see Will on his own. Rosie got the message. She was just the woman who kept William warm in bed at night. It galled Rosie. She had been the only one sitting by William's bed in between her shifts on her new job as a clippie all over Christmas and the New Year.

Hesitantly, Rosie took Will's hand in hers and looked at him. "Trisha wants to come and see you."

William's face contorted with rage. He balled his fists as much as the bandages would allow. "She's the devils spawn," William snarled.

"I haven't heard that expression—the devils spawn—since I was at Sunday school," a voice said, yanking back the curtain at the side of the bed.

Rosie face flamed. "I'm very sorry, doctor. Will is just a bit upset…"

"Any particular reason?" the doctor said, picking up William's notes from the end of the bed.

"His daughter, Trisha…" Rosie stammered. "She wants to come and see 'im."

"I don't have a daughter," William bellowed, beating his fists on top of the yellow counterpane on the bed. He glared at the doctor "Where's the other one?" he rasped.

"What other one?" Doctor North said briskly, motioning for the nurse to draw the curtains around the bed.

"He means the other doctor what's been looking after 'im since he came in," Rosie said.

"And you would be…?"

"Will's common-law wife for the past three years," Rosie retorted, surprising herself.

"I see. Wait outside while I examine my patient. I need to have a word with you," the doctor said with a dismissive nod of her head.

"What's this about Mr Armstrong's daughter?" the doctor asked. To Rosie's surprise, the doctor had poured her a cup of hot tea out of a flask.

"Every time her name's mentioned, he gets in a strop. That's all I know," Rosie said. "Except Will was in the army and was a POW. But he never talks about it. He just has nightmares about it."

The doctor looked Rosie straight in the eye. "Does William have aggressive mood swings?" She watched Rosie's hand twitch on the strap of her handbag.

Waiting for the train on the Piccadilly Line, Dr Heather North thought about William calling his daughter the devil's spawn. "He may well be suffering from trauma," she mused. One thing was certain, she thought as she sprinted up the stairs from the underground: Rosie Kitchenn had a soft spot for him. "But how long will she be able to endure the moods swings and the drinking that inevitably follows mental health brought on by war trauma?" she murmured, dropping a coin to a limbless man begging on the corner.

Chapter 67

"Why am I surrounded by effing eejits?" Mickilo growled as a tray laden with food wobbled precariously in the hands of the latest trainee waiter.

"Stay a bit later tonight, Armstrong. Can't you see there are customers waiting to be fed, including bloody Marta?" Mickilo scowled. "She's turned into a right wee slapper," Mickilo muttered. "I don't want her about the place."

"Oh, so you realise she's a manipulative, scheming easy lay," George had said sardonically. "Pity you didn't realise that before you stood up and swore…"

"Aye, and it's a pity you couldn't keep your thieving hands to yourself in Smithfield Market in Belfast, and then maybe…"

"Is this a private argument, or can anybody join in?" a voice said, interrupting yet another heated argument between them.

"Detective Maloney, me oul mucker," Mickilo exclaimed. "I thought with all the civil rights marches in the North, the Royal Ulster Constabulary would need you at home," Mickilo sighed.

"Yeah, it's getting serious now, alright. Car bombs are a daily occurrence," Tomas agreed.

George swore voraciously under his breath. "Fuck! He had planned tonight as the night." The vision came to him again: Mickilo, in full chef's uniform, mouth gaping open, hanging by the neck on one of the butcher hooks in the walk-in freezer among all the other dead carcasses. The image in his mind's eye made him smile.

No way could he chance locking that bastard Mickilo in the freezer with the cop hanging about on the pretence of wanting a steak.

"You off then?" Thomas Maloney said, disappointed. He had hoped to talk to George.

"Ma Higgins doesn't like to be kept waiting for her drink," George sneered, indicating the brown paper bag in his hand.

A dim light was shining from under Ma Higgins' bedroom door. George listened for the raucous laugh and her usual string of obscenities when he didn't come straight in with the bottle he'd brought her home.

The house smelled foul but somehow he didn't notice it as much now. "That's what comes of spending years sharing a cell with slop-out bucket every day," he mused.

Jail had taught him to trust his instincts; follow his gut feelings. It wasn't the smell that was bothering him tonight. It was the silence. Tonight, his gut was telling him something was wrong.

He went down the hall and knocked on Ma Higgins' door. No response. He knocked louder. "You there, M?," he called, turning the handle. *Maybe she had no callers tonight and had gone out to get the drink herself,* he thought.

To his surprise, the handle of the door opened under his hand. The hairs on his arms stood up. It was very rare for Ma Higgins, drunk or hungover, not to put on the army of bars and locks she kept on her door.

"You here, Ma?"

A rancid smell filled his nostrils. He fumbled for the light switch. The old-fashioned black Bakelite switch clicked, but nothing happened.

"Must be no money in the meter," he muttered. Holding his hand over his mouth and nose, he went further into the room and flicked his lighter.

Then he saw her. She lay upside down behind the old iron bed like a bundle of old rags. There was a big gaping hole between her two eyes.

"Who did you say you were?" the doctor on duty at St Christopher's Hospital asked.

George cursed his stupidity in coming in the ambulance with Ma Higgins… He had spent the time since his release keeping a low profile.

"Her lodger—came in from work and found her."

"You'd better have a word with the police before you leave," she said, nodding her head in the direction of the corridor where a uniformed officer stood waiting.

"How… bad is she, doctor?"

The doctor shook his head. "If she makes it through the night, she might have a chance. But she has lost a lot of blood… and she has a large amount of alcohol in her system."

George's heart plummeted. If Ma Higgins died, the cops wouldn't go to too much trouble to find her killer. Not when they had a readymade ex-con like him living in the house where she had been attacked.

Nurses bustled in and out, their stiff starched aprons and caps bristling and rustling in the still of the night. In a nearby ward, someone cried out in their sleep. The fear-filled cry set George's already jagged nerves on edge. It reminded him of how his father used to cry out in his sleep. He wondered if Rosie chucked his father out after his visit to her.

"She soon showed you the door, Georgie boy," he scowled to himself.

"Get out o' my 'ouse before I call the peelers," she ordered, poking her finger in his chest, her cold blue eyes staring into his. "And 'ere," she had shouted after him defiantly, "don't you go botherin' me and your old man—unless you want to end up back in the clink."

The clicking of the monitor and the gurgle of the array of tubes and machines that were keeping Ma Higgins alive was the only sound in the room.

He moved over and looked out on the lights of the city. Traffic still trundled, and the lament of a late train could be heard.

He walked back and looked down at the still figure of Ma Higgins in the bed, thinking Stella should be here.

Ma Higgins gave a low gurgle in her throat as if she agreed with him.

"You have to leave now," the nurse commanded, bustling in as the emergency lights on the machines started to flash.

"Stella needs to be here," he blurted out as the doctor rushed past him, letting the ward door shut behind him.

George stood for a minute. Then he started down the corridor. "Stella should be here," he said again, stopping beside the policeman.

"Stella? Is she Ma Higgins' daughter?" the grey-haired, tired-looking copper asked, taking out a small black notebook.

"No! Yes!" George stammered.

"Well, what's it to be? Is she her daughter or not?" Constable John Deere watched the mix of emotions flash across George's features. Licking the stub of a pencil, he started to write. "Do you know where we can find this Stella?"

George shook his head. He suspected the reason Stella had wanted him back living in Birch Hill Avenue was because she had wanted to get away and needed someone who would keep an eye out for Ma Higgins. How could he explain that Stella had been a missing child that Ma Higgins had found kept without informing the Old Bill or Social Services? If Ma Higgins survived, she'd be done for kidnapping.

"I haven't seen her in over a year. She used to lodge, sort of permanent, with Ma Higgins, but she moved on," he said.

"What age is she?" John shot out.

George shrugged. "Don't know, thirty, maybe."

PC Deere furrowed his brows. He'd had a word with the ambulance crew who had brought Ma Higgins in.

"Haven't seen or smelt nothin' like that house for a while," the driver had commented.

"It was bad, then?"

"A hobo's paradise," his colleague said, shaking his head.

"I think you're not being straight with me, mate. I think you know a lot more about this Stella and the mugging of that poor wrecked mare than you're letting on," the PC stated, pocketing his notebook.

George's gut was urging him to get away, to sprint out into the night and disappear. But his legs refused to move. He had a feeling if he left, he'd never see Ma Higgins alive again. His glance slid back to the closed ward door. He'd slip in and see her again before she died; whisper thank you in her ear for taking him in when nobody else wanted him.

"It's nearly daylight," he said, watching the purple and orange dawn colours spread across the sky. "The doctors said if Ma Higgins made it through the night, she might have a chance."

Despite himself, PC Deere felt a stab of pity for the lad. "If he doffed the old woman, he's a bloody good actor," he mused. He studied him: clean-cut, stylish clothes, baby-faced, blond hair curling around the collar of his coat, tense body. "I'll bet my pension he's been in trouble with the law before; might even been inside," he mused.

"Kind of fond of your old boozy landlady, ain't ya? For a young lad," he stated.

George stared at the ward door. "Last time I heard, there was no law against that," he retorted, watching the ward door open as the doctor he'd spoken to earlier came towards him.

"I was just going off night duty. I thought you would be still here," the doctor said, looking at George. "I'm sorry to tell you, Mrs Higgins has just died."

PC Deere stood up. "You'd better come down to the station with me. It won't take long. Just a formality—since you found her."

Chapter 68

"You have a track record of vicious attacks on old, vulnerable 'um. Didn't think you went in for old ladies; thought you were more of a cock and balls man. Handy with a kitchen knife, an' all I hear."

"I told you. I found her lying in her bedroom when I came back from work, and I called an ambulance. I never harmed a hair on her head. She was a guzzler. But she was good to me."

"What were you doing in your landlady's bedroom?"

"I bring her drink," George admitted.

The copper snorted. "Yeah, that figures—typical Irish! Pay your rent that way, did you? Steal drink from Mickilo Martini—the hand that feeds you?"

George clenched his teeth together. "It was to keep her from goin' out…"

"You were keeping her a prisoner? She went out when you told her not to? When she got back, you decided to teach her what's what?"

George put his head in his hands. He could hear the clang of the prison gates as they closed behind him. These two were going to stitch him up.

"I never laid a hand on her… She was like a… kind of mother to me." He lifted his head and stared in shocked disbelief at the impassive faces of the two policemen. Fuck! He couldn't believe he had just blurted that out.

"You're free to go… for the time being. Don't go anywhere, Mr Armstrong. We'll be seeing you again."

Every step up the corridor was like a mile. Every second, he expected a hand on his shoulder and a voice saying he was under arrest for the murder of Ma Higgins.

His bag of clothes hit him full force as he pushed open the swinging doors into the restaurant's kitchen. "You're out of here. I must have been bloody bonkers to think you'd wise up," Mickilo bellowed, his eyes out on stalks.

George felt his hands start to twitch. He could almost feel them squeezing the life out of Mickilo. He glanced around at the other staff. Everybody was suddenly very busy. His eyes fastened on the walk-in freezer at the back of the kitchen. An image of the chef hanging from a meat hook among all the other dead meat rose up and mocked him. There was no chance of that plan working now.

He looked to where Mickilo was standing beside the hot plate. It would be sizzling hot at this time of the evening. He could rugby tackle Mickilo, smash his face on the red-hot cooker. It would do until he finished him off.

Moving, Mickilo picked up a meat cleaver and started to pummel a piece of steak. "It has your hands all over it. The cops think so too," he said, beating the steak viciously. "That's your game; you go about picking on the old and defenceless—them that are helpless to protect themselves."

George opened his mouth to say, *All that will change when I get the chance to kill you, you bastard.* He snapped his mouth shut. *Why warm him? The element of surprise will give me the advantage,* he thought. Picking up his bag of clothes from where it had rolled under a table, he turned on his heel and started out the door.

Macklin's cursing obscenities followed him. "Fuck you, half-breed," he yelled, almost toppled Det Maloney on his way out. Pushing past him, George lengthened his stride.

"There's no point in goin' back to Birch Hill Avenue," the detective said, catching up with him. "The forensics boys have it sealed off as a crime scene."

George thumped the bag on the pavement and cursed. Lack of sleep and the death of Ma Higgins were beginning to catch up with him. His head throbbed and his bones ached. "What the fuck are you doing here?" he snarled at the detective, certain Maloney had been sent to babysit him until his friends in the MET could drum up something to pin on him around Ma Higgins' death.

"Go easy on the oul bag," Tomas said. The chef Mickilo had been keeping him up to date. He'd phoned, ranting and raving about the police taking George in for question for the death of his landlady.

It wasn't the best of timing to get time away. Things were beginning to heat up in Belfast, with people from the Shankill and the Falls Road getting fighting to protect themselves from each other; his chances of getting leave to keep an eye on George Armstrong in London were running out.

"Tell you what, we'll eat first and then see about getting your things out of Ma Higgins' house. I'm staying in a B&B with a wee Belfast woman. She'd give you a bed for the night. You look like you could do with it."

George's teeth clenched on the bone of the chop he was eating. This guy was like a bloody sticking plaster—a real pain in the arse! Slowly, he put the chop down and placed his clenched fists on either side of his plate. "What the fuck is it with you? Every time I turn round, you're bloody there! You one of them Special Branch, out to keep an eye on me because I'm from Northern Ireland?"

Tomas scooped up the last of the peas on his plate and laughed. Then his face sobered. "I think you might be the son of an old girlfriend—back in the day…"

George's eyes bored into the detective's. "You know nothing about my mother! So, keep your bloody mouth shut."

The detective stilled. George was in a foul mood. *But this opportunity might never come again,* his inner voice warned him. Reaching into his inside pocket, he withdrew the small, grimy picture of a woman from his wallet.

George clamped his jaws into a hard line and clenched his fists. "You sick bastard. This is some kind of trick, isn't it? You got it out of some file or something," George scoffed, staring at the small black-and-white photo of his mother.

She was laughing into the camera. He was struck with the resemblance to himself. Pain squeezed his heart. He gulped. She hadn't been happy like that when she lived with his father.

"Where did you get it? Can I keep it? I don't have any photos of her."

Tomas ran his thumb over the face in the photograph before carefully putting it back into his wallet. He rose and turned his back on George. "She gave it to me the night before I left Waterford to go up North to join the Inniskilling Fusiliers. I helped defeat Hitler. But your father married my girl," he said inaudibly.

George stared at the detective's back. He'd never met anybody, except his Aunt Lisa, who had known his mother. He wanted to know more about her.

Chapter 69

Trisha's back and arms ached, and her feet felt like two blocks of ice. It had been a long, long day.

"It's too set, too theatrical. I want factory—working class, not Hollywood dolls," Claude, the photographer, fumed, dissatisfied with what he saw through the lens of his camera.

Lisa knew she was lucky that Miss Thomas even permitted her to do photoshoots for catalogue clothes after what she had been stupid enough to get entangled with Seymour.

"I want the natural look—hair blowing in the wind, like the girl with the sticky-up hair that resembled a curly afro. The girl you were too ashamed to be seen shopping with for her wedding dress."

"You mean our Isobel?"

Claude ran his fingers through his hair impatiently. "Yes! When women look at you—at the clothes—I want them to see them wearing them."

Trisha thought of Isobel with her mop of appallingly badly cut hair. She shuddered. "I'd throw myself in the Thames before I'd be seen looking like Isobel," she muttered.

Isobel and her boyfriend Ewan had arrived unannounced and uninvited to Claude's studio in fashionable Knightsbridge. "Ma says you know all the best places to shop," Isobel had said, flashing a tiny diamond engagement ring.

Trisha's eyes swept over Ewan and then back to Isobel. They looked like hillbillies. *She wouldn't be seen dead in any of the places she could take them now that Seymour was dating her,* she'd thought.

Seymour, handsome, filthy rich and, as it turned out, slimy. He had almost cost her modelling career. Despite his betrayal, even thinking about him sent a tingling feeling through her. Seymour had introduced her to a lifestyle she could have only dreamt of. The clicking of the photographer's camera shutter faded away as she relived those few heady months dating Seymour.

With his privileged, moneyed background, he had brought her to a world of high-class restaurants, high-society parties and sleazy hippie squat where LSD and marijuana were offered and used as a matter of course. "And all I had to do was be photographed romping about with him." She sighed deeply. "I thought he was going to ask me to marry him," she murmured. She had seen the perfect engagement ring in Tiffany's the weekend he had taken her to New York. She imagined the scene: the soft, lighting of a classy rooftop restaurant, Seymour down on one knee, a head waiter hovering discreetly with flutes of champagne.

"Miss Thomas is right. I'm a stupid cow," she said aloud.

Claude scowled at her. "You need to stay focused. Give me more of a mixture of glamour and the girl next door," he said irritably. "If you can't, I'll get one of the other models who can."

Trisha gritted her teeth. She wanted to strip off the stupid, revolting denim maxi pinafore and hideous cowboy boots that made her feet look like the boxes they boot had come in and fling them in Claude's face, but she daren't. She knew after the scandal and uproar the photography had unleashed, she was lucky that Claude was prepared to use her as a model.

"Change into the swimwear now," Claude ordered.

"It's blowing a gale…"

"Get changed and try to l look as if you are having fun. The shot is supposed to show that despite the British weather, you can have fun wearing off-the-peg clothes. Do you get it?"

"If you think women believe that, you're a bigger fool than I am," Trisha snapped, rammed the straw boater with its coloured streamers on her head and slipped the see-through mac over her two-piece swimwear.

Clenching her jaw to keep her teeth from chattering with cold, she clambered up the slippery stone steps in the weak December sun and clung to the rough steel rail of the promenade. Plastering a smile on her face, she looked out over the windswept empty beach. Waves as big as breakers crashed on to the shore, leaving foamy white shaving puddles dribbling in the sand.

Her mind went back to the days she had spent making love to Seymour, lulled into a mellow happiness as he told her he couldn't live without her. Ecstatic to be photographed with a top model and delighted his friends were jealous of his photo in *Vogue,* he wore me on his arm like a piece of expensive jewellery and discarded me like his outdated Saville Row cast-offs, she fumed. "But how was

I to know he would sell the photographs when I refused to be photographed doing more graphic stuff?"

"I'm losing the light," Claude called. "Don't forget about the Heathrow shoot; be on time and don't be hungover."

On impulse, Trisha decided to have something to eat at the Mayfair, Seymour's favourite place to eat.

"Evening, Miss," the doorman smiled, brushing the peak of his cap with his forefinger. He had once told her that his father before him had also worked at the hotel.

She smiled back at him. The flutter of nervousness she felt at dining alone receded a little.

"The usual, Miss?"

Trisha hesitated. Claude had made her sign a contract stating that any drinking while she was working on a set assignment with him would render her unemployed.

"Why don't I bring you a glass of the newest French champagne?"

I'll have a one glass, she thought. *I'll order a salad and some of the delicious fish chef does and then I'll go home, have a scented bubble bath and an early night,* she promised herself.

Her attention was caught by a brash laugh. She could see part of a man's arm and shoulder. *Whoever he is, he has a lot to say for himself,* she thought.

Her thoughts turned back to Seymour "Daddy's money sent him to prep school and then to Oxford. And later, it had secured him a place on the Trading Floor of the City. Money couldn't make the child in him forget that was all his father had ever given him," she murmured into the champagne.

I wonder, was that what attracted us to one another? Did we recognise the desperate longing in each other to be loved?

Placing her meal on the gleaming damask tablecloth, her waiter arranged her fish dish and a selection of small salad dishes.

"Bon appetite," he smiled. Breathing in the aroma of the fish, Trisha realised she was ravenously hungry as she began to eat.

"The gentlemen at the far table sent this, with their compliments," the waiter said.

Trisha looked at the glass of strange-coloured liquid.

"What is it?"

"It's a Wall Street Banger," the waiter said, the tips of his ears beginning to turn pink.

Trisha stilled. It was an obvious reference to the caption *Playboy Magazine* had used under the photo of her and Seymour romping naked. Miss Thomas' screaming words reverberated in her head like pistol shots.

"You wanton... slut! You will pay for this with your career," she'd screeched, flinging the magazine picture into Trisha's lap. "The fashion world is not forgiving. They have a long memory," she'd thundered. "How dare a little gutter snipe like you try to bring down the House of T'ASS? It has taken me years, years to get where I am today, and you dare to make it crumble." She'd screamed, towering over Trisha. "Your days of modelling couture collections are over. No decent fashion house will ever employ you again!"

Miss Thomas had scraped her nails, like talons, along the desk and bared her teeth. "You are a model of the House of T'ASS. I wish with all my heart you were not."

Trisha had leapt to her feet. Miss Thomas recoiled from her outstretched hand. Trisha had clung on. She had nothing to lose now. "Please, Madam! Give me a second chance," she pleaded. "It will never happen again."

"Enjoying your dinner?" Bennett, the head waiter, asked, gliding up to her table.

Trisha involuntarily glanced in the direction of the other table.

Bennett followed her gaze. He fiddled with the cuffs of his immaculate white shirt. Then he leaned towards her, and adjusting the cutlery, murmured, "I have had occasion to visit the Albert and Victoria Museum," he said sagely. "Not a lot different from the body art you find in popular magazines nowadays, in my opinion," he murmured gently. "It is unfortunate that some people don't see it that way," he said, gazing at the hooting men at the far table.

"It's very kind of you to say so," Trisha choked out. Bennett's fatherly face wobbled and flushed. Clasping her bag tightly, Trisha prepared to leave.

"If this is the way London beauties treat their visitors, I'm not surprised it's still a one-horse town," the voice behind her boomed, making her jump. Uninvited, the man sat down and pushed the unwanted drink at her. Trisha gave him one of Miss Thomas' famous icy stares.

"Little spitfire, aren't you, honey? My friends want to see the London nightlife. And we reckon you're just the gal to show us. Or anything else you fancy showing us," he chortled.

Something about his flushed, drunken face nagged at her memory. Had she met him at one of Seymour's parties?

"Last time I checked, I was neither a tour guide nor a prostitute," she said, pushing back her chair.

"True, but you do like having your face and your pretty little tutsy splashed across the front pages."

Incensed, Trisha lifted her hand and smashed it cross his face. There was a horrifying silence, then the click and the blinding light of a flashbulb.

Trisha stared in horror at the drink and glasses on the table and the horrified, bloodied face of the man across from her. She knew the photographs would be on Claude's desk by midnight and in the papers by morning.

Chapter 70

The buzzer on her intercom was blaring as Trisha fumbled her key in the lock. "You have a gentleman called," the doorman of her apartment building intoned. "He says he's your brother…"

"What the hell is going on? That old bugger should be in the Military Police. Where have you been? I've been waiting for hours…"

"What do you want, George?"

"Do I have to want something now before I can come and see you?"

Trisha eyeballed him. "Yes. Last time you wanted to shag Lara."

"What the hell kind of modelling were you doing today? Your hair looks as if somebody pulled you through a hedge backwards," George sniggered. "You go for the Isobel look now?"

Trisha ran into the bathroom and slammed the door.

"Why are you here, George?" she asked, coming back out while the bath water ran hot.

George shifted uneasily. "My landlady, Ma Higgins, was found with her head bashed in. Nothing to do with me; I only found her." he rushed on as Trisha startled. "I just need a place to stay. I'll kip on the couch. It's only for a few days. I was thinking about going home for a while. I thought you might want to come with me," he lied.

"I can't; Claude, the photographer, is in the middle of shooting the 70s, spring collection of dresses and beachwear." She stood up. "I'm going have a bath, and then I'm going to bed. I have to be at work early tomorrow. The sofa bed is the only bed there is."

George grinned. "We'll share."

Fully clothed, he lay beside Trisha in the narrow pull-out couch, resting his arm around her like he used to do when she was small. Through the quilt, he could feel her ribs. *Jesus, she's nearly a skeleton,* he thought.

"Granda's quilt—still your wee comfort blanket," he teased her, tucking it around both of them.

Trisha nodded. "Sometimes I roll myself up in it and try and see if I can still get the smell of the tobacco he used to put in his pipe."

"Golden Virginia, Mild blend," they both said in unison.

Trisha felt the warm feeling she always got when she thought about her Granda. "His favourite patch was the silky patch with the pink roses. It was from the pink blouse granny wore when she married him." In the darkened room, George felt her body relax into a giggle.

"Lisa had made me a laundry bag with a pull string to keep it in. I'll never part with it," she murmured.

"You ever think about home and the farm… about Mammy and when we used to live there?" Trisha asked.

"Not very often," George admitted. His hand brushed his pocket where a copy of the photo of his mother Detective Maloney had given him. He'd share it with her another time. "You go and see Da since he moved in with the barmaid?"

Trisha shook her head. "I went to see him in the hospital when the navvies beat him up, but he didn't want to see me."

"You got shot of slimy what's-his-name," George said quietly.

He thought back to when Trisha had shared a flat with Lara, one of the other models. Lara had taken him to the party downstairs in the hippies' flat. Trisha and a soaped-up guy with a posh accent had been kissing hot and heavy as they shared a joint. He'd tackled her about it the next day. Trisha had given him one her haughty looks. "I'm moving in with Seymour as soon as he asks me."

Lara had snorted. "He has her parading around like Lady Godiva… with him as the horse."

Trisha had glanced at George. "Seymour knows people… business people. He's promised to get me a part in a film." She'd turned cold, dark, hooded eyes on George. "I don't want you interfering in my life." If she'd slapped him across the face, George wouldn't have been more hurt.

"What happened?" he asked now.

"Seymour? He found another model to do the part in the film."

"Why didn't you do it?"

"It was… too gross."

George clamped his jaws together. "So, he lived up his name then, slimy see-more," he growled.

They lay listening to the creaks of the old house and the street outside quietening down.

"Uncle Billy wants me to go home for Hogmanay," Trisha said sleepily.

"I could stay for Christmas and go to Aunt Lisa's with you for the New Year," George offered. *That will get me out of London for a few more days—long enough for Detective bloody Maloney to piss off back to Belfast,* George thought.

Chapter 71

William snapped off the BBC News when he heard Rosie's key in the door.

"It's bitter cold out—cold enough for snow." Rosie shivered as she hung up her coat and came over, holding out her hands to the blazing fire. "Turn the news back on," she said, giving him a quick kiss. "It's been blaring out all day—about Northern Ireland and the rioting." Her heart had jumped in fear when she saw the news coverage of rioting and burning buses. She had serious doubts about going to Ireland, even for a short holiday.

"It'll not change your mind about going to Fermanagh?"

Rosie put her arm protectively around William's slumped shoulders. The beating in the 'Hair O' the Dog' had taken its toll.

"It'll be nice to see where you were born," she lied, handing him *the Daily Telegraph* and an old copy of the *Sunday Times.*

"No hats or scarves found the day, then?" William joked, holding on to her hand for a minute.

Rosie giggled like a schoolgirl. "Somebody left a packet of French letters—condoms," she said, her face going pink. "Must have been a disappointing weekend for 'im; still plenty left in the packet."

"Did you mention to your sons that you were going to Ireland?"

Rosie nodded.

Reggie had looked at her perplexed. Ron, her youngest had snorted. "If ya ask me, he's on to a good thing. Free rent, good grub and… all his home comforts," he ended in a rush.

"Well, nobody's askin' ya—either of ya. You 'ave homes and family o' your own. Don't ya think I deserve a bit of company?"

"She's beginning to lose 'er marbles," Ron had spluttered at his brother.

Rosie stilled. "Why are ya both here… together?" she asked.

Reggie shifted in his chair.

"We're going to Australia," Ron stated baldly. "We could get on the £10 fare the government is giving away."

Rosie had felt the kitchen tilt, then right itself.

"Australia?"

"Mum, it's mainly for the kiddies," Reggie, her firstborn said softly. "At least they'll have some kind of future there. What's here? Demonstrations about the Yanks fighting in Vietnam, drugs and stabbings, and the Irish fighting and arguing about religion."

Rosie felt her heart crack open at the thought of not seeing her grandchildren again; lips quivering, she swallowed down her tears.

"Do what you think is best for yourselves and the kiddies," she'd finally murmured.

"Did you 'ave your meeting with the doctor about how ya get in a strop over Trisha?" she asked. William dragging her mind back from the boys' impending sailing date to Sydney.

For an answer, William folded the paper over and shuffled out of the chair. "I think I'll have a kip." Rosie watched him start up the stairs, his hand on the rail like an old man.

"Will," she called gently, "I'll bring up a nice cuppa."

When the doctor at the hospital advised her William would benefit from seeing a psychiatrist, she had almost busted a gut. "Will 'as 'is odd ways but he ain't mad. He doesn't need to see a shrink," she had protested.

"I think you have Mr Armstrong's welfare at heart. With your support, he can attend as an outpatient."

"And she was right," Rosie mused as she carried the steaming cup of tea and a slice of currant loaf up the stairs. But this, Trisha thing, that might be a horse of a different colour, she mused.

"Don't go to sleep, darlin," she smiled, handing him the tray. William pretended to sigh but Rosie knew he liked it when they made love.

She lay curled into his side; her arm straddling his waist. "The doctor says I have some kind of… disorder," William's voice said into the semi-darkness.

Rosie snorted. There had been talk about giving William some kind of 'shock treatment.' This time Rosie had stuck to her guns. "No way are ya goin' to let them quacks mess about with ya—sticking' in them wires and fings in your 'ead."

She could feel the soft rise and fall of Will's chest. He was asleep. She always marvelled that William was such a kind and considerate man when they made love. She sat up in the bed. *Wonder what the shrink meant about Will 'avin' a 'disorder',* she mused.

She was still awake when the tinny shrill of the alarm went off. Quickly, she knocked it off. She let her lips rest lightly on Will's forehead where the scars of the beating were still visible and slipped out of bed.

Waking, William ran his tongue over his dry lips. The sleeping tablets, like his memories of the war, left a bitter taste in his mouth.

He heard the faint sound of scraping at the back door. Going downstairs, he let the stray cat in. The black cat rushed into the heat of the kitchen and wounds its tail around his legs. He bent down and stroked its thick fur. "You out on the tiles all night?" he said, giving it a pet. "You like getting petted now, don't you Puss," he said, watching it scoff down its breakfast. *In the beginning, it had shied away as if it expected to get hurt or be thrown out,* he thought. *Just like me.*

William stood stock still. The thought was so clear in his head it was as if someone had turned on a light. The smell of burning filled his nostrils. Dumping the blackened toast, he threw open the kitchen window.

Buttering the heel of the currant loaf, his unspoken words, *just like me,* reverberated in his head. "I've expected people, even my father and Lisa, to cast me off," he said aloud, the realisation shocking him.

The ringing of the hall phone jarred into his thoughts. He hesitated. He hated speaking on the phone.

"Hello," he mumbled.

"Can I speak to Rosie—Mrs Kitchenn, please?" a female voice asked.

"She's at work."

"Is that you, Mr Armstrong?"

"Aye, it's me, doctor," he sighed.

"Good. I'm glad I caught you. How are you getting on with the outpatient visits to Dr Friskily? I had a letter to say they were nearing an end."

"Aye, grand. We're… Rosie and me… goin' to Fermanagh for a holiday."

He heard a surprised intake of breath. "I could set the extra sessions for when you come back," the doctor said.

"Aye, right ye are, doctor," he said.

It occurred to him that the doctor respected him and Rosie's opinions. That was the thing he'd missed from his days in the army. "It was the first place where ah really felt in charge; feeling respected, looked up to," he murmured.

The purring cat turned green shiny eyes on him as if it agreed, then curled up and went to sleep.

Chapter 72

The black-mantilla-headed women dipped their fingers in the holy water font and bent their knees to the altar before taking their seats for Ma Higgins' funeral Mass, as Father Agnew prayed the coffin into the church.

George stared at Ma Higgins' coffin laid across the two wooden pews in front of the altar. He'd requested that he be allowed to help to carry the coffin but had been refused.

"Father Agnew didn't find any relatives, then," Tomas murmured, nodding to the empty pews at the front beside the coffin. George searched the faces, hoping to see Stella. If he did, he would insist she be permitted to be the chief mourner. Somewhere near the back, a baby cried out.

"I'm going up to sit beside the coffin," George hissed at the detective. "She shouldn't be up there by herself with everybody gaping at her."

"You can't—you're not family," Tomas Maloney hissed.

George joined the line of people queuing for Holy Communion and found himself at the centre of a small mêlée. The oncoming people for communion were blocked by the people who had just received.

George looked at the glut of people turning right. There was no way he was going to get into the aisle beside Ma Higgins' coffin without receiving communion.

Father Agnew nodded him to come forward.

George fumbled to his knees at the altar rails and opened his mouth.

"Receive the body and blood of Christ."

Red-faced, George pushed his way through the knot of people and sat down heavily in the seat beside the coffin. His heart thumped like a Lambeg drum on the Twelfth of July.

He could have sworn he heard Ma Higgins' sniggering laugh in the coffin.

The smell of incense rose up and hung for a minute in the early spring air. "In the Lord's name, let us take our sister Margaret Higgins to her place of rest." The priest intoned.

"What did you do that for?" Tomas hissed as they prepared to carry the coffin out of the church.

"She was up there with no main mourners as if she was of no importance," George said. "Well, to me she was important. She gave me a roof over my head and took me in after I served my time. Something even my own family wouldn't do. I was only paying her back—giving her a bit of respect. What are the harms in that?"

Outside, the pallbearers prepared to hoist the coffin on their shoulders for the short journey to the nearby graveyard. George stepped up to the pallbearer nearest to him. "I'll do this lift," he asserted.

"It all about balance... ye see, son," the man said, eyeing George's build. "I'll manage," George retorted, slipping his shoulder under the coffin.

The early daffodils in the small, well-tended graveyard shook in the biting March wind that blew in from the small lake below the graveyard. The pallbearers stopped beside a large community grave.

George clenched his jaw. "Why didn't you tell me? I'd have bought her a grave of her own!"

Tomas kept his eyes fixed on the priest's moving lips. The wind had got up, and the prayers were like a bad radio connection. "You'll need all the money you have."

George rounded on him. "Listen, Det Maloney, I've been making my own decisions—including what I do with my money—since Da dragged me to this hole when I was fourteen. Now, fuck off."

The priest motioned it was time to lower the coffin. The pallbearers closed rank, and George was left to watch Ma Higgins' coffin slowly disappear into the gaping hole. He held his breath. Any minute now, he expected to hear the banging on the lid of the box and Ma's voice yelling, "You sanctimonious old farts. You didn't give a toss if I had a pot to piss in when I was alive. Now bugger off and leave me in peace."

The wind caught the last blessing with the sprinkling of holy water and blew it back towards the few parishioners gathered around the grave.

George sniggered. "I knew she'd have the last word. She always did," He turned away. He didn't want to watch the final sods being battered into place by the gravediggers' spades.

Chapter 73

William's heart lifted as he waited in the Arrivals at Belfast Docks. Rosie was coming for Easter. The early spring sun was too weak to be warm, but it made him feel happy to be out of Gallaher's cigarette factory—the job he had been lucky enough to get when he'd decided to come back and live on the farm again.

"Must be a new regiment comin' in. Security's tight today," a man standing near him said.

William could see an army patrol checking car registrations and licences on the main road leading out of the Docks.

A young woman smiled at him. "William?" She hesitated. "Sorry. I'm Kathy—Annie Swanton's granddaughter. She used to be postmistress in Ballet post office." She saw recognition dawn on William's face.

"Aye, aye, you used to work after school in the Kielty's hotel," he said, his eyes flicking back to the Arrivals board.

Kathy followed his gaze. "I hope Jay, my fiancé, gets here before any trouble starts," she said, sitting down beside him.

Feeling uncomfortable, William wanted to get up and move seats.

"There's a place that sells tea," Kathy said. "C'mon, it'll be warmer than sitting here."

"I've paid for two chicken sandwiches," she said, placing two mugs of steaming tea on the table. "Will you go and get them?"

William marvelled at the confidence of the young girls nowadays.

"New suit?" Kathy enquired, biting into her sandwich.

William shook his head. "Ah sent it to the dry cleaners. Ah work in Gallaher's Tobacco Factory in York Street. It leaves yer clothes stinkin'."

Kathy laughed. William noticed she had little gaps between her two front teeth, but somehow they suited her.

"The smell of nicotine is nothing to the stench of Jay's farm in Texas. I've been living over there and in London since Jay and I graduated from Trinity College in Dublin."

William took another swallow of his tea. It was coming back to him. She was the girl who was marrying oul Kielty's Yankee grandson. He'd heard it was going to be a mixed marriage like his and Margaret's had been.

"I'm glad I bumped into you. I wanted to come up and see you, but Granny Swanton said that would be… very forward," Cathy said hesitantly. "You had a mixed marriage, didn't you?"

William felt his stomach lurch up into his throat. "Ah did—a long time ago—during the war. Your granny must be getting on. Asking nosy questions never bothered her before." As soon as he said it, he felt like biting off his tongue. *That's why it's better if I avoid people. Ah always end up saying the wrong thing,* he thought.

Kathy nodded. "Granny was always minding people's business."

Kathy hung her head. "It's been delay after delay. First, Reverend Snodgrass couldn't find my papers. Then Jay's clergy had to get permission from the Bishop for him to marry me, a Protestant. Then he was called up for service in Vietnam," she said, tears welling up in her eyes. "Now, we're supposed to be getting married in the Catholic Church here, on Easter Monday, but Granny is objecting to me having to promise to bring any children we have up as Catholics," Kathy said in exasperation. "I've tried to explain to her it's not like that anymore…"

William felt the collar of his shirt pressing against his Adam's apple. Annie Swanton had been the very woman who led the outcry about him marrying Margaret, causing them to be outcasts in the village.

"I'll get us more warm tea," he said hastily. Standing in the small queue, William felt his heart start to settle into its familiar feeling of despondency. "The wedding day and the church—that's only the start of her problems," he murmured.

Handing over the money for the teas, he wondered what he could say that might help. With old hatred stirred up again with the Troubles, the IRA and the UVF paramilitaries were threatening they'd deal with anybody who steps outside their own community.

"Jay's Granda, Mac Kielty, is not well." Kathy murmured. "I know this sounds terrible, but if he dies it'll delay the wedding again."

William was saved by the garbled announcement that Rosie's boat would soon be docking. "Good luck with your weddin'," he said, rising hurriedly to his feet.

Kathy stood up too, a determined look on her face. "I'll marry Jay in any church or no church if that's what it takes," she said, buttoning up her coat.

Momentarily stunned, William watched her retreating back, her words echoing in his head. They were almost the exact same words he had roared at his mother thirty years before.

"The place is looking better now you're whitewashed the outhouses," Rosie observed from her seat on the large stone planter outside the back door of the farmhouse kitchen.

"Rev Snodgrass has asked me about letting some of the outhouses to Lillian, his daughter. She's setting up some kind o' arts and crafts thing for the tourists to raise money for charity."

"Charge him plenty. These religious types think they should get things for nowt. Charity, my ass," Rosie snorted, standing up.

"It's a lovely day. What about walk—take a picnic down by the lakes?"

William looked at the April sun shining on Rosie's grey hair. *She looks lovely,* he thought. He wished it was night so that he could feel her soft plump body in bed close to him.

"Davy Dobbs wants me to join the new community vigilantes they've set up," William said as they walked along.

Rosie thought about the night over Christmas when they'd been coming home. They'd been stopped by a group of men, their faces blackened, carrying thick cudgels. It had been very intimidating and scary on the lonely back road. She'd clung to William's arm trembling with fear.

Davy Dobbs had been one of them.

"They'll not harm us," William had said, squeezing her arm. "It's the IRA they're after," he had assured her. She'd wanted to say, *why they don't leave it to the army and the police, then?*

She had been considering coming to live with William on the farm, but news of running battles between the Catholic and Protestant communities, especially in Belfast and Londonderry, was on the radio and television daily.

"Don't worry—it's far from us," William always assured her.

"Any news from Ron and Reggie?" William asked, taking the picnic basket and helped Rosie over the ditch into the next field.

Rosie shook her head. "It takes six weeks at sea to get there. Imagine, all that time on a ship with small kiddies. I'd be waiting for them to fall overboard. Ten Pounds Poms, that's what they call them. I might never see them or the kiddies again," she gulped, wiping her eyes with the sleeve of her cardigan.

William wanted to comfort her, but he didn't know what to say to her. It occurred to him he had never felt the way about George, and definitely never about Trisha, the way Rosie felt about her sons. He never missed them the way Rosie missed her family. He sometimes wondered what George was doing. He was now the age for inheriting the farm, but it was only a passing thought.

Ellen Callahan and other people in the village often said, "You must be very proud of Trisha. She's a very beautiful girl." She had been one of the reasons he come back to live in Fermanagh. Here, there was less chance of Trisha turning up wanting to see him.

Rosie's voice brought his thoughts back to her.

"It'll be years before my boys can afford the fare home," she was murmuring. William rubbed her back and awkwardly patted her on the shoulder.

Rosie's muffled sobs turned into a strangled chuckle. "I used to do that when my boys were kiddies and 'ad a fall on the old bombed-out 'ouses where they used to play. I'd rub their back, and then I'd give them a smacker like this," she grinned. Standing on her tiptoes, she kissed William full on the lips.

William tasted her lipstick and smelled the scent of the lavender talcum powder she used.

"Lisa still coming?" she asked, tucking her arm into him.

William nodded.

"Oh, bugger the picnic," Rosie said. "Let's go 'ome and 'ave an early night while we 'ave the house to ourselves."

Putting the basket down, William encircled her in his arms. "What do ye mean, an early night? It's not even the middle of the day yet," he smiled, stroking her cheek with his finger.

William poured them both a mug of tea from the flask. "You're a wanton woman sitting there in your petticoat, and not a cow home from the fields yet," he teased her.

Rosie giggled like a schoolgirl. Crumbs from the buttered scone fell into her cleavage as she sat propped up against the bed pillows.

"All the years I was married to Arnold, we only made love on a Monday and a Friday. And that was in the dark of night," she chortled. Finishing her tea, she turned. "I 'ave sommit' ta ask ya. William Armstrong, will you marry me and make a respectable woman of me?"

"All your finery for Kathy Swanton's big day," William asked, nodding at Lisa's case as he met her off the train. "It might never come off."

Lisa looked enquiringly at him across the table in the new little café that had opened on Main Street.

"Why? Is it because she's marrying a Catholic?"

William shifted in his seat. "Aye, there's that, but oul Mac Kielty's is waiting on. If he dies, Mary Kielty will not let her son marry straight after his grandma's funeral."

"You sure Rosie doesn't mind me staying?" Lisa asked, tucking into chicken and chips. "Maybe she'd like to have you to herself for the wee while she's in Ireland."

"She's asked me to marry her," William blurted out.

Lisa nearly choked on the buttered piece of bread she had in her mouth. *No wonder William was so pleasant. He was getting laid,* she thought.

"Did you accept? Margaret will be dead thirteen years this November," Lisa said.

"It doesn't seem right."

"Why not? You lived with Rosie in England…?"

"Aye, but oul Snodgrass wouldn't us live together here."

"Go back and live with Rosie in England?" Hastily, Lisa changed the subject. Look what had happened the last time she'd encouraged William to marry Margaret.

William toyed with his food. "Ah was hopin' Rosie would come and live here. But all the things on the television about the Troubles are puttin' her off."

Lisa sliced down her chicken. She could understand that. BJ hadn't wanted her to come home either.

"It'll no go down well, those Proddy lass whose Granda is a member of the Lodge, marrying a Catholic. There'll be bother over it," he'd fretted, his words ending in a chesty cough.

She pulled her mind back to William. "You coming to Scotland in September for Isobel are wedding?" she asked as they waited for the bus out to the farm.

William nodded. "Is it alright if Rosie comes wi' me?" he asked.

"William, Lisa," Davy Dobbs gave them a mock salute as they climbed on the bus.

"Ah have that wee waiterin' job lined up for George at the army barracks," Davy shouted back to William.

Lisa twisted around in her seat to stare at William. "George is home?"

There was no mention of him coming back when he was up with Trisha at the New Year, Lisa thought, wondering what he was up to.

Chapter 74

George looked out the bus window. In this part of Belfast, Protestants and Catholics lived in adjoining streets, kept apart by a heavy security, armed police, and the "Peace Wall" topped with barbed wired and locked gates. Protestants loyalists from the Shankill Road were attacking Catholics in the adjoining Lower Falls Road. A curfew had been declared, and the army had thrown up a barricade of barbed wire to keep the two communities from killing each other.

Heavily armed policemen of The Royal Ulster Constabulary (RUC) ordered the driver out, slammed him up against the bus and body-searched him. Finger on the safety catch of his rifle, ever ready for any unexpected attack, a soldier walked down the centre of the bus.

George moved so that the touristy camera slung across his shoulders was in clear view and focused on the map of Belfast lying open in his lap.

"Name," the soldier said, cradling his gun across his chest.

George noticed the soldier was young, about eighteen, he guessed—not long joined up, judging by the fresh look on his cap badge of the Scottish King's Regiment and the high polish on his boots.

Smile, be friendly, Dobbs had drummed into him. *Don't make them suspect anything.*

He'd had no interest in joining Davy's vigilante Ulster Vanguard, but Davy had been insistent. "Support the cause and show them there's more Prod than Taig blood in your veins, man," Davy advised.

At the start, it had just been drilling and patrolling their own and neighbouring farmland. Now it was different.

"All Catholics are fair targets," Sandy, the new leader, had announced at one of the recent training sessions.

A gaggle of laughing girls outside the bus window drew the young soldier's attention. Factory girls, out on their lunch break, were passing through the security check, raising their arms to be searched by the female searchers and opening their bags to disclose their personal belongings as if it were the most natural thing in the world when a bomb or a bullet could kill them at any moment.

"What's the camera for?" the soldier asked in a thick Scottish accent.

"Some holiday snaps of Belfast," George said evenly.

"Right mate, move," an older soldier, an officer, ordered the bus driver, motioning to the young soldier that the search was over.

The driver climbed back into his seat, and the bus moved on moved, passing behind the security lines. This part of the Falls Road was, according to Davy, a republican stronghold. Being friendly to the police was a surefire death wish.

"Don't engage in conversation," Davy had warned him. "Keep your mouth shut and your eyes peeled. See what you can see, listen to conversations, and report back to me. The wrong question could mean a gunman waiting for ye around the next corner."

"If I was sendin' an armed combatant in there, I'd tell him to save a bullet for himself."

George had tried to hide his smirk. He'd thought Davy was laying it on a bit thick.

"You think I'm winding you up, Armstrong? If the IRA gets you on the Falls Road with a camera hung around yer neck pretending to be a tourist, they'll take it you're working for Special Branch," he ground out. "After they interrogate ye, ye'll be begging them to shoot ye dead."

A barricade of burnt-out cars, tyres, twisted metal girders, and rusting barrels filled with cement was blocking the road.

George wished he were back in the safety of London. And that was exactly where he was going when he got off this bloody bus, he thought.

He wondered whether, in his disguise as a tourist, he should attempt to take photographs. The group manning the barricade were young teenagers, except for a few men standing beside the shell of a burnt-out house.

The two women who had berated the police earlier were looking too. "See, I told you them Limey lovers would be burnt out," the woman nearest George said to her companion. "Down there dancin' in the Legion Hall with the soldiers," she snorted.

"Is it true she was tarred and feathered?" Before her companion could answer, the bus door got a thump, and a masked man wearing a balaclava stepped onto the bus.

George's blood froze in his veins.

"Don't you be worrying, son," the woman opposite him said, reaching over and patting his knee with a friendly hand. "It's only our Tommy."

"Thank," George mumbled into his chest.

She looked at the camera lying on his lap. "Would you like a wee photo—for your album—when you get back to America?" George's throat was too constricted with fear to speak. *They obviously get more American tourists here than Brit,* he thought.

The woman waved at the masked man. "Here's a wee fella come to see how we live in West Belfast," she trilled. "Stand up straight, till he gets a picture of you."

George felt the sweat on his upper lip and heard the veiled sniggers of the other passengers. The masked man stalked down the bus and stopped dead beside him. His eyes riveted on George from the cut-out slits in the mask. For what seemed an eternity, he didn't speak.

George waited to be dragged off the bus. All the things Davy had told him about the IRA crowded into his mind. He was sure the man could smell his fear.

"Nice bit of kit," the man finally said, reaching out his gloved hand for the camera. Satisfied it wasn't a decent enough camera to belong to a journalist, he tossed it back into George's shaking hands.

"Want to get out and get a few shots of the barricades?"

George shook his head vehemently. No way was he getting off the relative safety of the bus.

"One of youse take a couple of photos for him," the woman ordered, turning around to the passengers behind her.

A hand shot across and grabbed the camera. George watched as the passenger took shots of the burnt-out cars and the burnt shell of the house. The youngsters manning the barricades, seeing a photo opportunity, gathered up armfuls of stones. Clambering onto the barricades, they started shouting and stoning the bus for the benefit of the camera.

The masked man jerked his head. Quickly, the passenger snapping the photos jumped back onto the moving bus and thrust the camera at George.

"Go home," he muttered. "There's nothin' to see here. This is no place to be playing' games."

Mistaking the terrified look on George's face for outrage, the woman patted his knee again.

"Pass no remarks on him," she said. "Visitors are always welcome here, son. Just make sure to tell all your American friends to keep sendin' us money to carry on the fight to get our country back from the Brits."

Disembarking from the bus in Great Victoria Street, George pocketed the camera and stuffed the street map in a bin. He had carried out Davy's orders, "Yeah, for the bloody last time," he muttered.

"Got another wee job for you, Armstrong. Pay a visit to that Yankee papist groom, you tell him he'll be shot dead if he turns for the wedding."

"No can do Davy… I'm going to England for Easter. I have a bit of unfinished business of my own," George grinned.

Davy swore viciously. He'd been the one who verified George as a sound man to have in the organisation. He owned the farm now and he was letting' the outbuildings be used for training and the farmhouse for meetings.

"Couldn't it wait till after the weekend when I get back?"

"God help Ulster if she has to depend on boys like you, Armstrong, to defend her."

"That's an order, Armstrong," Davy bawled.

"How will I warm him off?"

Davy stepped so close George could smell the cheese and onion crisps on his breathe. "I don't give a fiddler's fuck how ye do it, as long as he gets the message that Kathy Swanton has plenty of her own kind to tie the knot wi'," he spat.

Chapter 75

Lisa was surprised to find the early bus from Enniskillen to Belfast was packed. She sank into a seat beside a man with his diary open on his lap, who was obviously trying to get a head start on his day. The bus trundled into Great Victoria Street. Brakes squealed in protest as the traffic ground to a standstill.

"You might be as well getting off here," the bus driver sighed over his shoulder to his passengers. "This might take a while, so it might."

Lisa's heartbeat quickened. Soldiers piled out of the armoured personal carrier and set up an impromptu check point across the street. Starting down Royal Avenue, Lisa decided she'd take a taxi to the hotel.

"That's Harland and Wolff, where the Titanic was built," the driver said, nodding in the direction of the giant crane that towered over the docks. Remembering the bus driver's advice, Lisa leaned forward. "I'm gled ta see Belfast taxis dinnae rip folks off," she said, imitating her old neighbour, Madge's broad Scottish accent. The driver eyed her in the mirror, then swung down a side street, dropping her at the door of the hotel.

Lisa stood for a minute, taking in the breathtaking glittering expansion of glass that was the front entrance of the hotel.

Trisha hadn't written or phoned for months. Now, here she is, writing to me and offering to pay for me to stay in a five-star hotel, Lisa thought sceptically.

Dear Aunt Lisa,

I'm sorry about the row Isobel and I had at Hogmanay. I do appreciate all you have done for me.

Claude has a client in Belfast over Easter. I'm going as his assistant. We are booked into the Hilton Quays Hotel. I would like to treat you to a few days' holiday at the hotel while I am there as a way of saying sorry and thank you at the same time.

Claude has agreed to come to Glasgow in September to photograph Isobel's wedding. It's my wedding present to her and Ewan.

Tell Uncle Billy I send my love.
Trisha.

The reception area was cool and almost soundless. It was hard to believe that she was only a short drive from Belfast city centre.

"For a town under siege, they're pretty laid back in this place," she murmured.

Trying to look as if she stayed in five-star hotels all the time, she made her way to reception. She could feel her shoes dragging on the plush, deep-pile carpet. She wondered if she should tap the little gold bell set into the gleaming mahogany reception desk—or was that only something people did in films, she thought.

"Can I be of assistance?" a voice said behind her.

Turning, Lisa hid a smile. She thought at any moment he would say, *Walk this way, madam.* Instead, he smiled graciously at her as if she was the most important guest in the hotel and murmured, "I'll get someone to bring you to your room right away."

Riding up in the lift, Lisa tried not to slump.

"If there is anything else you need, madam—just ask," said the young porter who had carried up her case. Lisa wondered whether they called them porters or concierges in a fancy hotel like this.

She hesitated. Should she tip him? She opened her bag and gave him a tip.

"Thank you," he said, a smile breaking out all over his face.

Lisa looked around, disappointed. It was an odd shape, as if a small room and a narrow walkway or hall had been knocked into one. "Maybe the bathroom will be lavish," she murmured. She caught sight of the small balcony outside her window. Her heart lifted. What did it mattered what the room looked like? She was here.

Running her hand over the crisp Egyptian bedsheets, she decided to have a rest.

A soft, persistent knocking penetrated her dreams.

"Housekeeping," a voice said. "Basket of fresh fruit and chocolates, courtesy of the Management," a youngish woman said, taking in Lisa's dishevelled hair and the rumpled bedclothes.

Lisa putt her hand to her throbbing temple. She'd had some kind of nightmare where somebody was chasing her.

"Are you feeling unwell?" the woman asked, noticing the beads of sweat on Lisa's face. "Would you like something for a headache?"

Lisa glanced in the direction of the bathroom. She'd better get tidied up. She didn't want Trisha to find her looking a mess.

"I'll let myself in—if that is alright with you, madam—and leave tea and aspirin on the side table."

Lisa nodded.

"Oh, and Reception asked me to give you this. They said there was no need for a reply," the woman said, holding out a cream embossed envelope.

Lisa turned it over in her hand. *It's probably from Trisha to say she can't make it to Belfast after all,* she fumed, tossing the message unopened onto to the bedside locker. *It'll keep till I have a good soak and get rid of this headache,* she moaned.

The complimentary bubble bath made the bathwater feel soft and silky. Lying back, Lisa let it sooth her. It was heaven. Usually, when she had a bath at home, it was with one ear listening out in case BJ needed something.

Wrapping her body in one of the big, fluffily bath towels, Lisa rubbed the steam off the mirror above the hand basin and studied her face and neck. "Not bad for middle age and the mother of two grown-up children," she smiled at her reflection.

She pulled the shower cap off and let her hair fall onto her bare shoulders. There was a sprinkling of grey hairs at her ears and temple, but otherwise it was still glossy and healthy-looking.

She let the towel drop and examined her breasts. She frowned. They were not as firm as she'd liked them to be. "But what woman's are at my age," she consoled herself, pulling on the complimentary white towelling dressing gown.

A tea tray sat waiting for her on the small side table. The bed had been turned down and a soft glow was coming from the two matching side lamps.

"This is the life," Lisa chuckled.

Piling the pillows into a pyramid against the quilted headboard, she poured the tea and lathered clotted cream on top of the buttered scone. After a second cup of tea and another scone, she picked up the message from where it had landed beside the bedside telephone.

For a minute, the one-line sentence jumped and danced in front of her eyes.

"I must see you tonight."

Scott.

Startled, Lisa slopped the tea into the saucer, sending a milky spray over the crisp white bed linen. Scott was here and he wanted to see her. Tonight! Shaking, she picked up the note and read it again. *I must see you tonight,* he'd written.

She scrabbled about in her handbag for a cigarette. Stepping out on the balcony, her eye was caught by a young woman jogging. It was Trisha.

Lisa's knees trembled. She couldn't let Trisha know she was meeting Scott. She might let it slip to BJ. They'd need to meet in his room. She'd ring Reception, explain he was an old friend of hers, and ask for his room number.

She scrambled into her clothes and scrutinised her image.

A flushed middle-aged woman stared back at her. She wrenched off the matching jumper and cardigan. "Maybe a blouse and just the cardigan," she muttered. "It'll have to do. It's all I have with me. At least my hair looks half decent," she sighed, toning down her flushed cheeks with her Yardley powder puff. She smacked her lips together and checked that her lipstick hadn't gotten on her teeth.

Her hand trembling, reached out for the bedside phone. "I'd be better going down to the desk. That way I can find out Trisha's room number as well. Make up an excuse—tell her I'm not feeling well and am going to have an early night. With Scott!"

Chapter 76

The door of the hotel suite gave a soft click as it closed. Ready for her jog, Trisha limbered up in the air-conditioned corridor. She inhaled the powerful, pungent scent of the flowers as she passed a man cradling a huge bouquet of blooms.

Scott checked the room number and whirled around. "Excuse me… Miss Armstrong?"

Trisha couldn't believe her eyes. It was the man who had accosted her in the London hotel.

"These are for you," he said tentatively.

Not waiting to hear his stammering apology, she jogged away from him. The door to the stairs banged behind her, cutting off his words and beheading some of the flowers as he rushed after her.

He fell into step beside her, still clutching the bedraggled blooms, as she slowed to walk through the foyer.

"Your photographer Claude said I owed you a personal face-to-face apology for my inexcusable behaviour. I wanted to get it all cleared up—out of the way before my son's wedding."

Trisha's heart jumped into her mouth. Oh my god, he was Claude's assignment—the father of the groom. No wonder she had thought there was something familiar about him that night in the hotel. He was her Aunt Lisa's old flame, who had taken her and Isobel to the seaside when they had been on holiday in Ireland. He'd been pig-ignorant to Lisa on the drive home that day too.

Trisha turned on him. "Do you really think a bunch of flowers will make up for the humiliation you caused me? And spare me the devoted family man and father bit!" she ground out, jogging away from him as they came out into the grounds.

"What about the damn flowers?"

"Give them to whoever you insult in the hotel tonight," she muttered, increasing her stride.

After a while, her outrage subsided, and she realised she had left the grounds of the hotel and was jogging in the adjoining golf course. She slowed to a walk and headed back into the hotel grounds.

Approaching the small Remembrance Monument to men lost in the WWII in the grounds of the hotel, she saw the man again. He was placing the flowers at the bottom of the cenotaph.

Letting the heavy glass door of the hotel slam behind her, she pounded up the stairs. The man followed.

Sweating with fear now, Trisha fumbled the key in the lock. Gasping for air, Scott lounged forward and leaned against the jamb of the door, his hand on his chest, his breath coming in short spurts.

"You a model or a damn Marine?" he wheezed. "I need to sit down—heart problems."

He looked at the mocking smirk on Trisha's face. *The sassy little trollop is enjoying this,* he thought as he slid down on the floor.

"Brandy… heart," he wheezed. *So this is it,* Scott thought. *Survived the war and the Japs, and I are going to take a heart attack and die half in and half out of this bitch's hotel room! Shit! He couldn't even remember her name.*

Trisha stood over him, her own heart jumping about. He was sweating profusely. His lips had a blue tinge to them, like her Uncle BJ's had sometimes.

"See this," she snarled, pulling a security alarm out of her pocket. "This can wake the dead. If you as much as move a limb from this spot while I get you a drink, I'm pulling the cord."

The neat brandy burned Scott's throat and made his eyes water. Trisha stood watching him, waiting for him to go.

"I only wanted to give you the damn flowers, apologise and explain…"

"Explain!" Trisha exploded. "You and your friends acted like horny, hormonal adolescences on their first bellyful of booze."

Scott Osbourne hung his head. The tightness in his chest was easing. "I deserve that. I did act like a pig," he murmured, running his hand over his sweating face. "We'd just closed a big deal on beef exports… out to have a good time our last night in London." He held up his hand as Trisha opened her mouth to speak. "I'm not… bullshitting you. The guys couldn't believe their eyes. Your photo was all over centre page of the tabloids. You must admit, the shots were pretty sassy. You can't blame the guys for jumping…"

"It wasn't my idea to put those photos in the papers. Not that it's any of your business." Trisha's hand shook as she gulped down her own drink. "It's not only women who take revenge," she sneered, the brandy beginning to calm her. "My so-called boyfriend did because I wouldn't do a porn film for him."

Scott shook his head. "What a god-awful thing to do. I hope you sued the bastard for every cent he has," Scott said, holding out his glass for a refill.

A hysterical giggle gurgled in Trisha's throat. This was ridiculous. He was defending her honour now.

Scott proffered his glass once again. This time she refilled it.

"I'm not making excuses, but things have been damn pressured this past year, what with my son's wedding and my wife's drinking…"

"Please! Spare me—things are tough and my wife doesn't understand me," Trisha snorted.

"May I?" Scott said, moving to close the door as another passing guest stole a curious glance into the room.

"Tell me about him—the boyfriend," Scott asked, refilling both their glasses and sitting again.

"He was a manipulative, egotistical rich shit. He used me to live out his twisted fantasies."

Trisha hand gripped her glass. Once she started talking, she found she couldn't stop. She told him about her plunge into depravity with Seymour, that had almost cost her her modelling career.

"Seymour used my body as a commodity, but when he was rational, the sex had been unbelievably great," she confessed. "I miss it," she said, eyeballing Scott.

"No! Let's not go there," Scott said hastily. He could hardly believe he was turning down this young, vibrant body. "We need something to eat to sober both of us up," he mumbled, reaching for the phone. "Let's book a table downstairs, get something to eat, and go out—see a bit of Belfast nightlife…"

Trisha started to strip off her sweaty joggers. Stretching up, she released her mass of black glossy hair from its ponytail. It cascaded down her back and over her breasts like a dark waterfall.

Scott's eyes riveted on the dark mound of pubic hair partially hidden by her zipped top. He watched hypnotically as the top fell on top of the discarded joggers. Desire shot through him. He wanted her.

And she knew it.

Suddenly, Scott was stone cold sober. It was a trap. A trick—in illusion—like the Japs used to torment the prisoners: mind games. This was her way of getting her revenge on him. As soon as he made a move towards her, she'd set off the damn security alarm and scream rape.

"Can I help you?" a voice said. Scott whirled around. Fuck! The damn receptionist was still on the line. He'd forgotten he was still clutching the phone in his hand.

"Can I help you?" the receptionist voice said again, a faint trace of irritability creeping in.

"No, no, I don't believe you can," Scott said weakly.

Chapter 77

Detective Maloney's leaving party was in full swing. Satisfaction ripped through Tomas. His transfer to Fermanagh had come through. In his ten years in CID, he had made some good friends—and some dangerous enemies, he mused, his eyes scanning the crowded room.

"Congratulations, we'll miss your banter and cool head around this place, not to mention that Waterford twang of yours," Bertie, an older man said. Sliding his hip on to the bar stool beside Tomas, he tried to catch the barman's eye.

"It's an odd location to transfer to, given your track record of successful undercover surveillance and arrests with the paramilitaries in Belfast," he said.

"Thanks, appreciate that," Tomas smiled, sipping his drink. *I wonder what he would think if I told him my reason for applying for the transfer wasn't entirely to do with policing,* Tomas thought.

George Armstrong had given him the brushoff since he returned home.

"Stay the fuck away from me. They're beginning to think you're my bloody handler," he'd snarled.

Tomas was jolted out of his reverie by Bertie offering to buy him another drink. Tomas shook his head. "Thanks, Bert, the missus has booked a table for a bite to eat in the Quays Quarter. It's more than my life's worth to turn up half-cut," he joked. "We think we have trouble with the vigilante boys and the boys at the barricades; they're a stroll in Botanic Gardens compare to Violet's temper. She's already champing at the bit about the transfer," he laughed.

Bertie looked a bit concerned. "Keep your personal weapon handy when you're out eating, son. We've walking behind too many coffins lately," he advised. "The Provisional IRA—and indeed others—would be glad to see the back of you, Tomas," he said. Tomas drained his glass and looked at him enquiringly.

"You heard something, Bertie?"

"You know your arrests of some of the fanatics who believe they are defending Ulster against the IRA are not always welcome in some quarters," he said, glancing across the room to where two plain-clothes men were drinking.

Tomas straightened his shoulders. "Killing is killing, regardless of what part of the community it comes from," he said, following Bert's gaze.

"Any word about that case at the Met you were interested in—where the old biddy got her head bashed in?" Bertie asked, catching Tomas off guard. "Wasn't there a lad from Fermanagh helping police with their enquiries?" he said, eyeing Tomas.

It took all of Tomas' police training to hide his startled surprise. *Old Bertie must have come across the reference to George's arrest in London,* he thought. Instinct told him his colleague had information to impart to him.

"I'll just have a mineral," he said.

"Fuck's sake. You can't stand there and let your parting glass be a mineral at your own leaving do, son."

"Was there something you wanted to tell me, Bertie?"

Bertie moved out of earshot of the barman.

"Your patch in Fermanagh takes in the village of Ballet?"

Tomas nodded.

"Intelligence has it that the Belfast boys are using a farm in Fermanagh as their country headquarters. It's owned by an ex-army veteran and his son. The father is a decorated WW2 veteran, not long back from England. The son has a bit of form, so he has."

"William Armstrong and his son is George," Detective Maloney said quietly.

Bertie nodded. "Once the IRA gets wind of their activities…" Bertie didn't need to say any more. Tomas knew the farm would be raided, and anybody there suspected of being a UVF member would be shot dead, including George. He'd have to try and get him out of there, fast.

"That's good to know," he said, getting up to leave.

In the restaurant, out of habit, he peopled watched. Knowing the nervous facial expressions and body language of terrorists had saved his life before. Pressing his arm to his body, he felt the comforting feel of his personal weapon. He tensed as a lone man walked in and unbuttoned his long black coat; *if he intended to pull out a submachine gun, he'd have worn a zipped jacket,* Tomas thought.

Chapter 78

The receptionist arched an enquiring eyebrow. "Mr Osborne has requested we hold all his calls," she said coolly.

"Yes. But he didn't mean me." Lisa said, trying not to waver under the woman's keen scrutiny.

"Is this your first stay with us, Mrs…?"

"Mrs Armstrong-McKnight," Lisa said, hoping the double-barrelled name would impress the woman enough to give her Scott's room number.

"I hope everything is to your satisfaction?"

Lisa could feel her resolve to remain calm slipping. "Mr Osborne's room number," she persisted.

"Would you like to speak to…?"

"I don't need to speak to anybody else. What I need is the number of Scott's room!"

"Mr Osborne is not in his room. But I can take a mess…"

Lisa's lips straightened into a thin line. "He sent me a message… he had to see me tonight!"

The woman lowered her gaze, but not before Lisa saw a pitying look flit across her face. "He's having… drinks with his… niece. I believe she's a model from one of the top London Fashion Houses."

Lisa gave the receptionist a perplexed look. Then the penny dropped. "You mean Trisha Armstrong?"

The receptionist's face remained impassive.

"Trisha is my niece, actually." Lisa said, as haughtily as she could manage.

"If you say so, madam," the receptionist murmured.

"I'll find him myself," Lisa muttered, turning in the direction of the bar.

The receptionist gave a soft cough. "They are not in the public bar, madam."

"Residents' lounge?"

The receptionist shook her head as she ran her eye down the guest register. "Oh, yes, I do beg your pardon, madam. I see your niece, Miss Armstrong, booked you in. Your niece is in 803. She has requested an extra key. I wonder, would you be kind enough to give her this," she said, proffering the key.

Lisa felt as if a swarm of butterflies had taken residence in her stomach. Scott must be having drinks with Trisha and Claude. That's why they were in Belfast. Claude must be the photographer for Jay Osborne's wedding. She'd have to be very careful. Trisha mustn't suspect there was anything between her and Scott. *That's how Scott knew I was here. Trisha must have mentioned it and Scott took the opportunity to be with me,* she thought.

She listened outside Trisha's door, expecting to hear the murmur of voices. There was only silence. She stood for a minute, debating what she should do. *I'll go back to reception and leave a message for Trisha to say I am tired and will see her at breakfast,* she thought.

She had her finger on the button to summons the lift when she realised she was still clutching the spare key to Trisha's room.

The door whined a little as it opened.

"Tidy as ever, I see," she muttered, stepping over the clothes on the floor. "Wow! This is pure luxury compared to my room," she gasped. Two small matching sofas covered in soft velvet faced each other. Between them, a marble-topped coffee table was littered with fashion and photography magazines and an assortment of empty glasses.

"Didn't take Claude long to get into the Irish liquors and brandy shots," she mused, noting the empty mini bar and leaving the spare key on the table.

She couldn't resist opening the door to the bedroom to have a peek.

Her eyes were immediately drawn to the bed. Trisha's hair was spread like a raven's wing against the stark white silken sheets; her long painted nails raking over a man's back, leaving long red railway tracks in their wake. Ecstatic moaning sounds filled the room.

"Say you love me. Say you love me," Trisha was moaning.

"Damm right I love you, babe. I haven't had ass like yours since I was a rookie," the man chortled.

Lisa froze like a deer caught in headlights at the sound of Scott's voice.

Chapter 79

Ma Higgins' old house looked as dilapidated as ever, except there was a clean pair of curtains in the downstairs room with the lock on the door he had 'flitted' his father from, the makeshift room in the attic, George thought.

Despite it being April, he was as cold and hungry as he had been on that first day in London in 1958. He had been sleeping rough since Ma Higgins had been battered to death, careful not to use the men's hostels or B&Bs in case the police were looking to blame him for her murder.

He knew it was a long shot that Stella had moved back after Ma's death, but he knocked the door anyway. There was a long silence, then the sound of feet, and the door was flung open.

"What the fuck do ya want?"

George felt the breath leave his body. For one wild, shocking moment, he thought Ma Higgins had come back from the dead. Stella leaned up against the jamb of the door, a cigarette in her mouth, breath smelling of drink, like a younger version of old Ma Higgins. Memories flooded back of Stella schooling him to be a thief and a pickpocket. *You're come a far way from that now, Georgie boy. Now you're stealing cars for to put bombs in and sending bullets in the post,* he thought.

"Irish?" Stella exclaimed, straightening up and opening the door wide.

George followed her down the hall. It smelled marginally better than he remembered, and into what had been Ma Higgins' bedroom-cum-living quarters and drinking den. His eyes were immediately drawn to where he'd found Ma with her head smashed in. He could still see the edge of a faint outline of bloodstains on the floorboards, partly hidden by a mat.

Stella followed his gaze. "Poor old bitch. 'Er old man bashed her 'ead in. Fink she must have told him she was leaving this dump to me," she sighed, casting her eyes around her. "I wish Ma 'adn't friggin' bothered," she sighed. "Like a noose around my neck it is."

"You back 'ere, Irish?"

George shrugged. "It depends. You still rent out the rooms?"

Stella nodded. "Sheamie Foy still comes with the Irish navvies. Landladies don't trust the Irish no more since they bombin' started 'ere. Ya need a bed, Irish? The attic room is still there—goin' cheap," she smiled, clocking his unkempt appearance.

George hesitated. The attic room would be a perfect place to stay while he searched for Mickilo Martini. "Not sure how long I'll be here," he said evasively. "Might need to go back…"

"You need a change of clothes. And sommit to eat—ya looked half starved. C'mon, we're going shopping," Stella ordered.

George recoiled. "I am not going shoplifting." It would just be his bad luck to get caught thieving and end up in the cells again.

Stella ignored him. "The Irish Centre 'as a soup kitchen and a place ya will get clean clothes."

It was as if time was in reverse. He'd been searching for Mickilo Martini for a month. He was back scouring the streets where he'd searched every day for better digs for him and his father. It was if the chef had fallen off the edge of the world. *I hope the fucker has,* he thought.

Ready to head out the next morning to continue his search, he was surprised to hear Sheamie Foy's familiar voice in Ma Higgins' hall.

"Jasus, is it yourself," Sheamie said, pumping George's hand. "What brings you back here?"

Before George could answer, Sheamie motioned to the man beside him to follow Stella down the hall.

"What the fuck is going on over there?" he said, turning back to George. "You're wrecking the North. Now you're starting here, and poor critters like yer man," he said, nodding at the retreating back of the navvy, "can't get a place to stay."

George laughed. "You don't know the half of it. Your safer over here than over there," he joked with Sheamie.

"Do you ever see any of the old crew? Or that Mickilo, the chef fucker who got me five years at her Majesty's Pleasure?" George asked, quickly changing the subject.

Sheamie shook his head. "The last I heard, the Donegal chef had struck it rich and was cooking for the boyos working on the oil riggs. And was saving like fuck to buy an eating place of his own. There's one for you, young Armstrong," he laughed, heading for the door.

George could hardly hide his disappointment. His dream of seeing Mickilo hanging by the neck from a meat hook amongst the rest of the circuses would have to wait. He'd be going home having failed, but he'd bide his time. As soon as Mickilo open an eatery he'd be back with a firebomb to burn it down—with him in it.

Chapter 80

Lisa curled into a ball on her bed and stared down at the long black strands of Trisha's hair tangled around her clenched knuckles. William was right. The devil in Trisha had bewitched Scott and lured him into her bed.

There was a knock on the hotel bedroom door. *Probably hotel security come to escort me out of the hotel,* she thought.

She dragged herself off the bed and opened the door a crack.

It was Scott.

"You didn't come down for dinner. I brought you a plate of cold meats, some oysters, and strawberries with fresh cream," he mumbled, avoiding eye contact.

Lisa felt a hysterical cackle rising in her throat. *The food of love,* she thought, crawling back into the bed.

"Now you can claim to have bedded two generation of Armstrong women," she hurled at Scott.

"Hand on my heart, Lisa; I didn't know she was your niece," he said, spreading out his hands in a gesture of helplessness. "It was nothing—meant nothing. I am under a lot of stress," Scott bleated.

Lisa gathered the bed sheets up in furious handfuls and glared at him. "What do you know about living a stressful life, Scott? Try living in a tenement building for years, scraping to get by, with walls so thin you can hear your neighbours making love. Or like my life now, listening to the gurgle of BJ's oxygen tank at the side of the bed, every night."

Scott stiffened. "I've seen my best friends—school pals—blown to pieces. I had to leave them where they'd fallen, move on with my men, and take care of the living men first," he rasped, stung by her words. "Fighting the Japs, I knew who my enemy was. In this damn guerrilla warfare here in Ireland, I don't bloody know. I look into people's faces and think, was it you, or you, or you who ordered a death sentence on my son simply because he's marrying a girl of another faith!"

Lisa roused herself from the pillows. "You sent me a message you wanted to see me tonight," she said, her words almost inaudible.

Scott looked at the ravaged face of the woman he'd had a romantic dalliance with when he and she were just kids in 1942. Lisa was the type of girl you had a good time. Mary was the kind you took home to your folks. Old Kielty had brought girls in from Belfast for to entertainment the squaddies, but he never let them near his own daughter. *No man was getting near his Mary until he walked her up the aisle, and she came down with a wedding ring on her finger,* he thought. More fool me, he grunted.

He took a deep breath. "I wanted to see you before Jay's wedding day… Talk to you about the past—clear everything up," Scott said, placing his hand over Lisa's, where it lay limply on the bed cover.

Lisa's heart stilled, and a small flame of hope fluttered in her chest.

"Scott, there's something you need to know… our time together…"

Scott put his finger on her lips. "Yeah, something good did come out of it. More than you realise. Lying in a bunker expecting to die any moment, the image of your face, your body, the good times we had splashing in the Lakes like crazy kids, and making love hidden from view under the laurel bushes in the gardens of the old castle, kept me sane," he stopped to draw breath. "Every day I didn't die, I thanked God for the memories of the beautiful sunsets, like huge orange balls slipping into the dark glass surface of the lakes. Their image kept me from giving up, kept me fighting to stay alive, kept me from coming home in a body bag."

Lisa didn't realise she was crying until she tasted the salty tears. "Oh Scott, I waited for you in our secret place night after night, hoping against hope you had been sent away on a mission but that you would come back."

Scott stood up abruptly. "I did come back. But you had married and were living in Scotland."

Despite her despair at finding him and Trisha in a storm of passionate lovemaking, Lisa felt her heart lift. He hadn't deserted her after all, like her mother had said he would.

"I should have waited…but… there wasn't time," Lisa whispered.

"It was for the best," Scott said heavily. "But sometimes when Mary is in a drunken spree… I think …about you, Lisa."

It was a small consolation for her shattered heart, but Lisa took it.

"I was always your girlfriend. How did you come to marry Mary?" she choked out.

Abruptly, Scott got up, walked away from her, and stood looking out over the balcony at the Belfast skyline, its lights twinkling in the dark evening sky.

"Mary wasn't as much fun to be with as you," he said with a small chuckle. "Old Mac Kielty wanted a man who was good marriage material for his plain daughter. And he had the money to make it happen. I persuaded him in Texas that Mary would have a good life."

Scott looked away from Lisa's stricken face. "I'm sorry, Lisa. I... needed to bring home a girl who had never known a man. Mary wasn't the kind to give up her favours without a marriage licence," he sighed, running a hand over his thinning hair.

Lisa felt as if he had stuck a knife in her and was twisting it in her gut. "You were the only one I ever made love with. You knew that, Scott. You were the first... and last man I made love with until I married BJ," she gasped out. "I flirted with the locals and BJ, but that's all it was—harmless flirting."

Scott turned back into the room and closed out the night air.

"You and BJ had been walking out..."

Lisa's mouth fell open with shock. "It was you that suggested that I walk out with BJ, so your Commanding Officer wouldn't suspect you were planning to marry me and take me back with you..."

The tips of Scott's ears grew red. "You thought that, Lisa. I never said I was taking you home to meet my folks."

Lisa looked at him, dumfounded. "Other GIs took Irish brides back home with them. Why not you, Scott? Why did you not say goodbye?" Lisa asked, a wobble in her voice.

Scott licked his lips nervously. He needed to get this over with.

"I sent you the note earlier because... I wanted to explain why I left without seeing you." Scott took a deep, shuddering breath. "The truth is I got spooked when I guessed you were going to have a baby."

Startled, Lisa's head shot up. She gaped at him, her eyes out on stalks.

"You knew! You knew I was having your baby, and you... ran away!"

Scott pulled a snow-white hanky out of his pocket and wiped at his forehead. "I couldn't be sure it was mine," he said resignedly.

"Maybe this will help you decide," Lisa cried, leaping out of the bed and thrusting the photos of Andrew at him.

Chapter 81

"Be upstanding for your bride and groom."

A loud cheer and clapping broke out as the bride and groom came in through the flower-decked marquee entrance to a champagne toast. Smiling like two children in a sweetie shop, they made their way under the canopy of gaily coloured lanterns, especially imported for the occasion, towards the elevated top table and the stunning-looking seven-tiered wedding cake decked out in silver and gold. Two figurines, arms entwined stood on the top tier waving a miniature Union Jack and a miniature Stars and Stripes.

Davy Dobbs snorted. "It's not every day ye get a bullet as a wedding present an' ignore a death promise," he growled under his breath. *And if I had any sense, I'd be miles from this bloody place,* he mused.

Cameras clicked as the bridesmaid fussed with Kathy's white lace veil and train on her silk dress until it was to the satisfaction of Claude, the photographer.

As one, Reverent Samson and Father Nuland moved towards the newly married couple to offer their congratulations. They had pulled a fast one and married Jay and Cathy in a church across the border in Donegal just as the sun was rising.

William went in search of Rosie. He found her checking out the laden table of wedding presents, her face as flushed as the bride's.

"Doesn't it all look so lovely? They 'ave definitely done them proud," Rosie enthused. "Weddin' presents piled three deep. It'll be years before they use the 'alf of them."

William gazed at the beautiful sets of cut glass, tea sets, and the usual collection of toasters, chip pans, tea towels and bales of blankets.

"They'll not care now they're finally got married," William murmured.

Rosie slipped her hand into William's. He knew she was wondering if the day would come when they'd be married. William looked around him. The whole village and most of the people from the outlying farms seemed to have been invited.

Small groups of soldiers, in uniform from the earlier security for the expected wedding service in the local Catholic Church, were enjoying what he suspected was their first wedding reception, Irish-style.

Involuntary, he shivered. It had been eerie to see the army in full riot gear and armed RUC policemen mingling with the guests and the media. The death threat against the groom had brought wide media coverage. Reporters and camera crews were trailing locals, looking for a good story.

"Good turnout," a familiar voice stated. William turned to see Dr Coles.

"Here's a seat, doctor," he said as the old man wavered about.

"Damm tremors. They're a bloody nuisance," John Coles muttered as William helped him to a chair.

"What are ye drinking?"

The old doctor beamed. "Whiskey, please, William." He hesitated. "Don't mention it to my son Aengus, will you," the doctor said, tossing back the Bushmills.

"If you're taking tablet for that shake," William blurted out, nodding at the doctor's hands as they twitched on the glass. "Maybe ye shouldn't mix them wi' whiskey."

John Coles laughed. "You know, William, I used to think you were poor at communicating," he said, putting a shaky hand in William's arm. "But if there was a bit of plainer talking about these parts, we mightn't have needed the army and police to protect a young couple in love," he said, glancing to where the bride and groom were posing with well-wishers for yet more photographs.

He patted William's knee. "You know only too well all about bigotry and hypocrisy. It'll not be an easy road they'll have to travel," he sighted.

William saw Annie Swanton making her way to the op table. She caught his eye and waved him over.

"I'm so glad to see you and Rosie here," she gushed, two pink spots lightening up her cheeks. William guessed she'd had a few extra sips of the sherry bottle to help her get through the early morning marriage service in the Catholic Church.

The round tables had been set out so that guests from both the Catholic and Protestant communities sat elbow to elbow. William held in the urge to snigger.

They did business and passed the time of day with each other, but they rarely socialised in the same circles.

"How is Lisa?" Faith Hamilton asked as the best man rose to his feet and cleared his throat to make his speech. "She was telling me in her last letter that Isobel is getting married too," Faith went on.

William fidgeted in his seat. He'd just seen Trisha and that photographer come in.

"Lisa was saying Isobel's brother Andrew has volunteered to work in special services with the army here," Faith continued.

"My son is serving with the army. He's from here," a man across from Faith said quietly. "His mother and I wait every night to hear he's been shot."

"I didn't think Catholics joined the British Army," Rosie said before William could stop her.

William felt his gut tightening. Rosie had no understanding of what went on in Northern Ireland.

"What about Robbie Black, Mrs Hamilton?" William interjected before Rosie could begin to ask questions.

Faith took a sip of water. "He's been transferred to a firm of solicitors in Co. Kerry." She fell silent for a minute. "I suppose you heard I have the farm up for sale. I'm going to live with my sister."

She lifted her head, and William saw the sorrow in her eyes. "Poor Robbie paid dearly for letting Dr Coles and your father convince him your mother wasn't in her right mind when she made her will. It cost him his job," she said as the hum of voices rose and the other people around the table began to relax and enjoy each other's company.

William nodded towards the newly married couple. "Mother's will took away my right to the farm because, like them, me and Margaret had a mixed marriage."

Faith twisted the napkin in her lap. "Your mother was only doing what she believed was right, William. That farm had been left to her by the old couple who reared her on the agreement she'd always keep the farm and the land in Protestant hands."

William looked at her incredulously. Faith paused and took a deep breath.

"Can't you see, William, you married outside your Protestant faith, and in time the farm would pass down to your children… who have papist blood in them," she said.

A terrible anger rose up in William.

"There wouldn't be a farm or lands to pass on to Catholics or Protestants if my Margaret hadn't kept the farm from going to seed when I was a POW."

Angrily, he scraped back his chair. Striding in the direction of the exit, he almost collided with a man coming in carrying a large gift-wrapped box. As he passed him, William's body jerked, and his skin prickled. *It was the same feeling I used to get when I sensed my army unit was in danger,* he thought shakily as his gut started to shake.

Whatever's in that box, it isn't a wedding present, he thought.

"Bomb," he croaked out.

"What's that, mate?" a young soldier asked, cracking open a bottle of beer with his teeth as he strolled out past the gaily wrapped box perched on the end of a table that, a short time ago had been lined with champagne-filled glasses.

William's voice deserted him. Frantically, he pointed at the box.

"Too heavy for ya, mate? Want me to carry it to the table where the rest of the wedding gifts are piled up?" the young soldier asked, putting down his glass and moving to lift the box.

"It's a bomb!" William bellowed.

"A bomb?" the young soldier said, half smiling. "It's a wedding present, sir."

"It's a bomb! It's a bomb!" Willian roared at the top of his lungs.

A hush fell over the chatter of the wedding guests nearest the entrance of the marquee. There was a snigger as William's hoarse-shouted warning was passed from one guest to another like a Chinese whisper.

"It's only William Armstrong having one of his bad turns," a woman said.

"There's wires coming out of it," the young soldier, who had offered to carry the gaily wrapped box in and place it with the rest of the wedding presents, stuttered out. "Shower of bastards, didn't get the groom at the church—thought they have another go."

A horrifying silence fell. Then pandemonium broke out as the panic-stricken guests streamed past the bomb.

Watching from across the street, Rosie pulled her light summer cardigan tightly across her chest and trembled as she watched the tense body and slow, measured steps of the bomb disposal expert, signalling it really was a bomb.

"I'm never comin' back 'ere, never again, William," Rosie said, her voice quaking and her body shaking uncontrollably.

Chapter 82

The latch of the milking shed grated as it lifted. A stream of weak sun raced across the milking bucket William had between his knees.

"Somebody here to see you, Da," George said brusquely.

William straightened his stiff back. "If it's that detective again, ah have no more to say to him," he grunted, going back to the milking.

George reined in the sharp retort. His father's fright at finding the bomb had brought his father's nightmares about the war back full force. He watched William trying to control the shambling shake he had developed. But the too-full milk bucket defied him, and milk slopped out onto the milking shed floor.

"Why don't you let Davy do his own bloody milking?"

"What do you want me to do? Sit in the kitchen and watch her belly growing bigger every day? What brought her home here? Why didn't she stay in London?" William growled. "Who's lookin' for me?"

"It's some young fella asking for you. He's not from around these parts. He's driving an old Toyota with a Tyrone registration," George said, trying to release his father's grip on the handle of the bucket. For a minute, a silent battle of wills ensued as the cows turned their big beseeching eyes on William, as if urging him to do as he was asked.

"It's Friday. Get out there and get rid of him before the boys get here," George warned. "And don't be arguing with Trisha when you go on there," he added.

"Is there a meeting of the Belfast boys tonight?" William asked.

"I'm just after telling you that, Da," George said in exasperation.

"If he's another one of them reporters, he'll get nothin' more out of me," William snarled, releasing his grip on the milk bucket and drying his hands on his trousers.

A strange sensation had come over George as his fingers had closed over his father's. A long-forgotten memory of his father's hands, strong and able, swinging him up on top of a load of hay as they headed home after a day's working in the fields. Startled, he sat down. What age had he been then? Maybe five or six, he mused. *Sarah was only a year younger than me. She must have been there too.* But he could only remember his father's strength as he swung him high in the air.

He reached for a fresh, empty milking bucket and fastened his hands on the cow's udders. She complained, swishing her tail at the rough handling.

"You're nearly as good at complaining as the merry widow," he said, blowing his hands to heat them before settling into a steady rhythm.

Chapter 83

A warm September sunbeam spread in through the stained-glass church windows, splashing Trisha's pale shift dress with warm red and blue dappled shapes, disguising her growing bump. She breathed a wordless prayer that, despite the hostility that existed now between her and Isobel, her cousin's big day wouldn't end in disaster like Kathy's and Jay's had, she thought casting her mind back to six months before.

It was hard to believe Scott Osborne was dead. He had been so alive...so sexy...

The lilting shrill of the Scottish piper broke into Trisha's reverie. It lingered poignantly, then died away as the organist struck the key, and the first strain of the wedding march floated on the air.

Trisha drew in a surprised breath. Isobel looked beautiful. Her drop-waist dress of floating taffeta with its lace sleeves gave her elegance and poise. Her unruly hair, beneath a short veil trimmed with white diamante rosebuds, had been teased, coaxed, and lacquered to a soft, submissive sheen. Trisha caught the scent of her bouquet of wild heather and lavender as she glided past.

She glanced at Lisa and BJ sitting in the front pews reserved for the bride's family, peeved she wasn't there. BJ's face was glowing with pride. For once, the ugly oxygen mask was not in view, but she knew it wouldn't be too far away.

Shakily, BJ got to his feet just as Isobel made her slow ascent up the aisle.

"My beautiful lass," BJ beamed. He put a trembling hand under her chin. "You ready to do this, darlin'?"

Isobel nodded.

"It's no' too late to change yer mind and stay wi' you're oul da. It's a long road wi' ne turns," he smiled.

"I'm sure, Da," Isobel said, smiling radiantly.

"Good lass. Granny Mac would be proud o' you," he said, swiping at a tear. Looking down into her upturned face, he linked her arm in his and walked her the last few yards to where Ewan, her groom, stood waiting.

Lisa shifted in her seat. She glanced at Claude, the photographer, busily snapping away. True to his word, he had come to the house and taken loads of shots of Isobel and her bridesmaid at different stages of the hair fixing and dressing. The girls had squealed and protested, but she knew that the photos would be well viewed and gloated over for years to come.

At least my daughter will have something to remind her of her big day, Lisa mused. *All I had was a handshake from the strangers who had stood as witnesses at my wedding in Gretna Green.*

Her heart aching, she glanced her son. Andrew, resplendent in full RAF officer's uniform, smiled down at his sister as he tucked her hand in the crook of his arm and started up the aisle of St Gregory's Methodist Church. *Scott would have been proud of his son if only he had had time to get to know him,* she thought. A searing pain shot through her gut. She wouldn't think of Scott today. She couldn't, because if she did, she might blurt it all out.

She could feel Trisha's eyes boring into the back of her head. BJ had objected vehemently when Trisha was seated with the rest of the guests and not in the family pew with them.

"She's not our family," Lisa had retorted angrily.

"Didn't we rear her? She should be Isobel's bridesmaid."

"She has a father and a brother. They're her family. And she has grandparents somewhere in Ireland."

Lisa had gritted her teeth and faced him down. "She's not going to be Isobel's bridesmaid, and she's not sitting up the front with us."

BJ had given her an odd look. "Something happened between you two when you were hame in Ireland for Mac Kielty's granddaughter's wedding to that Yank's son at Easter," he'd said. "And it wasne just that damn bomb," he mused.

The vicar's prayers interrupted Lisa's thoughts. "Repeat after me…" She heard Isobel's clear responses as she took her wedding vows.

Tears choked Lisa's throat. She felt the comfort of her son's hand as it slipped over hers. She wondered what he say would if he knew she was crying for her lost, unrequited love—for the father he would never see in person. How was she going to tell him now?

She glanced at BJ. The lack of oxygen was beginning to tell. His lips had a blue tinge to them and his wheezing was becoming audible. *It'll be just him and me after this,* she thought. *Isobel will have her own life; and Andrew will go back to his career in the Air Force.*

I'm free to live my own life now. But what use is it without the dream of Scott and I being together, she thought.

A sob escaped her just as Ewan slipped the slim gold band over Isobel's knuckle.

"I feel like an outsider," Trisha said, squeezing in beside George while the bride and groom went to sign the register.

"Why aren't you sitting with the family?" George asked. "They still sore about that row at Hogmanay."

Trisha nodded.

"What about asking that fancy photograph of yours if he'd take a few shots of us getting' married," Isobel had challenged her. "Make up for treating me and Ewan like hillbillies that time in London."

"Claude only photographs models," Trisha had said. As soon as the words left her lips, she wanted to claw them back.

"Oh, Claude only takes photos of models," Isobel had mocked. "Like you, you jumped up bisims! Ye hadnea a pair o' drawers to yer name when yer Da dumped ye on Ma, when ye were a bairn!"

Lisa gave George a quick hug. "Never mind Isobel and Lisa. You and Uncle Billy are always there when I need you."

George looked around the wedding reception, drained his pint, and wondered how much longer he'd be expected to play the dutiful cousin before he could leave. He'd sat through the best man's long-winded speech; clapped as BJ coughed his way through little whimsical tales of Isobel's babyhood and school days; smiled and bought Old Gordon and Mary a wee dram as they tripped down memory lane.

He slipped out to the bar in the foyer. Mary Kielty and Lisa were there. Mary was untying a gold string on a box.

"Claud brought Jay's wedding album," she said, her voice slurred. "My poor Scott never lived to see his only son's wedding photos," she said.

George checked if the photographer had accidently caught a shot of the man who carried the bomb into the wedding reception. A tremor passed through him.

It was a godsend that the timer hadn't gone off when it should. Most of the guests were able to get out before the army blew it up.

"The police think they might know who posted the bullet to my son," Mary said, putting the wedding album carefully into its cream embossed box.

George gulped at his drink. *Bloody hell! Were the cops on to him?*

Chapter 84

Andrew filled a glass with water leaned and back nervously against the draining board. "Da, I need to talk to you and Ma—tell you… something."

"Oul Gordie is callin' to go for a bit o' a dander and blether. Will it keep 'til after, son?"

A sense of love rose up in Andrews's chest. *I work alongside hard, tough men every day, but I'd put my father above any of them for his courage and tenacity any day of the week,* he mused. *He's battled and struggled against a debilitating lung disease for years without grumbling. And put up with Ma,* he thought.

"You're looking a lot better, Da, since I was home last," he said.

BJ laughed. "Still some fire in the oul belly yet," he joked.

His face sobered. "Your mother hasnea been keepin' well since she was caught in that damn bomb at the weddin'." BJ hesitated. "She has somethin' on her mind," he sighed, his face hidden in the flapping folds of his trousers as he bent to lace up his shoes. "She maybe wants a wee word wi' you, son," he said evasively.

The water shook in the glass Andrew was holding. "Is Trisha keeping OK?"

"Trisha? Is she no' well? Your Ma nivir said."

"She's having a bairn."

BJ jerked upwards. "She nivir!"

Andrew cursed under his breath. Shit, his father didn't know!

His father gave a wheezy laugh. "You're drinkin' too much o' that oul English ale, son. It's affecting yer heed."

He chuckled at his own joke. "It's Isobel that's expectin' the bairn. She's havin' a honeymoon baby—just like us when you we had you, son," BJ murmured. "Maybe if we're lucky, Isobel's bairn will be born early too on 25th January."

Andrew laughed. "That's poet Robbie Burn's birthday, Da."

"Aye, that's right, son. That be something, wouldn't it," BJ mused. "Gordie aye bumming his load about his Kenny's bairns. Aye, me first grandbairn born on Robbie Burns birthday—that'd be hard to beat, wouldn't it, son," BJ chortled.

Old Gordon shook Andrew's hand. "Good te see ye hame. Will ye be staying a few days?"

Andrew nodded.

"Ne lassie yet?"

Andrew shook his head.

"Why haven't you told Da about Trisha being pregnant?" Andrew asked, turning back from watching Gordon and his father take the towpath along the riverbank.

Lisa's hands trembled as she lit up a Sweet Afton. She took a deep drag and waited for the nicotine to calm her shaking insides. "I'm not telling him, and neither are you," she said vehemently. "Trisha's not stealing the limelight off my daughter this time. Isobel is a married woman. She should be first in her father's eyes. If I had told him about that tramp, he'd have her back here living, instead of going to Ireland to live with her father and brother."

Andrew startled at his mother's vehement attack on Trisha.

He looked at his mother's shaking shoulders. For a minute, he thought she was laughing, and then he realised she was crying.

"What wrong, Ma?" he said, alarmed.

Fat tears coursed down Lisa's cheeks and dripped onto her clenched hands. It crossed Andrew's mind that he couldn't remember his mother's hair looking so neglected or her ever wearing such an old, baggy, washed-out jumper and skirt like she was wearing today.

Lisa wrapped her arms around herself. Sobs racked her body. She gazed up at son. With his fair eyebrows pulled down, Andrew looked the spit of his father. The breath in her throat constricted. She wondered how BJ or Andrew himself never noticed that not one feature on his face resembled BJ's.

"What wrong wi' ye, Ma?" Andrew said, lapsing back into his Glasgow accent unconsciously. "Da said you hadn't been well since that terrible scare with the bomb at the Yank's wedding."

Swiping at the tears, Lisa nodded. "Mary Kielty's husband, Scott, died from a heart attack the day of their son's wedding. The ambulance crew couldn't get through because of the bomb," she gulped, her voice cracking with emotion. "I knew Scott when I lived at home in Fermanagh. He was a GI stationed at Castle

Archdale." Overcome with grief and guilt, she broke down completely and couldn't go on. How could she tell Andrew the man she was telling him about had been his father?

Andrew looked at his mother, not sure what to think. *Why would his mother be so clearly affected about the death of a man she'd known years ago—before she met my father and before I was born, he wondered? Had there been something between his mother and the man who had died? Had he been an old love? His mother had always been tight-lipped about her background before she married Da,* he thought.

"Ma, there's something you're no' telling me. What is it? You need to tell me," Andrew said. "You were always secretive about when you were young. You never ever took me or Isobel to see our grandparents in Fermanagh. I always wanted to see the farm where you were born. Isn't Trisha living there now with Uncle William? If I go, will you come with me... make it up with Trisha?" Andrew asked.

Hysterical laughter bubbled up in Lisa's throat. Her son was searching for his roots. *It must be your father's American blood in you, she almost blurted out. The next thing you'll want to do is go to Texas to find Scott's family,* she thought.

"We had no money to go anywhere. And there was always Granny Mac to see to. Anyway, your Da never wanted me to go back."

A sense of foreboding penetrated Lisa's grief over Scott's death. She knew now what Andrew wanted to tell her and BJ. Seeing Andrew's lip open, she covered her ears with her hands. No, no please don't let him say it. As long as he didn't say it, she wouldn't have to believe it was true.

It had been simmering at the edge of her mind ever since he had told her months ago that Trisha was pregnant. That bitch was going to take Andrew from her just as she'd taken Scott.

"Has all my doing without and making do so you could stay on at school and get your exams so you could join the RAF and end up with your full cousin!"

"Ma, it was you who begged and borrowed from Madge and Gordon so that you could go to Ireland and bring Trisha to live with us. Da didn't want her, but you brought her to live with us just so you could pull Uncle William out of a tight spot," Andrew said defensively.

He ran his hand through his hair. "I'm only trying to do the right thing," he said. "There are enough skeletons in this family's cupboards as it is. Trisha and me... we... met a few times after she had that roaring row with Isobel," he admitted, his words stumbling over each other in his rush to get them out before he lost his courage. "But I've have met someone… else now. That's what I wanted to talk to you and Da about."

Lisa wasn't listening.

A frisson of excitement was stirring in her. "That bairn that bisim's is expecting is not yours. It's Claude's."

Andrew gasped. "Claude? The photographer Trisha works for?" Andrew shook his head emphatically. "That's impossible, Ma. Claude doesn't sleep with women."

Lisa wondered fleetingly why Andrew had such a shocked look on his face. *It must be because Trisha had slept with Claude while she was sleeping with him,* she thought. She shrugged. He'd learn soon enough the type of woman Trisha was.

"What? Why are you shaking your head, Andrew? She was two-timing you… with Claude," Lisa said sharply. "He shared a hotel penthouse with that bitch at Easter."

"Ma! Claude is… homosexual… a fairy… gay… whatever words you want to call him," Andrew hissed.

Lisa ran her mind's eye over what she remembered of Claude at Isobel's wedding.

"He's never!" She smirked. "He hasn't got that girly, handbag look, and he doesn't do those mincing steps…" She stopped when she saw the stricken look on Andrew's face.

"You don't believe Trisha would sleep with other men? Believe me, son, she would," Lisa said with a harsh, brittle laugh.

An image thundered into her mind of the opulence of the bedroom with its silk sheets and satin pillowcases. And the sensuous smell of a man and a woman's body coupling in wild, abundant lovemaking. Trisha had had a whole afternoon of sex with Scott!

Lisa's thoughts shuddered to a sudden halt.

The baby in Trisha's belly wasn't the photographer's. It was Scott's. She begin to tremble violently. "Andrew, you can't be a father to Trisha's baby… because… because you're too closely related already," she gasped, choking on the words.

Andrew snorted irritably. "I know. You've told me that already."

"No! Listen to me Andrew," Lisa screeched. "There's something else I didn't tell you…"

"What the blazes is going on in here?"

The sudden loudness of BJ's voice startled them both, making them whirl around.

"Ma's hysterical," Andre said, relieved to see his father back.

"She's crying about that American guy she knew when she was young—the one who had the heart attack and died at that wedding."

BJ said the first thing that came into his head. "It's them tablets that daft doctor is givin' her for her nerves. Pay no attention, son. She's in the, ye know, *the change* o' life—that thing women go through. That's the way they get, sometimes…"

"I didn't mean to talk about Trisha and upset you, Ma," Andrew said, seeing the state his mother was in. He licked his dry lips and thrust his hair back with a shaky hand. "I want to tell you both—about…"

"Away ye go," BJ wheezed. "Slip down the pub and get a blether and a few drams of good Scottish whiskey," BJ said, forcing a smile. "It's no' the best time for yer mether. What was it ye wanted to tell us about anyway? Is it something important?"

Andrew shrugged into his overcoat. "It'll keep," he said, resignedly. "Until I come back from seeing Trisha."

Breathing hard with agitation, BJ stood over Lisa. "You're no' to tell him the dead Yank was his feather."

Lisa startled. "How long have you known?" she whispered.

BJ sat down beside her and put his arms around her. "From the day he was born. Go on, lass. Away up and put on that new dress ye made. We're away up the pub to have a good drink with my son—our son. You've grieved long enough for the Yank. He's no' worth your tears," BJ said quietly.

Chapter 85

George stamped his feet to keep warm while he waited for Trisha.

"See you tonight," he heard her call back to Davy. The shape of her protruding stomach was prominent now. He wondered if she'd told Davy who the father was. The way Davy was fussing about her, you'd think it was him, George smirked.

"Who owns the car?" Trisha asked.

George swore. "It's that fella whose father was a POW with Da. He's nearly here as often as that as that bloody detective Maloney," he sneered.

The man looked past George and smiled at Trisha.

"How're you doin'? Jack Donnell," he said, rising to his feet and stretching out his hand. "Your father served with my father in Malta. My mother saw on the telly about the bomb at the wedding. She thought William might be the man who was a good friend to my father when they had to surrender to Hitler."

"It's long past time you should have been on your way, mate," George ground out.

"He just came to bring me these," William said, pointing to letters on the kitchen table.

Jack Donnell nodded. "I never knew my father. Mammy was expecting me at the time," he said, glancing at Trisha's belly.

"After three sons, your father hoped when he got home, he'd get a girl. He even had a name picked out for her," William said quietly.

"It's time he was going, *Father,*" George hissed, glancing at the clock on the kitchen wall, hoping his father got the message and remembered about the vigilantes' meeting. If they made good time out of Belfast, they could be here any minute.

Jack Donnell stopped in his step. He knew if the son had his way, he wouldn't be back again. His eyes swivelled to William. "The army told us my father died as a POW... in the line of duty. But how did he really die?"

William groped for a seat. "He died saving my back," he quacked. "It torments me every day why a bastard like me was allowed to live and a good man like your father died. Ah even got a medal for my cowardly action," he muttered, beginning to shake.

Trisha felt the baby jump. She stared at the tears in her father's eyes. A huge lump rose up, constricting her throat. She had never imagined her father could feel enough or care about somebody enough to cry. She reached her hand out towards him.

"What happened?" Jack Donnell asked.

William's body slumped further into the chair.

"The German's made the POWs work. I couldn't take the starvation and burying the mountain of dead bodies from the bombin'. I tried to run away, to escape, and ah took your father wi' me," he gulped, his Adam's apple bobbing in his throat. "We were nearly clear…" William paused. "They shot your father where he stood." A sob wracked William. "Ah left him and made a run for it. I got caught and got solitary in a black hole. The only way I could tell day from night in the pitch darkness was when the guard pushed the slops that passed for rations under the door."

"Da! Get him out of here before it's too late!" George ordered, sure he'd heard the soft click of a car door carried on the frosty air. If it was Davy, he'd check out the car registration with his contact in the Bullrich police. But if it was the Belfast boys, Jack Donnell would be shot before they took the time to find out he was a serving British soldier.

William began to shake. "I'm sorry, young Donnell. I know it's not enough, but ah made a pact with God." He stopped and covered his face with his hands. "I should have known better. The only God I knew was my mother's: a god of vengeance and retribution." William gasped out his words, almost incoherent. "I promise Him and your dead father the day ah buried him if ah had another girl, I'd give her the name he'd picked out for his daughter." He raised his head and looked at Jack Donnell. "It was not a name you'd hear much about these parts, but I kept my promise. It was all I could do to make it up to him for leading him into danger and leaving him to face the enemy," he choked out.

A gust of icy air invaded the kitchen as George flung the door back against the wall. "Go now, fella!"

"What name did my father pick?" Jack Donnell asked, as if George hadn't spoken.

"Her name," William said, pointing at Trisha.

Jack Donnell looked from William to the heavily pregnant, visibly shocked girl.

"Trisha. He called me Trisha. And he's hated me from the day I was born," she said inaudibly.

"It was great to get a chance to chat with you again," Jack said, shaking William's hand. "I hope the letters give you a bit of peace of mind." He added. "I'll call back and get them another day. I'd like to hear more about my father."

George swore under his breath.

William staggered to his feet. "I couldn't save your father's life, but maybe I can make it up to him and your mother by saving yours," he moaned, reaching for his legally held shotgun. "Get in your car and don't stop for anything or anybody till you're in Beragh," he warned.

"You're too late, Da," George sneered, as the lights of a car lit up the hedges at the mouth of the lane to the farmyard.

Chapter 86

"They're here," Trisha said, heading upstairs. The kitchen door opened without the customary knock or rattle. Sandy, the self-styled CO of the vigilante group, stood there, black gloved thumb silencing the latch.

"Any drink in this place? Or did your visitor with the Tyrone registration clean you out?" he asked, smiling malevolently at William.

He took a slug of the beer George gave him. "You're an old 'Skins' man, right? Like your visitor who nearly ran us off the bloody road."

William silently willed his trembling limbs to be still. "He's a son of an old army mate and a serving British soldier," he retorted.

"A son of your old mate's Catholic? That figures. You were always fond of tegs; you married a Catholic, didn't you, Armstrong," Sandy smirked.

Feeling the survival of the old soldier rise up in him, William stumbled to his feel. "You listen to me, young fella. You get that bomb-makin' stuff out of my barn before the cops come back wi' the army and raid the place. Did Davy Dobbs not tell you the CID boys are keepin' a close eye on the farms about here these parts these days?" He paused. "I had no bother wi' the local boys doing a bit of drillin' and so on, but am havin' nothing to do with stealin' cars and puttin' bombs in them to blow people to pieces."

George mouth fell open. "Your friend Detective Maloney passing on bits of information to you?" he hissed when Sandy and the Volunteer moved to the sitting room.

"He wanted to speak to you. Your granda Furlong's not keepin' well. Maloney wants you to go down south. Bring her upstairs with you when ye go."

George swung around. "You have to be kiddin' me! You never wanted us to have anything to do with Ma's family."

Mumbling into his chest. William thrust the simmering kettle on top of the open range. It spat and sizzled as the water boiled over onto the hotplate.

George's eyes widened. "What did you just say?"

"I said I was wrong to keep your mother from her family." William barked. "Is that clear enough for you?"

George was so stunned at his father's admission that for a minute he was speechless. "If you are really sorry, apologise, really apologise to Trisha. You had no bother laying your soul bare to Jack Donnell, your old army buddy's son. So, it should be easy for you to tell your own daughter you're sorry for bloody up her life," George paused. "You tell Trisha you're sorry for all the senseless beatings and neglect, and I'll go to Waterford and take her with me out of your sight," George snarled as Trisha came back into the kitchen.

"Davy's here," she said.

Silence sat like a heavy dark thing between her and her father. With the security of Davy and George down the hall, Trisha felt brave enough to sit down opposite him. "Was it true what you told Jack Donnell—about his father wanting my name for his daughter?" she demanded.

"You were always the same," her father said, shoving the poker into the heart of the fire. "Always askin' question, wearin' your mother out," William mumbled. The silence grew and lengthened like the black shadows in the yard cast by the outbuildings.

"You screeched day all night—never lettin' me forget the terrible death all around me—men callin' out for their mothers," William mumbled, pulling the red-hot poker from the fire and sitting, staring at it.

The poker glowed red, like iron ready to be beaten and hammered into shape on a blacksmith's anvil. Afraid to move or make a sound, Trisha sat rigid and motionless.

"You're Donnell's ghost daughter. Ye have his eyes. It was the first thing I noticed," William said now with conviction, remembering how he'd looked down into Trisha's newborn face and saw Spud Donnell's dead eyes staring back at him. Slumping back into his chair, William let the poker drop with a sudden clatter into the coal bucket at the side of the range.

Trisha shivered involuntarily. Was it possible to be born with the eyes of a dead person?

"Listen to them. They're down in the room planning a bomb that will kill the innocent. It's my fault for lettin' them use the farm's barn," William said in an anguished, mumbled voice. Rising, he reached for his coat and flat cap hanging on the back of his chair.

"Da, its pitch dark out there," Trisha said as he struggled to open the new deadlock bar Davy had fitted. William stopped struggling and turned towards her. Trisha shrank away from him and put her arms protectively over her bump.

"It's the same pitch dark it was when I shoved you in the byre in the night. It was only when, after I tried to escape, and the Germans threw me into the black hole without food or light, that I knew the terror of the dark with only the vermin for company," he muttered. "It was a terrible thing to do to ye," he muttered. "Am sorry," he said, going back to the door. "I can't bring Donnell or any of the men I killed in the name of war back. But I can stop Davy and Sandy from more senseless killing," William gasped out.

Startled, by her father's acknowledgement of what he had done to her, Trisha stood transfixed. Then she screamed for Davy.

Chapter 87

Davy's mother had his clothes all laid out and ready for him.

"Don't let this one go, son," she said as she stood him up and brushed down the shoulders of his coat with the clothes brush. "She's the one for you."

"She's a model. She wouldn't look at the likes of me," Davy retorted, looking down at the bog muck under his nails and grass stains on his trousers.

"She's a woman in need of a husband… and father," his mother said. "You're old enough to be both. She's the one. She's comin' into that farm along wi' her brother when the court case is settled, and from what I hear, he mightn't be around that long."

Davy whirled around. "Where did you hear that?"

His mother shrugged. "I hear plenty. Faith Hamilton's farm runs alongside the Armstrong place. Marry the model, get a bank loan, buy the Hamilton place and you'd have both farms of land and all the rights to the fishing on the Lakes."

Davy looked in amazement at his mother.

"And what about…"

"What about what's in her belly?" his mother said.

His mother puffed out as she carried the pot of boiled potatoes over to the white Belfast sink to drain. "There was plenty around here who asked the self-same question when your da—God be good to him—married me," she retorted, wiping a beefy arm across her sweating forehead. Davy watched with consternation as the steam from the potatoes wafted up, obscuring his mother's face. He had always known that the man his mother had married had not been his father. It had been thrown up to him often enough over the years.

"She's the one, son," his mother said, sinking into a chair and fanning herself with the end of her apron.

Davy looked at her. A heavy-set woman now, he knew she had been almost as good-looking as Trisha in her day. He'd seen the black-and-white photographs she kept secreted away.

"Aye, a confirmed bachelor the folks about here advised me about your da; twenty years older than me. I got a good man and a good father for you, son," she murmured.

"Maybe she'll not take me," Davy mused, pounding down the flowery balls in the pot.

"She'll take you," his mother said confidently. "Annie Swanton was up here the other day…"

Davy gave his mother a dark look. "You shouldn't listen to oul gossips like Annie, Ma."

Davy filled his plate with the potatoes and cabbage. His mother was still talking. He knew it was useless trying to get her off the subject until she ran out of steam. *That might take a while,* he thought, looking fondly across the table at her.

"…Couldn't beat the craft o' them Catholics," his mother was saying. "William's new wife is supposed to be sufferin' with her nerves." She snorted. "Sufferin' from a broken heart over her old soldier boyfriend—our new CID man, if you ask me."

"What about Trisha's papist blood?" Davy asked.

His mother wiped her mouth with the end of her apron. "The youngster she's carryin' belongs to a good British subject from when she was doin' all that modellin' in England. A son to carry on your name and the farm, Davy," she said, reaching across and patting his hand.

"What if it's a girl?"

"It's a boy. I know from the way she's carrying it," his mother said, combing his hair with her hand as he got ready to go to meet Trisha.

Chapter 88

William was dreaming about Rosie. He could feel her hand and hear her softly whispering his name.

He stiffened. Trisha was there too. "Dad, Da," she was calling. He shoved her away.

"Da, wake up! The army and police are hammering the door in!" The urgency and fear in her voice dragged him up from his dream. He could feel the bulk of her stomach looming over him, feel her breath on his face. He struggled against consciousness. Rosie had felt so real, so near. He closed his eyes, willing her back.

"Da!"

He fumbled for the bedside clock, forcing his heavy eyes to focus on the luminous green hands. The hammering reverberated through the house. Stumbling into his trousers, he yanked back the bedroom curtains and pushed up the lower panes of the sash window. The smell of oil and cooling engines from army trucks hung in the early dawn air. He could see dark outlines lined up, sealing the mouth of the lane. "Open it or we'll break it down," a voice ordered in an English accent.

William zipped his fly and searched in the dark for his shoes.

"Break it down," he heard a voice command.

Scuttled in socked feet down the stairs, he yanked at the dead bolts. They grumbled, resisting his shaking fingers. William's knees knocking against the sturdy door were lost in the noise the pounding fists. Conceding defeat, the bolt slid out of its keeper.

The door was immediately forced inwards. William found himself staring into a pair of cold eyes in a blackened face.

"What is it you want at this time of the morn'?" William started to say. He heard Trisha's cry of fear as soldier boots thundered past her on the stairs.

Uncertain what to do, Trisha stood on the stairs. She could see, down the hall in the room where Davy held the meetings, a soldier's head and shoulders up the chimney.

"Clear here, sir," he called, his face freshly blackened by soot.

"Who else is in the house?" the officer in charged barked.

"Nobody—just her and me. Here, stop that!" William bawled as a soldier knocked over a small side table and upended the chair Rosie had covered in a nice fresh floral pattern. He could see large soot handprints on the cushions already.

"In the kitchen," the army officer ordered, prodding Trisha down the stairs with his rifle. Snapping back into old soldier mode, William set his face against the sharp eyes of the officer who was barking out orders. "Let her be. There's no need for that. What do you think you're going to find?" William said, his voice coming out in a hoarse quack.

"We know this house and farm is being used for paramilitary activities," a familiar voice stated from the kitchen door.

William let out a sigh of relief. "Detective Maloney, will you tell this crowd to stop wreckin' the place?"

He stopped speaking as Tomas Maloney's words sunk in. Expletives flowed from his mouth. "You sleeked bastard, hangin' about the place—sucking up to George. Using havin' known my Margaret as an excuse to get your arse in here," he said, taking an angry step towards the detective. The soldier guarding them raised his gun. William shrank back. He had a clear, vivid memory of the feel of the boot on his throat when the soldier had flung him to the ground after he'd found the bomb at Kathy Swanton's wedding.

The young soldier fixed his gaze on Trisha's belly. "Sir," he said in a low, guttural voice to the officer. "She's hiding sommit."

Trisha blushed and tried in vain to tighten her dressing gown.

The officer gave the young recruit a withering look. "Shut the fuck up. She's pregnant."

William could hear the legs of the beds upstairs scraping like loose teeth on the wooden floorboards. Bed springs protested as the soldiers dragged them off the mattresses, their boots trampling over the exposed springs.

Detective Maloney watched Trisha surreptitiously. Heavily pregnant or not, she was still a very beautiful girl. He wondered why she was wasting her time on the likes of Davy Dobbs, a dirt farmer twenty years older than her.

Smothered laughter came from the young rookie soldiers. He guessed they were having a bit of fun going through Trisha's underwear drawers. Realising what they were up to, silent dry, sobs clogged her throat. Beneath the gaping dressing gown, her belly jumped and jerked as the baby kicked.

At the sight of her obvious distress, a strange sensation filled William's chest. He stretched out a comforting hand towards her. Trisha shrank back. William persisted and gripped her hand tightly. "Don't cry… It's not good for the… baby. It'll be over soon," he promised. He looked down in wonder and astonishment as his trembling hand covered her clenched one. It struck him that this was the first time he had touched his daughter without anger.

The noise of splintering wood and the tramping of heavy boots reverberated overhead as the soldiers ripped up the floorboards and searched below them.

William rubbed his thumb over Trisha's knuckles. "I'm sorry," he whispered. "I never hated you… I was afraid of your… eyes," he stuttered in a strangled voice. "I always thought Spud Donnell's eyes could see the coward inside me."

"My, ain't this a cosy little father and daughter scene," the soldier guarding them sneered.

"Give it a rest," Detective Maloney snapped. "Is it a house search or a kiddie's romper room, you're running here?" he said, fixing the officer in charge with an unblinking stare, his eyes moving to the ceiling.

Outside, the bird's dawn chorus had been overtaken by the lowing of the cows clamouring for milking. Tomas could hear the beginning of the morning traffic making its way into Enniskillen.

Word would soon spread about the presence of the security forces in the area. It didn't take long for the paramilitaries on either side to seize the opportunity to take a pot shot or place a roadside bomb, hoping to score a death of a policeman or a soldier.

"They've literally taken the place apart. If they haven't found anything before now… It'll soon be daylight—time to wrap this up. RUC orders—don't spend too much time in one location," he said, addressing the OIC, rising to his feet. He had done what was necessary. *It was time he was going,* he thought.

"Game over," the OIC bawled up the stairs.

Booted feet trampled everything in their path as they trundled down the stairs and into the convoy of army vehicles. A rookie soldier fell over the rock planter outside the back door of the farmhouse and cursed profusely.

William stared at the proffered form. "What's that for?"

The officer sneered. "I keep forgetting. Half of you Irish bastards can't read or write," he sneered. "It states that my *men* have done no damage during the search," he barked out.

William's blood boiled. "I was readin' and writin' when you were a scabby-arsed…"

"Sign it," Detective Maloney advised.

William straightened up as best he could, his muscles stiff from sitting in the cold, hard kitchen chair all night. He aimed for his authoritative corporal's tone but missed by a mile. "From the racket going on up the stairs, I'll be surprised if there's a stick of furniture…"

"That's nothing to what I'm going to do to your bloody farmland," the officer promised grimly. "Where's your son, George, tonight, Mr Armstrong.?" he hissed.

William blinked.

"At the big meet on the Shankill, taking a bow for the car he stole from the IRA boys on the Falls Road. The word is, the whole bloody lot of them are comin' for George. You couldn't make it up, so you couldn't." he smirked.

"Sign the bloody form," Detective Maloney urged. "Time is running out." Snapping the form from the officer's hand, he thrust it at William. "Sign it," he said in a voice that brooked no argument.

Chapter 89

Trisha glanced at Davy. He'd obviously made an effort. His black hair was freshly shampooed and slicked down neatly in its usual middle parting. He had lost his six o'clock shadow, and the smell of Old Spice aftershave wafted up her nose. His tweed jacket was freshly brushed and a perfect match for his grey slacks. She giggled. "I love the high army finish on your shoes," she chortled, slipping her arm through his. Davy puffed out his chest.

"Right, here we are; mind your step," he fussed as they alighted from the bus in the centre of Enniskillen. Trisha inhaled deeply. It was far from the smells, sights, and sounds of bustling London, but it was great to get the smell of town living, even if it was only a country town.

"George told me about the plans to adopt the baby, but I have another plan," Davy said, laying his hand on her protruding belly. Trisha gave an exasperated sigh. Her plans were already made. The baby was due at the end of January. Claude was expecting her back. That was his plan. She planned to be in shape to buy a whole new wardrobe of clothes from the new Easter Paris Collections.

Davy held her arm as they crossed the street. "Do you like that ring?" he said, stopping to point at a small engagement ring in a jeweller's window. Trisha wondered if they had a toilet and whether they would let her use it.

She nodded.

Delighted with himself, Davy pushed open the door. A bell clanged above their heads.

"Could we see the ring in the window?" Davy said, puffing up his chest.

"Certainly, sir," the middle-aged female assistant smiled. Taking a small key from her pocket, she unlocked a small door into the window display and withdrew the tray of rings.

What is a beautiful girl like her doing with an old codger like him, she wondered.

"Could I use your ladies?" Trisha asked in a low voice from behind her gloved hand.

"Certainly, miss… madam. I'll just show you," the assistant stuttered in confusion. *So that's how it is,* she thought. *She needs a husband before it's born, which won't be long by the look of her.*

Davy fumbled for Trisha's hand. "I know it's not as fancy as you're used to," he mumbled, giving her fingers a tight squeeze.

Trisha could feel the rough texture of his hands. Thoughts of the feel of Seymour's silky manicured hands on her body and Scott's stubby fingers stroking her into a frenzied orgasm leapt into her mind.

"A perfect fit. It was just made for you," the sales assistant beamed, sensing a sale. *She wondered was the baby his. Probably not—bloody old eejit,* she thought.

"Try on the matching wedding ring," she smiled. Colour flooded Trisha's face as she slipped on the wedding ring.

"You mean get married sooner than later before this little bundle of joy is born a bastard?" Davy said, glowering at the shop assistant.

The shop assistant's neck went a deep crimson. "I didn't mean… I was just saying…"

Davy's face hardened into a mask of blotched purple and red fury. A vein throbbed in his neck. "Stick your rings up your…"

"Davy!" Trisha said sharply, tugging him towards the door. It was only when they were outside that she realised she still had the matching engagement and wedding rings on her finger.

"Keep them," Davy said, tucking her arm through his as he marched her up the street.

"Ice cream… and real Italian cuisine," Trisha read from a menu outside a restaurant with a marble-covered front. Davy's eyes shot out on stalks when he saw the prices. Trisha flashed the rings; "Ice cream, please."

"It's the first of December," Davy spluttered. They stood for a moment, the bulk of the baby between them.

Trisha seated herself at a marble-topped table. Davy rubbed his hands together as the waitress placed two heaped oblong-shaped dishes of Banana Split ice cream before them. Little blobs of golden honey glistened against the white of the tiny biscuits that stuck up like sails. A cherry nestled, red and luscious, its vibrant coloured enhanced by the light of the small flickering table candle.

Davy cleaned his dish and looked around him. If he hadn't had Trisha with him, he'd have gone to his usual wee tea shop beside the cattle mart. It was cheap and cheerful—just the way he likes it.

He watched Trisha running her finger around the edge of the glass, her long dark eyelashes fanning down in a state of intense enjoyment. He inhaled as she raised her fingers one by one and sucked them clean, her red lipsticked mouth making a perfect circle. Yes, he wanted her, but he wanted her to be only his. He didn't want other men ogling her. The strength of his feelings for her startled him. *For the first time in my life, I love a woman other than my mother,* he thought. *And odder still,* he mused, *Ma and Trisha get on like a good fire on a winter's night.*

Trisha's giggling brought him out of his reverie. "Do you remember the first day we met?" she said, reaching across and stroking the inside of his wrist with her finger. "I was nine. You let me sit on your knee and drive the tractor." Davy turned her palm upwards and traced the lifeline in her hand.

"You were a wee beauty even then," he said, embarrassed, his face going red.

"You're a good, hardworking man, Davy Dobbs," Trisha murmured. "Not like some of the scumbags I have been in contact with. But you don't know me or anything about me," she said softly.

"I was just thinking about the banana and how it was split down the middle."

"Aye.?"

"If that… sheath hadn't split, I wouldn't be expecting, and I wouldn't be sitting with you here today, showing off an engagement and matching wedding ring," she said, smiling into his eyes.

Davy heart thudded in his chest. Maybe she would marry him after all. He'd go back and pay for the engagement and wedding ring.

Chapter 90

George was back, and so was Tomas Maloney when William returned from bringing in the cows in the early evening.

He glowered at George and ignored Detective Maloney. "Where were you? Your sister Trisha could have been done with having you here."

George snorted. "Since when did you give a fiddler's fuck about Trisha? Where is she? I wanted to see her before I go." It was only then William noticed the packed bag at his son's feet.

"Where will you go?"

"He's going to Waterford with me… to see his grandparents."

William caught the lie in Tomas' eyes before he could hide it. William experienced a strange tightening sensation in his chest. Pain and regret squeezed his heart, making it difficult to breathe.

"Sandy and his crowd want you dead, and the IRA Falls Road boys could be on their way to get you right now," William stammered out.

Detective Maloney grabbed the bags. "We don't have time to stand around playing happy families at this stage," Tomas barked.

George looked towards the stairs.

"Trisha's away to Enniskillen with Davy. He's had shopping to do for his Main Rogan's hardware shop," William said.

A look of pure horror washed the colour from George's face.

"The car bomb I nicked from the IRA is on its way to Rogan's… they served the police and soldiers," he stuttered, blanching visibly.

"That's where you were the last couple o' night with that cur Sandy," his father whispered, beginning to tremble violently.

Tomas Maloney spun around and lunged for the phone in the hall. He dropped it back in its cradle and raced for the door. "Don't use your phone. It's tapped. I've called in a bomb warning," he bawled as George followed him out the door and into his car.

Chapter 91

Something wet and sticky was clinging to Davy's chest. He fought wildly against the blackness that swamped him. "Trisha, Trisha," he moaned, scrabbling the hands that tried to restrain him.

"It's alright, mate." A khaki uniform and a concerned face with what appeared to be a head with a badge on it swam into his line of vision. "Can you tell me your name?" a voice asked.

"Davy, Davy Dobbs," he gasped out. A cacophony of sounds and voices overwhelmed him. He smelled what he thought was something burning. English accents mingled with local tongues.

He heard the murmur of a hurried short prayer. A face loomed over him again. "You were caught in a bomb blast. You're in the Erne Hospital in Enniskillen," a female voice said. "You're being moved to the Royal Victoria Hospital in Belfast as soon as we can get an ambulance."

A bomb! "Davy!" he moaned, calling Trisha's name.

"The army paramedics took your daughter straight to Belfast City Hospital," the voice said.

Sirens shrieked as they sped past. Davy couldn't be sure if they were police or ambulances or both.

"Davy," a stunned familiar voice said close to him.

"It's Benny"

"Benny. You in the bomb…"

"Am here w' St John's Ambulance taking people to hospital. But I never expected to be takin' my old mate," Benny said, his voice thick with emotion.

Trisha eyelids felt weighted down. Her body, strange, detached. She forced her eyelids up and stared at the bright glare of a strip light.

"Good, you're awake—at last," a woman's voice said. "You're in the City Hospital. How do you feel?"

"City hospital," Trisha's croaked. "Why am I…"

"You were caught in a bomb blast six days ago, Mrs Dobbs. It's OK. You're being moved out of Intensive Care to the High Dependency ward." Lights slipped by, the obscure shape of an arm and a swaying bag of liquid floated close to her face.

Trisha moved her hand to her stomach. There was no bump. "You have a neck and body brace on. You're a very lucky young woman," the nurse said crisply. "Now, Mrs Dobbs, you must be hung…"

"Why are you calling me Mrs Dobbs?"

A furrow deepened Sister Eleanor Smith's black pencilled eyebrows. She placed her thumb and finger lightly on Trisha's wrist and consulted the small mother-of-pearl watch pinned to the bib of her uniform. Her plump face creased into a concerned gaze. It was always difficult to assess just how much a patient was affected until they recovered fully from the sedation.

"Would you prefer the nurses to call you by your Christian name? Its Trisha, isn't it?"

Trisha nodded. She had no recollections of any bomb. The last thing she remembered was Davy smiling across the table, taking her hand and asking her to marry him. Panic assailed her. Had she said yes? *Davy must have told them I was his wife,* she thought as she drifted into confused oblivions.

The ward was in semi-darkness when she woke again. "How are you feeling now?" a soft, cultured voice asked. "It's Doctor Coles. Doctor Aengus Cole," he said after a short pause.

"I was supposed to come and see you," Trisha mumbled, trying to remember what she was supposed to go to see him about. There was something wrong with her head. Panicked, she tried to touch her face. She felt a scream rising in her throat. "Something is wrong with my face… with my eyes…"

The smell of soap and aftershave wafted over her as the doctor pulled his chair closer to her bed.

"The bones in your head, face and neck were crushed when a wall fell in on you after the car bomb explosion," he said quietly. He thought it was pointless to burden her with the severity of her injuries yet. He was silent for a few seconds. "You were very lucky. The marble-topped table in the restaurant saved you from the worst of the building collapsing in around you."

"My baby…"

Aengus Coles moved back from her one-eyed glassy stare. "I'm sorry to tell you your baby didn't survive the blast," he murmured. He paused and gave a dry cough. "William, your father, asked me to come and see you. He asked me to give you this." He groped in his inside pocket. "I would have waited, but I'm going away for a pre-Christmas break, and I wanted to give it to you before I went," he said, placing a small object in Trisha's palm. Trisha cried out in pain as she tried to close her fingers on it.

"It's your mother's wedding ring," Aengus said, a stricken note in his voice. Cursing his father and William Armstrong for getting him involved in their complicity, Trisha's fingers lost their grip and the ring made a tinny sound as it rolled under the bed.

Aengus ducked out from under the bed to the amused glint in Sister Eleanor Smyth's eye. *Nice ass. Pity about his sour puss,* she thought.

"I'll get it put on a chain for you. Then you can wear it around your neck," she offered.

"Why is he giving it to me now? I have… my own rings." Spittle leaked out of the corner of Trisha's mouth as she spoke.

Aengus felt his ears redden. Ever since he had attended this girl when she was found wandering in the fields near his home, suffering from severe frostbite, he seemed destined to be involved with her in one form or another. He cursed his father again for his overly zealous involvement with the Armstrong family, simply because he and Samuel, Trisha's grandfather, had survived the First World War together.

"Here, put it on this for the time being," Eleanor said, unhooking a small silver chain and cross from around her neck. "Just keep the cross on it too," she whispered in Aengus' ear. "Pity that's not the only cross she'll have to carry…"

Her voice trailed off as she looked at the thick bandages covering the left side of Trisha's head and face. *I wonder how she'll cope when she realises her head has been shaved of all that beautiful black ebony hair and she'll be blind in at least one eye and scarred for life,* she thought sadly. "Mrs Dobbs—about your baby… It was a boy," she said gently. "You can have him christened posthumously, if that is what you had planned… What name…?" Relief washed over Trisha. There was no more need to wait. She was free to take up her modelling again.

"I want to see Davy," she said, focusing her unbandage eye on Aengus Coles. There was a beat of silence as the nurse smoothed an imaginary wrinkle in the counterpane. "I'll be in my office if you need me," she said, quietly to the doctor, swishing the curtains around Trisha's bed. *I don't envy him his task,* she thought

Telling a patient at any time that their loved one has died is no easy task. But when they have already been buried—at least what was left of him—it's even worse, she thought, hurrying out of the ward.

Aengus Coles cursed into his sweating palms. William had arrived in his surgery earlier in the day. He'd shifted from one foot to the other. Then he had proffered the small gold ring. "I want you to give this to Trisha. It's her mother's wedding ring."

"I want you to go yourself and tell her... Davy's dead," William said hoarsely. "I don't want you to leave it to some young thing that knows nothing about death to tell her," he'd said angrily.

Aengus had curled his lip. "I'm not my father. I don't do for the Armstrong's what they should do for themselves," he'd spat.

Aengus reached across and stroked Trisha's hand. "I have some very distressing news to tell you. Davy died in the ambulance on the way to hospital in Belfast. I am very sorry and about the loss of your baby boy too... if there is anything I can do..."

Trisha bit her lower lip until she drew blood. Davy was dead. What would his old mother do now? She realised Doctor Coles was talking.

"... Car parked down the street from the restaurant and across from the Town Hall. Wilbur Wilson, the Registrar, was also killed and his secretary, Miss Moss. Apparently, they'd stayed in during their lunch hour waiting for a couple to come back to be married."

Trisha's sobs turned into a hysterical scream. "It's our fault he was caught in the bomb," she cried out, sobbing wildly.

Davy had wanted to go to the Town Hall to ask one of the local councillors if he would back him in a bank loan to buy the Hamilton farm. The door to the Registrar's outer office had been standing open. Playfully, Davy had pulled her inside. "Let's get a look at what it would be like to be married in this place," he'd joked. A buzzer had sounded and a middle-aged woman thrust back a glass panel.

"Names," she'd asked.

"Davy Dobbs and Trisha Armstrong," Davy blurted out. Her eyes widened when she saw Trisha's advanced state of pregnancy. She'd clucked her tongue. "I can't find your names on the list. No doubt our new trainee university graduate has forgotten to update it again," she'd sighed. "Come back in an hour," she sniffed, sliding the glass panel shut.

Giggling and laughing like two giddy love-struck teenagers, Trisha had taken the wedding ring she was supposed to be returning to the jewellers, and Davy had slipped it over her knuckle. They'd linked arms and sashayed down the wide carved staircase, flashing the ring pretending to be newlyweds. The elderly doorman had smiled at them indulgently and wished them all the best.

Aengus took out a big white hankie and dabbed at the trickle of blood that oozed from a cut that had reopened in Trisha's upper lip from her sobbing. A sense of guilt flashed his mind back to the day he had let his father talk him out of contacting Social Services to have George and Trisha taken into care. It was a regret that haunted him to this day.

They both listened in silence to the bleep of the heart monitor and the plop of the intravenous drip. "Davy asked me to marry him. The Registrar was there because he thought we were coming back to add our names to the wedding dates. If that bomb hadn't exploded, Davy and I might have gotten married and we'd be home waiting for our son to be born," Trisha moaned. She let the lie hang in the air.

Aengus stared into Trisha's tearful one-eyed gaze. All of a sudden, the ward felt confining and airless. He distanced himself from her and stood up. *Whoever the father of her son was, it certainly wasn't Davy Dobbs,* he thought.

"What is a marriage certificate anyway?" Trisha muttered. "Just a piece of paper with two names on it…"

Aengus thought of Davy's broken-hearted old mother; her work-worn hands clutching at her son's coffin as it was lowered into the frozen ground. "Without Davy to take care of, she'll not be long after him," a mourner had whispered behind him.

"And not another soul to leave the land to or to look after her," someone whispered back. Aengus cast the whispered conversation from his mind. *No! I will not give credence to a lie,* he fumed. *My father did that too many times for the Armstrong family down the years.*

"Davy wanted a son to leave his farm and land to," Trisha whispered beginning to sob again.

"She's right," Sister Eleanor Smyth's voice murmured low behind Aengus. "She'll be better off as a widow of a war veteran. The Legion and the Lodge will support and help her; and from what I saw at Davy's funeral, he was a paid-up member of both."

Doctor Cole stumbled in his haste to get away. *No! I will not be party to another Armstrong deceit,* he told himself fiercely.

How different would her life have been if you had had the courage of your conviction as a doctor and reported William Armstrong's abuse of her to the proper authorities? A small inner voice sneered.

Aengus let his shoulders slump in defeat. It was partly his fault that Trisha Armstrong had turned out the way she had. If he had faced down his father, she'd have been in care, away from her father's madness, and lived a very different life.

"As soon as the Town hall is open again, I'll see about getting the death of your baby registered as Davy's son," he grated out from behind clenched teeth, his back turned on Trisha.

"And the wedding certificate?" Trisha pressed.

"A lot of the Town Hall records were lost in the fire that broke out after the bomb," the nurse who was checking the monitors above Trisha's bed said.

Aengus tore at the floral curtains, searching for the opening. "Will you give my father, William, a message from me, Doctor Coles?" Trisha's rasping voice asked, following him out through the opening. Aengus's footfall stilled.

"Tell him I said thanks—for nothing!"

Chapter 92

William watched the specialist army teams digging up the far field where the Nissan huts were. He had been expecting them to search the fields and the outhouses since the house raid.

An army helicopter whirred overhead. He glanced upwards. They had been checking the layout of the farm from a helicopter all day for any sighting of potential booby traps. It reminded him of the recommission mission his unit had carried out during the war—always on the lookout, always aware of enemy attack in whatever form it took.

He went back inside and started his final tour of the house. The kitchen was bare and empty now. Heartless was the word that sprung into William's mind. An empty shell bereft of life, shadows gathering in the lengthening gloom. He'd have to be going soon if he wanted to catch the boat train. He made his way upstairs and stood on the landing. A faint smell of Trisha's perfume hung in the air. Dr Coles had given him her message. He had gone to see her to beg her to forgive him for the terrible childhood she'd had to endure because of his madness.

A plump nurse had bustled up, two red spots high on her cheeks. "I'm sorry, Mr Armstrong, Mrs Dobbs says she doesn't feel up to any visitors today," she murmured, fixing her eyes somewhere behind his head.

"Mrs Dobbs? So that's what she was calling herself now. You got what you wanted, after all, Davy boy," William muttered—the daughter and the farm. It's all Trisha's now.

The silent house seemed to mock him. "She paid me back in my own coin, didn't she?" he whispered to the gaping open doors of the empty bedrooms. "She disowned me. She's going to live with Davy's mother when she gets out of hospital," he murmured.

He stepped into what he always thought of as his father and mother's room, then into George's room.

The words of the news reports were like fresh ink marks in his mind. They had reported that the bomb had gone off prematurely before it reached Rogan's, its intended target.

The two bombers in the car were killed instantly, and a motorist and his passenger travelling behind the car bomb were badly injured and died later, the news had said. "One was a local man, George Armstrong, and the other man was a CID police officer, Det Tomas Maloney, new to the area," William intoned to the silent house.

A chilling stillness crept over William's trembling limbs. His eye twitched, and his hands shook. He moved downstairs and outside to where the stone flowerpot Margaret had loved to plant daffodils and snowdrops stood.

Visiting George in hospital, he'd leaned close to his son to hear his dying words.

"Think I'm your son, Da? Think again," George had gasped out…

William looked towards the well in the far field. Sarah was there.

There was the shrill sound of a car horn. It was his taxi. He signalled; he knew it was there. But he had to say goodbye to Sarah before he left for good. She was all he had left now.

He pulled the farmhouse door closed behind him for the last time, taking one last lingering look in the direction of the graveyard. Without Reverend's Snodgrass' permission, he'd had Margaret's body exhumed and reburied in the Armstrong family plot beside their daughter.

Old Kielty's granddaughter, Hannah, had moved on from doing crafts to lettering headstones. He would never see Margaret and Sarah's name in letters, but he'd know it was there. He had been warned it was only because of his status as a veteran and his father's bravery at the Battle of the Somme in 1916 that his name wasn't on the gravestone too.

He hadn't told Rosie he was coming. This time, he wouldn't wait for her to ask him to marry; he would ask her.

THE END